Two Unforg

LOVE
AFFAIRS

An Independent Woman by Betty Neels

Julia Gracey has always stood on her own two feet,
but lately Professor Gerard van der Maes is always
on hand with a perfect solution to every problem.
And now, when she loses her home, he sweeps her
off her feet with an irresistible proposal – marriage!

&

Husband For Real by Catherine George

Years after their wedding of convenience, Rose
could admit that she *had loved* James. But she
didn't expect him to turn up on her doorstep
to say that he wanted to *stay* married to her.
Their physical attraction was undeniable, yet she
needed more than just a Valentine lover...

*Read one novel then flip the book
and read the other.*

*And don't miss our romantic, hot tips
for your own Valentine's Evening!*

Betty Neels spent her childhood and youth in Devonshire before training as a nurse and midwife. She was an Army nursing sister during the war, married a Dutchman, and subsequently lived in Holland for fourteen years. She lived with her husband in Dorset, and had a daughter and grandson. Her hobbies were reading, animals, old buildings, and writing.

Betty started to write on retirement from nursing, incited by a lady in a library bemoaning the lack of romantic novels. She then became one of Mills & Boon's most prolific and best-loved authors. Over her thirty-year writing career Betty wrote more than 134 novels, was published worldwide and brought pleasure to millions. She has left us all the lasting legacy of her heart-warming novels.

Catherine George was born in Wales, and early on developed a passion for reading which eventually fuelled her compulsion to write. Marriage to an engineer led to nine years in Brazil, but on his later travels the education of her son and daughter kept her in the UK. And instead of constant reading to pass her lonely evenings she began to write the first of her romantic novels. When not writing and reading she loves to cook, listen to opera, browse in antiques shops and walk the Labrador.

Valentine
LOVE
AFFAIRS

BETTY NEELS
& CATHERINE GEORGE

All the characters in this book have no existence outside the
imagination of the author, and have no relation whatsoever to anyone
bearing the same name or names. They are not even distantly inspired
by any individual known or unknown to the author, and all the
incidents are pure invention.

VALENTINE LOVE AFFAIRS © by Harlequin Books SA 2006

Husband For Real and *An Independent Woman* were first
published in Great Britain in separate, single volumes.

An Independent Woman © Betty Neels 2001
Husband For Real © Catherine George 2001

ISBN 0 263 84982 1

118-0206

Printed and bound in Spain
by Litografía Rosés S.A., Barcelona

AN INDEPENDENT WOMAN

BETTY NEELS

CHAPTER ONE

THE street, like hundreds of other streets in that part of London, was shabby but genteelly so, for the occupants of the small turn-of-the-century houses which lined it had done their best; there were clean net curtains at the windows and the paintwork was pristine, even if badly in need of a fresh coat. Even so, the street was dull under a leaden sky and slippery with the cold sleet.

The girl, Ruth, looking out of the window of one of the houses, frowned at the dreary view and said over her shoulder, 'I don't think I can bear to go on living here much longer...'

'Well, you won't have to—Thomas will get the Senior Registrar's post and you'll marry and be happy ever after.'

The speaker who answered, Julia, was kneeling on the shabby carpet, pinning a paper pattern to a length of material. She was a pretty girl, with a quantity of russet hair tied back carelessly with a bootlace, a tip-tilted nose and a wide mouth. Her eyes under thick brows were grey, and as she got to her feet it was apparent that she was a big girl with a splendid figure.

She wandered over to the window to join her sister. 'A good thing that Dr Goodman hasn't got a surgery this morning; you've no need to go out.'

'The evening surgery will be packed to the doors...'

They both turned their heads as a door opened and another girl, Monica, came in. A very beautiful girl, almost as beautiful as her elder sister. For while Julia, she of the russet hair, was pretty, the other two were both lovely, with fair hair and blue eyes. Ruth was taller than Monica, and equally slender, but they shared identical good looks.

'I'm off. Though heaven knows how many children will turn up in this weather.' Monica smiled. 'But George was going to look in...'

George was the parish curate, young and enthusiastic, nice-looking in a rather crumpled way and very much in love with Monica.

They chorused goodbyes as she went away again.

'I'm going to wash my hair,' said Ruth, and Julia got down onto her knees again and picked up the scissors.

The front doorbell rang as she did so, and Ruth said from the door, 'That will be the milkman; I forgot to pay him...I'll go.'

Professor Gerard van der Maes stood on the doorstep and looked around him. He had, in an unguarded moment, offered to deliver a package from his registrar Thomas, to that young man's fiancée—something which, it seemed, it was vital she received as quickly as possible. Since the registrar was on duty, and unlikely to be free for some time, and the Professor was driving himself to a Birmingham hospital and would need to thread his way through the northern parts of London, a slight deviation from his route was of little consequence.

Now, glancing around him, he rather regretted his offer. It had taken him longer than he had expected to find the house and he found the dreary street not at all to his taste. From time to time he had listened to Thomas's diffident but glowing remarks about his fiancée, but no one had told him that she lived in such a run-down part of the city.

The girl who answered the door more than made up for the surroundings. If this was Ruth, then Thomas must indeed be a happy man.

He held out a hand. 'Van der Maes, a colleague of Thomas. He wanted you to have a parcel and I happened to be going this way.'

'Professor van der Maes.' Ruth beamed up at him. 'How kind of you.' She added, not quite truthfully, 'I was just going to make coffee...'

He followed her into the narrow hall and into the living room and Ruth said, 'Julia...'

'If it's money you want there's some in my purse...' Julia didn't look up. 'Don't stop me or I'll cut too much off.'

'It's Professor van der Maes.'

'Not the old man from across the street?' Julia snipped carefully. 'I knew he'd break a leg one day, going outside in his slippers.'

Ruth gave the Professor an apologetic glance. 'We have a visitor, Julia.'

Julia turned round then, and looked at the pair of them standing in the doorway. Ruth, as lovely as ever, looked put out and her companion looked amused. Julia got to her feet, looking at him. Not quite her idea of a professor: immensely tall and large in his person, dark hair going grey, heavy brows above cold eyes and a nose high-bridged and patrician above a thin mouth. Better a friend than an enemy, thought Julia. Not that he looked very friendly…

She held out a hand and had it gently crushed.

'I'll make the coffee,' said Ruth, and shut the door behind her.

'Do sit down,' said Julia, being sociable.

Instead he crossed the room to stand beside her and look down at the stuff spread out on the carpet.

'It looks like a curtain,' he observed.

'It is a curtain,' said Julia snappishly. It was on the tip of her tongue to tell him that by the time she had finished with it it would be a dress suitable to wear to an annual dance which the firm she worked for gave to its employees. A not very exciting occasion, but it was to be held at one of London's well-known hotels and that, combined with the fact that it was mid-February and life was a bit dull, meant that the occasion merited an effort on her part to make the best of herself.

She remembered her manners. 'Do you know Thomas? I suppose you're from the hospital. He's Ruth's fiancé. He's not ill or anything?'

'I know Thomas and I am at the same hospital. He is in splendid health.'

'Oh, good. But horribly overworked, I suppose?'

'Yes, indeed.' His eye fell on the curtain once more. 'You are a skilled needlewoman?'

'Only when I am desperate. What do you do at the hospital? Teach, I suppose, if you are a professor?'

'I do my best…'

'Of what? Professor of what?'

'Surgery.'

'So you're handy with a needle too!' said Julia, and

before he could answer that Ruth came in with the coffee.

'Getting to know each other?' she asked cheerfully. 'Thank you for bringing the parcel, Professor. I'm sorry you won't see Monica—she runs the nursery school here. Luckily I've got the morning off from the surgery, and Julia is always here, of course. She works at home—writes verses for greetings cards.'

Ruth handed round the coffee, oblivious of Julia's heavy frown.

'How very interesting,' observed the Professor, and she gave him a quick look, suspecting that he was amused. Which he was, although nothing of it showed on his face.

Ruth asked diffidently. 'I suppose Thomas hasn't heard if he's got that senior registrar's job? I know he'd phone me, but if he's busy...'

'I think I can set your mind at rest. He should hear some time today. He's a good man and I shall be glad to have him in my team in a senior capacity.' He smiled at Ruth. 'Does that mean that you will marry?'

She beamed at him. 'Yes, just as soon as we can find somewhere to live.' She went on chattily, 'An aunt left us this house, and we came here to live when Mother and Father died, but I think we shall all be glad when we marry and can leave it.'

'Your other sister—Monica?' encouraged the Professor gently.

'Oh, she's engaged to the local curate; he's just waiting to get a parish. And Julia's got an admirer—a junior partner in the firm she works for. So you see, we are all nicely settled.'

He glanced at Julia. She didn't look at all settled,

for she was indignantly pink and looked as though she wanted to throw something. She said coldly, 'I'm sure the Professor isn't in the least interested in us, Ruth.' She picked up the coffee pot. 'More coffee, Professor?'

Her tone dared him to say yes and delay his departure.

He had a second cup, and she hated him. And she thought he would never go.

When he did, he shook hands, with the observation that the dress would be a success.

Ruth went with him to the door. When she came back she said, 'He's got a Rolls; you ought to see it.' She glanced at Julia's kneeling form. 'You were a bit rude, dear. And he's such a nice man.'

Julia snipped savagely at a length of curtain. 'I hope I never meet him again.'

'Well, I don't suppose you will. He's a bit grand for us…'

'There's nothing wrong with a rising young surgeon and a member of the clergy.' She'd almost added *and a junior partner in a greetings card firm,'* but she didn't, for Oscar, accepted as her admirer by everyone but herself, didn't quite fit. Curiosity got the better of her.

'Why do you say he's grand?'

'He's at the very top of the tree in the medical world and he's got a Dutch title—comes from an ancient family with lots of money. Never talks about himself. Thomas says he's a very private man.'

'Huh,' said Julia. 'Probably no one's good enough for him.'

Ruth commented mildly, 'You do dislike him, don't you?'

Julia began to wield her scissors again. 'Dislike him? I don't even know him. Shall we have Welsh rarebit for lunch? I'll make some scones for tea. Monica will be ravenous when she gets home; she never has time to eat her sandwiches. And if you're going to the shops you could bring some steak and kidney and I'll make a pudding.' She added, 'Filling and cheap.'

She spoke without rancour; the three Gracey sisters, living together for the sake of economy in the poky little house a long-dead aunt had bequeathed to them, had learned to live frugally. The house might be theirs, but there were rates and taxes, gas and electricity, clothes and food to be paid for. None of them had been trained to do anything in the business world, having been left suddenly with nothing but memories of their mother and father, killed in a car accident, and a carefree life in a pleasant old house in the country with never a thought of money worries.

It had been Julia who'd got them organised, refusing to be daunted by unexpected debts, selling their home to pay off the mortgage, arguing with bank managers, solicitors, and salvaging the remnants of her father's ill-advised investments. Once in their new home, it had been she who had urged the rather shy Ruth to take the part-time job as a receptionist to the local doctor while she looked for work for herself and Monica joined the staff of the local nursery school. But Julia had had no luck until, searching through the ads in the local paper, she'd seen one from the greetings card company.

Nothing ventured, nothing gained, she had decided, and had sat down to compose a batch of verses and send them off. Much to her surprise, the firm had taken her on. It was badly paid, but it meant that she could work at home and do the housekeeping and the cooking. And they managed very well.

Ruth had met Thomas when she had gone to the hospital to collect some urgent path. lab. Results for Dr Goodman, and soon they would marry. Monica, although she liked children, had never been quite sure that she wanted to stay at home, especially in such alien surroundings, but then George had come one day to tell the children Bible stories and all ideas of going out into the glamorous world to find a job more to her liking had faded away. They would have to wait to marry, of course, until George had a parish. In the meantime she was happy.

Which left Julia, twenty-four years old, bursting with life and energy. Because she had a happy nature she didn't allow herself to dwell on what might have been, but wrote her sentimental little verses, kept the house clean and tidy and, being clever with her needle, dressed herself in a style which, while not being the height of fashion, was a passable imitation.

It was fortunate, she supposed, that Oscar, her admirer—for he was only that at the moment, although he promised to be rather more when it was convenient for him to be so—had absolutely no taste in clothes. That horrible professor might sneer in a well-mannered way at the curtain, but Oscar wouldn't suspect. Indeed, even if he did, he would probably approve, for he was of a frugal nature when it came to spending money. He was persistent too. She had tried, over and over again, to shake him off, to suggest that she would make him a most unsuitable wife, but he refused to be shaken and, despite the countless excuses she had given, she was committed to attend the annual dance given by the greetings card firm.

Rightly, Ruth and Monica had urged her to go and enjoy herself. But neither of them had met Oscar, and she had given way because she knew that they both felt unhappy at the idea of her being left alone when they married. When she allowed herself to think about it she felt unhappy about that too.

She put away her sewing and started on the household chores, and found herself thinking about the Professor. He seemed a tiresome man, and she suspected that it would be hard to get the better of him. Probably he was horrid to his patients.

Professor van der Maes, contrary to Julia's idea, was treating the endless stream of patients attending his clinic with kindness and patience, his quiet voice reassuring, his smile encouraging. He was a tired man, for he worked too hard, but no patient had ever found him uncaring. But that was a side which he seldom showed to anyone else. The nursing staff who worked for him quickly learnt that he would stand no nonsense, that only their best efforts would suit him, and as for his students—he represented the goal they hoped to obtain one day. A good word from him was worth a dozen from anyone else, just as a quiet reprimand sent them into instant dejection. They called him the old man behind his back, and fiercely defended any criticism anyone was foolish enough to utter.

The Professor remained unmoved by other people's opinion of him, good or bad. He was an excellent surgeon and he loved his work, and he had friends who would be his for life, but he had no use for casual acquaintances. He had a social life when his work permitted, and was much sought after as a dinner party guest. Since he was unmarried, he could have taken his pick of any of the women he met. But, although he was a pleasant companion, he showed no interest in any of them. Somewhere in the world, he supposed, there was the woman he would fall in love with and want for his wife, but he was no longer young and he would probably end his days as a crusty old bachelor.

It wasn't until he was driving back to London a few days later that he thought about the three Gracey sisters. Ruth would make Thomas a good wife: a beautiful girl with her shy smile and gentle voice. He thought only fleetingly of Julia. Pretty, he supposed, but sharp-tongued, and she made no effort to be pleasant. She was the last person he imagined would spend her days writing sentimental verses for greetings cards, and what woman in her senses wore dresses made from curtains? He laughed, and forgot her.

The dance was ten days later, and, since the firm had had a good year, it was to be held at one of the more prestigious hotels. There was to be a buffet supper before everyone went to the hotel ballroom, and Ruth and Monica, anxious that Julia should enjoy herself, lent slippers and an old but still magnificent shawl which had belonged to their mother. They sent her there in a taxi—an unnecessary expense, Julia protested; the journey there would have been a lengthy one by bus but far cheaper. However, they insisted, privately of the opinion that Oscar could have come and fetched her instead of meeting her there...

The dress, despite its origin, was a success, simply made, but it fitted where it should, and unless anyone had actually seen the curtain, hanging in the spare bedroom, one would never have known...

Julia walked out of the taxi feeling quite pleased with herself, straight into the Professor's person.

He set her tidily on her feet. 'Well, well, Miss Julia Gracey. Unexpected and delightful.' He looked around him. 'You are alone?'

She bade him good evening in a choked voice. 'I am meeting someone in the hotel.'

She glanced around, looking without much hope for Oscar. There was no sign of him, of course. He had said that he would be at the hotel entrance, waiting for her. She supposed that she would have to go inside and look for him. She was not easily daunted, but the hotel's imposing entrance and the equally imposing appearance of the doorman daunted her now, and how and by what misfortune had the Professor got here? Surely he hadn't anything to do with greetings cards?

It seemed not. He said easily, 'I'm meeting friends here. We may as well go in together.' He paid the cabby and took her arm. 'Your friend will be looking for you inside?'

He was being kind, with a casual kindness it was impossible to resent. She sought frantically for something to say as the doorman opened the doors with a flourish and they joined the people in the foyer.

There was no sign of Oscar. She had been a fool to accept his invitation; she didn't even like him much.

'Let me have your shawl,' said the Professor. 'I'll let the girl have it.' And he had taken it from her and left her for a moment, returning with a ticket which he tucked into the little handbag hanging from her wrist.

She found her tongue then, 'Thank you. I'll—I'll wait here. Oscar will find me…'

'Oscar?' She mistrusted his casual voice. 'Ah, yes, of course. And if I'm not mistaken this must be he…'

She should have been glad to see him, and she might well have been if he had expressed regret at not meeting her promptly. But all he did was thump her on the shoulder and say heartily, 'Sorry old lady. I got held up; so many people wanted to have a chat.'

He looked her up and down. 'Got yourself a new dress for the occasion? Not bad, not bad at all…'

His glance fell upon the Professor, who had made no attempt to go away.

'Do I know you?'

Julia, aware of the Professor's eyes fixed on the curtain, said tartly, 'No, Oscar, you don't. This is Professor van der Maes. He knows Ruth's fiancé.'

Oscar looked uneasy under the Professor's cool gaze. 'Nice to meet you. Come along, Julia, I'll find you somewhere to sit; I've one or two important clients to talk to, but we'll be able to dance presently.'

He nodded in a condescending manner at the Professor, who took no notice but said pleasantly to Julia, 'I do hope you have a happy evening,' and, as Oscar turned away rudely to speak to a passing couple, 'but I doubt it.' He looked amused. 'I can't say that I agree with Oscar about your dress, but then I know it's a curtain, don't I?'

He was sorry the moment he had said it; for a moment she had the look of a small girl who had been slapped for no reason at all. But only for a moment. Julia stared up into his handsome face. 'Go away, Professor. I don't like you and I hope I never see you again.'

She had spoken quietly but she looked daggers at him. She turned her back then, surprised at how upset she felt. After all, she hadn't liked him the first time, and she couldn't care less if he jeered at the dress or liked it. If Oscar liked it, that was all that mattered, she told herself, not believing a word of it. But presently, when Oscar had finished his conversation, she went with him to the hotel ballroom, to be sat on one of the little gilt chairs and told to wait awhile until he had the leisure to dance with her.

A not very promising prospect—but quickly lightened by a number of men who, seeing a pretty girl sitting by herself, danced her off in rapid succession. Which served Oscar right by the time he found himself ready to partner her.

'Some of these modern dances are not dignified,' he told her severely, propelling her round the ballroom with correct stiffness. 'You would have done better to have sat quietly until I was free to come to you.'

'But I like to dance, Oscar.'

'Dancing in moderation is splendid exercise,' said Oscar, at his stuffiest.

They came to a dignified halt as the music stopped.

Julia spoke her thoughts out loud. 'Do you want to marry me, Oscar?' she asked.

He looked at her with astonishment and displeasure.

'My dear Julia, what a very—very...' he sought for the right word '...unwomanly remark to make. I must only hope it was a slight aberration of the tongue.'

'It wasn't anything to do with my tongue; it was a thought in my head.' She looked at him. 'You haven't answered me, Oscar?'

'I have no intention of doing so. I am shocked, Julia. Perhaps you should retire to the ladies' room and compose yourself.'

'You sound like someone in a Victorian novel,' she told him. 'But, yes, I think that would be best.'

The ballroom was at the back of the hotel; it took her a few moments to find the cloakroom where the Professor had left her wrap. She would have to take a bus, she hadn't enough money for a taxi, but it wasn't late and there were plenty of people about. She wrapped the vast mohair shawl she and her sisters shared for evening occasions round her and crossed the foyer, comfortably full of people. And halfway to the door the Professor, apparently appearing from thin air, put a hand on her arm.

'Not leaving already?' he wanted to know. 'It's barely an hour since you arrived.'

She had to stop, his hand, resting so lightly on her arm, nevertheless reminding her of a ball and chain. She said politely, 'Yes, I'm leaving, Professor.' She looked at his hand. 'Goodbye.'

He took no notice; neither did he remove his hand.

'You're upset; you have the look of someone about to explode. I'll take you home.'

'No, thank you. I'm quite capable of getting myself home.'

For answer he tucked her hand under his elbow. 'Your Oscar will come looking for you,' he said mildly.

'He's not my Oscar...'

'Ah, I can't say that I'm surprised. Now, come along. This is indeed a splendid excuse for me to leave with you—a pompous dinner with endless speeches to which I have been bidden.'

He had propelled her gently past the doorman, out into the chilly night and, after towing her along gently, popped her into his car, parked nearby.

Getting in beside her, he asked, 'Are you going to cry?'

'Certainly not. And I have no wish to be here in your car. You are being high-handed, Professor.' She sniffed. 'I'm not a child.'

He looked at her, smiling a little. 'No, I had realised that. Are you hungry?'

She was taken by surprise. 'Yes...'

'Splendid. And, since you are not going to cry and I'm hungry too, we will go and eat somewhere.'

'No,' said Julia.

'My dear girl, be sensible. It's the logical thing to do.' He started the car. 'Let us bury the hatchet for an hour or so. You are free to dislike me the moment I see you to your front door.'

She was hungry, so the prospect of a meal was tempting. She said, 'Well, all right, but not anywhere grand—the curtain...'

He said quietly, 'I'm sorry I said that. You look very nice and it was unforgivable of me. We will go somewhere you won't need to be uneasy.'

He sounded kind and her spirits lifted. Perhaps he wasn't so bad… He spoilt it by adding, 'Is your entire wardrobe made up of curtains?' He glanced at her. 'You must be a very talented young lady.'

She was on the point of making a fiery answer when the thought of a meal crossed her mind. She had no idea why he had asked her out and she didn't care; she would choose all the most expensive things on the menu…

He took her to Wilton's, spoke quietly to the *maître d'*, and followed her to one of the booths, so that any fears concerning her dress were instantly put at rest.

'Now, what shall we have?' asked the Professor, well aware of her relief that the booth sheltered her nicely from the other diners. 'I can recommend the cheese soufflé, and the sole Meunière is excellent.' When she agreed he ordered from the waitress and turned his attention to the *sommelier* and the wine list. Which gave Julia a chance to study the menu. She need not have bothered to choose the most expensive food; everything was expensive.

When it came it was delicious, and cooked by a master hand. She thought fleetingly of Oscar, and applied herself to her dinner, and, being nicely brought up, made polite conversation the while. The Professor replied suitably, amused at that and wondering what had possessed him to take her to dinner. He went out seldom, and when he did his companion would be one of his numerous acquaintances: elegant young women, dressed impeccably, bone-thin and fussing delicately about what they could and couldn't eat.

Julia, on the other hand, ate everything she was offered with an unselfconscious pleasure, and capped the sole with sherry trifle and drank the wine he had ordered. And that loosed her tongue, for presently, over coffee, she asked, 'If you are Dutch, why do you live in England?'

'I only do so for part of the time. My home is in Holland and I work there as well. I shall be going back there in a few weeks' time for a month or so.'

'How very unsettling,' observed Julia. 'But I suppose you are able to pick and choose if you are a Professor?'

'I suppose I can,' he agreed mildly. 'What are you going to do about Oscar?'

'I dare say he won't find me a suitable wife for a junior partner...'

'And will that break your heart?'

'No. He sort of grew on me, if you see what I mean.'

He said smoothly, 'Ah—you have a more romantic outlook, perhaps?'

She took a sip of coffee. 'It's almost midnight. Would you take me home, please?'

Not one of the women he had taken out to dinner had ever suggested that it was getting late and they wished to go home. On the contrary. The Professor stifled a laugh, assured her that they would go at once, and signed the bill. On the journey through London's streets he discussed the weather, the pleasures of the English countryside and the prospect of a fine summer.

The street was quiet and only barely lit. He got out and opened the car door for her, before taking the door key from her. He opened the door and gave her back the key.

Julia cast around in her mind for something gracious to say. 'Thank you for my dinner,' she said finally, and, since that didn't sound in the least gracious, added, 'I enjoyed the dinner very much and the restaurant was—was very elegant. It was a very pleasant evening…'

She didn't like his smile in the dimly lit hallway. 'Don't try too hard, Julia,' he told her. 'Goodnight.'

He pushed her gently into the hall and closed the door soundlessly behind her.

'I hate him,' said Julia, and took off her shoes, flung the shawl onto the floor and crept upstairs to her bed. She had intended to lie awake and consider how much she disliked him, but she went to sleep at once.

The Professor took himself off home, to his elegant Chelsea house, locked the Rolls in the mews garage behind it, and let himself into his home. There was a wall-light casting a gentle light on the side table in the hall and he picked up the handful of letters on it as he went to his study.

This was a small, comfortably furnished room, with rows of bookshelves, a massive desk, a chair behind it and two smaller ones each side of the small fireplace. Under the window was a table with a computer and a pile of papers and books. He ignored it and put the letters on his desk before going out of the room again and along the hall, through the baize door at the end and down the steps to the kitchen, where he poured himself coffee from the pot on the Aga and acknowledged the sleepy greetings from two small dogs.

They got out of the basket they shared and sat beside him while he drank his coffee: two small creatures with heavily whiskered faces, short legs and long, thin rat-like tails. The professor had found them, abandoned, terrified and starving, some six months earlier. It was apparent that they weren't going to grow any larger or handsomer, but they had become members of his household and his devoted companions. He saw them back into their basket, with the promise of a walk in the morning, and went back to his study. There were some notes he needed to write up before he went to bed.

He sat down and pulled the papers towards him and then sat back in his chair, thinking about the evening. What had possessed him to take Julia out to dinner? he wondered. A nice enough girl, no doubt, but with a sharp tongue and making no attempt to hide the fact that she didn't like him. The unknown Oscar was possibly to be pitied. He smiled suddenly. She had enjoyed her dinner, and he doubted whether Oscar rose much above soup of the day and a baked potato. He acknowledged that this was an unfair thought; Oscar might even now be searching fruitlessly for Julia.

When Julia went down to breakfast in the morning, Ruth and Monica were already at the kitchen table, and without wasting time they began to fire questions at her.

'Did you dance? Was it a splendid hotel? What did

you eat? Did Oscar propose? Did he bring you home?'

Julia lifted the teapot. 'I danced three and a half times, and the hotel was magnificent.'

She shook cornflakes into a bowl. She didn't like them, but, according to the TV ad, the girl who ate them had a wand-like figure—a state to which she hoped in time to subdue her own generous curves. She said, 'I didn't eat at the hotel.' She took a sip of tea. 'Oscar didn't propose. I don't think he ever will now. And he didn't bring me home.'

'Julia, you didn't come home alone?'

'No, Professor van der Maes drove me back.'

She finished the cornflakes and put bread in the toaster.

'Start at the beginning and don't leave anything out,' said Ruth. 'What on earth was the Professor doing there? He doesn't write verses, does he?'

'No. Though I'm sure he is very handy with a needle.'

Her sisters exchanged glances. 'Why did you dance half a dance?' asked Ruth.

Julia said through a mouthful of toast, 'Oscar was annoyed because I hadn't stayed on my chair to wait for him, so I asked him if he wanted to marry me.'

'Julia, how could you…?'

'He told me to go to the ladies' room and compose myself, so I found my shawl and left, and the Professor was at the entrance. He said he was hungry and asked me if I was, and when I said yes, he took me to Wilton's.'

'Wilton's?' chorused her sisters, and then added, 'The dress…?'

'It was all right. We sat in a booth. It was a nice dinner. And then, when I asked him to bring me home, he did.'

Two pairs of astonished blue eyes stared at her. 'What about Oscar?'

'He was shocked.'

'And the Professor? Whatever did he say?'

'He said he wasn't surprised that Oscar wasn't mine. You will both be late for work...'

'But why should the Professor take you out to dinner?' asked Ruth.

'He said he was hungry.'

'You can be very tiresome sometimes, Julia,' said Monica severely.

When they had gone Julia set about the household chores and then, those done, she made coffee and a cheese sandwich and sat down to write verses. Perhaps Oscar would be able to get her the sack, but on the other hand her verses sold well. The senior partners might not agree. For it wasn't the kind of work many people would want to do and it was badly paid. She polished off a dozen verses, fed Muffin, the family cat, and peeled the potatoes for supper. Oscar, she reflected, wouldn't bother her again.

CHAPTER TWO

OSCAR came four days later. Julia was making pastry for a steak pie and she went impatiently to the front door when its knocker was thumped. Oscar was on the doorstep. 'I wish to talk to you, Julia.'

'Come in, then,' said Julia briskly. 'I'm making pastry and don't want it to spoil.'

She ushered him into the house, told him to leave his coat in the hall, and then went back into the kitchen and plunged her hands into the bowl.

'Do sit down,' she invited him, and, when he looked askance at Muffin the household cat, sitting in the old Windsor chair by the stove, added, 'Take a chair at the table. It's warm here. Anyway, I haven't lighted the fire in the sitting room yet.'

She bent over her pastry, and presently he said stuffily, 'You can at least leave that and listen to what I have to say, Julia.'

She put the dough on the floured board and held a rolling pin.

'I'm so sorry, Oscar, but I really can't leave it. I am listening, though.'

He settled himself into his chair. 'I have given a good deal of thought to your regrettable behaviour at the dance, Julia. I can but suppose that the excitement of the occasion and the opulence of your surroundings had caused you to become so—so unlike yourself.

26

After due consideration I have decided that I shall overlook that…'

Julia laid her pastry neatly over the meat and tidied the edges with a knife. 'Don't do that,' she begged him. 'I wasn't in the least excited, only annoyed to be stuck on a chair in a corner—and left to find my own way in, too.'

'I have a position to uphold in the firm,' said Oscar. And when she didn't answer he asked, 'Who was that man you were talking to? Really, Julia, it is most unsuitable. I trust you found your way home? There is a good bus service?'

Julia was cutting pastry leaves to decorate her pie. She said, 'I had dinner at Wilton's and was driven home afterwards.'

Oscar sought for words and, finding none, got to his feet. 'There is nothing more to be said, Julia. I came here prepared to forgive you, but I see now that I have allowed my tolerance to be swept aside by your frivolity.'

Julia dusted her floury hands over the bowl and began to clear up the table. Listening to Oscar was like reading a book written a hundred years ago. He didn't belong in this century and, being a kind-hearted girl, she felt sorry for him.

'I'm not at all suitable for you, Oscar,' she told him gently.

He said nastily, 'Indeed you are not, Julia. You have misled me…'

She was cross again. 'I didn't know we had got to that stage. Anyway, what you need isn't a wife, it's a doormat. And do go, Oscar, before I hit you with this rolling pin.'

He got to his feet. 'I must remind you that your future with the firm is in jeopardy, Julia. I have some influence...'

Which was just what she could have expected from him, she supposed. They went into the hall and he got into his coat. She opened the door and ushered him out, wished him goodbye, and closed the door before he had a chance to say more.

She told her sisters when they came home, and Monica said. 'He might have made a good steady husband, but he sounds a bit out of date.'

'I don't think I want a steady husband,' said Julia, and for a moment she thought about the Professor. She had no idea why she should have done that; she didn't even like him...

So, during the next few days she waited expectantly for a letter from the greetings card firm, but when one did come it contained a cheque for her last batch of verses and a request for her to concentrate on wedding cards—June was the bridal month and they needed to get the cards to the printers in good time...

'Reprieved,' said Julia, before she cashed the cheque and paid the gas bill.

It was difficult to write about June roses and wedded bliss in blustery March. But she wrote her little verses and thought how nice it would be to marry on a bright summer's morning, wearing all the right clothes and with the right bridegroom.

A week later Thomas came one evening. He had got the job as senior registrar and, what was more, had now been offered one of the small houses the hospital rented out to their staff. There was no reason why he and Ruth shouldn't marry as soon as possible. The place was furnished, and it was a bit poky, but once he had some money saved they could find something better.

'And the best of it is I'm working for Professor van der Maes.' His nice face was alight with the prospect. 'You won't mind a quiet wedding?' he asked Ruth anxiously.

Ruth would have married him in a cellar wearing a sack. 'We'll get George to arrange everything. And it will be quiet anyway; there's only us. Your mother and father will come?'

Julia went to the kitchen to make coffee and sandwiches and took Monica with her. 'We'll give them half an hour. Monica, have you any money? Ruth must have some clothes…'

They sat together at the table, doing sums. 'There aren't any big bills due,' said Julia. 'If we're very careful and we use the emergency money we could just manage.'

Thomas was to take up his new job in three weeks' time: the best of reasons why he and Ruth should marry, move into their new home and have a few days together first. Which meant a special licence and no time at all to buy clothes and make preparations for a quiet wedding. Julia and Monica gave Ruth all the money they could lay hands on and then set about planning the wedding day. There would be only a handful of guests: Dr Goodman and his wife, George, and the vicar who would take the service, Thomas's parents and the best man.

They got out the best china and polished the teaspoons, and Julia went into the kitchen and leafed through her cookery books.

It was a scramble, but by the time the wedding day dawned Ruth had a dress and jacket in a pale blue, with a fetching hat, handbag, gloves and shoes, and the nucleus of a new wardrobe suitable for a senior registrar's wife. Julia had assembled an elegant buffet for after the ceremony, and Monica had gone to the market and bought daffodils, so that when they reached the church—a red-brick mid-Victorian building, sadly lacking in beauty—its rather bleak interior glowed with colour.

Monica had gone on ahead, leaving Julia to make the last finishing touches to the table, which took longer than she had expected. She had to hurry to the church just as Dr Goodman came for Ruth.

She arrived there a bit flushed, her russet hair glowing under her little green felt hat—Ruth's hat, really, but it went well with her green jacket and skirt, which had been altered and cleaned and altered again and clung to, since they were suitable for serious occasions.

Julia sniffed appreciatively at the fresh scent of the daffodils and started down the aisle to the back views of Thomas and his best man and the sprinkling of people in the pews. It was a long aisle, and she was halfway up when she saw the Professor sitting beside Mrs Goodman. They appeared to be on the best of terms and she shot past their pew without looking at them. His appearance was unexpected, but she supposed that Thomas, now a senior member of the team, merited his presence.

When Ruth came, Julia concentrated on the ceremony, but the Professor's image most annoyingly got between her and the beautiful words of the simple service. There was no need for him to be there. He and Thomas might be on the best of terms professionally, but they surely had different social lives? Did the medical profession enjoy a social life? she wondered, then brought her attention back sharply to Thomas and Ruth, exchanging their vows. They would be happy, she reflected, watching them walk back down the aisle. They were both so sure of their love. She wondered what it must feel like to be so certain.

After the first photos had been taken Julia slipped away, so as to get home before anyone else and make sure that everything was just so.

She was putting the tiny sausage rolls in the oven to warm when Ruth and Thomas arrived, closely followed by everyone else, and presently the best man came into the kitchen to get a corkscrew.

'Not that I think we'll need it,' he told her cheerfully. 'The Prof bought half a dozen bottles of champagne with him. Now that's what I call a wedding gift of the right sort. Can I help?'

'Get everyone drinking. I'll be along with these sausage rolls in a minute or two.'

She had them nicely arranged on a dish when the Professor came into the kitchen. He had a bottle and a glass in one hand.

He said, 'A most happy occasion. Your vicar has had two glasses already.'

He poured the champagne and handed her a glass. 'Thirsty work, heating up sausage rolls.'

She had to laugh. Such light-hearted talk didn't

sound like him at all, and for a moment she liked him. She took her glass and said, 'We can't toast them yet, can we? But it is a happy day.' And, since she was thirsty and excited, she drank deeply.

The Professor had an unexpected feeling of tenderness towards her; she might have a sharp tongue and not like him, but her naïve treatment of a glass of Moet et Chandon Brut Imperial he found touching.

She emptied the glass and said, 'That was nice.'

He agreed gravely. 'A splendid drink for such an occasion,' and he refilled her glass, observing prudently, 'I'll take the tray in for you.'

The champagne was having an effect upon her empty insides. She gave him a wide smile. 'The best man—what's his name, Peter?—said he'd be back...'

'He will be refilling glasses.' The Professor picked up the tray, opened the door and ushered her out of the kitchen.

Julia swanned around, light-headed and light-hearted. It was marvellous what a couple of glasses of champagne did to one. She ate a sausage roll, drank another glass of champagne, handed round the sandwiches and would have had another glass of champagne if the Professor hadn't taken the glass from her.

'They're going to cut the cake,' he told her, 'and then we'll toast the happy couple.' Only then did he hand her back her glass.

After Ruth and Thomas had driven away, and everyone else was going home, she realised that the Professor had gone too, taking the best man with him.

'He asked me to say goodbye,' said Monica as the pair of them sat at the kitchen table, their shoes off, drinking strong tea. 'He took the best man with him, said he was rather pressed for time.'

Julia, still pleasantly muzzy from the champagne, wondered why it was that the best man had had the time to say goodbye to her. If he'd gone with the Professor, then surely the Professor could have found the time to do the same? She would think about that when her head was a little clearer.

Life had to be reorganised now that Ruth had left home; they missed her share of the housekeeping, but by dint of economising they managed very well.

Until, a few weeks later, Monica came into the house like a whirlwind, calling to Julia to come quickly; she had news.

George had been offered a parish; a small rural town in the West country. 'Miles from anywhere,' said Monica, glowing with happiness, 'but thriving. Not more than a large village, I suppose, but very scattered. He's to go there this week and see if he likes it.'

'And if he does?'

'He'll go there in two weeks' time. I'll go with him, of course. We can get married by special licence first.' Then she danced round the room. 'Oh, Julia, isn't it all marvellous? I'm so happy…!'

It wasn't until later, after they had toasted the future in a bottle of wine from the supermarket, that Monica said worriedly, 'Julia, what about you? What will you do? You'll never be able to manage…'

Julia had had time to have an answer ready. She said cheerfully, 'I shall take in lodgers until we decide what to do about this house. You and Ruth will probably like to sell it, and I think that is a good thing.'

'But you?' persisted Monica.

'I shall go to dressmaking classes and then set up on my own. I shall like that.'

'You don't think Oscar will come back? If he really loved you…?'

'But he didn't, and I wouldn't go near him with a bargepole— whatever that means.'

'But you'll marry…?'

'Oh, I expect so. And think how pleased my husband will be to have a wife who makes her own clothes.'

Julia poured the last of the wine into their glasses. 'Now tell me your plans…'

She listened to her sister's excited voice, making suitable comments from time to time, making suggestions, and all the while refusing to give way to the feeling of panic. So silly, she told herself sternly; she had a roof over her head for the time being, and she was perfectly able to reorganise her life. She wouldn't be lonely; she would have lodgers and Muffin…

'You'll marry from here?' she asked.

'Yes, but very quietly. We'll go straight to the parish after the wedding. There'll be just us and Ruth— and Thomas, if he can get away. No wedding breakfast or anything.' Monica laughed. 'I always wanted a big wedding, you know—white chiffon and a veil and bridesmaids—but none of that matters. It'll have to be early in the morning.'

Monica's lovely face glowed with happiness, and Julia said, 'Aren't you dying to hear what the vicarage is like? And the little town? You'll be a marvellous vicar's wife.'

'Yes, I think I shall,' said Monica complacently.

Presently she said uncertainly, 'Are you sure you'll be all right, Julia? There has always been the three of us...'

'Of course I'll be fine—and how super that I'll be able to visit you. Once I get started I can get a little car...'

Which was daydreaming with a vengeance, but served to pacify Monica.

After that events crowded upon each other at a great rate. George found his new appointment very much to his liking; moreover, he had been accepted by the church wardens and those of the parish whom he had met with every sign of satisfaction. The vicarage was large and old-fashioned, but there was a lovely garden... He was indeed to take up his appointment in two weeks' time, which gave them just that time to arrange their wedding—a very quiet one, quieter even than Ruth's and Thomas's, for they were to marry in the early morning and drive straight down to their new home.

Julia, helping Monica to pack, had little time to think about anything else, but was relieved that the girl who was to take over Monica's job had rented a room with her: a good omen for the future, she told her sisters cheerfully. Trudie seemed a nice girl, too, quiet and studious, and it would be nice to have someone else in the house, and nicer still to have the rent money...

She would have to find another lodger, thought Julia, waving goodbye to George's elderly car and the newly married pair. If she could let two rooms she would be able to manage if she added the rent to the small amounts she got from the greetings card firm. Later on, she quite understood, Ruth and Monica would want to sell the house, and with her own share she would start some kind of a career...

She went back into the empty house; Trudie would be moving in on the following morning and she must make sure that her room was as welcoming as possible. As soon as she had a second lodger and things were running smoothly, she would pay a visit to Ruth.

A week went by. It was disappointing that there had been no replies to her advertisement; she would have to try again in a week or so, and put cards in the windows of the row of rather seedy shops a few streets away. In the meantime she would double her output of verses.

Trudie had settled in nicely, coming and going quietly, letting herself in and out with the key Julia had given her. Another one like her would be ideal, reflected Julia, picking up the post from the doormat.

There was a letter from the greetings card firm and she opened it quickly; there would be a cheque inside. There was, but there was a letter too. The firm was changing its policy: in future they would deal only with cards of a humorous nature since that was what the market demanded. It was with regret that they would no longer be able to accept her work. If she had a batch ready to send then they would accept it, but nothing further.

Julia read the letter again, just to make sure, and then went into the kitchen, made a pot of tea and sat down to drink it. It was a blow; the money the firm paid her was very little but it had been a small, steady income. Its loss would be felt. She did some sums on the back of the envelope and felt the beginnings of a headache. It was possible that Oscar was behind it… She read the letter once again; they would accept one last batch. Good, she would send as many verses as she could think up. She got pencil and paper and set to work. Just let me say on this lovely day…she began, and by lunchtime had more than doubled her output.

She typed them all out on her old portable and took them to the post. It would have been satisfying to have torn up the letter and put it in an envelope and sent it back, but another cheque would be satisfying too.

The cheque came a few days later, but still no new lodger. Which, as it turned out, was a good thing…

Thomas phoned. Ruth was in bed with flu, could she possibly help out for a day or two? Not to stay, of course, but an hour or two each day until Ruth was on her feet. There was a bus, he added hopefully.

It meant two buses; she would have to change halfway. The hospital wasn't all that far away, but was awkward to get to.

Julia glanced at the clock. 'I'll be there about lunchtime. I must tell Trudie, my lodger. I'll stay until the evening if that's OK.'

'Bless you,' said Thomas. 'I should be free about five o'clock.'

Trudie, summoned from a horde of toddlers, was helpful. She would see to Muffin, go back at lunchtime and make sure that everything was all right, and she wasn't going out that evening anyway. Julia hurried to the main street and caught a bus.

The house was close to the hospital, one of a neat row in which the luckier of the medical staff lived. The door key, Thomas had warned her, was under the pot of flowers by the back door, and Julia let herself in, calling out as she did so.

It was a very small house. She put her bag down in the narrow hall and went up the stairs at its end, guided by the sound of Ruth's voice.

She was propped up in bed, her lovely face only slightly dimmed by a red nose and puffy eyes. She said thickly, 'Julia, you darling. You don't mind coming? I feel so awful, and Thomas has to be in Theatre all day. I'll be better tomorrow...'

'You'll stay there until Thomas says that you can get up,' said Julia, 'and of course I don't mind coming. In fact it makes a nice change. Now, how about a wash and a clean nightie, and then a morsel of something to eat?'

'I hope you don't catch the flu,' said Ruth later, drinking tea and looking better already, drowsy now in her freshly made bed, her golden hair, though rather lank, it must be admitted, neatly brushed. All the same, thought Julia, she looked far from well.

'Has the doctor been?' she asked.

'Yes, Dr Soames, one of the medical consultants. Someone is coming with some pills...'

Thomas brought them during his lunch hour. He couldn't stop, his lunch 'hour' being a figure of speech. A cup of coffee and a sandwich was the norm on this day, when Professor van der Maes was operating, but he lingered with Ruth as long as he could, thanked Julia profusely and assured her that he would be back by five o'clock. 'I'll be on call,' he told her, 'but only until midnight.'

'Would you like me to keep popping in for a few days, until Ruth is feeling better?'

'Would you? I hate leaving her.'

He went then, and Julia went down to the little kitchen, made another hot drink for Ruth and boiled herself an egg. Tomorrow she would bring some fruit and a new loaf. Bread and butter, cut very thin, was something most invalids would eat.

It was almost six o'clock when Thomas returned, bringing the Professor with him. The Professor spent a few minutes with Ruth, assured Thomas that she was looking better, and wandered into the kitchen, where Julia was laying a tray of suitable nourishment for Ruth.

'Get your coat,' he told her. 'I'll drive you home.'

Julia thumped a saucepan of milk onto the stove. 'Thank you, but I'll get a bus when I'm ready.'

Not so much as a hello or even a good evening, thought Julia pettishly.

His smile mocked her. 'Thomas is here now. Two's company, three's none.'

'Thomas will want his supper.'

Thomas breezed into the kitchen. 'I'm a first-rate cook. We're going to have a picnic upstairs. You go home, Julia. You've been a godsend, and we're so grateful. You will come tomorrow?'

'Yes,' said Julia, and without looking at either of the men went and got her coat, said goodnight to her sister and went downstairs again.

The two men were in the hall and Thomas backed

into the open kitchen door to make room for her, but even then the professor took up almost all the space. He opened the door and she squeezed past him into the street. Thomas came too, beaming at them both, just as though he was seeing them off for an evening out.

The Professor had nothing to say. He sat relaxed behind the wheel, and if he felt impatience at the heavy traffic he didn't show it. Watching the crowded pavements and the packed buses edging their way along the streets, Julia suddenly felt ashamed at her ingratitude.

'This is very kind of you,' she began. 'It would have taken me ages to get home.'

He said coolly, 'I shan't be going out of my way. I'm going to the children's hospital not five minutes' drive away from your home.'

A remark which hardly encouraged her to carry on the conversation.

He had nothing more to say then, but when he stopped before her house he got out, opened the car door for her and stood waiting while she unlocked the house door, dismissing her thanks with a laconic, 'I have already said it was no trouble. Goodnight, Julia.'

She stood in the open door as he got into the car and drove off.

'And that's the last time I'll accept a lift from you,' she said to the empty street. 'I can't think why you bothered, but I suppose Thomas was there and you had no choice.' She slammed the door. 'Horrid man.'

But she was aware of a kind of sadness; she was sure that he wasn't a horrid man, only where she was concerned. For some reason she annoyed him...

She got her supper, fed Muffin, and went to warn Trudie that she would be going to Ruth for the next few days. 'No one phoned about a room, I suppose?' she asked.

'Not a soul. Probably in a day or two you'll have any number of callers.'

But there was no one.

For the next few days Julia went to and fro while Ruth slowly improved. Of the Professor there was no sign, although her sister told her that he had come frequently to see her. Dr Soames came too, and told her that she was much better. 'Though I look a hag,' said Ruth.

'A beautiful hag,' said Julia bracingly, 'and tomorrow you're going to crawl downstairs for a couple of hours.'

Ruth brightened. 'Tom can get the supper and we'll have it round the fire, and I dare say Gerard will come for an hour...'

'Gerard?'

'The Professor. I simply couldn't go on calling him Professor, even though he seems a bit staid and stand-offish, doesn't he? But he's not in the least, and he's only thirty-six. He ought to be married, he nearly was a year ago, but he's not interested in girls. Not to marry, anyway. He's got lots of friends, but they're just friends.'

'You surprise me...'

Ruth gave her a thoughtful look. 'You don't like him?'

'I don't know him well enough to know if I like or dislike him.'

Ruth gave her a sharp look. 'I'm feeling so much

better; I'm sure I could manage. You've been an angel, coming each day, but you must be longing to be let off the hook.'

'There's nothing to keep me at home. Trudie looks after herself and keeps an eye on Muffin. And if you can put up with me for another few days I think it might be a good idea.'

'Oh, darling, would you really come? Just for a couple more days. I do feel so much better, but not quite me yet...'

'Of course I'll come. And we'll see how you are in two days' time.'

After those two days Julia had to admit that Ruth was quite able to cope without any help from her. It was all very well for her to spend the day there while Ruth was in bed, but now that she was up—still rather wan—Julia felt that Ruth and Tom would much rather be on their own.

The moment she arrived the next morning she told Ruth briskly, 'This is my last day; you don't need me any more...'

Ruth was sitting at the table in the tiny kitchen, chopping vegetables. She looked up, laughing. 'Oh, but I do. Sit down and I'll tell you.'

Julia took a bite of carrot. 'You want me to make curtains for the bathroom? I told you everyone could see in if they tried hard enough.'

'Curtains, pooh! Dr Soames says I need a little holiday, and Thomas says so too. He wants you to go with me. Do say you can. You haven't got another lodger yet, and Trudie could look after Muffin.'

'You're going to Monica's?' It would be lovely to

go away from the dull little house and duller street. 'Yes, of course I'll come.'

'You will? You really won't mind? Thomas won't let me go alone...' She added quickly, 'And we're not going to Monica. We're going to Holland.'

Before Julia could speak, she added, 'Gerard has a little cottage near a lake. There's no one there, only his housekeeper. He says it's very quiet there, and the country's pretty and just what I need. Thomas wants me to go. He's got a couple of days due to him and he'll drive us there.'

'There won't be anyone else there? Only us?'

'Yes, you and I. Tom will stay one night and come and fetch us back—he won't know exactly when, but it will be a week or two. You're not having second thoughts?'

Which was exactly what Julia was having, but one look at her sister's still pale face sent them flying; Ruth needed to get away from London and a week in the country would get her back onto her feet again. Although early summer so far had been chilly and wet, there was always the chance that it would become warm and sunny. She said again, 'Of course I'll love to come. I'll fix things up with Trudie. When are we to go?'

'Well, Thomas can get Saturday and Sunday off—that's in three days' time. We shan't need many clothes, so you'll only need to bring a case—and I've enough money for both of us.'

'Oh, I've plenty of money,' said Julia, with such an air of conviction that she believed it herself.

'You have? Well, I suppose you have more time to

work for the greetings card people now, and of course there's the rent from Trudie…'

Which was swallowed up almost before Julia had put it into her purse. But Ruth didn't have to know that, and she certainly wasn't going to tell anyone that she no longer had a market for her little verses. There would be another lodger soon, she told herself bracingly and she would find a part-time job; in the meantime she would enjoy her holiday.

The nagging thought that it was the Professor who had been the means of her having one rankled all the way home. For some reason she hated to be beholden to him.

She felt better about that when she came to the conclusion that he didn't know that she would be going; beyond offering the use of his house, he wouldn't be concerned with the details.

The Professor, phoning instructions to his housekeeper in Holland, was very well aware that she would be going with Ruth; he had himself suggested it, with just the right amount of casualness. He wasn't sure why he had done so but he suspected that he had wanted her to feel beholden to him.

He was an aloof man by nature, and an unhappy love affair had left him with a poor opinion of women. There were exceptions: his own family, his devoted housekeeper, his elderly nanny, the nursing staff who worked for him, life-long friends, wives of men he had known for years. He had added Ruth to the list, so in love with her Thomas—and so different from her sharp-tongued sister. And yet—there was something about Julia…

*   *   *

No need to take a lot of clothes, Ruth had said. Julia foraged through her wardrobe and found a leaf-brown tweed jacket, so old that it was almost fashionable once again. There was a pleated skirt which went quite well with it, a handful of tops and a jersey dress. It was, after all, getting warmer each day. As it was country they would go walking, she supposed, so that meant comfortable shoes. She could travel in the new pair she had had for the weddings. She added undies, a scarf and a thin dressing gown, and then sat down to count her money. And that didn't take long! There would be a week's rent from Trudie to add, and when she got back there would be another lot waiting for her. She went in search of her lodger and enlisted her help.

Trudie was a quiet, unassuming girl, saving to get married, good-natured and trustworthy. She willingly agreed to look after Muffin and make sure that the house was locked up at night.

'You could do with a holiday. No doubt when you get back you'll have a house full of lodgers and not a moment to yourself.'

A prospect which should have pleased Julia but somehow didn't.

Three days later Thomas and Ruth came to fetch her. They were to go by the catamaran from Harwich, a fast sea route which would get them to their destination during the afternoon. Julia, who had received only a garbled version of where they were going, spent a great part of their journey studying a map— a large, detailed one which the Professor had thoughtfully provided.

Somewhere south of Amsterdam and not too far

from Hilversum. And there were any number of lakes and no large towns until one reached Utrecht.

Ruth said over her shoulder, 'It's really country, Julia. Gerard says we don't need to go near a town unless we want to, although it's such a small country there are lots of rural areas with only tiny villages.'

It didn't seem very rural when they landed at the Hoek and took to the motorway, for small towns followed each other in quick succession, but then Thomas turned into a minor road and Julia saw the Holland she had always pictured. Wide landscapes, villages encircling churches much too large for them, farms with vast barns and water meadows where cows wandered. And the further they drove the more remote it became. The land was flat, but now there were small copses and glimpses of water. Julia looked around her and sighed with pleasure. Maybe there were large towns nearby, and main roads, but here there was an age-old peace and quiet.

Ruth, who had been chattering excitedly, had fallen silent and Thomas said, 'See that church spire beyond those trees? Unless I've read the map wrongly, we're here...'

CHAPTER THREE

WHEN they reached the trees Thomas turned into a narrow brick lane between them which opened almost at once into a scattered circle of houses grouped around the church. Any of the houses would do, thought Julia, for they were really all cottages, some larger than others, all with pristine paintwork, their little windows sparkling. But Thomas encircled the church and went along a narrow lane, leading away from the road.

'Hope I'm right,' he said. 'The Prof said it was easy to find, but of course he lives here! Five hundred yards past the church on the right-hand side…'

They all chorused 'There it is,' a moment later. It was another cottage, but a good deal larger than those in the village, with a wide gate and a short drive leading to the front door.

It had a red-tiled roof, white walls and small windows arranged precisely on either side of its solid door, and it was set in a garden glowing with flowers, all crammed together in a glorious mass of colour. Julia, standing by the car, rotated slowly, taking it all in. She hadn't been sure what kind of a house the Professor would have—something dignified and austerely perfect, she had supposed, because that would have reflected him. But this little cottage—and not so little now that she had had a good look—was definitely cosy, its prettiness fit to grace the most sentimental of greetings cards. She tried to imagine him in his impeccable grey suiting, mowing the lawn…!

The door had been opened and a short, stout lady surged to meet them.

She was talking before she reached them. 'There you are—come on in. You must want a cup of tea, and I made some scones.'

She shook hands all round, beaming at them. 'Mrs Beckett, the housekeeper, and delighted to welcome you. Such a nice day you've had for travelling, and it's to be hoped that we'll get some fine weather. A bit of sun and fresh air will soon put you back on your feet, Mrs Scott.'

She had urged them indoors as she spoke. 'Now, just you make yourselves comfortable for a minute while I fetch the tea tray, then you can see your rooms. A pity Mr Scott can't stay longer, but there, you're a busy man like Mr Gerard. Always on the go, he is, pops in to see me whenever he can, bless him. He's so good to his old nanny.'

She paused for breath, said, 'Tea', and trotted out of the room.

Thomas sat Ruth down in one of the small armchairs and went to look out of the window. Ruth said, 'Oh, darling, isn't this heavenly? I'm going to love it here, only I'm going to miss you.'

Thomas went and sat beside her, and Julia wandered round inspecting the room. It was low-ceilinged, with rugs on the wooden floor, comfortable chairs and small tables scattered around a fireplace with a wood stove flanked by bookshelves bulging with books. Julia heaved a sigh of contentment and turned round as Mrs Beckett came in with the tea tray.

They were taken round the cottage presently—first to the kitchen, with its flagstone floor and scrubbed table and old-fashioned dresser, its rows of saucepans on either side of the Aga and comfortable Windsor chairs on either side of it. And on each chair a cat.

'Portly and Lofty,' said Mrs Beckett. 'Keep me company, they do. Mr Gerard brought them here years ago—kittens they were then; he'd found them.'

She led the way out of the kitchen. 'There's a cloakroom here, and that door is his study, and there's a garden room...'

Upstairs there were several bedrooms, and two bathrooms luxurious enough to grace the finest of houses.

'He does himself proud,' murmured Julia, leaning out of the window of the room which was to be hers.

They strolled round the garden presently, and then Julia went to her room again on the pretext of unpacking, but really so that Thomas and Ruth could be together. And later, after a delicious meal of asparagus, lamb cutlets, new potatoes and baby carrots, followed by caramel custard and all washed down by a crisp white wine, she excused herself from taking an evening stroll with the other two on the plea of tiredness. Not that she was in the least tired. She slept soundly, waking early to lie in bed examining the room.

It wasn't large, but whoever had chosen the furniture had known exactly what was right for it: there was a mahogany bed with a rose-patterned quilt and a plump pink eiderdown, pale rugs on the polished floor, a small dressing table under the window and a

crinoline chair beside a small table. There were flowers on the table in a Delft bowl.

Like a fairy tale, decided Julia, and got up to lean
out of the window.

Mrs Beckett's voice begging her to get back into
bed and not catch cold sent her back under the eiderdown to drink the tea offered her.

Breakfast would be in half an hour, said Mrs
Beckett, sounding just as an old-fashioned nanny
would sound. 'Porridge and scrambled eggs, for I can
see that Mrs Scott needs feeding up.' Her small twinkling eyes took in Julia's splendid shape. 'Women
should look like women,' observed Mrs Beckett.

I shall get fat, thought Julia, buttering her third
piece of toast. Not that it mattered. Now, if she were
married to someone like Thomas she would go on a
diet; men, so the TV advertisements proclaimed with
such certainty, liked girls with wand-like shapes...

Declaring that she wanted postcards, she took herself off to the village and didn't get back until lunchtime. Thomas was to leave shortly and Ruth did most
of the talking: clean shirts, and mind to remember to
change his socks, and to wind the kitchen clock, and
she hoped that she had stocked the fridge with enough
food...

'I'll be back in just over a week, darling,' said
Thomas.

When he had gone Mrs Beckett sent them to the
village again, to buy rolls and croissants for breakfast,
and they strolled back while Ruth speculated as to
Thomas's progress. Julia put in a sympathetic word
here and there and ate one of the rolls, still warm from
the bakery.

'You'll get fat,' said Ruth.

'Who cares?' The strong wish that someone would care kept her silent; it would be very nice if someone—someone who didn't even like her very much, like the Professor—would actually look at her and care enough to discourage her from eating rolls warm from the oven.

There was no reason why she should think of him, she told herself. It was because she was staying at his home, and it was difficult to forget that. I don't like him anyway, she reminded herself.

Between them, she and Mrs Beckett set about getting Ruth quite well again. It was surprising what a few days of good food, temptingly cooked, walks in the surrounding countryside and sound sleep did for her. After five days Ruth satisfied her two companions; she was now pink-cheeked and bright-eyed and, although she missed Thomas, she was willing to join in any plans Julia might suggest.

Another four or five days, thought Julia, getting up early because it was such a lovely morning, and we shall be going home again. But she wouldn't spoil the day by thinking about that. She skipped downstairs and out of the front door.

The Professor was sitting on the low stone wall beside the door. He didn't look like the Professor; the elderly trousers and a turtle-necked sweater had wiped years off him. He said, 'Hello, Julia,' and smiled.

She stood staring, and then said, 'How did you get here? It's not eight o'clock yet.' A sudden thought struck her. 'Is Thomas ill? Is something wrong?'

'So many questions and you haven't even wished me good morning. Thomas is in the best of health;

nothing is wrong. I came to make sure that you were both comfortable here.'

'Comfortable? It's heaven! How did you get here?' 'I flew.''

'You flew? But how? I mean, do planes fly so early in the morning?'

'I have my own plane.'

'Your own plane?'

'This conversation is getting repetitive, Julia.'

'Yes, well, I'm surprised. Are you going to stay?'

'Don't worry, only for an hour or so.'

'And you'll fly back? You mean to say you've come just for an hour or so?' The Professor smiled, and she hopped onto the wall beside him. 'When we got here I was surprised—it didn't seem your kind of home. But now you're in slacks and a sweater I can see that it is. I just couldn't picture you in grey worsted and gold cufflinks being here…'

He didn't allow his amusement to show. 'You make me feel middle-aged.'

'Oh, no. Ruth told me that you're thirty-six or so, but you're remote, indifferent…' She paused to look at him. He was smiling again, but this time it was a nasty smile which sent her to her feet. 'I'll tell Ruth you're here.'

Indoors, flying up the stairs, her cheeks burning, she wondered what on earth had possessed her to talk to him like that. It was because he had seemed different, she supposed, but he wasn't, only his clothes. He was still a man she didn't like. She would make some excuse to go to the village after breakfast and stay there until he had gone again.

When, at the end of the meal, she stated her intentions, he told her carelessly to enjoy her walk, while Ruth said, 'Get me some more cards if you go to the shop, Julia.'

Mrs Beckett observed, 'You'd best say goodbye to Mr Gerard; he'll be gone before you get back.'

So Julia wished him goodbye, and he got up and opened the door for her—a courtesy which she was convinced was as false as his friendly, 'Goodbye, Julia.'

She spent a long time in the village—buying things she didn't need, going the long way back, loitering through the garden—for he might still be there.

He wasn't. 'How kind of him to come and make sure we were all right,' said Ruth. 'And he's arranging things so that Thomas can spend the night here before we go back next week. I've loved being here, but I do miss Tom…'

She glanced at Julia. 'You haven't been bored? We haven't gone anywhere or done anything or met any-one…'

Julia was replaiting her tawny hair. A pity she hadn't put it up properly with pins that morning; a pigtail over one shoulder lacked dignity.

'I've loved every minute of it,' Well, this morning was something best forgotten. It was obvious that the Professor had no intention of being friendly—some-thing which she found upsetting and that considering she didn't like him in the least, was puzzling. All the same, just for a little while she had enjoyed sitting there on the wall beside him.

It had turned warm, warm enough to sit in the gar-den or potter around watching things grow. She would have liked to have weeded and raked and

pulled the rhubarb and grubbed up radishes and lettuce from the kitchen garden at the back of the house,
but the dour old man in charge wouldn't allow that.
Whatever the language, it was obvious he objected
strongly to anyone so much as laying a finger on a
blade of grass.

Thomas phoned each day. The professor had arrived back safely, he told Ruth, and had gone straight
to his late-afternoon clinic. News which Julia received
without comment and an inward astonishment at the
man's energy.

The week passed too quickly. Thomas would come
on Saturday morning, so they must be ready to leave
soon after breakfast. Julia, packing her few things,
looked round her charming room with real regret; she
was going to miss the comfort and unobtrusive luxury
of the cottage, and still more she would miss Mrs
Beckett's company. She was a contented soul, only
wanting everyone else to be contented—the kind of
person one could confide in, reflected Julia, who had,
in truth, told her a good deal about her hopes and
plans. And quite unwittingly revealed her uncertainty
as to the future.

Mrs Beckett had listened with real sympathy and
some sound advice. It wouldn't be needed, of course;
if ever two people were made for each other they
were Julia and Mr Gerard. Of course, they hadn't discovered that yet, but time would tell, reflected Mrs
Beckett comfortably.

The sun shone on Saturday morning, and the garden had never looked so lovely. Julia, dressed and
ready to leave, had gone into the garden to wish it
goodbye. Ruth was in the kitchen with Mrs Beckett,

but Julia didn't want to wish her goodbye until the very last minute. She strolled round, sniffing at the flowers and shrubs, and, coming upon a patch of white violets, got down on her knees to enjoy their scent.

'My mother planted those,' said the Professor from behind her.

Julia shot to her feet in shock and whirled round. 'Why are you here again?' she demanded.

'This is my home,' he said mildly.

Julia went red. 'I'm sorry, that was rude, but you took me by surprise.'

When he didn't speak she added, 'Have you come to stay? We are so grateful to you for inviting us to stay here. We've had a glorious time. You must be very happy living here; the garden is so beautiful too.'

'What a polite little speech.' The faint mockery in his voice brought the colour back into her cheeks once more. 'I'm glad that you have enjoyed your stay. Are you ready to leave? Mrs Beckett will have coffee waiting for us.'

She went into the house with him, not speaking, and Ruth came running to meet them.

'Julia, isn't it wonderful? Thomas can stay until tomorrow. We're going to fly back—we shall have a whole day together.' She put a hand on the Professor's sleeve. 'You've been so kind...'

'Thomas is due a couple of days off, and this has given me a good excuse to arrange things to suit all of us. I'm only sorry I can't stay longer.'

He took the mug of coffee Mrs Beckett offered him. 'I'll see Julia safely home.'

She was swallowing hot coffee...choked, and had

to suffer the indignity of having her back patted and being mopped up. Then she said frostily, 'Is this something I should know about?'

Ruth laughed. 'Oh, didn't the Professor tell you? He's driving you back.' Before Julia could utter, he said, 'We need to leave in five minutes or so. I've patients to see later on today.'

Julia said childishly, 'But you've only just got here. I'm sure you must want to stay.'

'Indeed I do. As it is, I can't. So, if you would do whatever you still need to do, we'll be on our way.'

They were all looking at her and smiling; the Professor's smile was brief and amused and he turned away to stroll to the window and study the garden. She fetched her jacket, and was kissed and hugged and escorted to the Rolls with exclamations of delight at her good fortune at having such a comfortable journey.

Ruth poked her head through the window. 'I'll phone you when we get back. Trudie will be there, won't she? You won't be alone?'

'Who is Trudie?' asked the Professor as she settled back after a last wave.

'My lodger. Which way are you going back?'

'From Calais by hovercraft. That should get us back by the late afternoon.'

She must make an effort to be an agreeable companion—probably he didn't want her company anymore than she wanted his. 'A long drive,' she observed, striving for an easy friendliness.

It was at once doused by his casual, 'Yes—doze off if you want to, and you have no need to make polite small talk.'

Rude words bubbled and died on her lips; she couldn't utter them; he was giving her a lift, and she depended on him until she was back on her own doorstep. She sat silently seething, staring out at the countryside. But once they had reached the motorway there wasn't a great deal to look at, only the blue and white signposts at regular intervals. She watched them flash past.

'Why are we going to Amsterdam?' she wanted to know. 'You said we were going to Calais; you ought to be going south.'

He answered her in a patient voice which set her teeth on edge. 'We are going to Amsterdam because I need to. From there we will continue on our way to Calais. Don't worry, we are in plenty of time to catch the ferry.'

'I'm not worried.' Since there was nothing more to be said, she lapsed once more into silence.

But once they reached the city and had driven through its suburbs and reached the heart of it she forgot to be quiet. The old streets were lovely, the houses lining them much as they had been three hundred years earlier. 'Look at that canal,' she begged him, 'and those dear little bridges—and there's a barge simply loaded with flowers—and I can hear bells ringing...'

'Carillons. The barge is moored close to the street so that people can buy the flowers if they wish. There are bridges everywhere connecting up the streets. We are going over the one you see ahead of us.'

The street on the other side of it was narrow, brick-built and lined with large gabled houses on one side and a narrow canal on the other side.

Halfway down it the professor stopped the car, got out and opened her door.

'Would you rather I stayed in the car?' asked Julia. 'Perhaps...'

He opened the car door wider. 'Come along, I haven't time to waste.'

She got out huffily then, and went wordlessly with him up the double steps to the solid front door with its ornate transom. She was hating every minute of it, she told herself, while admitting to a longing to see inside the house. Friends of his, she wondered, or some kind of business to do with his work?

The rather bent elderly man who opened the door broke into voluble Dutch at the sight of them, which was of no help at all. It was obvious that he knew the Professor, and that the Professor held him in some regard, for he had clapped him gently on the back as they went in and addressed him at some length.

She allowed her gaze to wander around their surroundings and felt a surge of pleasure. They were in a long narrow hall with doors on either side and at its end a curving staircase. The walls were panelled, and it was all rather dark, but it was sombrely rich, she told herself, with a brass chandelier, undoubtedly old, a black and white tiled floor strewn with rugs of colours faded with age and a console table upon which someone had set a porcelain bowl of flowers.

The Professor's voice recalled her to her surroundings.

'This is Wim. He looks after the house and everyone in it.' When she offered a hand it was gently shaken and she was made welcome in his thin reedy voice.

The penny dropped then. 'This is your house?' said Julia.

'Yes. My home. We will have coffee and then I must ask you to excuse me while I deal with one or two matters. We must leave in half an hour or so.'

Wim was going ahead of them to open a door, into a long narrow room, panelled, like the hall, and furnished with comfortable chairs grouped round a vast fireplace. Its walls were lined with cabinets, a great long-case clock and a walnut bureau bookcase. There were small tables too, bearing gently shaded lamps, their glow enough, with the firelight, to bathe the room in soft light. And the room had an occupant, for a large dog came bounding to meet them, large and woolly with fearsome teeth.

'It's all right; he's only smiling,' said the professor, bracing himself to receive the delighted onslaught of the devoted beast.

'This is Jason, he's a Bouvier, a splendid chap who will guard those he loves with his life. Offer him a fist.'

Julia liked dogs, but she tried not to see the teeth as she did as she was told—to have her hand gently licked while small yellow eyes studied her face from under a tangle of hair. She said, 'I'm Julia,' and patted the woolly head.

'You must miss him,' she said, and sat down in the chair the Professor was offering.

'Yes, but I plan to spend more time here than in England. In the meantime, I snatch a few moments whenever I can.'

A casual remark which left her feeling vaguely disquiet.

Wim came in with coffee, and presently the Professor excused himself on the grounds of phone calls to make.

'We must leave in fifteen minutes. Wim will show you where you can tidy yourself.'

He went away, Jason at his heels, and Julia was left to finish her coffee before going slowly round the room, inspecting its treasures. She supposed that it was the drawing room, but there were several other doors in the hall. It was a large house; if all its rooms were as splendidly furnished as this one then the Professor must live in some style.

'Ancestors going back for ever and ever,' said Julia, addressing a portrait of a forbidding gentleman in a wig, 'and loaded with money.'

She became aware of a wet tongue on her hand. Jason was standing silently beside her. She turned quickly; the Professor would have heard her... But apparently he hadn't; he was across the room, looking out of a window. She sighed with relief and said quickly, 'You want to go? If I could ask Wim...?'

'By the staircase. The door on the right. Don't be long.'

He sounded much the same as usual: polite, detached, faintly amused. She joined him after a few minutes with the polite remark that she hoped she hadn't kept him waiting, bade goodbye to Wim and was swept out to the car without any further delay. Jason, standing in the hall, had rumbled goodbye when she had bent to stroke him, and on impulse she had bent down and thrown her arms around his neck and hugged him.

'You mustn't mind,' she'd said softly. 'He'll be back soon.'

She had turned away then, not wanting to see the parting between master and dog.

The Professor drove through the city and onto the motorway, giving her little opportunity to look around her. She sat silently beside him, sensing that he didn't wish to talk. No doubt he had a great many important matters to think about. She settled down to watch the countryside. He was driving fast and she was enjoying the speed; it was a pity that the motorway bypassed the villages and towns, but there was plenty to hold her attention and she kept a sharp eye open for road signs—a map would have been handy...

'There's a map in the pocket beside you,' said the Professor. Was he a thought-reader or did he want to keep her occupied so that there was no need to talk? The latter, she decided, and opened the map.

South to Utrecht, on to Dordrecht and then Breda, where they stopped at a roadside café just outside the town. As they went in he said, 'Fifteen minutes. Coffee and a *Kaas broodje*?'

Julia had spied a door at the back of the cafe with Dames written above it in large letters, 'Anything,' she told him as she sped away.

The Professor got up and pulled out a chair for her when she returned to the table. The coffee was already there, so were the cheese rolls. Obviously this wasn't to be a social meal; they ate fast and silently and were away again with her mouth still full.

'Sorry to rush you,' said the Professor laconically.

To which she replied, 'Not at all, Professor.'

To tell the truth she was enjoying herself.

They bypassed Antwerp, took the road to Gent, by-passed Lille and flew on to Calais.

'Just nicely in time,' observed the Professor, going aboard the hovercraft with two minutes to spare.

He settled her at a small table by a window and said, 'Run along and do your hair; I'll order tea.'

It was early for tea, but the sight of the tea tray and a plate of scones gladdened her heart. The Professor, watching her pour second cups, thought how pretty she looked and how uncomplainingly she had sat beside him. The seat beside him might have been empty. Upon reflection he was glad that it hadn't been. A pity they couldn't like each other…!

They talked during the crossing, careful to talk about mundane things, and when he suggested that she might like to have a brief nap before they landed she closed her eyes at once, thinking that it was a polite way of ending their conversation. She wouldn't sleep, she told herself, but if she shut her eyes she wouldn't need to look at him…

A gentle tap on her shoulder woke her. 'Ten minutes before we land,' the professor told her. 'Run along before there's a queue.' He paused. 'And your hair's coming down.'

How was it, thought Julia, that her hair being untidy and going to the loo should seem so normal and unembarrassing between two people who didn't even like each other? She remembered with a shudder Oscar's coy references to powdering her nose, and the disapproving frown if she needed to stick a pin back into her hairdo.

There was no time to pursue the thought; they were

going through Dover and speeding along the motorway to London without loss of time.

Saturday, she thought. She would have to race to
the shops and get some food for the weekend. The
idea of a cold house and an empty fridge didn't appeal, but of course a man wouldn't think of such
things. No doubt, she reflected peevishly, the professor would go to wherever he lived when he had seen
his patients and have a splendid meal set before him.
She peeped at his calm profile; he appeared unhurried
and relaxed but he certainly hadn't dallied on the
way...

As they slowed through London's sprawling suburbs she began her rehearsed thank-you speech. 'It
was very kind of you to give me a lift,' she began.
'I'm very grateful. I hope it hasn't held you up at all,
me being with you. If you want to drop me off at a
bus stop or the Underground...'

'You live very close to the hospital; it will be easier
to take you to your house. Stopping anywhere here
will hold me up.'

So much for trying to be helpful. She held her
tongue until he stopped before her door. The house
looked forlorn, as did the whole street, but she said
brightly, 'How nice to be home—and so quickly.'

A remark which needed no comment as he got out
of the car, took her case from the boot, the key from
her hand, opened the door and ushered her into the
narrow hall.

'Don't wait—' and that was a silly thing to say
'—and thank you again.'

'A pleasure. Goodbye, Julia.'

He drove away without a backward glance.

'He's a detestable man,' said Julia fiercely, standing on her doorstep. 'I hope I never meet him again. Rushing me back home just because he was in a hurry. Well, I hope he's late for whatever it is.' She added rather wildly, 'I hope it's a beautiful woman who will make him grovel!'

He would never grovel, of course, and she didn't mean a word of it, but it made her feel better.

She went indoors then, and into the kitchen to be greeted by Muffin, and a moment later by Trudie, coming downstairs to meet her.

'I knew you'd be back. The man who brought the box said you'd be here some time today.'

Julia went to fill the kettle. 'Box? What box?'

'It's from some super shop in Jermyn Street. It's on the table.'

They went to look at it together. It was a superior kind of box, very neatly packed under its lid; tea and coffee, sugar, milk, a bottle of wine, croissants, eggs, cold chicken in a plastic box, a salad in another plastic box, orange juice, smoked salmon…

Julia unpacked it slowly. 'There must be a mistake.'

Trudie shook her head. 'I asked to make sure. The delivery man said there was no mistake. A Professor van der Maes had ordered it by telephone late yesterday evening to be delivered this afternoon.'

'Oh, my goodness. He never said a word. He gave me a lift back so that my sister's husband could stay in Holland for a day. We had to hurry to get to Calais and we only stopped once on the way. He had to get back by the late afternoon.'

'Well, it's a gorgeous hamper,' said Trudie cheerfully.

'It's coals of fire,' said Julia.

'Well, I'm going out this evening,' Trudie went on. 'You'll be all right?'

'Me? I'm fine, and thank you for keeping an eye on Muffin and the house. No one called about a room?'

'No. You had a good time?'

'It was heaven. I'll tell you some time.'

Presently, alone in the house, she unpacked, fed Muffin and got her supper. The contents of the box might be coals of fire, but they made splendid eating.

Presently, in bed, she lay awake composing a letter to the Professor. Fulsome thanks would annoy him, considering the coolness between them, all the same he would need to be thanked. She slept at last, only to wake from time to time muttering snatches of suitable phrases.

The letter, when it was at last written, was exactly right. Neatly phrased, politely grateful—and it would have served as a model letter for a Victorian maiden to have written. The Professor read it and roared with laughter.

The house, after the charming little cottage, was something Julia would have to get used to. Ruth, back home, had phoned her, bubbling over with the day she had spent with Tom and happy to be back in her little house. Julia had assured her that she was fine, that there was the prospect of a lodger and that the garden was looking very pretty. None of which was true. She didn't feel fine. For some reason she felt depressed.

And I'll soon deal with that, Julia told herself, and went off to the newsagent's to put a To Let sign in his window, and then back to mow the small square of grass in the garden.

There were two applicants for the room the next day. A foxy faced middle-aged man who smelled strongly of beer and wanted to cook his meals in the kitchen, and a youngish woman, skilfully made up, with an opulent bosom and very high heels, who said coyly that she was expecting to get married and would Julia have any objection to her boyfriend calling from time to time?

She told them that the room was already let and watched them go with regret. The rent money would have been useful...

Something would turn up, she told herself, and in the meantime she got a temporary job delivering the local directory. It was dull business, for the neighbouring streets all looked alike, as did the houses, but she enlivened the tedium of it by memories of the cottage, and at the end of the week there was a little money in her pocket and she had written in reply to six vaguely wanting help with houses and small children—something she could surely do without any kind of training. And it wouldn't be for long, she told herself. If she could let a room—two rooms at a pinch—she could sleep in the box room.

She went to Ruth's for lunch on Sunday, and Thomas came over from the hospital for an hour or two. After the meal Ruth said, 'While you're here, Julia, would you look at that little chair I was going to cover? It's in the other bedroom and I've tried to do it, but it doesn't look right. You're so good at that kind of thing.'

So Julia went up the little stairs and into the second bedroom, which was small and unfurnished save for suitcases, a bookcase which was too large to go anywhere and the chair. It was a pretty little chair, and Ruth had pinned the velvet onto it in a haphazard fashion. Julia got down on the floor, undid it all to cut and fit, pinned and tacked, and sat back on her heels to study her work. It would do, but Ruth wanted a frill, she thought.

She was on the stairs when she heard Ruth's voice. The sitting room door was open and the house was small, with thin walls.

'Oh, Thomas, I can't ask Julia. Where would she go? But it would be wonderful. We'd have the money to start buying our own house, and Monica and George need central heating and a new bathroom— the house would sell for enough money for that?'

'Oh, yes, darling. Split three ways you would each get a very useful sum. But we mustn't think about it. If Julia marries you could suggest it then, but not before.'

Julia crept back into the room, closed the door quietly and sat down on the chair. Of course she had thought of it before, but had put it out of her mind. How could she have been so stupid? There was nothing remarkable about the house, but it had three bedrooms, and although the street was shabby it was quiet, and those who lived in it were law-abiding— striving to keep so. Moreover, there were buses and the Underground into the City. It would fetch a fair price—Ruth and Thomas could get a house of their own; Monica could have her central heating. As for herself…a small flat somewhere, and the money to take a course in something or other. She could think about that later. She would have to wait for a few days and then broach the subject…

Steps on the stairs sent her onto her knees, fussing with the frill.

Ruth put her head round the door. 'You had the door shut. You didn't hear me?'

'No. Were you calling? Look, do you want a frill? I think it would be too much.' She got to her feet. 'Has Thomas gone back? I'll come down, shall I?'

CHAPTER FOUR

THE opportunity to do something about the house came sooner than she had expected. Monica phoned to ask abut their stay in Holland, and when that subject had been exhausted she talked at length about George and the house and the village. 'I'm so happy, Julia…'

It seemed to be the right moment. Julia knew exactly what to say; she had rehearsed it carefully and now she made her suggestion with just the right amount of eagerness. 'I can't think why I haven't thought of it before. I haven't said anything to Ruth yet. Do you think it's a good idea? It's only an idea, anyway…'

She could hear the excitement in Monica's voice. 'But what about you?'

'I'd get a small flat and take a course in dressmaking. You know how I love making clothes.'

'Would we get enough from the house for all of us?'

'Yes, but perhaps Ruth wouldn't like the idea…'

'I'll talk to her and find out. Is this what you really want, Julia?'

'Oh, yes. Just think, I wouldn't have to depend on lodgers. I'd be free—have a holiday when I wanted to, come and go as I pleased and work at something I enjoy doing.'

She rang off presently, knowing that she had convinced Monica. Now she must wait and see what Ruth would decide, and let the news come from Monica.

She didn't have long to wait, Ruth phoned that evening. 'Monica rang and told me you'd suggested selling the house. But, Julia, what about you?'

So Julia repeated her carefully thought out words and added, 'Do you like the idea? It's only an idea…'

'You really want to? You'd be happier somewhere else? There would be enough money for you to feel secure?'

'I don't feel secure now,' said Julia. 'I need three lodgers to keep this house going and so far I've only got one; I didn't tell you that I got the sack from the greetings card people—but then I expected that; Oscar, you know. I could train as a dressmaker, live in a small flat…'

'Oh, my dear, I didn't know. I think it's a marvellous idea.' Ruth paused. 'As a matter of fact, Thomas and I have seen a house near the hospital—in a cul-de-sac, and so quiet. It's for sale…'

'You see,' said Julia bracingly. 'It's the hand of fate!'

Of course there was a good deal to discuss during the next few days. Julia, striking while the iron was hot, had the house valued, and the price the agent suggested clinched the matter. He had people on his books waiting for just such a house to come on the market. Ruth and Thomas, inspecting the house they so wanted to buy, had no doubts.

'A pity the Prof is away,' Thomas observed. 'By the time he gets back we'll probably have moved.'

'Will he be in Edinburgh much longer?'

'No, a few days more, but he's going straight to

Vienna to give lectures and then a week or two in Holland.'

'He'll have a nice surprise. Oh, Thomas, I do hope the house sells quickly.'

Something Monica hoped too, with her writing desk awash with central heating brochures and magnificent bathroom catalogues.

As for Julia, unaware that the Professor was away, she went to see the solicitor who held the deeds of the house, bullied the house agent in the nicest possible way, explained everything to Trudie and hoped that the hand of fate she had been so sure about would point a finger at her. Now that they were selling the house she wanted to be gone quickly, to start a new life. That she woke in the night to worry about that was something she did her best to ignore.

The house sold within a week. Moreover, it was a cash sale, and the new owner wanted to move in as soon as Julia could move out. Monica and Ruth came, and, helped by a cheerfully co-operative Trudie, they all set to work to pack up the house.

It wasn't just the packing up. There was the furniture—what was left after they had each decided what they wanted to keep and, since Trudie hoped to marry soon, she had had her share—and then the removal men, the gas, the electricity, the telephone, the milkman—an unending stream of things which needed her attention.

With three days left before the new owners took over Julia found herself in an almost empty house. Trudie had moved in with the other teacher at the kindergarten, George had driven up in a borrowed van and taken the furniture Monica had chosen, and the local odd-job man had collected the tables and chairs and beds which Ruth wanted for her new home. Which left Julia with a bed, a number of suitcases, a box of books, the kitchen table and two chairs. The fridge and cooker had been sold with the house, so meals were no problem although lack of comfort was. Ruth had wanted her to go and stay with them, but to leave the house empty was risky. And it was only for two nights.

Tomorrow, thought Julia, getting into bed with Muffin for company, she would go in search of a room to rent. She knew what she was going to do: find a small flat in a quiet street in a better neighbourhood. Islington would be nice, if she could find something to suit her purse. Perhaps a basement flat with a bit of garden at the back—or Finsbury—somewhere not too far from Ruth and Thomas. She wished that she had someone to advise her.

The Professor's face flashed before her closed eyes and she said out loud, 'What nonsense. He's not even in the country, and in any case he hasn't the least interest.'

Ruth had said that he was away, and that they hadn't told him that they were moving. 'We're going to surprise him,' said Ruth happily. 'He'll be back soon.'

'Not before I've gone,' reflected Julia now. 'Disagreeable man.'

She went in search of a room the next day and returned home disappointed. She had been to several likely addresses, but most of them had proved to be top-floor attics which wouldn't do at all for Muffin. One or two had been grubby, and the only one which would have done at a pinch she'd been denied. 'Not cats!' the lady of the house had said. 'Nasty, dirty creatures.'

'We'll try again tomorrow,' she told Muffin, inspecting the fridge for their suppers.

She was just finishing breakfast the next morning when there was a thump on the door. And when she went to open it there was the Professor.

She was aware of delight at seeing him, and that was something she would have to think about later on. For now she stared up at him wordlessly. His 'Good morning Julia,' was coolly friendly.

Since he stood there, obviously expecting to be asked in, she said, 'Oh, do come in—has something happened to Ruth or Thomas?' She shut the door behind him with something of a snap. 'It's very early…'

'This has nothing to do with Ruth or Thomas. I wished to talk to you.'

He stood in the hall, looking around him at the empty place. 'Is there somewhere…?'

She led the way to the kitchen, angry that he should see its poverty stricken appearance: the milk bottle on the table, a loaf of bread beside it, her mug and plate with a slice of bread and butter half eaten…

'Do sit down,' she begged him in a voice of a polite hostess who must entertain an unwelcome guest, and when he had taken the other chair at the table she asked, 'Would you like a cup of tea? There's still some in the pot.'

His mouth twitched. 'Yes, please,' he responded as his eye fell on the loaf.

'Would you like some bread and butter?' she asked.

'Breakfast is always such a pleasant meal,' he observed, before he cut a slice and buttered it.

'There's no need to be sarcastic,' said Julia. 'Why have you come?'

'It must be obvious to you that this is not a social visit. Unfortunately it is the only time of day when I'm free…'

She interrupted him. 'Ruth said you weren't in England.'

'I got back yesterday evening. Tell me, Julia, have you any plans for your immediate future?'

'Why do you want to know?'

'If you will answer my question I will tell you.'

'I can't see why you should ask, but since you have, no.'

'You have somewhere to go tomorrow? A flat or rooms?'

'No. I intend to find something this morning.' She frowned. 'I don't see that it's any of your business—and we're not even friends…' She blushed scarlet the moment she had said it and mumbled, 'Well, you know what I mean.'

'I hardly think that friendship has anything to do with it, and it is my business in so far that I am asking for your help.'

'Me? Help you?'

'If you would refrain from interrupting, I will explain.'

He drank his tea and looked at her. She was untidy, for she had done some last-minute packing; her hair was in a plait over one shoulder, she had a shiny nose, and was wearing a cotton top faded from many washings. But she looked quite beautiful, he thought. Her sisters were beautiful too, but Julia was full of life, impulsive, refusing to admit that life wasn't quite what she had hoped for. She had a sharp tongue, and a temper too...

He said gently, 'Indeed you could help me if you would consider it. You haven't forgotten Mrs Beckett? I have been with her for a day or two. She is ill—pneumonia—and in hospital. It is a viral infection and she isn't so young. Would you consider going over to Holland and minding the cottage while she is away, and then staying for a while when she gets back until she is quite well and I can arrange some sort of help for her?'

It was so unexpected that she could only gape at him.

'Go to Holland?' said Julia at length. 'But does Mrs Beckett want me—and how long would I be there?'

'Mrs Beckett will be very happy to see you again,' said the Professor smoothly. 'I cannot say for certain how long your stay might be. But she will be in hospital for at least two weeks, and when she returns home she will need a good deal of cosseting.'

'She is in hospital now?'

'Yes, in Leiden. A colleague of mine is the consultant physician there. I have arranged for someone to look after her cats and the cottage but it is a temporary arrangement. I want someone with no other commitments so that I can be sure that both Mrs Beckett and the cats and cottage are in the hands of a person who is willing to remain until she is quite fit.'

'But why me?'

He ignored that. 'I am aware that this may interfere

with whatever plans you have made. You would, of course, receive a salary and any expenses.'

'Well, I haven't any real plans. I mean none that can't be put off for a few weeks. There is no reason why I shouldn't go. When do you want me to be there?'

It was impossible to tell whether he was pleased or not. 'Within the next day or so. I will arrange for you to fly over. You will be met and taken to the cottage. You will be kept informed as to Mrs Beckett's condition and taken to visit her if you wish.'

He got up and she, perforce, got up too. His goodbye was brief and he had gone before the dozen questions tumbling around in her head could be uttered.

She had been glad to see him, she couldn't deny that, and not having to decide about her future for another few weeks was a relief she didn't admit to. It was while she was going through her scanty wardrobe that she started to wonder how he had known that she was leaving the house. Had he been back in England earlier and had Ruth told him? Surely he hadn't made up his mind to ask her in the space of a few hours?

It wasn't until she was getting her lunch that her eye fell upon Muffin...

The phone hadn't been transferred yet, thank heaven; moreover, she was put through to the Professor at once.

'Muffin,' she began without preamble. 'I can't go to Holland—Ruth's far too busy moving house and he'll pine in the cattery.'

'No problem. My housekeeper in London will be delighted to look after him. I have arranged for you to fly over tomorrow afternoon. I will come for you at midday and we can leave Muffin with her as we go.'

And he had hung up without giving her a chance to say anything.

She addressed Muffin. 'I've been a fool. I have allowed Professor van der Maes to make use of me. I must be losing my wits.' Although, she reflected presently, it would be delightful to stay in that cottage again, and it would give her time to decide exactly what she intended to do next.

She was ready for him when he came; the new owners were moving in later that afternoon, everything was signed and sealed, the money was in Ruth's care, and her share would be waiting for her when she got back. In the meantime she had enough of her own to keep her going. The Professor had mentioned a salary, but probably it had just been a passing thought.

He greeted her in a businesslike manner and stowed Muffin on the back seat, her case in the boot and herself beside him without more ado. She didn't look back as he drove away. She and her sisters had lived in the house but it had never been home to any of them.

She sat without speaking as he drove through the busy streets. Presently he said, 'I shall have to drive straight to Heathrow.'

He had shown no signs of impatience at the slow progress they were making, but a glance at the clock told her that at the rate they were going they would never get to the airport on time. All she said was, 'Muffin?'

'I will take the cat to my house as soon as I have seen you on to the plane. I promise you that I will see that he is in safe hands.' He gave her a quick look. 'Trust me, Julia.'

'Yes,' said Julia, knowing that she meant it.

She was the last to board the plane; there had barely been time to bid Muffin goodbye before she was hurried away, told that she would be met at Schipol and would she telephone him that evening?

'The phone number is in the envelope with your ticket. Goodbye, Julia.'

Schipol was overflowing with people; Julia stood for a moment, wishing wholeheartedly that she hadn't come, then a short, thickset man, bearing her name on a placard he was holding before him, came to a halt in front of her.

'Miss Gracey? Sent by Professor van der Maes? I am Piet, to drive you to his house.' His English was strongly accented but fluent.

Julia held out a hand. 'How do you do? Is it a long drive?'

'No, I drive fast.' He picked up her case and led the way through the crowds, out to the car, which was an elderly Mercedes. Its appearance, she quickly discovered, was deceptive; it was capable of a fine turn of speed which, coupled with Piet's obvious wish to be a racing driver, took them at a hair-raising speed to the cottage.

As she got out Piet told her that he would call for her in the morning and take her to see Mrs Beckett at Leiden. He took her case into the cottage, gave her a broad grin and was gone.

There was someone in the cottage, waiting for her:

a small woman with an old-fashioned hairdo, wearing a severe black dress. She smiled a welcome and broke into voluble speech, unfortunately in Dutch.

Julia smiled in return, offered a hand and mustered her few words of that language.

The woman was amused. 'I go. I come at morning, early.' She thought for a moment. 'Work, cook.'

'All day?'

'Mornings. Professor van der Maes tell.'

'I should hope so. How like a man,' said Julia crossly and her companion smiled and nodded. 'Nice man. Food ready. *Dag.*'

She trotted off in the direction of the village and Julia closed the door and found Mrs Beckett's cats staring at her.

'Well, at least I can talk to you,' said Julia, and at that moment the phone rang.

'You had a good journey?' enquired the professor. 'Mevrouw Steen was at the cottage?'

'Is that who she is? Why are you ringing me? You told me that I was to phone you this evening.'

'I thought that you might be anxious about Muffin. Why are you cross?'

'I am not cross.' She sounded peevish. 'I am in an empty house with two cats, I want a cup of tea, and *Mevrouw*'s English is as basic as my Dutch.'

'An excellent opportunity for you to improve your knowledge of the language.'

'I have no wish to do so,' said Julia haughtily. 'Is there anything you wanted to say to me? Because if there isn't I'm going to put the kettle on...'

He took no notice. 'Piet will take you to see Mrs Beckett tomorrow morning. Arrange with her or the doctor when you wish to visit her and let him know. Piet will drive you wherever you should wish to go and do any odd jobs or errands for you

She said stiffly, 'Thank you. Is Muffin all right?'

'Settled down very nicely. I hope you will do the same, Julia.' With which he rang off.

'Rude man,' said Julia.

She had every intention of wallowing in self-pity as she went into the kitchen, but the sight of the tea tray standing ready on the kitchen table made her hesitate. There wasn't only a pretty teacup and saucer and plate on it, matching the teapot, sugar bowl and milk jug, but also a plate of buttered scones and a little dish of jam, and when she opened the fridge door while the kettle boiled she found salmon, ready to eat, and salad and a bowl of potato straws. Moreover, there were strawberries and cream and a bottle of white wine.

She made the tea, carried the tray through to the sitting room and wondered uneasily if she had been a bit too off-hand with the Professor...

Her bedroom welcomed her: flowers on the dressing table, a pile of books and magazines on the bedside table, a carafe of water and a tin of biscuits, and in the bathroom towels and soaps and a delicious selection of oils for the bath. Somebody had been very thoughtful about her well-being, she reflected, going downstairs and taking the bottle of wine from the fridge. She didn't feel lonely or hard-done-by any more; it was as though she had been warmly welcomed even if there had been no one there to do that.

Presently she ate her supper, drank the rest of her glass of wine, fed the cats and, accompanied by them both, went upstairs to lie in the bath and then get into bed. Her two companions settled each side of her and she hoped that Muffin was being as well cared for. She would be all right, she decided sleepily; the Professor had said that he would look after her...

She woke to a splendid morning; hanging out of the window, she looked down at the garden, which was a riot of colour, and beyond it to the flat, peaceful countryside... She showered and dressed and skipped downstairs, intent on breakfast. She had fed the cats and was eating her boiled egg when Mevrouw Steen arrived.

She greeted Julia with a cheerful *'Dag'* and then added, 'Piet comes; I stay.'

So Julia gobbled down the rest of her breakfast, found her handbag, got into Piet's car and was driven to Leiden—a trip she would have enjoyed if she hadn't been so scared of the speed at which Piet drove. But he was a splendid driver, and of course the road ahead of them was flat as far as the eye could see. He put her down at the hospital, rather shaken and glad to feel solid ground beneath her feet. He would return in an hour, he told her, and wait until she came. She was not to hurry.

Mrs Beckett, looking half her normal size, was propped up against her pillows with an oxygen mask clamped over her nose. But she smiled and nodded to Julia and waved a languid hand.

'Don't talk,' said Julia urgently. 'I'm going to sit here and tell you all the news!'

Mrs Beckett listened, nodding from time to time, then asked, 'Portly and Lofty—how are they?'

'Both in splendid health; they slept on my bed. You don't mind?'

Mrs Beckett smiled. 'I'm glad. Mr Gerard has been to see me. He'll come again; he's so good to me.'

'He's organised everything,' Julia assured her. 'As soon as you're well again you are coming home, and I'll stay until you are perfectly fit.'

'You'll want to go home,' whispered Mrs Beckett. 'To your own home.'

'I haven't got one. We've sold it. I'll find somewhere to live when I get back. It's lovely being here again. The cottage looks lovely and I'll look after everything.' She bent and kissed the pale cheek. 'I'm going now. I shall phone every day and come and see you again in a day or two. You are going to get well quickly; the Professor told me so.'

Which wasn't true, but a lie in a good cause…

'If he said so, then I shall.'

It was a relief but no surprise to find that the doctor she asked to see spoke English as good as hers. Mrs Beckett was making good progress, he assured her. She had been seriously ill—pneumonia in the elderly was not to be treated lightly—but she had responded well to treatment.

'You are a friend of Professor van der Maes?'

It would save a lot of explanations if she agreed…

'May I come at any time? Not every day, perhaps, but I will phone each morning and you will let me know at once if it's necessary.'

'Of course.'

He walked with her to the entrance, where Piet was waiting, and watched her getting into the car. A delightfully pretty girl, he reflected. Gerard had told him that she was a sensible young woman, very well able to look after herself and deal with any situation which might arise. And of course Gerard would come at once in an emergency....

After that first day Julia slipped into a gentle pattern of days. Visiting Mrs Beckett, even beginning to enjoy Piet's breakneck driving, cherishing Portly and Lofty, filling the cottage with flowers because she knew that Mrs Beckett would like that, weeding and tending the flowerbeds when the gardener allowed, practising her sparse Dutch on Mevrouw Steen and each evening listening eagerly for the phone to ring. The Professor never had much to say but his voice was reassuring.

She had been there for several days when he said, 'The question of your salary. I have arranged for my bank to send it to you each week in guilders.'

'I don't need any money,' said Julia.

'Money is something which everyone needs from time to time,' said the Professor, and hung up before she could utter another word.

When the postman brought it she sat at the kitchen table and counted it. There seemed to be a great deal, even when she did careful mental sums and changed it into pounds. 'For a month, I suppose,' she said and, feeling rich, went to the village and bought postcards, stamps and chocolate.

The following week the same amount arrived, so that evening when he phoned she pointed out to him that there had been a mistake; she already had her salary.

'Did I not make myself clear? Each week you will receive your money from my bank...'

'But it's too much.'

'I must beg you not to argue. When are you going to see Mrs Beckett?'

'Tomorrow, in the morning. Why?'

'If you will give me time to speak, I will tell you. She is so much better she will probably be able to come home within the next few days. She will need to convalesce in a leisurely fashion. I rely upon you to see that she does.'

'I'll take the greatest care of her. How will she come home? Shall I go with Piet and fetch her?'

'I will tell you in due course. In the meantime you will see her doctor tomorrow.'

'Very well.' Then she added, 'Don't you ever say goodbye?'

'Not to you, Julia.' And he hung up!

Mrs Beckett was sitting in a chair by her bed when Julia got to the hospital. She looked weary and far too pale, but Julia was pleased to see that she was taking an interest in life once more.

'I'm coming home soon,' she told Julia. 'I've missed it so…' Her eyes filled with tears.

'Won't it be fun? Lofty and Portly will be so glad to see you…the garden looks lovely, and so many people have asked me how you are. You have so many friends. They'll want to come and see you, but the doctor says you must be a bit quiet for a little longer.'

'I know. Mr Gerard told me. I'm to do what you say just for a time; he's promised that everything will be just as it always was.'

'Well, of course it will. And I promise you that I

won't make you do anything that you don't want to do.'

She hugged Mrs Beckett because she looked so small and frail.

'If the weather is warm and fine, you shall sit in the garden and tell me what to do.'

Four days later Julia was awakened by a thunderous knocking on the door.

'Mrs Beckett—something's happened,' she told the cats as she tore down the stairs, tugging on her dressing gown as she went, her feet bare.

The professor was on the doorstep.

'I didn't use my key; I didn't want to disturb you…'

'But you have disturbed me. You've given me the fright of my life—I thought something had happened to Mrs Beckett. And why are you here?'

'If I might come in?' he asked meekly. 'This is my home!'

He sounded meek, but he gave her a mocking smile as she stood aside to let him pass.

'Oh, well—sorry,' said Julia. 'You could have phoned.'

He agreed blandly; he hadn't known until the very last minute that he could snatch twenty-four hours away from his work; too late to warn her of his intention.

'Tea? Breakfast?' Julia went ahead of him into the kitchen and turned to look at him. It was then she saw how tired he was…

'You've had no sleep. How did you come? When do you have to go back?'

'Tonight. I've come to bring Mrs Beckett home.'

'You'll have a cup of tea, then go and sleep for an hour or so while I get breakfast. What time do you plan to go to Leiden?'

'Shortly after midday.'

She had the kettle on, was setting out mugs, sugar and milk. 'Mevrouw Steen won't be here before eight o'clock.' She got the loaf and butter and cut him a generous slice. 'What a good thing I made the beds up yesterday…'

He sat at the table, watching her. Her hair was all over the place, her dressing gown had come untied, her feet were bare. She was, he decided, just what a man would want to see after a sleepless and tiring night.

Julia, far too busy to bother about appearances, put his tea before him, cut him more bread and butter and poured herself a mug. 'There's plenty of hot water,' she told him. 'Did you bring the car?'

'Yes. I'll have a shower and a nap. Breakfast about nine o'clock?'

It was barely seven. 'Yes, would you like it in bed?'

He choked back a laugh. 'The last time I had breakfast in bed I was nine years old, suffering from the mumps.'

When she looked at him, he added, 'That was twenty-seven years ago.'

He smiled, and the smile made her suddenly aware of the flyaway dressing gown and no slippers. She said briskly, 'I will call you at nine o'clock.'

He went away then, and she saw to the cats, put everything ready for breakfast and went quietly upstairs. The bathroom door was open but the three bedroom doors were closed. She had a shower, dressed, then made her bed and went downstairs again. Just in time to say *dag* to Mevrouw Steen.

There was no need to tell her that the Professor was there; the car was before the door. Mevrouw Steen broke into voluble talk, smiling widely.

'Mrs Beckett is coming home today.' Julia thought for a moment and added in Dutch, 'This afternoon.'

Mevrouw Steen nodded. 'I clean house…'

She trotted off, but not before Julia had warned her not to go upstairs until the Professor was awake. 'No sleep,' she told her in her fractured Dutch. 'Driving all night.'

Mevrouw made sympathetic clucking noises, went into the sitting room and shut the door on the sound of the Hoover.

Julia began to get breakfast. Bacon and eggs, tomatoes, mushrooms, fried bread. There was no lack of food in the house. Toast and marmalade to follow, and tea or coffee. And while she was busy she considered lunch. Salad, and there was ham in the fridge, and in the evening before he went back she would cook him a meal. A Spanish omelette, potatoes in their jackets and a salad—a bread and butter pudding, perhaps, or a sponge pudding with custard…

The bacon was sizzling in the pan and it was nearly nine o'clock. Time to rouse him…

He came into the kitchen through the door leading to the garden.

'You're up,' said Julia, and frowned because that had been a silly thing to say.

'I wanted to have a quick look at the garden. Something smells delicious.'

He looked as though he had slept all night—shaved and immaculately turned out. Of course he would have clothes here, thought Julia, and, suddenly conscious that she had been staring at him, she blushed.

The Professor studied the blush with interest and decided that it made her even prettier than she already was.

'Can't I help?' He sounded casual.

'If you would make the toast?'

Mevrouw Steen came in then. She had a great deal to say and it was frustrating, for Julia only understood one word in a dozen. The dear soul paused for breath presently and Julia offered her a mug of coffee and she trotted off with it. She would go upstairs, she said, and clean.

'A good soul,' said the Professor as he speared a mushroom. 'When you leave here I must find some kind of help for Mrs Beckett. Mevrouw Steen's a splendid worker but she doesn't like responsibility.'

Julia looked down at her plate. 'I expect you would like me to go once Mrs Beckett is settled here.'

'Now, why should you think that? Mrs Beckett is going to need you for another three weeks at least. You wish to go home?'

'No, no. I love it here,' she burst out. 'I don't know how you can bear to live anywhere else. Well, I dare say that's not true, for you have your lovely house in Amsterdam.'

'You liked that too?'

'My goodness me, indeed I did.'

'Then we must find time to go there again.' He added casually, 'I am planning to do rather more work

over here—go over to Scotland from time to time
when necessary.'

'You mean you won't live in London?' The
thought filled her with a dismay she couldn't understand.

The professor watched her face. 'From time to
time,' he repeated gently. 'I'm going down to the village to see Piet. Shall we have lunch before we go to
Leiden?'

'We? Wouldn't it be better if I stayed here and had
everything ready—tea—and the cats waiting.' She
looked at him. 'A welcome, if you see what I mean.'

He agreed readily, and presently she watched him
walking along the lane. Even from the back he looked
full of energy—a man who had had a good night's
sleep and with not a care in the world.

CHAPTER FIVE

THE Professor didn't come back until she was putting lunch on the table. 'Well,' said Julia to Portly, sitting beside her while she made a salad, 'I'm sure if he doesn't want my company I couldn't care less. After all, I'm only a kind of housekeeper.'

She wallowed in a comforting self-pity for a few minutes, and then forgot about it as the Professor came into the kitchen.

'Piet will come each day,' he told her without preamble. 'He'll do anything you want him to do and if you wish to leave the place he will stay with Mrs Beckett and Mevrouw Steen.'

'Thank you, but I'm happy to stay here. Will Mrs Beckett be able to sit outside for a while each day?'

'Dr de Groot—you saw him at Leiden—will come and see her in a day or so and let you know what he wants done.'

'I see. When will you go back?'

'Anxious for me to be gone, Julia?' He sounded amused. 'I'm going back this evening.'

'But you've only just got here. You've had no sleep; you'll be dead on your feet.'

'I'm going back from Harwich on the night ferry. I'll sleep then.'

He drove away after lunch and she tidied up, put the tea things ready and went up to her room. She wasn't a vain girl, but she had the sudden urge to make the most of herself. It would have to be the same blue denim skirt, because she hadn't another, but there was a newly washed and ironed cotton blouse, and she wasted a good deal of time trying out various ways of doing her hair, only to tug out the pins and bundle it up on the top of her head. 'He won't notice anyway,' she told Lofty, watching her from the bed.

Of course he noticed, the moment he got out of the car and saw her waiting on the porch. He lifted Mrs Beckett out of the car and carried her into the cottage, and as he passed Julia he observed, 'I like the hair. Is it in my honour?'

She went pink, going ahead of him to open the sitting room door as he bore his housekeeper in and settled her in the chair Julia had put ready. Mrs Beckett said in a wispy voice, 'My dear, how well you look—such lovely pink cheeks. I do hope I'm not going to be too much of a nuisance.'

Julia gave her a gentle hug. 'What nonsense. I love being here and I shall love looking after you. I'm going to get the tea; you must be dying for a cup.'

She got herself out of the room and Mrs Beckett settled back in her chair and nodded her head. 'A dear girl, don't you agree, Mr Gerard?'

He grinned at her. 'Don't fish, Nanny. When we've had tea you're going to bed, and mind you do exactly what Julia tells you. I must give her all the details of your treatment before I go.'

Tea was quickly over, which was a good thing for Julia could think of very little to say. The Professor made gentle small talk, addressing her from time to time and staring at her in a way which both annoyed and disturbed her. His remark about her hair had shaken her calm—perhaps she should have taken more pains with it.

He'll be gone in a few hours, thought Julia, and for some reason her spirits sank.

Getting Mrs Beckett to bed took time. There were her things to unpack and put away and frequent pauses while she discussed the hospital and her illness. When Julia finally went downstairs she found the Professor in the kitchen.

'I must leave in just over an hour,' he told her. 'Come here and listen carefully to what I have to say.'

'You must have a meal before you go. You can still tell me while I'm cooking it.'

She had her nose in the fridge. 'A bacon omelette? Asparagus? New potatoes?'

'Excellent. If you are as handy with the frying pan as you are with the needle I am indeed a lucky man.'

'You have no reason to be sarcastic...'

'What do you intend to do when you get back to London, Julia?'

'Be a dressmaker. Only I must be taught properly first.'

'And where will you live?'

'Oh, somewhere...'

Since he didn't answer, and the silence got a bit lengthy, she added, 'Ruth and Thomas have found such a nice house; I expect you've seen it. And of course Monica and George have a lovely old vicarage...'

'And you, Julia—do you not wish for a home and a husband and children, or is the fashioning of garments the acme of your ambition?'

'I don't like you when you talk like this,' said Julia fiercely. 'Never mind me, and much you care anyway, just tell me what I must do to get Mrs Beckett on her feet again.'

He didn't speak for a moment, but looked at her with lifted eyebrows, and when he did speak he was Professor van der Maes, giving courteous instructions to a patient's attendant.

She listened carefully while she beat eggs and chopped bacon and mushrooms, and when he had finished said, 'Thank you, that's all quite clear, but please write her medicines down so that I can be quite sure.'

'And here is Dr de Groot's phone number. Don't hesitate to ring him if you feel the necessity.'

She set the potatoes to cook. 'Will you come again to see Mrs Beckett?'

'If it's possible. I have complete faith in de Groot. As for yourself, I think that Mrs Beckett will be fully recovered in three weeks. I shall arrange for suitable help before you return.' He wandered to the door. 'Will you let me know when my supper is ready? I'm going to sit with Nanny.'

It's my own silly fault, reflected Julia. Why can't we be friends? And why did he want me to come here if he dislikes me so much? Once I leave here I won't see him again; I'll find somewhere miles away.

Somewhere where—hopefully—she could make a living, find friends, perhaps meet a man who would want her for his wife. There must be any number of men around not in the least like Oscar, or, for that matter, the Professor. There was no one like him, she added...

She laid a place for him at the table, tossed the potatoes in butter and mint and had the pan hot ready for the omelette. She could hear the murmur of voices as she went into the hall when she called him and he came at once.

'There are strawberries and cream,' she told him, 'and I've made coffee.'

'Thank you. I've said goodbye to Nanny; she's a bit tearful, so I think a glass of claret might do her good before her supper. And you too, of course.'

He didn't talk much as he ate, and presently he went and got his bag.

She said awkwardly, 'I hope you have a safe journey and won't be too tired.' She had gone to the door with him. 'I promise I'll take good care of Mrs Beckett.'

He stood looking down at her. 'I'm sure of that. Look after yourself, Julia.'

He got into the car and drove away and she stood in the porch staring down the now empty lane. She felt empty too.

There were letters from Monica and Ruth in the morning; it was nice to know that selling the house had brought them so much happiness. And Monica wanted her to go and stay after she'd spent time at Ruth's, which solved the problem as to where she would go next. Somehow the future had seemed vague and far off, but the Professor had mentioned three weeks. In that time she must make up her mind what she intended to do.

Mrs Beckett was a model patient and, like a trusting child, did everything asked of her without question. Julia cooked her small tasty meals, helped her with the slow, tiring business of dressing and undressing, and after a few days led her carefully downstairs to sit and watch the TV or chat. Talking was something she enjoyed, and Julia was soon in possession of the professor's family history.

Old family, said Mrs Beckett, wealthy and respected. 'His father was a surgeon, you know. Retired now. His mother's a sweet lady. He has brothers and sisters too. A brother in Canada and two sisters in New Zealand. All married. His parents are visiting them and will be away for some months.'

'They live in Amsterdam?'

'No. No, dear. In den Haag. Mr Gerard took over the Amsterdam house when he came of age. Lovely old house too, but he needs a wife to run it...'

'I should have thought that the Professor would have had no difficulty in finding someone; he's rich and good-looking and well known in his profession.'

Mrs Beckett peered over her specs. 'Yes, dear, but Mr Gerard will never marry unless he finds his dream girl—he told me that a long time ago.' Before Julia could pursue the subject she added, 'I fancy a cup of tea. Make it in the brown pot, dear, it tastes so much better.'

It was in one of the numerous magazines Mrs Beckett had sent from England that Julia, idly leafing through its pages, saw the advertisement.

Skilful needlewomen were required to help in the repair of old fabrics and upholstery at a stately home in the north of England. Small salary and accommodation on the estate property. References would be required and full details as to the applicant's skill.

Interviews would be held in London in one month's time.

Just what I'm looking for, reflected Julia, and miles away from London. Although why that should be so vital a need was something she didn't enlarge upon, even to herself. That evening she sat down and wrote a letter...

The weather was delightful and Mrs Beckett, spending quiet hours in the garden with Lofty and Portly in close attendance, began to look like her former plump self. As for Julia, cooking tasty meals, washing and ironing, pottering around the garden, she found life was a pleasure which she would have liked to continue for ever.

Mevrouw Steen and Piet smoothed her path, and if they found her Dutch inadequate and frequently laughable, they were too kind to say so. She had little time to herself, though, for Mrs Beckett liked to have company and was sometimes fretful at having to sit quietly and watch activity which she would normally have enjoyed herself. But as the days passed and she began to take up her normal life again Julia gradually handed over to her. In another week she would be back to her normal state of health.

The thought of leaving depressed Julia, although she told herself that it was time she went back to England and got on with her own life. After all she had money now, and soon she could decide what she wanted to do...

A problem solved for her for one morning, when a letter arrived for her. If she cared to present herself at a certain London hotel on a day three weeks from now, she would be interviewed with the possibility of being employed at the stately home. She should bring with her two references and a sample of her needle-work. She would be good enough to acknowledge the letter…

Which she did, without saying anything to Mrs Beckett, trusting to luck that she wold be free by then. That done, she expressed a wish to do some embroidery. 'So that I can sit with you and not feel guilty while you knit,' she explained, and wished that she could take Mrs Beckett into her confidence.

Mrs Beckett was enthusiastic: there was a box in the attic, full of bits and pieces. Julia could rummage around and take whatever she fancied.

She found the ideal thing: a piece of patterned damask and a bundle of silks. She set to work, embroidering the pattern in a variety of stitches and various colours, and Mrs Beckett, examining it, declared that it was a lovely piece of embroidery.

'What a clever girl you are,' she observed. 'It's almost professional.' And she smiled so fondly at Julia that she almost told her of her plans. But she couldn't, of course, otherwise Mrs Beckett might feel that she was anxious to be gone—which thought was followed by another: if she told her companion what she hoped to do, the Professor might come to hear of it, and it seemed of the utmost importance that he should be unaware of her plans for the future.

He came a few days later, coming unhurriedly into the garden where they were having tea. Mrs Beckett saw him first.

'Mr Gerard—what a sight for sore eyes. And just in time for tea!'

He bent to kiss her. 'You're well again, Nanny. You look splendid…'

He nodded to Julia, half smiling. 'Julia has done a splendid job.'

'I'll get a cup and saucer and more tea,' she said, and took herself off indoors. So she was to go, and quite soon. And was he staying? Because if he was she would have to make a room ready and reorganise supper. She put the kettle on and warmed a teapot, found a cup and saucer and plate and a tray to put them on, and picked up a knife to cut the cake on the table.

It was taken from her and the Professor cut an enormous slice and began to eat it.

'Are you hungry?'

'For a home made cake? Always—don't you know that the way to a man's heart is through his stomach?'

She spooned tea into the pot. 'Are you staying?' Her voice sounded wooden in her own ears. Why, oh, why did she feel so awkward with him?

'For supper. I flew over; Piet will drive me back to the airfield later. I wanted to see how Nanny was getting on. She's fit again, but I have asked Dr de Groot to come tomorrow and give her a check-up. If he agrees with me, I'll be over in a few days with a nice middle-aged woman who will take over from you. You will be glad to go home, Julia?'

He had eaten the cake so she cut him another slice. 'Oh, yes, although I've been happy here, but Mrs Beckett wants to get back to her normal life. This lady who is coming—does Mrs Beckett know her?'

'Yes. She used to work for my mother. They were

good friends and she will stay for as long as Nanny wants her to. I have told her and she's delighted.'

He picked up the tray and Julia followed him, the rest of the cake on a plate. She hoped that he would have time to tell her how Thomas and Ruth were and, more importantly, how she was to get back home. 'Home,' she muttered to herself. 'I haven't got a home…'

There was no talk of the return as they had tea, and it was Mrs Beckett who did most of the talking.

'I have never felt better,' she assured the Professor. 'This dear girl has looked after me as though she were my own daughter—all the delicious food she has cooked for me—I have grown quite plump. She chuckled. 'Julia says she has grown fat, but I tell her that she is just right—I like a woman to have a shape…'

Julia went pink and looked away, but not before the professor had caught her eye. 'You take the words out of my mouth, Nanny.'

Julia found his smile so disquieting that she jumped to her feet, declaring that she must see what there was for supper, and nipped smartly into the cottage. Safe in the kitchen, she shut the door, muttering to herself, and poked her head into the fridge, glad that she had something as prosaic as supper to take her mind off that smile.

She had made watercress soup earlier that day; there would be just enough for the three of them if she served it carefully. She had intended omelettes for the two of them, but now she took lamb chops from the fridge, scrubbed new potatoes, baby carrots and added to the broad beans. These on the Aga, she turned her attention to a pudding. Egg custards with plenty of cream...

That dealt with, she laid the table in the dining room. She and Mrs Beckett ate their meals in the kitchen, but for this evening Julia set the table as Mrs Beckett liked it, with flowers and a starched table-cloth, polished silver and the best glasses. It looked nice when she had finished it and it had been a good excuse to stay in the cottage. She went back to the kitchen, inspected the chops, and the Professor asked from the door. 'Can we talk now, or shall it be after supper?'

'Well, everything will be ready in ten minutes.'

'Ample time. You will want to know how you are to return home; it will take only a few minutes to tell you.'

So much for wanting the pleasure of her company, thought Julia, and clashed the saucepan lids with unnecessary noise.

She said, 'Well?' in an icy voice, and didn't look at him.

'If everything is as I hope it will be, I will come on Saturday—that's three days away. I shall bring with me Miss Thrisp, who has been here before and is already in possession of the facts of Nanny's illness. I want to leave after lunch. I shall have the car and we will go back by ferry.'

'Very well.' She added, 'Thank you.'

'Where will you go?'

'I'm staying with Ruth and Thomas for a while, and then Monica's asked me.'

'And after that?'

When she didn't answer he said carelessly, 'Oh,

that isn't any of my business, is it? If supper's ready I'll pour us some sherry. When does Nanny have her glass of red wine?'

'With supper. Piet brought a case of claret; we've had some of that.'

'Good. I'll fetch Nanny in and bring you your sherry.'

Julia gave the potatoes a prod. 'Thank you.'

He came back presently with the sherry and put it on the table. 'You're as cross as two sticks,' he observed cheerfully. 'Was it because I admired your shape?'

Julia, her back to him, tossed back the sherry. 'Certainly not. I hope I'm not so childish…'

'Not childish, Julia, but very much a woman. Give me those dishes; I'll carry them to the table.'

It must be the sherry, decided Julia, making her feel peculiar. And she had every intention of forgetting what the Professor had said, or rather the manner in which he had said it. Had he been poking fun at her? Trying to annoy her? She found that hard to believe; he wasn't that kind of a man.

He left soon after their meal, thanking her pleasantly for his supper. He might annoy her but she had to admit that he had lovely manners. When he had gone she cleared away and settled Mrs Beckett in her chair, then sat and listened to that lady's reminiscences of the van der Maes family and the Professor in particular. 'Always knew what he wanted to do, yet he found the time to backpack round the world, spent his holidays working for them poor starving children in Africa, and a year or so ago he went with a team to Bosnia. Not a word to anyone, mind you.'

Mrs Beckett settled herself more comfortably in her chair. 'You'd never think it to look at him, would you? And he don't lack for social life, either. Could have married half a dozen times, and when I remind him—respectful, of course—that it is time he settled down with a wife and had children, all he says is he hasn't found his dream girl. Although goodness knows it wasn't lack of trying on the part of various young ladies.'

She peered at Julia over her specs. 'I dare say you've wondered about him, Julia?'

A truthful girl, Julia pondered her reply. 'Well, a bit, sometimes. But you see, Mrs Beckett, we don't know each other very well. Circumstances brought us together, but once I've left here I dare say I shan't see him again. You see, I have nothing to do with hospitals, and I don't know anyone he might know.'

'Such a pretty girl. I can't believe that you haven't had a boyfriend.'

'Well, hardly that…' She told her about Oscar then, and Mrs Beckett nodded her head when Julia explained why she had run away from the hotel. 'Quite right too, nasty man. How fortunate that Mr Gerard happened to be there.'

'Yes, he was very kind and helpful. Now, I'm going to get your hot milk and see you to your bed; it's been a busy day.'

'Yes, but a most interesting one,' said Mrs Beckett thoughtfully.

Lying cosily in her bed presently, Mrs Beckett reflected that the pair of them were ideally suited. It was to be hoped that they would discover that for themselves as soon as possible, though it seemed likely that Mr Gerard had already done that...

Ruth phoned in the morning. It would be lovely to have Julia to stay, and she was to make herself at home for as long as she wanted to. Thomas was busy at the hospital, but they could go shopping and there was such a lot of talking to do. 'And then Monica wants you to go and stay with them, so don't hurry to get yourself settled. I'm not sure when you'll arrive exactly, but I'll be home waiting for you.'

Julia should have felt happy and content that her future was arranging itself so pleasantly. First Ruth, then Monica, and then, if she was lucky, the job at the stately home.

'I'm free as air,' said Julia, and wished that she weren't.

Three days had never gone so fast. Julia and Mevrouw Steen got a room ready for Miss Thrisp, and while Mevrouw Steen polished and Hoovered Julia did the flowers, stocked the fridge with the food Piet went to buy for her and then did her own packing. That didn't take long, for she had had no chance to buy anything other than small necessities from the village. She would buy clothes when she got home; the money she had been sent each week was almost untouched. She allowed her mind to dwell on the pleasant prospect of buying the kind of clothes she hankered after. No more curtains, she promised herself. She would gather together an elegant wardrobe. It was a pity that the Professor would never see her in it...

There had been no word from him, but she hadn't expected it. Dr de Groot had seen Mrs Beckett, pronounced himself satisfied, observed that Julia had taken good care of his patient and gone again. Presumably the Professor didn't think it necessary to add to that.

She was up early, anxious to have everything just so before he and Miss Thrisp came; she organised fresh flowers, salad and cold meat in the fridge, strawberries and cream, plus a selection of cheeses; Miss Thrisp might not want to spend time in the kitchen after her journey. Julia had coffee ready too, and some of the little almond biscuits Mrs Beckett had shown her how to bake. As for that lady, Julia had made sure that she looked her best, sitting now in the sitting room, a good breakfast inside her, her hair just so…

Julia went to do her own hair then. There was too much of it, she thought impatiently, tugging it viciously. Perhaps she would have it cut really short. It was the fashion, and it would be nice to be fashionable.

The Rolls stopped without a whisper of sound and the professor got out and opened the car door for Miss Thrisp. Julia, who had conjured up several mental pictures of her, was pleased to see that she was exactly as anyone with a name like that would look, being tall, and thin, with a long face and a long thin nose, very dark eyes and a mouth which would stand no nonsense. But her smile was warm and friendly, and Julia thought that, despite the nose, she was rather nice. Well, she would be, she reflected, ushering the pair of them into the cottage, otherwise the Professor wouldn't have allowed her near Nanny.

And why should I be so sure of that? she wondered. She left them in the sitting room after their brief introduction and a casual nod from the Professor, and went to the kitchen to fetch the coffee. She dawdled over that to give them time to exchange their first greetings, and presently, when she took the tray in, she found the two ladies sitting side by side, both happily talking their heads off. The Professor had gone to the open window and was looking at his garden.

He turned to face her as she put the tray down.

'We shall leave directly after lunch,' he told her. 'You're ready?'

She wondered what he would say if she said that no, she wasn't; he so clearly expected her to be waiting, case in hand.

She said, 'Yes. At what time do you want lunch?'

'Noon. So that there is ample time for goodbyes.'

She said tartly, 'Will you come and sit down for your coffee?' Once everyone had coffee and biscuits, she sat down herself and joined in the ladies' conversation.

Miss Thrisp was shown to her room, then went to the kitchen with Julia to make sure she knew where everything was. Before she went back to the sitting room she put a bony hand on Julia's arm. 'You've taken such good care of Mrs Beckett; I couldn't have done better myself. I'd have come the moment the Professor told me she was needing someone, but I was getting over a nasty attack of flu myself and I was real bothered as to what would happen. But he was right, you're worth your weight in gold—he never makes mistakes about people. You look exactly as he described you.'

It would have been nice to have known just what that was, thought Julia.

Lunch was a cheerful meal, but they didn't linger over it. Julia helped Miss Thrisp clear the table and then, obedient to the Professor's look, fetched her case and made her goodbyes.

Mrs Beckett was inclined to be tearful. 'But of course you'll come again?' she asked hopefully, and Julia mumbled that perhaps she would, if and when she had got settled.

'You must get Mr Gerard to bring you over for a weekend.'

Julia mumbled again, shook Miss Thrisp's bony hand, and got into the car, to turn and wave to the two ladies and the cats as they drove away.

The Professor had had little to say, but he had been pleasant in a remote kind of way and there were several things that she wanted to know.

'Where does the ferry leave from and at what time?'

'The catamaran—it leaves tomorrow around two o'clock, and gets to Harwich in the early evening.'

'Tomorrow? You mean today?'

'I mean tomorrow. We are spending the night in Amsterdam.'

She sat up very straight. 'You may be Professor, but I'm going back today.'

'Why are you making a fuss? A few hours more or less can't make a difference to your plans, but it is a matter of urgency that I stay until tomorrow.'

'I should have been told; I could have made other arrangements. I have no wish to stay in Amsterdam. And where am I to go, pray?'

'To my house, of course. Where else? And don't worry; I shan't be there. Wim and my housekeeper will take care of you.'

'Why won't you be there?' she asked sharply.

'I shall be at the hospital, operating early this evening, and I shall be there all night until I judge my patient to be in a stable condition. I hope that satisfies you?'

She felt mean. 'I'm sorry I snapped, but if you'd told me that when I first asked I wouldn't have said anything more about it.'

He didn't answer, and she added cautiously, 'Won't you be too tired to travel tomorrow?'

His 'no' discouraged her from saying another word.

But presently she asked, 'Why do we quarrel?'

'I never quarrel, and nor, I think, do you. We strike sparks off each other, Julia.' He turned his head briefly and smiled at her, 'And that's as good a beginning as any.'

She was about to ask him what he meant, but then thought better of it, and they stayed silent as they neared Amsterdam, but it was a friendly silence.

The quiet street by the canal seemed remote from the bustling streets of the city, the old houses silent under the trees which bordered it.

It's like coming home, reflected Julia as Wim opened the door to them and greeted her as though he had known her all his life.

The Professor spoke to him quietly and he nodded and went away, to return with a solidly built elderly woman who listened to what the Professor had to say, smiled at Julia and beckoned her to follow.

'This is Getske, my housekeeper,' the professor

said. 'Go with her; she will show you to your room.
We have time for tea before I have to go.'

Julia followed the housekeeper along the hall and
up the staircase at its end. It opened onto a circular
gallery with passages leading off it and any number
of doors. Getske opened a door and stood aside for
her to go into the room beyond. It wasn't a large room
but was instantly welcoming, with its canopied bed,
the dressing table to one side, a small upholstered
chair with a table beside it under the long window
and a soft carpet underfoot. Through a door in the far
wall there was a bathroom, and leading from it a
wardrobe fit to house more clothes than Julia would
ever buy.

Alone, she prowled round, picking things up and
putting them down again. Then, remembering that the
Professor might want to leave, she tidied her person,
stuck a few more pins in her hair, dabbed powder on
her nose and went back downstairs.

He was waiting with well-concealed impatience in
a little room leading from the hall. Really, the house
was a rabbit warren, she thought, but a very luxurious
one and very much to her taste.

Tea had been laid out on a small table between two
chairs. The Professor got up from one as she went in
and Jason pranced to meet her.

'He will keep you company this evening.' The professor drew up a chair for her. 'Will you be Mother?'

She sat down and picked up the silver teapot. She
would miss this elegance, she reflected. It was something she had become accustomed to during the last
few weeks. The thought saddened her.

The Professor had his tea, ate a slice of cake and got up to go.

'I'll see you tomorrow morning,' he told her. 'Wim will take you round the house if you would like that—ask for anything you want.'

He was standing in front of her, looking down at her upturned face.

'Oh, I should like that; it's a lovely old house.' She smiled at him, and he bent down and kissed her. It was a gentle kiss, so why did it arouse such strong feelings in her person? She wondered, watching the door close behind his vast back.

Wim's English was as sparse as her Dutch, but they contrived to understand each other well enough. He had been with the Professor's family, he told her, for fifty years or more, and they and the house were his life. With Jason at their heels, they went from room to room, taking their time, while he pointed out the plasterwork ceilings, the heavy brocade curtains at the tall windows, the bow-fronted display cabinets filled with porcelain and silver, the exquisite marquetry on a long-case clock. Julia looked at it all with delight, wishing that the Professor was there too, so that she could tell him what a splendid home he had.

The house was surprisingly large, with rooms opening from one to another until the final one opened onto a long narrow garden. Tomorrow, she promised herself, she would explore the garden early in the morning, before the professor got home.

Wim took her upstairs then, waiting patiently while she poked her nose round each door on each landing, until they reached the final narrow staircase to the attic. When Wim smiled and nodded she took a look, then climbed up to the small door and opened it. The attic was long and narrow, with small windows at each end and a steeply sloping roof. It wasn't empty, containing odds and ends of furniture, rolled up rugs, a row of ice skates hanging from hooks on the wall and a baby's cradle. In one corner there was a stack of framed pictures and old photographs. She bent to look and picked up the top one. A boy, a quite small boy. She didn't need to read the date and name on it. She put it down again, feeling as though she had pried into the Professor's private life. He was smiling in the photo and his smile hadn't changed...

She had dinner in the same small room where they had had tea: watercress soup, duckling in an orange sauce and *pofferjes* light as air and smothered with cream. There was a light white wine, and coffee to follow, and a beaming Wim to serve her.

It was a reward for looking after Mrs Beckett, she supposed; he had paid her wages, but he could hardly tip her...

She offered a morsel of the little sugary biscuit which had come with the coffee to Jason and allowed herself to daydream. But presently she sat up. She had allowed her thoughts to run away with her just because the professor had kissed her.

'I shall go to bed,' she told Jason, and did so.

She was awake after a dreamless sleep when a stolid young girl brought her tea. She showered and dressed and went down to the hall and found Wim. Breakfast would be in half an hour he told her; the Professor wasn't home.

So she went into the garden and walked with Jason up and down its narrow paths in the morning sun. It was full of old-fashioned flowers, with a circular rose bed and flowering shrubs against the brick wall at its end. She could have stayed there, sitting on the rustic seat, surrounded by honeysuckle and wisteria, but breakfast waited.

The Professor was standing by the window of the room leading to the garden. His good morning was pleasantly friendly, his enquiry as to whether she had had a good night uttered in the tones of a thoughtful host. He was immaculately dressed and one would have supposed that he had enjoyed a good night's sleep too, but Julia saw the tired lines in his face.

'Have you had any sleep?'

'Enough,' he told her, and smiled so that she remembered the little boy in the photo.

I must forget that, she told herself, and went with him to eat her breakfast. They ate in silence for a time until she asked, 'Was it successful? The operation? Or would you rather not talk about it?'

He didn't answer at once, and she said quickly, 'All right, you don't have to tell me. I'm not being curious, you know.'

He loaded butter onto toast. 'It was entirely successful. And I don't mind you asking, Julia.' He stared at her across the table. 'I think that I would have been disappointed if you had not done so.' He passed his coffee cup. 'A mutual interest is to be desired.'

'Oh, is it?' said Julia, bewildered. She had a feeling that things were moving too fast for her to understand, but she was aware of a pleasant excitement. And they had the rest of the day together.

CHAPTER SIX

JULIA'S pleasant speculations about the morning were quickly cut short.

'We shall need to leave here after an early lunch,' said the Professor. 'I shall go back to the hospital presently, and I'll take Jason with me and give him a run. Perhaps you want to explore or go to the shops? I would be easier in my mind if you stayed here…'

She said brightly, 'I shall sit in the garden. I can do all the shopping I want when I get home.'

So he went away with Jason and she went into the garden again and sat down with the newspapers Wim had handed to her. She could so easily have gone with him, she thought; perhaps waited in the car while he was at the hospital, and then gone with him and Jason. He was deliberately avoiding her…

'I couldn't care less!' said Julia, and picked up the *Daily Telegraph* and read it from front to back page. She was none the wiser when she had. She tried the *Haagsche Post* next—she might as well improve her Dutch while she could—although it was a complete waste of time. She was puzzling out the small ads when the Professor joined her.

He said affably, 'Oh, splendid, you're improving your Dutch.'

'I have very little Dutch to improve,' said Julia coldly. 'I hope your patient is improving.'

He sat down beside her with Jason squeezed between them.

'Yes, I think he has a very good chance. I've left him in good hands.'

'Was he someone important?' She turned to look at him. 'Did they send for you specially?'

'Yes, and yes. Will you be sorry to leave Holland?'

'Oh, yes, although I've not seen anything of it. I'm sorry to leave the cottage and this splendid house, but they'll be lovely memories.'

'You would like to come back some time?'

'Perhaps.' She put an arm round Jason's woolly shoulders and he licked her hand gently. 'Jason is going to miss you.'

'Yes, and I shall miss him, but I shall be here again very shortly and he is used to my coming and going.'

He glanced at his watch. 'We had better have our lunch.'

The day which had seemed to stretch before her for hours of delight had telescoped into an all too short day. The professor might not like her, but that couldn't prevent her from enjoying his company. She supposed that she didn't like him either, but she was no longer quite sure about that. Of course, there was still the journey back to London…

Which was disappointing, in so far that the Professor, while thoughtful for her well-being, made only the most casual conversation, giving her no opportunity to get to know him better. On board, he excused himself smiling and began to study a case full of papers—first, however, making sure that she had something to read and a tray of tea.

She leafed through the magazines and wondered what he was thinking about.

She would have been astonished to know it was herself. Usually so sure of himself, the Professor found himself uncertain. That he had fallen in love with Julia and wanted her for his wife he now freely admitted, but she had shown no preference for his company; he thought that she liked him a good deal more than she was prepared to admit, but he wasn't prepared to rush her. Once back in London, he would have the opportunity to see her frequently. In the meantime, it was only by maintaining a casual disinterested manner that he was able to keep his hands off her...

They discussed the weather, the countryside and the state of the roads as he drove back to London. All safe subjects which lasted them nicely until he drew up before Thomas's and Ruth's new home.

They were warmly welcomed but the Professor didn't stay. He had a brief smiling chat with Ruth, observed that he would see Thomas at the hospital in the morning, and got back into the Rolls, brushing aside Julia's careful little speech of thanks.

He couldn't have been pleasanter, she thought, or more remote.

Mrs Potts, his housekeeper, and the two dogs were waiting for him. His housekeeper was middle-aged, brisk and devoted to him, and as for Wilf and Robbie, their welcome was estatic.

He took the car round to the mews at the back of

the house, promised to be back for his dinner and took the little dogs for a run. The streets were quiet; London on a summer's evening could be delightful. He thought about the cottage—he would have to ring Nanny when he got back—and he wondered if Julia was thinking of it too. She had loved the house in Amsterdam; she would fit so easily into his life…

Despite his casual goodbye, Julia had expected to see him again while she was staying with Ruth, but, beyond saying that he was working too hard, Thomas had nothing to say about him. Ruth wondered from time to time why he hadn't come to see them or at least phoned, but Julia's monosyllabic replies led her to a rather thoughtful silence. Julia looked splendid: full of fresh air, nicely tanned, apparently well pleased with life—and yet there was something wrong…

Ruth entered into the plans Julia had for an entire new wardrobe, and when she wasn't there phoned Monica. 'She looks marvellous, but there is something wrong. Do you suppose she met someone in Holland? She's coming to stay with you—try and find out.'

Getting ready for bed, Ruth asked Thomas, 'Has Gerard said anything about Julia?'

'Only that she has been a splendid help with Mrs Beckett. He's off to Glasgow tomorrow. He'll be gone for a couple of days.' Thomas gave her a sharp look. 'Why did you ask?'

'Oh, nothing, darling. They don't get on, do they?'

Thomas got into bed. 'Don't they? It isn't something I'd ask him—or Julia, for that matter.'

There were still ten days before her interview for the job. Beyond telling Ruth vaguely that she had heard of something, Julia had said nothing; instead she and Ruth went shopping.

With money in her purse Julia ignored the High Street chain stores and poked around boutiques, and, egged on by her sister, spent a good deal more than she had intended to. But the results were worth it; she bought well-cut jersey dresses, elegant tops and skirts, dresses for summer and a silk dress suitable for the evening. She thought that she might never wear it, that it would probably hang in the cupboard forgotten and regretted, but there was always the chance that she might need it—supposing the Professor should ask her to dine with him one evening?

It was highly unlikely—and even if he asked her she might refuse...

There were undies to buy too, shoes, a raincoat, a short jacket, a sensible outfit to wear if she got that job...

Afterwards she went to stay with Monica and George. She had a long weekend in which to explore their home and the village and listen to George preaching a splendid sermon. He had a good congregation too, said Monica proudly and she herself ran the Mothers' Union and Sunday School. Village life suited her, and now there was money to see to the plumbing and refurbish the vicarage. There was so much to see and talk about that no one noticed that Julia had almost nothing to say about her stay in Holland once she had given a brief account of it— and an even briefer reference to the professor.

Back with Ruth, she dressed in one of the jersey

dresses and, for once very neat about the head, went to her appointment. It was to be held in one of the smaller hotels and, urged by the porter to take the first door on the left of the foyer, Julia did so. There were five or six other women there, all armed as she was with specimens of their handiwork. They paused in their talk to stare at her, answer her good morning with nods and then resume their chatting. There was one older woman who had smiled at her, but others were young, smartly dressed and discreetly made up. Julia decided that she had very little chance against their self-assurance. Probably they had all been to a needlework school and had diplomas and marvellous references.

They were called in, one after the other, and came out looking pleased with themselves. The older woman went in, looking anxious, and when she came out she said nothing, only smiled again as Julia opened the door in her turn.

There were three women sitting behind a table. They greeted her pleasantly, told her to sit down, and the one in the middle, middle-aged and looking how one would imagine a strict schoolteacher would look, asked her why she wanted the job.

This was unexpected; there was no time to prepare a speech. Julia said, 'I want to get away from London,' and then wished that she hadn't said it, so she added, 'And I like needlework and sewing and making things out of things.'

The three women looked at each other. 'Will you show us your work?'

So she unwrapped the tapestry, its pattern picked out with the silks Mrs Beckett had given her, and spread it out on the table and sat down again. It was passed from one hand to the other, looked at through magnifying glasses and held up to the light. She was asked which stitches she had used and why she had chosen to embroider the tapestry.

'I hadn't anything else. I was in the country with no shops for miles. So I used what I found in the attic.'

'You understand that this is temporary employment? A week's notice on either side. Tedious work, repairing very old curtains. Quite long hours and the remuneration is small. Bed and board is free, of course. We are prepared to employ you on those terms.'

Julia didn't give herself time to think. She said, 'Thank you; I should like the job.'

'It will be confirmed by letter and you will be given directions as to how to reach the estate. You will need to go to Carlisle and then to Haltwhistle, where you will be met. Are you free to travel within the next day or so?'

'Yes, I can be ready in two days' time.'

Back in the waiting room, she found the older woman still there.

She said hesitantly, 'I waited. I thought they might take you. I've got a job there.'

'You have? I'm glad—so have I. Perhaps we could travel up together. Do you know that part of the world?'

'I was born near the estate. I came to London with my husband. He died and I wanted to go back home.'

'I'm sorry about your husband. I just wanted to get away from London.'

They were standing on the pavement outside the hotel 'Do you have a phone number? Perhaps we could meet at the station?'

The woman nodded. 'My name's Woodstock— Jenny. It would be nice to travel together.'

It wasn't difficult to convince Ruth that the job was something which was exactly what she had hoped for. 'And,' she pointed out, 'it isn't a permanent one; I expect that once the repairs are made we shan't be needed. And while I'm there I can decide where I want to live and what I want to do.'

Ruth said, 'Yes, dear,' in an uncertain way. Something was wrong. Perhaps Julia *had* met someone in Holland? She was about to ask when Julia said casually, 'Ruth, don't let the Professor know where I am. Don't look like that. It's just that he has this way of turning up with some offer of a job or something...'

It sounded pretty feeble but Ruth, thinking her own thoughts, said at once, 'I won't say a word. It sounds rather fun, this job. It's a long way away, of course, but probably it will be a lovely old house full of treasures and you'll meet lots of people.'

The day before she was due to leave the Professor came. Ruth had gone to the hairdresser and Julia was in the kitchen getting lunch when he knocked on the door. She had opened it expecting the postman, and the sight of the Professor standing there, smiling a little, did things to her breath. She had wanted to see him just once more, for after she had gone from London she had every intention of forgetting him. On the other hand she would have liked to have gone away before he found out that she was no longer at Ruth's.

She said now, 'Oh, hello. Did you want Ruth? She's out…'

'I came to see you.'

There was nothing for it but to ask him in. 'I'm getting lunch,' she told him, and led the way to the kitchen. It would be easier to calm down if she had something to do. And why should she need to calm down? she wondered.

'You're glad to be back?' he asked.

She whisked eggs in a bowl and didn't look at him. 'Yes, yes, I am.'

'Will you have dinner with me tomorrow evening, Julia?'

It was so unexpected that she put the bowl of eggs down with something of a thump on the table. 'Tomorrow? No—no, thank you.'

She looked at him then, wishing with her whole heart that she wasn't going miles away, knowing suddenly that she loved him and that the thought of not seeing him again was unbearable.

She said carefully, 'I'm sorry, I can't…I wasn't going to tell you—I'm going away—tomorrow morning.'

Something in his quiet face made her add, 'I've got a most interesting job. I want to get away from London…'

'You were not going to tell me?' His voice was as quiet as his face.

'No—no, I wasn't.' She had spoken too loudly, and now added recklessly, 'Why should I?'

'Indeed, why should you?' He smiled gently. 'I hope that you will be very happy.'

'Of course I shall be happy,' said Julia in a cross voice, wishing that he would go so that she might burst into tears in peace.

Which was exactly what he did do, blandly wishing her goodbye, telling her cheerfully that he would see himself out.

She wept into the eggs then, and, since she couldn't see to do anything for a moment, sat down and buried her face in Muffin's furry body. Muffin, who loved her in his own cat fashion, bore with the damp fur and Julia's incoherent mutterings, but it was a relief when she settled him back in his chair. Feline instinct warned him that she was unhappy, that she was probably going away. But she would be back, and in the meantime he was quite comfortable with Ruth. He settled down for a nap and Julia went and washed her face, and then went back to the eggs.

Ruth, back home again, took a quick look at Julia. 'You don't have to go, dear. You know you can stay here as long as you like, and if you want to get away from London, Monica would love to have you.'

She went to the fridge and poured two glasses of white wine. 'Is that a soufflé? It looks delicious…'

Presently Julia said, 'The Professor came. I told him I was going away but he doesn't know where I'm going. Don't tell him, Ruth.'

'Of course not, love.' Ruth was brisk. 'Did he want to know?'

'No,' said Julia bleakly. She added, 'He didn't even say goodbye.'

Ruth forebore from pointing out that he was a man

who never said anything he didn't mean. She began
to talk instead about the morrow's journey.

Jenny Woodstock was at the station in the morning,
mildly excited and happy at the thought of going back
to her home. She talked in her quiet way about it
during their journey and Julia was thankful for that,
for it kept her own thoughts at bay. And she was glad
to have someone with her who knew her way about
once they reached Carlisle and, finally, Haltwhistle.
    Even then their journey wasn't over. There was a
middle-aged man, stocky, with a Land Rover waiting
for them, and they drove for what seemed like hours
through the wide countryside until he turned into a
wide gateway and onto a long drive. They could see
their destination now, an imposing mansion with a
few trees around it. Even on a summer's day it looked
bleak, but as they neared it Julia could see that it was
lived in and that there were cars parked to one side
of the house and people going in and out of the great
entrance.
    Mrs Woodstock enlightened her. 'They're open to
the public twice a week.'
    And the driver said over his shoulder, 'I'll drive
you round to one of the side doors. The housekeeper
will settle you in.'
    A surly man, thought Julia. She hoped that the
housekeeper would be more friendly.
    Her hopes were realised. Mrs Bates was large and
stout, with twinkling eyes and a wide smile. She offered tea and then led them out of the house and
across a wide courtyard. 'Most of the sewing ladies
come from the village,' she explained. 'I've put you

here, Mrs Woodstock.' She opened a door in one of the outbuildings. 'It's a nice little room and there's a bathroom and a gas ring and so on, so's you can be cosy.' She looked at Julia. 'If you'll wait here, Miss...'

She was back in a few minutes. 'You're over here, up these steps.' She observed, 'The place is used for storage but you won't be disturbed.'

She surged up the steps and unlocked the door at the top, and Julia followed her. The room was quite large, with a low ceiling and a wide window. It was comfortably furnished—a divan bed, a table and two chairs, an easy chair and bookshelves. There was another door leading to a shower room and an alcove with a gas ring and cupboards.

'You'll eat over in the house but I'll see you have tea and milk so that you can have a drink in your own room. You'll be wanted in half an hour or so. Will you come back to me and I'll take you?'

Left alone, Julia took another look around her; it was nice to have a room of her own, away from the house, and once she had unpacked and put her small possessions round the place it would look more like home. She tidied herself and then went in search of Jenny.

Jenny was delighted. 'It's like a hotel,' she observed happily, 'and I'm only a few miles from where I was born.'

They followed the housekeeper through endless corridors until they reached a small staircase tucked away in a narrow passage. They climbed to the second floor before they were finally ushered into a vast attic with overhead lighting and a row of windows overlooking the front of the house. The severe woman who had interviewed them was waiting and they spent the next hour or so being led along the long tables where the repair work was being done. A cup of tea would have been nice, reflected Julia, being shown the wall tapestry she would be working on.

There wasn't much of the afternoon left. The half-dozen women around her began to pack up presently, and thankfully she and Jenny were shown the way to a room on the ground floor where tea was waiting. It was more than tea; there were eggs and ham, several kinds of bread, butter, pots of jam, a splendid cake and a great pot of tea. Julia, eating with a splendid appetite, wondered if this was the last meal of the day, for it was almost six o'clock.

As they got up from the table one of the women said in a friendly voice, 'You're new, aren't you? There's sandwiches and hot drinks about eight o'clock. Some of us live in the village but two of us live here in the house.'

It was going to be all right, Julia decided, going sleepily to her bed later that evening. Everyone was friendly, she had a pleasant room, good, wholesome food and she would be working at something she enjoyed doing. Nevertheless she cried herself to sleep, and her last thoughts were of Gerard. He would forget her, of course. Probably by the time she got back to London he would have gone back to Holland and got married into the bargain.

The Professor went about his work in his usual calm manner. For the moment there was nothing to be done; first he had to find out where Julia had gone.

It was some days before he saw Ruth and enquired casually as to whether she had heard from Julia. And Ruth blushed because she was longing to tell him where Julia was, but a promise was a promise...

'She's very happy...'

'Splendid. What kind of a job is it?'

There would be no harm in telling him that. 'Repairing old tapestries.'

'And where is she?'

Ruth blushed again. 'She asked me not to tell you and I promised.'

'Then I won't bother you. I hope she will settle down and enjoy life. How fortunate that she heard of something so soon after coming back.'

'Oh, it wasn't sudden; she told me she'd applied for the job while she was still in Holland with Mrs Beckett—she saw it advertised in a magazine.'

Now he had one or two clues. He said casually, 'And how are Monica and George getting on? Will you be visiting them now that you're nicely settled in here?'

So Ruth told him all about the new bathrooms and the central heating in the vicarage, pleased that she had given nothing away about Julia.

It was the following day before the Professor had the leisure to phone Mrs Beckett. He listened patiently to her detailed account of her progress and when she paused for breath he asked, 'Nanny, which magazines do you read?'

'Now there's a funny question,' observed Mrs Beckett. 'English ones, of course, they get sent each week.' She named them and added, 'Why do you want to know, Mr Gerard?'

'Do any of them advertise jobs?'

'Not all of them. The *Lady* does—pages and pages of them.'

'Nanny, have you heard from Julia?'

Mrs Beckett looked out of the window and smiled. 'Well, yes, bless the dear child. Sent me a long letter but forgot the address. Got a lovely job, she says, embroidering and suchlike. The post mark was Carlisle. Seems a long way from home, but I dare say she was visiting friends.'

His 'Probably' was non-committal, and she put down the phone with another smile. The path of true love never did run smooth, she informed a rather surprised Miss Thrisp.

True enough. But that wasn't going to deter the Professor from his own particular path. His secretary was bidden to obtain back copies of the *Lady* and he searched the advertisements until he found what he sought…

Life was very different for Julia now. The work was interesting and she enjoyed it; the other women were friendly and they were well looked after. There was a vast park to walk in when she had finished work in the evening, and an estate Land Rover took the staff to the village or Haltwhistle when they were free. All the same, she was lonely. It was a splendid job, she told herself. The country around was vast and lonely and very much to her liking, and although she didn't regret leaving London it was impossible to forget Gerard. She consoled herself with the thought that he would have forgotten her by now, but that couldn't stop her loving him.

She took to getting up early and walking in the park before breakfast. It was peaceful there: birds singing, distant sounds coming from the Home Farm, subdued noise from the great house waking to another day. It was such a vast place that she had only seen a little of it, and nothing of its owners.

She had been there for almost two weeks when a particularly splendid morning got her out of bed earlier than usual. She showered and dressed and drank her early-morning tea and let herself out of her room. There was no one about and she crossed the courtyard and went into the parkland beyond. Part of it was wooded, and there was a lake which dribbled into a small stream, and on such a morning it was a delight to the eye.

She wandered along and presently sat down on a tree stump, allowing her thoughts to wander too. She supposed that sooner or later she would go back to London, find herself a small flat and put her talents to good use. At least she would have a reference, and there were museums and art galleries and private houses who would employ her. And, although she might never see the Professor, she would be near him...

A cheerful 'Good morning' got her to her feet. A man was coming towards her, a young man with a pleasant rugged face. There were two dogs with him who crowded round her, tails wagging.

'You'll be one of the needlewomen,' said the man cheerfully. 'I heard Mother saying that there were one or two new ladies.' He held out a hand. 'Menton—Colin Menton.'

Julia smiled at him, warmed by his friendliness.

'Gracey,' she said in her turn. 'Julia. How do you do?'

They shook hands and he asked, 'Where are you from?'

'London.'

'You're a long way from home. Do you like it here? It is really rather different.'

'I didn't live in a very nice part of London; this seems like heaven.'

'It is.' They were strolling back towards the house. 'But it's not to everyone's taste—too quiet.'

'That's why it's heaven.' They had reached the courtyard. 'I must go.'

'Nice meeting you. Perhaps we shall see each other again. Do you go walking each morning?'

'Well, yes.'

'Then we'll meet again.'

She thought about him while she stitched patiently. It had been pleasant to talk to someone of her own age; the other needlewomen were really friendly, and she got on well with them, but they were twice her age and Jenny went to her home when she was free. Julia explored when she was free. Haltwhistle was near enough for her half-day expeditions. It was a small market town with a fine church, and she sent picture postcards to Ruth and Monica, quite forgetting that they might be shown to the Professor.

One day she got a lift to the small village of Greenhead. The road running through it was close to the Roman Wall and she walked for miles until she found a side road which took her back to Haltwhistle and eventually back to the estate. It was a long walk and she enjoyed every minute of it. She didn't feel

lonely in the country and she had her thoughts of
Gerard to keep her company.

She had done the right thing, she told herself; she
had no intention of mooning after a man who hardly
noticed her. Once or twice she had thought they could
have been friends, but that had been a flash in the
pan. And anyway there was always the possibility that
Gerard would have gone back to Holland.

The thought of never seeing him again was unbearable, but she would have to learn to bear it and
it would surely be easier as time passed. There was
always the chance that they might meet... She would
stay at the estate for as long as there was work for
her, and then she would have to decide her future and
what better place in which to do it than this remote
countryside?

She wrote cheerful letters to Ruth and Monica,
though both of them were mystified as to why she
shouldn't want anyone to know where she was. But
since she seemed so happy and content with the job,
and they were both fully occupied with their own
lives, they didn't pursue the matter further. Perhaps
if the Professor had mentioned her on one of his in-
frequent visits they might have given it more
thought...

A few days later Julia met Colin Menton again. The
day's work was finished and she was crossing the
courtyard to go to her room. It was late afternoon and
still warm. She would go for a walk before supper
and then write letters.

He met her halfway. 'Hello, finished work for the
day? I don't suppose you feel like a walk? I'm going
to the other end of the park to see if the trees we

planted are doing well.' He smiled at her. 'Do say yes.'

Julia laughed. 'Well, all right, yes.'

The park was vast, merging now and again into fields of rough grass. Close to the house the gardens had been skilfully laid out, and there was a lake bordered by trees, but presently they followed a path into the trees on the edge of the park. It was pleasant walking and they found plenty to talk about. He begged her to call him Colin and told her that he'd been spending a month or two at his home before taking up a post abroad as an agricultural adviser. 'I shall be getting married before we go,' he confided.

Julia sensed a wish to talk about his fiancée. 'Is she pretty?' she asked.

The rest of their walk was taken up with a detailed description of his fiancée's perfections, and as they neared the house again he said awkwardly, 'Have I been boring you? Only I do like to talk about her.'

'Well, of course you do. She sounds a perfect dear, as well as being so pretty. I'm sure you'll both be very happy. How much longer will you be here?'

'Ten days. We're being married from her home in Wiltshire. We didn't want a big wedding, but you know what mothers are.'

They were standing in the courtyard. 'I enjoyed our walk. I suppose you wouldn't like to drive over to Hexham? I have to see someone there but it shouldn't take too long. There is a splendid abbey there that you might like to visit if you're interested.'

'I should like that. I get two half-days in the week—Tuesday and Thursday, both in the morning.'

'Next Tuesday? It's no distance—fifteen miles or

so. If we left around nine o'clock we could have coffee before I see this fellow. You can look round and visit the abbey and I'll meet you for lunch.'

'I have to be back at work by two o'clock.'

'Easily done. We can lunch early.'

Julia agreed; the prospect of an outing was inviting and there might be time to do some shopping.

Jenny, working beside her on the worn tapestry they were patiently repairing, gave her a quick glance as they started to stitch.

'How are you getting on?' she wanted to know. 'This is a grand job. If we ever get our time off together you must come home with me. You've no idea how marvellous it is to be back with the family. You look perky. Have you made any friends?'

Julia nodded. 'And I walk miles—I love walking and the country is beautiful. I met Mr Menton one morning. He's offered me a lift to Hexham—I'd like to see the abbey and do some shopping.'

'Young Mr Menton? He's nice—getting married soon, did you know?'

'Yes, he told me about his fiancée and the job he's going to. He's leaving very shortly. Will the family go to the wedding? What happens here if they do? Will we still be open to the public?'

'I shouldn't think so. We'll be told, I suppose.' Jenny gave Julia an enquiring look. 'It's likely that there will be enough work for us until early next year. There are the curtains in the drawing room to mend and that wall tapestry in the hall. It'll be cold here after London. Will you stay?'

'Why not? Unless I have a good reason to go back

to London. I have two married sisters; they might have babies or need me for something or other.'

She spoke cheerfully but, much though she liked her surroundings, the prospect of being there for almost another six months was daunting. After all she had money now, enough to get a mortgage on a small flat—not necessarily in London—and find work. She choked back dismay at the prospect. She was letting herself drift; she who had never been faint-hearted in her life before.

That evening she borrowed an atlas. She mustn't be too far away from Ruth and Monica, but far away enough from London and Gerard. She made a list of likely towns and went to bed feeling that she had at last begun to organise her future.

And on Tuesday afternoon, bending over her stitching, she went over the trip to Hexham. It had been a success. She and Colin had fallen into an easy friendship and there had never been a lack of something to talk about during the short drive. They had had coffee before parting, and she had spent a happy morning looking round the abbey and then looking at the shops, buying some books and other small items on a list she had made. They had met at a pleasant old pub and had an early lunch before driving back. It had been a pleasant morning and she would miss his cheerful face and casual friendliness. He was leaving on Thursday, and she had said that she would say goodbye to him before she set off on a walk before starting work that afternoon.

He was to leave early, but she had breakfast before she went out to the yard. He had already said goodbye to his family and his car, an Aston Martin, was there, with him in the driving seat.

Julia lent over to shake his hand. 'Go carefully, and have a lovely wedding.'

'Oh, we will. I'm glad we met, Julia. I hope you will have a lovely wedding to some lucky chap one day.' He kissed her cheek just as the Professor drove the Rolls into the yard.

CHAPTER SEVEN

JULIA straightened up with a laugh—and saw the Professor's car. The wild rush of delight at the sight of him turned at once to a mixture of panic and bad temper. Panic because he might have bad news of her sisters, and temper because she was wearing an old skirt and a cotton top, suitable for a walk in the country but not for meeting him of all people.

She waved in answer to Colin's wave, and watched the Professor get out of his car and come towards her. She would have liked to have run to meet him, but something in his leisurely approach stopped her. Yet when he reached her his, 'Hello, Julia,' was uttered in the mildest of voices.

She asked breathlessly, 'How did you know I was here?' She frowned. 'I asked Ruth…'

'Who told me nothing. But rest assured that I am quite capable of finding you if I wish to do so.'

'So why did you?'

'There would be no point in telling you that at the moment. I'm glad to see that you have found friends. Or should I say a friend.' His voice was silky.

'Colin?' She wanted to shake his calm. 'Oh, yes, we've had some pleasant walks. He is the son of the house.' She added, without much truth, 'We've seen quite a lot of the surrounding country—Hadrian's Wall…'

When he didn't speak she asked uneasily, 'Do you have friends in this part of the world?'

'Colleagues at the hospital in Carlisle.'

'Oh, you're doing something there?'

He didn't answer, only asked, 'When do you work?'

'From nine in the morning until five o'clock. We get breaks for meals and two half-days.' She added defiantly, 'I'm loving it.'

'And is this a half-day?'

She said Yes so reluctantly that he smiled.

'Then perhaps you will spend it with me? We could drive to Hadrian's Wall and have a walk and an early lunch. When must you start work?'

'Two o'clock.'

'An hour or two in the fresh air and a brisk walk will do you good.'

'I go walking each morning...'

He said smoothly, 'Ah, yes, but now that you will be walking alone it is never as inviting, is it? Go and do something to your hair. I'll wait here. Ten minutes?'

'I haven't said I would come...'

He smiled and her heart turned over. 'But you will!'

She went to her room then and got into a cotton jersey dress, and did her hair again and made up her face nicely, all the while telling herself that she was mad to be doing it. On the other hand, he would soon be gone again, back to London. Surely an hour or so in his company wouldn't make any difference to her resolve not to see him again. She wondered briefly how he had discovered where she was... She didn't waste time thinking about it; half-days were precious, and every minute of them had to be enjoyed. She hurried back to the yard and found the Professor leaning against his car, talking to Jenny, on her way to start her morning's work.

'Lucky you,' she called cheerfully. 'Don't forget the time, though in your shoes I would.'

Julia tried not to see the wink which accompanied the remark.

The Professor stowed her into the Rolls and drove away, embarking at the same time on a casual conversation which put her instantly at ease. She reflected that this unexpected meeting should have bothered her, but it hadn't. It seemed the most natural thing in the world that Gerard should have appeared out of the blue, as it were, and that they should be spending the morning together as if they were old friends. But, of course, it wasn't that at all; he had felt the need of company and had an hour or so to spare.

The Professor glanced at her puzzled face and smiled to himself. Just for once Julia had lost her tongue.

He took her to Brampton, not many miles away, gave her coffee at the hotel there, parked the car, booked a table for lunch and marched her off briskly. Hadrian's Wall was no distance, and when they reached it they walked beside it. It was quiet and the countryside was empty; the road was nearby but there was little traffic, and it was cool enough to make walking a pleasure. And they talked.

It was surprising how easy it was to talk to him, thought Julia, discussing her future, her doubts and problems until at a certain moment she stopped abruptly. She was a fool, telling him all this; he wouldn't be in the least interested. He might even be bored.

'Do you know this part of the world?' she wanted to know.

'Not well enough.' He had seen her sudden reluctance to talk about herself and so slipped easily into a casual discussion of the country around them. Presently she was lulled into the idea that he hadn't been listening, had shown no sign of interest. She had been a fool, telling him of her plans when she had made up her mind not to see him again. She supposed that being in love made one foolish…

Back at the hotel they had lunch in a delightful restaurant, its windows overlooking a well-kept garden. The place was half full and the service friendly. Julia, hungry after their walk, made a splendid meal. The food was well cooked and plentiful on the estate, but the food set before her now was something of a treat: game soup, a meal in itself, roast beef with Yorkshire pudding to dream of, roasted parsnips, crisp and golden brown, and a crème brulée which melted in the mouth.

'I'm not going to offer you wine,' said the Professor, 'or you'll droop over your curtains!' So they drank tonic water.

He drove her back afterwards, making casual small talk, and back in the court yard, when she would have uttered her carefully rehearsed thank-you speech, he said abruptly, 'I'm glad you enjoyed the morning. You must get Colin to take you again while the weather is good.'

Julia could think of nothing to say but, 'Yes', and

watched him drive away while all she wanted to say crowded her tongue unuttered. Perhaps it was just as well, she thought unhappily. For a short time she had thought that perhaps he had sought her out because he had wanted to see her again, but that wasn't so; he had had a morning to spare and had used it to make sure that she was all right so that he could tell Ruth. It was a lowering thought...

The Professor drove himself back to London deep in thought. Julia had been glad to see him, he had seen the look on her face, but had the delight been at the sight of him or because he was someone from home? And this man, this young man, reflected Gerard, deeply aware that at thirty-six he could no longer be considered young. Though a man of no conceit, he was aware that he could make her fall in love with him—but he had no intention of doing that; she must learn to love him of her own free will. That they were meant for each other was something he never doubted.

He didn't think that she was happy; she liked her work and the surroundings in which she lived but she was sad about something. There was nothing he could do for the moment only have patience.

He phoned Ruth when he got back and gave her a reassuring account of Julia.

'I suppose he went to the Carlisle hospital,' she told Thomas, 'and discovered where she was.'

And Thomas, who knew better, agreed with her.

A week or two went by. The weather was unusually warm and dry, even in the north of the country, and sitting for long hours stitching was tiring. Julia, taking her solitary early morning walks, made plans for the future and then discarded them. There was a rumour that once the tapestry they were working on was finished they would be asked to work at the town-house the family owned in London. The local women wouldn't go, but Jenny and she might be offered work there. That wouldn't do. Forgetting Gerard was harder than she had thought it would be. And how could she forget him when she loved him? The only thing to do was to go away, as far as possible...

She wrote cheerful letters to Ruth and Monica and scanned their replies for a mention of the Professor, but it was as though he had never existed.

It was some time after four o'clock in the afternoon when the fire broke out. A sightseer, disregarding the 'No Smoking' notices, had lighted a cigarette and tossed the still burning match to one side. It had fallen onto the curtains shrouding the state dining room windows. Dry as dust, and fragile with age, they had smouldered unnoticed for some minutes and then suddenly burst into flames which had swept across the room and into an adjoining salon. From there it leapt from wall-panelling to tapestries, to chairs and tables, through the wide archway and into the music room beyond...

It was a large, rambling mansion, and there was no one in that wing when the fire started. By the time the alarm was raised it had spread, burning the telephone cable and the fire alarm which connected it to the police station at Haltwhistle.

There was a certain amount of panic and great confusion, so that no one remembered that up on the fourth floor, under the roof, there were seven women, stitching…

Sounds from outside the house were muted in the attics; cars and coaches arriving with visitors were sounds so frequent that they were disregarded, as were the voices. The windows at the front of the house were kept shut on open days, since fumes from the cars might harm the delicate materials they were working upon, but that afternoon Julia's ear caught another sound: voices raised in alarm—more than alarm, terror: And seconds later she smelled the smoke. She went to a window and looked out and saw one wing of the house in flames, people getting into cars and buses and a confused mass of those who didn't know what to do…

By then the other women had left their work and joined her at the window.

'We'd better make haste and get out.' One of the women from the village, older than the rest, spoke urgently. 'We're quite safe if we go down the back stairs.' And indeed the fire was reassuringly distant from them.

But when they reached the second landing it was to find the staircase below already alight.

So far there had been no panic, they weren't women to do that, but now the sight of the smoke and the flames creeping around the staircase on the floor below shattered their calm. Someone screamed.

'The garden door at the back of the house—there's a small staircase…'

Someone told the screamer to be quiet, in a voice rendered hoarse by anger and fright, and they ran through the main part of the house along corridors and passages Julia had never seen before and found the staircase. It was still intact, but the floor below was well alight.

Julia caught one of the older women by the arm. 'If we go back to the attics we can break the windows—there's a narrow parapet, isn't there? Someone will see us; there will be a fire escape…'

The woman nodded. 'We're going back,' she shouted above the panicky voices. 'They'll get us off the roof.'

They went back the way they had come, and although there was a smell of burning and wisps of smoke and a great deal of noise the fire was out of sight. And once back in the attics they set about breaking the glass in the windows at the front of the house, shouting for help as they did so.

The fire had spread to the centre of the house by now, and there were a great many people running to and fro, but the noise of the fire carried away the voices of the women in the attic and no one saw them.

It was Julia who picked up a stool and hurled it over the parapet, and within seconds they were all tossing anything they could carry into the sweep below. And now they could see upturned faces, waving arms, people running and the heartening sight of the first of the fire engines belting up the drive. The third floor was alight now and the hoses were turned on to it. If the fire could be halted there, thought Julia, we'd have a good chance of getting out. She said so, loudly, and the little band of terrified women took heart.

It was five minutes—the longest five minutes of her life, reflected Julia later—before the fire rescue team arrived, and another five minutes saw the first of them being edged over the parapet and into the arms of the fireman perched on the end of the fire escape. In unspoken consent, the women who had children were the first to be rescued, then the two elderly ladies who were married to estate workers, and lastly Jenny and Julia.

And Julia, waiting alone in a blur of held-back terror, allowed herself to scream—for there was no one to hear above the roar of the flames below. She felt better once she had screamed; she had nothing to be frightened about now, the firemen would be back for her in a few minutes. Only she wished with her whole heart that Gerard was there beside her telling her not to worry...

The attic was filling with smoke when she was helped over the parapet.

The Professor was home early. He went to his study with Wilf and Robbie, closely followed by Mrs Potts and the tea tray, and sat down at his desk. He had a good deal of paperwork to do, and notes for a lecture to write. He drank his tea, gave his dogs the biscuits and turned to the pile of papers on his desk. But before picking up his pen, he turned on the radio.

Just in time for a news flash that an estate in the north of England was on fire. No casualties had been reported so far, said the voice, but it was feared that there might be people trapped in the house.

The Professor's instinct was to leap from his chair into his car and drive north within seconds. Instead he picked up the phone and dialled the hospital; Thomas was still on duty. He didn't waste words.

'I'm flying up within half an hour,' he told Thomas. 'Tell Ruth that I will bring Julia back here.'

'You're sure it's where Julia is?'

'They gave the name on the radio.'

The rush hour hadn't started. The Professor, as good as his word, left his house within minutes, outwardly calm, and made for the airport. He concentrated on flying, firmly keeping other thoughts at bay.

Almost at his journey's end, after picking up a hire car, he could see the glow of the fire ahead of him, and shortly after he turned into the drive leading to the house. He was stopped before he was halfway there.

'Sorry, sir, you can't go any further. Can I help?'

'Indeed you can. My future wife works here. She would have been on the top floor. I've come to take her back home.'

At the officer's look of enquiry, he said 'London. I've flown up. I'm a surgeon at one of the hospitals there.'

'Then you'd best find her. There's a rare old muddle checking everyone's out of the building, and quite a few have been taken off to hospital for a check-up or been taken home—local folk.' He nodded at the Professor. 'I'll phone through.'

The Professor drove on, parked the hire car and got out. The sweep in front of the house was crowded with people: firemen, police, estate workers and people from the village. The officer he spoke to was helpful; everyone had been got out and had been sent home, if they lived in the village, or into hospital at Carlisle... It was an elderly man standing near them who interrupted.

'Not all of 'em,' he said. 'There's one of the sewing ladies over at my place with the missus. Not from hereabouts, she isn't, and got nowhere to go.' He added, 'I'm the head gardener here.'

He glanced at the Professor. 'You'd best go and take a look. It's the end cottage, on its own.' He waved an arm. Tell the missus I sent you.'

The Professor thanked him and made his way through the throng, holding down his impatience and anxiety with a firm hand. When he reached the cottage he paused for a moment as an elderly woman came to the door. She was a sensible woman, who listened to his quick explanation and told him to go into the kitchen. 'If it's a girl called Julia, it's her,' she told him softly. 'She's not hurt, but she was the last to be rescued and it's shook her up badly.'

He thanked her quietly and pushed open the kitchen door. Julia was sitting in a chair by the old-fashioned stove, and when she looked up at him the Professor forgot that he was tired, hungry and thirsty. He would have flown ten times the distance he had to see that look on her face.

He spoke quickly, because he could see that she was struggling with tears.

'It's all right, my dear. We'll go home just as soon as I've let someone know that you are in safe hands.' He smiled down at her with the kindliness of an old family friend or elder brother.

She found her voice. 'Gerard, oh, Gerard. I've been so terrified and I didn't know what to do—and then you came...'

She gave him a lop-sided, watery small smile, and

perhaps it was as well that the gardener's wife came in then.

'You could do with a cup of tea. You'll just have to see the police—the one who got the others sorted out is in that car with the blue light.' She turned to Julia. 'You do know this gentleman, miss?'

Julia nodded. 'Oh, yes, we're...' She stopped and added, 'He knows my family too; he'll take me home.'

'Then I'll boil the kettle, sir, and you come back as soon as you can. I dare say you've got a way to go.'

The Professor only smiled and went away, and Julia said, 'London.'

'You mean to say he's come up from London?'

'No, no. He sometimes comes to Carlisle, to the hospital—he's a surgeon.'

'Well, that's good fortune indeed. Here's your tea. Drink it hot; you're still all of a shake.'

Which was true enough. She had drunk half of it when the Professor came back. He drank his own tea, thanked the gardener's wife and walked Julia to the car. He had an arm around her and she was glad of it, for her legs felt like jelly. When they reached the car, he picked her up and popped her in, and fetched a rug from the boot and wrapped her in it. And all this with the air of an elder brother...

The car was warm and comfortable and she closed her eyes, only opening them when a police officer put his head through the open window.

'You're Miss Julia Gracey? I'm just checking that everything is OK.'

She managed a smile. 'Yes, that's me, and this is

Professor van der Maes, who is a friend of my family.'

He nodded. 'There'll be someone round to see you at home, just to make sure that you are fit and well—get the record straight.' He grinned at her. 'You had a lucky escape, miss.' He turned to the professor. 'Safe journey, sir.'

Gerard got into the hire car and drove back down the drive and on to the road. They would have to stop on the way to the airport. He was tired and hungry, and Julia, even if she slept, would need a break and food. He glanced sideways at her, cocooned in the rug.

'We should be back in a couple of hours. We will stop on the way for a hot drink and something to eat. Are you all right?'

He sounded reassuringly normal. 'Yes, thank you. Oh, Gerard, how fortunate that you were here—I mean, at the hospital in Carlisle.' When he didn't answer she said, 'You were there, weren't you? I mean, how else could you have come so quickly?'

'I heard the news when I got home…'

She peered at him over the rug. 'You came all the way from London?' Her voice was an unbelieving squeak.

'Yes. Now go to sleep, Julia.'

And, while she was still feeling indignant about that, she did.

The professor looked at Julia's sleeping face. She was pale and smelled of smoke and her hair was in a tangle, but she was here, beside him, safe and sound. He kissed her grubby cheek and drove on.

At a service station he woke her gently. 'I'll get us

tea and something to eat,' he told her. 'But first I'll walk you to the facilities.'

Julia, feeling better, was soon shovelled back into the car and told to stay awake.

The tea was hot and sweet and there were sandwiches, cut thick and filled with corned beef. They ate and drank in comfortable silence, the quiet dark around them.

Later, halfway through their short flight, Julia said, 'Would you mind if I went to sleep again for a little while? I'm tired.'

He had expected that, and had already tucked a rug round her. He held his own tiredness at bay while he considered plans and discarded them. Once Julia had recovered from her fright and shock she would probably disappear again; the last thing he wanted was for her to feel beholden to him.

In London, he had to stop once more. 'I'm going to be sick,' said Julia, suddenly awake. He stopped, hauled her briskly out of the car and held her while she heaved and choked and then burst into tears. He mopped her face, popped her back into the car, tucked her up once more and gave her a handful of paper tissues. 'You'll feel better now, try and rest again.'

She closed her eyes but she didn't sleep. She thought about him. He had been quick and gentle and matter-of-fact and impersonal, and she sensed a professional remoteness. And why should it be otherwise? she reflected sadly. The only times they met hadn't been because they had wanted to but by force of circumstances. *Why* had he come all the way from London? She was too sleepy to think about that, but just as she was dozing off she muttered, 'Ruth would have been worried—and he likes her and Thomas.'

The Professor smiled to himself. It was as good a reason as any.

It was late when he stopped before his house. He had phoned before they had left the estate and asked Mrs Potts to get a room ready for Julia. 'And go to bed,' he had told her, 'for we shall be back after midnight.'

Julia was awake again. He got out of the car and, with an arm round her, opened his front door. There was a wall lamp alight and as they went in Mrs Potts, cosily wrapped in a woolly dressing gown, came down the staircase.

'There you are,' she observed, 'and tired to death, I'll be bound, sir. Now, just you go to the kitchen and eat and drink what's there while I take miss upstairs. She'll have a nice warm bath and bed, and a glass of warm milk.' She nodded her head. 'And you'll go to bed too, sir.'

The Professor smiled at her. 'You're an angel, Mrs Potts. Have you had any sleep yourself?'

'Bless you, sir, I went to bed early, seeing as how things were.'

He picked up Julia and carried her upstairs and laid her on the bed in a small bedroom.

'Don't go,' said Julia, clutching his arm. 'I haven't thanked you.' She sounded meek and tearful, and later she would feel ashamed of herself for being so silly.

'We will talk in the morning,' said the Professor bracingly, and went away. Next she heard Mrs Potts's soft voice. 'Now, we'll have these clothes off you. You just sit there while I help you. Then a nice bath, and I'll wash your hair, and then bed and a good sound sleep. The Professor's going to bed too and you can both have a nice chat in the morning.'

So Julia was bathed and shampooed, and all the while Mrs Potts talked in a soothing voice and finally tucked her up in bed and told her to go to sleep. Which she did.

She woke to hear dogs barking and the muted sounds of a household getting ready for the day and, reassured, went back to sleep.

It was mid-morning when she sat up in bed, feeling perfectly well again, and found Mrs Potts standing by the bed with a breakfast tray.

'Oh, I could have got up for breakfast,' said Julia. 'I've given you so much trouble already and I feel fine…'

Mrs Potts arranged the tray on a bed table. 'Now just eat your breakfast, Miss Gracey. Your sister will be here with some clothes for you presently.'

'Ruth? How did she know that I was here?'

'Why, the Professor phoned her before he went to the hospital this morning. She's to stay for lunch.'

'Lunch? What's the time, Mrs Potts?'

'A little after ten o'clock.'

'The Professor said he'd see me in the morning. He's still here?'

'Lor' bless you, Miss, he's been gone these past two hours.' Mrs Potts shook her head. 'There's no stopping him. A couple of hours' sleep and he's off again. I'm to tell you he'll see you some time.'

Julia drank her tea and swallowed tears with it. 'Yes, of course. I've given him a lot of trouble. I'll go back with my sister after lunch. Is there somewhere I could write him a note?'

'I'll have pen and paper ready for you,' promised Mrs Potts, and left Julia to finish a breakfast which tasted of sawdust. He had gone to a great deal of trouble to rescue her, but now that was accomplished he would forget her—a momentary nuisance in his ordered life.

'But I'm not going to cry about it,' said Julia, and ate the breakfast she no longer wanted, then got up and showered. Wrapped in a voluminous dressing gown produced by Mrs Potts, she went downstairs, where she was shown into a small, cosily furnished room. There was a small writing desk with paper and pen set ready for her.

'Your sister will be here presently,' said Mrs Potts comfortably, and left her to write her note.

Not an easy thing to do, Julia discovered. She had to make several attempts before she was satisfied, but she hoped that her warm thanks coupled with the assumption that she was unlikely to see him—his work—her intention to leave London as soon as possible—would strike the right note. She had just sealed the envelope when Ruth arrived, bringing clothes and agog to hear exactly what had happened.

When Julia had finished telling her everything she said, 'I didn't know anything about it until Gerard phoned Thomas to say that he had found you and that you were safe…'

Julia said slowly, 'I thought he had come because you were worried about me?'

'No, no. Thomas told me that Gerard phoned him

around half past four—he'd heard a newsflash about the fire. He was on the point of leaving.'

She saw the look on Julia's face and said quickly, 'You'll stay with us, of course, love, until you decide what you want to do.'

Julia said slowly, 'Would you mind if I went to Monica for a while?'

'No, of course not. It will be quiet there; you will have time to think.'

Something Julia didn't want to do, for she would only think of Gerard, who had rescued her and left a laconic message that he would see her some time. Well, that was something she could deal with. If she went to Monica he could forget her, something he must be wanting to do, only fate seemed intent on throwing her in his path.

They had their lunch, thanked Mrs Potts for her kindness and took a taxi to Ruth's home. Thomas was at the hospital and Julia seized the opportunity to phone Monica and invite herself to stay. 'Just for a week. I won't be in the way, but it would be nice to have a few days while I make up my mind what I'll do.'

'Come for as long as you like,' said Monica largely. 'No one will bother you. It must have been horrible, Julia, and so far away. You must have been glad to see Gerard.'

'Yes,' said Julia. 'I was. He's been very kind...'

'More than kind,' said Monica dryly. 'Come when you like, Julia; there's a room ready for you. The nearest station is Cullompton. George will meet you with the car.'

Thomas came home presently. He was glad to see

her, and wanted to know about the fire—and never mentioned Gerard. She said in a carefully casual voice, 'I haven't seen Gerard since we got back here. I hope he wasn't too tired...'

'Gerard's never tired,' said Thomas. 'He's done a day's work and he's dining out this evening with the widow of one of his patients who has been angling for him for some time.'

Well, thought Julia peevishly, I don't need to waste any concern on the man. I hope she catches him and leads him a simply horrible life. She smiled brilliantly at her brother-in-law and wished she could go and shut herself somewhere dark and lonely and cry her heart out.

And Ruth made it worse by observing that Olivia Travis was one of the most beautiful women she had ever met. 'If I were a man I'd fall in love with her the moment I saw her.'

Thomas grunted, which could have meant anything.

Julia stayed for three days at Ruth's. She had to buy clothes and be interviewed by someone from the police, who assured her that they merely wished to be sure that she was quite unharmed and safe with her family. And each morning when she woke she wondered if she would see the Professor. But he didn't come. Nor did Thomas speak of him. She told herself that she was glad. He could at least have acknowledged her note, though. Perhaps he hadn't read it. His secretary might have put it with the junk mail and all the invitations which he didn't wish to accept.

On the third day she made arrangements to go to Monica. Ruth asked worriedly, 'Will you stay for a while, love? Come back here when you want to.'

'I'm being a worry for them,' Julia told herself as she got ready for bed. 'I must find something somewhere and settle down.'

Perhaps in some small town in the West Country. A small flat—she could rent one—or a shop. She had money enough; there was no reason why she shouldn't make a pleasant life for herself. She might even marry...

Out of the question, of course. She loved Gerard and no one else would do.

Up until the very last minute, until the train was leaving the station, she had the forlorn hope that she would see Gerard. But there was no sign of him. He'd be in Holland, thought Julia despairingly, and then, as the train swept past the suburbs and through green fields and trees, That's it, she told herself. You're going to forget him just as he's forgotten you. You're wasting your life hankering after a person who doesn't care a straw for you.

After which heartening speech she picked up the magazine she had bought and began to read it. It was full of artfully posed teenagers wearing what looked like fancy dress costumes, and they were all painfully bony, with sharp elbows and jutting collarbones. Julia felt fat and almost middle-aged just looking at them. She handed the magazine over to a young woman who had been peering at it from the opposite seat and then looked out of the window. The country looked lovely and she felt a sudden surge of interest in the future.

You never know what's round the corner, thought Julia.

CHAPTER EIGHT

GEORGE, driving Julia away from Cullompton station, didn't bother her with questions. He thought that she looked tired and, despite her bright chatter, unhappy. He would leave the questions to Monica, he decided.

Monica was waiting for them with a string of questions and they had a cheerful lunch together.

'I'll take you over the house again, now that we've had the alterations done,' said Monica. 'It's far too large for us, of course, but we love it. And now we've got central heating and the plumbing works, it's easy to run.'

They had gone to Julia's bedroom after lunch and Monica was sitting on the bed while Julia unpacked.

'Is Ruth all right? And Thomas? And have you seen the Professor since you got back? What a man—going all that way to fetch you home. I expect he must have seen how worried Ruth was, but it was a noble thing to do, especially as you don't like each other much.'

Julia had her head in a drawer. 'Yes, it was. I haven't seen him since, though, but I didn't expect to.'

'Ruth told me that there's a beautiful woman lurking!'

'Yes.' Julia emerged rather red in the face. 'I had a present for you, but of course I lost it in the fire. Perhaps we could find something to take its place.

This really is a lovely old house, isn't it? Ruth's house is nice, too…'

Monica said concernedly, 'But you haven't a home, love. We do worry about you.'

Julia closed her case and put it tidily under the bed. 'Well, don't. I know exactly what I want to do. Leave London, for a start, and settle in a town between the two of you. I'll rent a flat to start with, and then find a small shop with living space. I shall sell everything to do with needlework and knitting and embroidery. While I'm here, if you don't mind, I shall take a look at some of the small towns round and about. I can hire a car. I know I haven't driven for years but I can't have forgotten how.'

Monica said suddenly, 'Do you ever wish that you'd married Oscar?'

Julia laughed. 'Monica, you must be joking! I'm happy as I am. "Footloose and fancy-free"—isn't that what someone or other wrote?'

Monica laughed too, and didn't believe a word of it.

It was delightful living in the country. The village was a large one with a widespread parish, and Monica and George made her more than welcome, but after a few days she declared her intention of exploring the surrounding countryside with an eye to the future.

Honiton seemed as good a place to start as any. A small market town straddling the main road from London to the West, it was famous for its lace-making and antiques shops, but she discarded it reluctantly. It was too near Monica and too far from Ruth. It needed to be somewhere between her sisters and far enough away from both of them so as not to encroach on their lives. She pored over maps and guidebooks and, sitting one morning with Monica in the garden asked, 'Where's Stourhead?'

'North of Yeovil. Not on a main road but easy to get at. It's a lovely place; we went there a month or so ago. Heavenly gardens and a Palladian house full of treasures.'

'There's an ad in your local newspaper. Guides for the house and people to repair and refurbish the furniture and the hangings. I know I want to start up on my own, but it looks rather inviting.'

She could see Monica's look of uncertainty and knew what she was thinking: that she was wasting time, drifting from one job to another, that she should settle down and make a secure future for herself— that was if she didn't marry, and that didn't seem likely.

Monica said worriedly, 'Yes, that might be a good idea. While you were there you might scout around and find a suitable shop in one of the small towns not too far away. There's Sherborne—the most likely, I should think. Yeovil is nearby, too, but that's quite large—too large for the kind of shop you're thinking of, I imagine. There's Warminster and there's Gillingham and Shaftesbury, but I'm not sure if you could make much of a living with the kind of shop you're thinking of. I'd opt for Sherborne...'

So Julia went to Sherborne and liked what she saw there. It was an abbey town with a well-known public school and the right kind of shops. For the first time since she had returned from the north she felt enthusiastic about her future. She supposed that all this time she had been hoping that she would see Gerard

again, that he might even discover that he liked her…
But that wasn't going to be the case. Once and for all
she would forget him.

Quite sure now that she knew what she wanted to
do, she wasted no time. A visit to the town's estate
agents left her with a handful of possible shops to
buy or lease. She would strike while the iron was hot,
she decided, viewing the future through rose-coloured
spectacles. And phoned Monica to tell her that she
was going to stay the night in Sherborne and inspect
what was on offer.

'You haven't got anything with you,' Monica reminded her, so she went out and bought a cheap
nightie and a toothbrush and booked in at a quiet hotel
five minutes' walk from the town centre. It was already late afternoon, but it was a small town and she
had no trouble finding the handful of addresses. The
first three were no use at all, tucked away down side
streets, but the fourth had possibilities; it was close
to the abbey and the main shopping street, tucked in
between an antiquarian book shop and a picture gallery. Its window was small, but it was in a good state
of repair and the paintwork was fresh. She peered
through the glass door. The shop was small too, with
a tiny counter and a door behind it. The leaflet
claimed that there were living quarters too.

She reached the estate agents as they were about
to close and arranged to inspect the shop in the morning.

Momentarily inflated with a strong sense of purpose, she took herself off then to the hotel, had a
splendid dinner and slept soundly.

The shop was small but it had possibilities. There

was a little room behind it and a kitchen beyond that, and upstairs there was a bedroom and a shower and a toilet. She could, she decided, make it home without too much expense. And she could rent it on a year's lease which meant that she wouldn't need to dig too deep into her capital.

She said that she would rent it subject to a surveyor's report. 'I'll need a solicitor,' she said, 'and I'd like to take possession as soon as possible.'

She went back to Monica's that afternoon, her head full of plans and ideas. She would stay in Sherborne, get the place fit to live in, buy her stock and move in at her leisure.

Monica, told the news, nodded her head in approval. 'If that is what you want,' she said cautiously. 'I've no doubt you'll make a success of it, and you're bound to make friends—if that is what you want?'

Julia assured her that it was. Which wasn't quite true, of course. What she wanted was for Gerard to fall in love with her, marry her and live with her happily ever after, but, since that was something which wasn't going to happen, she must turn herself into a successful businesswoman.

'You'll probably meet a nice man,' said Monica.

There was no point in telling her that she already had.

'I'll have to go back to London to see the solicitor and the bank. May I stay here for a few more days while the agent gets organised at Sherborne? I'll have to sign papers and so on.'

'Stay as long as you like, love. You know you'll always be welcome here. You're not far away, and if you get a car... Could you afford that?'

'I think so. A small second-hand one.'

Several days later she went back to London and told herself that she felt relief to hear that the Professor was in Holland.

The solicitor was helpful in a cautious way; he hoped that she had thought about the drawbacks as well as the advantages of setting up a small business.

'A young lady on her own,' he said, shaking a grey head. He hadn't moved with the times, but she liked him for his fatherly concern. And the bank manager was cautious too. He would have liked her to have invested her money in something safe, so that she would have had a small steady income, and possibly lived with one or other of her sisters...

While she had been working on the estate she had picked up quite a lot of information about the wholesale firms which had supplied the materials for the work there, and it had given her some idea as to how to contact them; she intended to sell tapestries, knitting wools, embroidery silks and patterns as well as canvases and embroidery frames and anything else needful to the serious embroiderer. She would also knit herself, and sell what she knitted. She wouldn't allow herself any doubts; she had always been able to cope and this was a challenge...

She was in Ruth's sitting room, and making yet another list, when the Professor opened the door and walked in.

She sat back and gaped at him, unable to think of anything to say.

'Close your mouth, my dear,' said the Professor. 'Why are you so surprised?'

'I thought you were in Holland.' Mingled with the

delight of seeing him again was annoyance that he had sneaked in on her without warning.

He sat down and stretched out his legs, the picture of ease. 'So you're about to become a business-woman? No doubt you will be very successful, make lots of money and fulfil whatever dreams you have...'

'Don't be sarcastic,' said Julia waspishly. 'and it's none of your business.'

'You're cross. Are you not pleased to see me? I thought that we might have dinner together this evening. We could talk over old times?'

She eyed him carefully. To spend an evening with him would be a dream come true, but on the other hand she had promised herself that she would forget him. The Professor, watching her face, said in just the right off-hand manner, 'I'm going back to Holland and you are leaving London.'

In that case, reflected Julia, there would be no harm done, would there? He was making it clear that they weren't likely to see each other again.

'All right. Though I'm sure we won't find anything to talk about.'

'No? The cottage? My home in Amsterdam? Mrs Beckett? I think we may be able to sustain some kind of conversation!' He got to his feet. 'I'll call for you at half past seven.'

'Shall I dress up?'

It was the kind of remark to make him fall in love with her all over again. One moment so haughty and the next as uncertain as a schoolgirl.

He said gently, 'Something short and pretty. We'll go to Claridge's.'

The moment he had gone she ran up to her room.

There was a dress which might do. She hadn't meant
to buy it but it had been so pretty: amber chiffon over
a silk slip, plain, high-necked, and long-sleeved and
elegant. She had bought it because it had seemed to
her to stand for all the pretty clothes she had never
been able to buy. Well, she would wear it—and even
if she never wore it again it would be worth every
penny of the money she had squandered on it.

Thomas and Ruth came in together and Julia said
at once with a heightened colour, 'I've done the veg
for supper and made a fruit pie. You won't mind if I
go out? Gerard has asked me to dinner.'

Ruth gave Thomas an 'I told you so' look, and said,
'Oh, nice. Where's he taking you?'

'Claridge's.'

Ruth was on the point of saying, Lucky girl, but
changed her mind. Having fallen in love with
Thomas, just as he had fallen in love with her, without
any doubts or complications, she found it hard to understand why two sensible people like the Professor
and her sister could be so slow in discovering that
they were meant for each other. She caught Thomas's
eye and said instead, 'You could wear that amber
chiffon dress…'

Studying herself in the dress later, Julia wondered
if she would ever wear the dress again. She knew no
one in Sherborne. It would take time to make friends,
and they might not be the kind to take her anywhere
as splendid as Claridge's. She would make the most
of her evening, she promised herself.

She was glad that she was wearing the dress when
the Professor came for her. In his sober, beautifully
tailored suits he looked the epitome of the well-

dressed man, but in a dinner jacket he looked magnificent.

He was standing in the hall talking to Thomas when she went down, but he turned and looked at her as she came down the stairs. 'Very pretty,' he observed, which left her doubtful as to whether he was referring to the dress or her person. She wrapped herself in the paisley shawl—the family heirloom she shared with her sisters—and bade him hello. She assured Ruth that she wouldn't be late back and went out to the car with him. She hoped that they would have the lovely time Ruth had wished them...

The streets were fairly free of traffic but their way took them through the heart of the city. Julia, mindful of good manners, made small talk from time to time, but since he replied in monosyllables she said coolly, 'You don't like me to talk?'

He glanced briefly at her. 'Why should you think that? You are determined to think the worst of me, Julia.'

Suddenly contrite, she said, 'I don't—really, I don't. You've helped me so often, even if you haven't meant to. I mean, circumstances...' She stopped. 'I've made a mess of saying that. I'm sorry. I would like us to part friends.'

'A most laudable notion. I hope that at last you are trying to overcome your initial dislike of me.'

Before she could think of an answer to that he had stopped before Claridge's entrance. And, after that, serious talk, even if she had wanted it, wasn't easy. She left the shawl in the hands of the haughty lady in charge of the cloakroom, rather deflated by the disparaging glance it was given, but her spirits were uplifted by the warm appreciation in Gerard's eyes when she joined him.

They didn't dine immediately but had their drinks in a magnificent room where a small orchestra played gentle background music. The surroundings were of a kind to make even the most uncertain girl feel cherished and beautiful, so that by the time they were seated at a table Julia felt both. Moreover, she was sitting opposite the man she loved, even if it was for the very last time. Nothing must spoil this, their final meeting...

She might be head over heels in love, but it hadn't spoiled her appetite. They had watercress soup, Dover Sole with lemon grass and tiny sautéed potatoes, and a lemon tart that was out of this world—and two glasses of champagne which gave her eyes a sparkle and her tongue a ready liveliness. She had, for the moment, quite forgotten that this was their last meeting...

The Professor, under no illusions as to that, led their talk from one thing to the other. He saw now that when Julia forgot that she didn't like him she was entirely happy in his company, so it was just a question of patience. He had no intention of forcing her hand, so he would let her have her shop for a while, and once the first flush of independence had worn off, she would turn to him. She was a darling, he reflected, but pig-headed, liable to be contrary. She must find out for herself...

So they had a delightful evening together, and it wasn't until they got back to Ruth's that Julia remembered that this really was their final meeting. All her good resolutions came tumbling back into her head, so that she said stiffly, 'Thank you for a lovely evening; I enjoyed it. I hope you will...' She began again. 'I expect you're glad to be going back to Holland. Please give my love to Mrs Beckett when you see her.' She couldn't help adding, 'Will you come back to England at all?'

'From time to time.' Indeed, he was going to Holland for a short time only, for consultations and hospital commitments there, but he had no intention of telling her that.

He got out of the car and helped her out and stood, her hand in his, looking down at her. 'A delightful evening, Julia, thank you for coming.'

She would never know what made her ask then, 'Are you going to get married?' She would have given a great deal to have unsaid her words, but they were spoken now, weren't they? And what did it matter, anyway?

The Professor studied her pink embarrassed face. He said evenly, 'Yes, that is my intention.' Idle curiosity? He wondered. Or could it be more than that?

Julia recovered herself. 'Well, I hope you'll be very happy,' she told him.

'And you, Julia?'

'Oh, I can't wait to do something I've wanted to do for so long...'

'And what is that?'

'Be independent.' How easy it was to tell fibs, she reflected, when one was desperate.

'Ah, yes, of course. I must wish you every success.' He bent his head and kissed her then. A kiss to drive all thoughts of independence out of her head. But he didn't wait for that. He pushed her gently through the door and closed it behind her, and she stood in the hall, listening to the gentle purring of the Rolls as he drove away.

She wasn't going to cry, she told herself, creeping silently to her room to hang up the pretty dress she supposed she would never wear again before getting into bed to weep silently all over Muffin, who had crept up with her. He was Ruth's cat now, but he had a strong affection for Julia and bore patiently with her snuffles and sighs.

Thomas had already left for the hospital by the time she got down to breakfast. Ruth took one look at her face and turned her back to make the toast.

'Did you have a lovely evening? We didn't hear you come in. Was the food good? I suppose it was all rather grand?'

'Well, it was, but you didn't notice it, if you see what I mean. It's a beautiful restaurant and the food was marvellous. It was a lovely evening.'

A remark which Ruth took with a pinch of salt, although she said nothing.

'Monica phoned yesterday evening. I'm to tell you that you're to go there if there is any kind of hitch at Sherborne. You have got everything fixed up?'

'Yes, I'll stay at a bed and breakfast place while I get the shop ready and buy some furniture. That ought not to take too long.'

She had been to a wholesaler and ordered her stock, packed her bags once more and there was nothing to keep her in London. And the Professor had gone back to Holland. The sooner she started her new life the better.

It was raining and chilly when she reached

Sherborne, and she was glad that the estate agent had been kind enough to recommend a place where she could stay. She had arranged to go there for a week, but probably it would be longer than that...

The house was in the centre of the town, one of a row of stone-built cottages of a fair size, and when the taxi stopped before its door Julia thought how cosy it looked. But the lady who answered the door didn't look cosy; she was immaculately dressed, not a hair out of place, a no longer youthful face carefully made up. Mrs Legge-Boulter welcomed Julia with chilly courtesy and within five minutes had made it clear that only most unfortunate circumstances had forced her to take in guests.

'It is not at all what I've been used to,' she observed, 'but beggars cannot be choosers, can they?' She laughed, but since she didn't look in the least amused Julia murmured in a non-committal manner as she was led upstairs to her room.

'I serve breakfast at half past eight,' said Mrs Legge-Boulter, 'and my guests are expected to be out of the house by ten o'clock. You may return after six o'clock. At the moment you are the only guest, so you may use the bathroom between nine and ten o'clock in the evening.'

'You don't offer evening meals?' said Julia hopefully.

Her landlady looked affronted. 'My dear Miss Gracey, you can have no idea of the work entailed in providing a room and breakfast for my guests. I am totally exhausted at the end of my day.'

Left alone, Julia examined her room. It was furnished with everything necessary for a bedroom, but the colour scheme was a beige and brown mixture unrelieved by ornaments or pictures. A place to sleep, decided Julia, and hoped that breakfast would be substantial. The sooner she could move into her little shop the better.

She unpacked her things and, since it was mid-afternoon, went into the town. She had tea and then went to take another look at her future home. Tomorrow she would see the estate agent and ask if he would let her have the key. She had signed the papers and paid over the money for the lease and the first month's rent. She sat over tea, making a list of all the things which had to be done, and then she wandered round the shops, looking for second-hand furniture and the mundane household equipment she would need. She earmarked several items, and then went in search of somewhere she could get her supper.

She found a small café near the abbey, serving light meals until eight o'clock, and she sat over a mushroom omelette and French fries and a pot of coffee until closing time and then returned to Mrs Legge-Boulter's house.

That lady opened the door to her with a thin smile, a request that she should wipe her feet and a reminder that breakfast was at half past eight. 'I must ask you to be punctual; I have my day to organise.'

Not only her day, reflected Julia, mounting the stairs, but the day of any unfortunate soul lodging with her. She had a bath and, mindful of the notice on the door, cleaned it and went to bed. She had a good deal to think about; the next few days were going to be fully occupied. But when she finally closed her eyes she allowed herself to think of Gerard. Even though she never intended to see him again, there was no reason why she shouldn't dream a little of what might have been…

She was tired, so that she slept well, and when she woke her only thoughts were concerned with getting down to breakfast. It was a frugal meal, served by Mrs Legge-Boulter with disdain, as though offering a boiled egg and two slices of toast was an affront to her social status. A miserable meal, decided Julia, gobbling everything in sight and shocking her landlady by asking for more hot water. The tea was already weak…

She left the house before ten o'clock, saw the estate agent, got the shop key and, fortified by coffee and a bun, let herself into what was now, for the moment, her property.

Not a great deal needed doing, she decided. A carpenter for the shop fittings, carpeting for the living room, and a good clean everywhere. So she went to the shops and returned presently with a bucket, broom, dusters and cleaning materials and set to. She paused for lunch and then went in search of a carpenter and a carpet shop.

It took a good deal of the afternoon but she found a carpenter who would come in the morning and also someone who would come and measure the floors. She went back to the café for a meal and then made her way back to Mrs Legge-Boulter's house, where she received the same tepid welcome as before. Really, thought Julia, lying in a hot bath and eating potato crisps, one wondered why her landlady chose to have lodgers when she obviously disliked them so much.

Breakfast was a boiled egg again. At least I shall get slim, thought Julia, and wondered if Gerard might like her better if she wasn't so curvy. A stupid thought, she told herself; he didn't like her whatever shape she was. She might be deeply in love, but it had made no difference to her appetite; she was still hungry when she left the house, and went along to the shop armed with a bag of currant buns, still warm from the oven at the bakers. Munching them, she went round the little place again, quite clear in her head as to what needed doing, so that by the time the carpenter arrived no time was lost. The floors measured, she took herself off to choose carpets, persuading everyone that everything had to be done as quickly as possible. A good morning's work, she decided, eating a splendid lunch in a friendly pub.

Buying a sewing machine and material for curtains took up her afternoon; tomorrow she would get them made and go in search of furniture. Hopefully she would be able to move in by the end of a week...

She had been busy all day, so that it had been fairly easy to forget Gerard. But now, back in her unwelcoming room, she forgot all about the shop and thought only of him. It wouldn't do, she told herself, sitting up in bed making yet another list. The sooner she got the shop open and had her hands full, the better. All the same, before she slept, in her mind's eye she roamed through the house in Amsterdam, remembering its age-old beauty and the endless quiet. She supposed that she would never forget them. She allowed herself a moment to wonder what Gerard was doing before she slept.

He was sitting in his magnificent drawing room and his mother was sitting opposite him, drinking after-dinner coffee by the small fire, for the evenings were cool.

Mevrouw van der Maes was a tall, imposing woman, elegantly dressed, not showing her age save for her white hair, worn in a French pleat. She had good looks still, and bright blue eyes. She sipped her coffee.

'This is delightful, Gerard; I see you so seldom. That can't be helped, I know. Den Haag is only half an hour's drive away, but that's too far if you've had a long day at the hospital. But I wish I saw more of you.'

'I'm thinking of cutting down on my work in England—not the London hospital but some of the provincial ones.'

'That means that you will make your home base here?' his mother asked, and added, 'You are thinking of getting married at last?'

He smiled. 'I've taken my time, haven't I? But, yes, that is my intention.'

'Do I know her? Oh, my dear, I shall be so happy...'

'An English girl; you may remember I mentioned her coming over here to look after Mrs Beckett?'

'And Nanny loved her, as I'm sure I shall. You will bring her to see me?'

'In a while, I hope.'

Something in his voice made her ask, 'She knows that you want to marry her?'

'No. When we first met it was hardly on the best of terms, and she has been at great pains to let me know that she is indifferent to me. At times she has allowed me to think that she likes me at least, but I think that has been due to circumstances...'

Mevrouw van der Maes asked quietly, 'You have told her that you love her?'

'No, and I've been careful not to show my feelings.'

His mother sighed silently. She loved Gerard deeply, and she was proud of him, his brilliant career, his good looks, his complete lack of pride in his success—and yet despite all those he was behaving like an uncertain youth in love for the first time. Men are so tiresome at times, reflected Mevrouw van der Maes.

There were a great many questions she wanted to ask him, but they must wait. When he had anything to tell her he would do so. Instead she began to talk about family matters.

The Professor, in Holland for a number of consultations, lectures and meetings with colleagues, found time to visit Mrs Beckett. He found her quite her old self again.

'Well, now,' said Nanny, offering a cheek for his kiss, 'how nice to see you, Mr Gerard. Miss Thrisp has been away for a week and I'm ripe for a gossip.'

So he told her all the news and gossip he knew that she enjoyed.

'And what's this I hear about Julia? She writes to me, bless her, but never a word about herself until this very day.' Mrs Beckett got out her specs. 'I had a letter this morning. Dear knows what the girl is doing—opening a shop, if you please. Full of plans, as bright as a button—and such nonsense. Why, she should be getting herself a husband instead of setting up on her own...'

The Professor asked casually, 'And where is this shop to be?'

'Sherborne—that's a small town in Dorset.' She took the letter from a pocket and re-read it. 'She's going to sell wools and embroidery and suchlike, and do a bit of dressmaking if there's a chance.'

Nanny turned the page. 'Here's a bit I missed. What does it say?'

She read it and looked worriedly at the Professor. 'She says not to tell anyone where she is—and now I've told you, Mr Gerard.'

He said placidly, 'Don't worry, Nanny, I won't tell a soul. I'm glad she still writes to you and that she appears to have such a bright future.'

'Future?' said Mrs Beckett pettishly. 'Nonsense. A lovely girl like her, selling wool to old ladies...' She added, 'And I thought you were taken with her...'

She looked at him, sitting at his ease, Jason at his feet, and saw his grin. And then she smiled herself while thoughts crowded into her elderly head: a wedding, babies and small children coming to stay with old Nanny.

But all she said was, 'Well, you've taken your time, Mr Gerard.'

CHAPTER NINE

SPURRED on by Julia, the carpenter made shelves and did some small repairs while two men laid a carpet in the living room; two more came to install a small gas stove and a gas fire. The little place was wired for a telephone and she had been promised that she would be connected as soon as possible. Everything was going smoothly, she thought with satisfaction, and took herself off to buy furniture.

She has already found a second-hand furniture shop down a small street, and she spent almost an hour there, searching out a nice small round table and two straight-backed chairs, a bookcase and a rather battered oak stand to hold a table lamp. She chose a chest of drawers too, and an old-fashioned mirror to go with it, and another little table which would do for a bedside stand with a lamp. Pleased with her purchases, she went back into the main street and bought a small easy chair. It cost rather more than she had expected, as did the padded stool for the bedroom and the bed, but she reminded herself that she could afford it.

She stopped for lunch presently, and then went in search of bed linen, towels and tablecloths, pots and pans, cutlery and all the small odds and ends which make up a home. She was tired by the evening, but she was getting everything done so far without a hitch; she slept like a proverbial log in her unwelcoming room and went downstairs in the morning to eat the inevitable egg, her head full of what still had to be done.

The little shop was ready to receive its contents; the first consignment of wool arrived that afternoon and she spent a long time arranging it on the shelves the carpenter had made. And some of the furniture had been delivered.

She saw Mrs Legge-Boulter, who, told that Julia would be leaving the next day, said with an unkind little titter, 'Well, I hope you won't regret opening a shop. I'm sure there isn't much call for wools and embroidery and so on, and that's not in the best shopping area.'

Julia, tired and to tell the truth a bit frightened of the future, said airily, 'I dare say I shall make more of a success of it than you with your bed and breakfast trade.'

To which Mrs Legge-Boulter took thin-lipped exception. 'Not a *trade*, Miss Gracey,' she explained coldly. 'A perfectly genteel way in which gentlefolk may add to their income.'

'Well, you're not adding much, are you?' observed Julia tartly. 'You'd do much better to put a few flowers in the rooms and offer some bacon for breakfast.'

She took herself off to bed and spent the next hour feeling ashamed of herself. She would apologise in the morning.

Which she did, for she was a kind-hearted girl even if her temper was a little out of hand at times. Her landlady ignored the apology, reminded her that she must be out of the house by ten o'clock and offered a boiled egg, not quite cold and rock-solid, and toast burnt at the edges.

There was no sign of her when Julia left the house. She had presented the bill at breakfast, waited while Julia paid, and then gone out of the room without a word.

A bad start to the day, thought Julia, although it had its funny side too. Only there was no one to laugh with her about it—the Professor for preference...

But once in the little room behind the shop she felt better. The odds and ends of furniture and the cheerful carpet and curtains made it quite cosy. She went into the tiny kitchen and arranged her few saucepans on the wall shelf and put the kettle on for a cup of coffee. There was no room for a table, only a worktop over the two small cupboards. Later, she promised herself, she would give the walls a coat of cheerful paint. She went through the shower room and loo and opened the back door. The patch of garden outside was neglected but the fences were sound and there was plenty of room for a wash-line.

The day went quickly; by the time she had made her bed and unpacked her things it was noon. She stocked her cupboard after lunch, made a cup of tea and sat by the gas fire drinking it. Tomorrow she would arrange the window, and then she would open the shop.

She phoned Ruth and Monica in the morning, after a sound night's sleep in her new bed, and warned them that until she had the phone connected they weren't to worry if she didn't ring for a day or two. The nearest phone box wasn't far away, but it would mean locking up the shop to go to it and she didn't want to miss the chance of a customer.

The window looked attractive, she thought: a small

display of knitting wools, embroidery silks and patterns, tapestry for canvas work, a little pyramid of coloured sewing thread... She sat behind the counter and watched people passing. Some stopped to look in but no one came into the shop. 'Well,' said Julia, 'I didn't expect anyone on the first day.'

Ruth and Monica had sent cards of good wishes, and Mrs Beckett had sent her a letter. The Professor, apprised of the opening date by Nanny, had restrained himself from rushing out and ordering six dozen red roses.

Julia had her first customer on the following day; an elderly woman came in and, after deliberation, bought a reel of sewing thread.

Her first customer and hopefully the start of many more.

Julia closed her little shop for the day and had tea and crumpets round the fire. The days were drawing in and the evenings were chilly; the housewives of Sherborne would be thinking of quiet evenings with their knitting or embroidery...

She hadn't expected instant success, but as the days went by with a mere trickle of customers her initial euphoria gave way to doubts which she did her best to keep at bay. Perhaps the ladies of Sherborne didn't knit? Perhaps they needed a little encouragement? She dressed the little window in a different fashion, with half-finished knitting arranged with careful carelessness in the corner, an almost complete tapestry opposite, and between them a basket filled with everything a knitter or needlewoman might need. And that brought customers—not many, not nearly enough!—but it was early days yet, she told herself.

Monica and George drove over to see her, and she led them round the shop and house, assuring them that everything was fine and that she was happier than she had been for years.

'So why does she look like that?' demanded Monica of her George as they drove back home. 'As though her world has come to an end? Oh, I know she was laughing and talking nineteen to the dozen, but that's not like her.' She frowned. 'Do you suppose...?'

George said, 'I agree that she isn't happy, but since she was at such pains to conceal that from us I feel that we should respect that.'

'She's in love,' said Monica, to which George said nothing. He was fond of his sister-in-law but she was a fiercely independent young woman. Any efforts to alter that, he considered, weren't for him or her sisters.

Monica, on the phone to Ruth, voiced her concern. 'And George says we mustn't interfere,' she added, with which Ruth agreed.

She wouldn't interfere, but she might drop a hint. She couldn't help but notice that whenever she saw the Professor he never once mentioned Julia. Ruth, sharing Mevrouw van der Maes' opinion that the best of men could be tiresome at times, bided her time.

A senior consultant at the hospital was retiring and she and Thomas had been invited to attend his farewell party—a sober affair, with sherry and morsels of this and that handed round on trays. Once the speeches had been made there was ample opportunity to mingle and chat. It took a little while to get the Professor to herself, and she wasted no time.

One or two remarks about the retiring consultant, a brief enquiry as to when Gerard would be going to Holland again, and then Ruth came to the point in what she hoped was a roundabout manner.

'So you're going to Holland…?'

She glanced up at him. He loomed over her, the picture of ease and she added, 'I expect you will go to your dear little cottage. That was a lovely holiday; Julia loved it too. She's quite settled, you know.'

'Sherborne is a charming little town, I'm told. I hear she has set up shop.'

Ruth gaped at him. 'You know? Who told you? She made us promise not to tell…'

He smiled down at her worried face. 'I thought that might be the case. It wasn't too difficult to discover where she was living.'

'Why do you want to know? I mean, you're not—that is, I didn't think that you liked each other much, even though you were always there when she needed someone.' She touched his sleeve. 'I'm sorry—I shouldn't have said anything. Only she's my sister and I love her very much.'

Two dignified members of the hospital committee were about to join them. 'So do I,' said the Professor gravely, and he turned to greet them.

She had no chance to speak to him again, and when a few days later she asked Thomas in a purposely vague manner if he had gone to Holland, Thomas answered just as vaguely that he was still at the hospital. 'Catching up on his work,' he added, but didn't mention that his chief was busy because he was planning a few days off.

Monica, at the other end of the phone, agreed that

there was nothing to be done. 'Julia can be as stubborn as a mule; if she got even a hint of all this she'd shut the shop and disappear. And as for Gerard, he'll sort everything out in his own good time. When you think about it, it's inevitable, isn't it? Only they've been at cross purposes ever since they met, haven't they? And they are so obviously suited to each other…'

A week later, on a fine, bright and chilly morning, the Professor bade Mrs Potts goodbye and, with Wilf and Robbie curled up in the back of the car, drove away from London going west.

Julia, totting up the week's takings, had to admit that business was slow. There had been several customers but none of them had bought more than a skein of wool or some embroidery silks. Even her simple arithmetic told her that she was running at a loss… And she had been open for three weeks now.

She rearranged the window display and added a notice that garments could be knitted, telling herself that it might be several months before she was established, then she made herself a cup of coffee, determined not to be downhearted.

She was rewarded not half an hour later by a customer who bought three ounces of wool and some knitting needles, and she was followed by a cross-looking woman who wanted a knitting pattern. She spent a long time sifting through the little pile Julia offered her, choosing with as much care as someone spending hundreds of pounds on a purchase. She still hadn't made up her mind when the shop door opened again and the Professor walked in.

Julia gave a gasp and the woman looked round and then back at the patterns. None of them, she told Julia, were what she wanted. She would do better if she went to a larger shop. And she swept out of the door.

The Professor eased his bulk from the door to the counter, his head bowed to prevent it coming in contact with the ceiling, and the little place was all at once overcrowded.

He said blandly, 'I hope that the rest of your customers are more profitable than that one!'

Julia glared at him. Her heart had turned over and leapt into her throat and she had only just managed to get it back where it belonged. She supposed that being in love made one feel giddy. But she was cross too; walking in like that without so much as a 'hello'—and if he hadn't then the woman might have bought something.

He leaned on the counter, disarranging the pile of patterns.

He said, 'You ran away...'

'I did no such thing. I have always wanted to own a shop and be independent...'

He leaned over the counter, opened the till drawer and looked at the handful of small change in it. 'Well,' he observed genially. 'You own a shop, but are you independent? Is that today's takings?'

It was a temptation to fib, but somehow she couldn't lie to him even if it was about something trivial. She said, 'The week's.'

He closed the drawer. 'It's a lovely day; will you have lunch with me?' And when she hesitated he asked, 'Have you ever been to Stourhead? There's a splendid lake there, with ducks and magnificent trees and all the peace in the world.'

He smiled slowly. 'Just for an hour or two? You must close for lunch; an extra hour won't make too much difference.'

'Well, it would be nice, but I must be back for the afternoon.'

She came from behind the counter and turned 'Open' to 'Closed' on the door, and asked, with her back to him, 'Are you on holiday?'

'Yes, for a day or two.'

'You aren't going to Holland?'

'Yes, but not immediately.'

She said, 'I won't be long—I must get a jacket.' She opened the door to the living room. 'If you'll wait here...'

She left him there and went up to her room, found a jacket and sensible shoes, poked at her hair and added lipstick and went downstairs. She was out of her mind, she told herself, seeing him sitting in the armchair, looking as though he belonged there. She wondered why he had come and how he had known where she was. Perhaps he intended to tell her that he was going back to Holland for good, to marry and live in his lovely old house in Amsterdam.

Doubtless she would be told over their lunch.

He had parked the car at the end of the little street and she was surprised and pleased to see Wilf and Robbie side by side in the back of the Rolls.

The Professor popped her into the car and got in beside her.

'We'll go to Stourhead; these two need a good walk.' He drove out of the town carrying on the kind of conversation which needed no deep thought and few replies. Their way took them through a quiet countryside with few villages and only the small town of Wincanton halfway. It was a bright day, and autumn had coloured the trees and hedges. The approach to the estate, with tantalising glimpses of its magnificent trees and shrubs over the high stone wall bordering the narrow road, was like a great tunnel, opening into a narrow lane leading to the gates.

There was a pub on one side, and a house or two on the other, and Gerard turned into the car park by the pub.

'We can lunch here. Shall we have coffee and then take the dogs for a walk? There's plenty of time.'

'Yes, please, I'd like that. Will Wilf and Robbie be allowed inside?' She looked down at the two whiskered faces and said, 'I never imagined that you would have dogs like these two.' And then went red because she had spoken her thoughts out loud and they had sounded rude.

He smiled a little. 'Neither did I; sometimes things happen whether one wants them or not. I wouldn't part with them now for a small fortune.'

They were walking to the pub entrance. 'And they're company for Mrs Potts when you're in Holland. Will you take them with you when you leave England?'

'They will go where I go,' he told her, and opened the pub door.

There was no one in the bar, but the cheerful man who was stacking glasses wished them good day and had no objection to Wilf and Robbie—and certainly, he told them cheerfully, they could have coffee.

I shouldn't be here, reflected Julia. I ought not to have come. But she knew that nothing would have stopped her; she felt as though she had left her mundane life behind and had gone through a door into a world where there was no one but Gerard. And this really is the last time, she told herself, forgetting how many times she had already said that.

The Professor, watching her thoughts showing so clearly on her face, had his own thoughts, but all he said was, 'Shall we go? If we walk all round the lake it will take an hour or so.'

There was a church by the pub, small and old, and while Gerard got their tickets from the kiosk at the gate she wandered up the path between the ancient tombstones and peered through its open door. It was beautiful inside, quiet with the quietness of centuries, and there were flowers everywhere. Presently she felt the weight of Gerard's arm on her shoulders and they stood together without speaking, then turned and went down the path together.

The dogs were waiting patiently, so they each took a lead and started along the path round the lake, not hurrying; there was too much to see—towering trees, bushes and shrubs, ducks on the water and, hidden away from the path, Grecian temples and presently a waterfall, and a wooden bridge under which there were shoals of small fish. They didn't talk much, but every now and then Julia clutched Gerard's arm to point out something she wanted him to see.

There weren't many people there and it was quiet save for the birds. They found the grotto presently, at the bottom of narrow steps, and then walked the short distance back to the gates.

There were a few people in the pub now, but they found a table in a window and Wilf and Robbie, refreshed with water and a biscuit, curled up at their feet while they ate a Ploughman's lunch and emptied a pot of coffee. And Julia, munching warm bread and cheese, didn't think of the past or the future, only the happy present.

She looked up and caught his eye. 'I feel happy,' she told him seriously, a remark which brought a gleam to his eye.

He drove her back to Sherborne presently, talking easily about their walk, and discussing what they had seen. When they got to the shop, he got out and unlocked the door for her, listened to her thanks, assured her that he had enjoyed himself as much as she had and then bade her a cheerful goodbye.

She watched him drive away and went through the shop and sat down in the living room. She wanted very much to have a good cry, but a customer might come. No one came. She locked the door at half past five and made herself a pot of tea. She wasn't hungry, and the memory of the Ploughman's lunch, eaten so contentedly in the Professor's company, would serve for her supper.

Of course she didn't sleep; she lay awake thinking of him driving back to London. He had had a free day and, having discovered where she was, had made her the purpose of a drive into the country. He had wished her goodbye in a most casual manner; now he had seen for himself where she was he would lose all interest—if he'd had any in the first place. But he had been kind to her on several occasions; perhaps he felt under an obligation to Thomas…

She dropped off to sleep at last and woke with a start. The shop doorbell was ringing—the postman must be getting impatient. She got into her dressing gown and slippers and hurried to the door, not stopping to pull up the blind.

Wilf and Robbie trotted in, and hard on their heels was the Professor. He shut the door behind him, turned the key in the lock and then stood for a moment, looking down at her sleepy face and tangled mane of hair. He had had a sleepless night too, but there was no sign of that in his quiet face.

He gathered her into his arms. 'Tell me truly,' he begged. 'Are you happy here?'

She shook her head against his chest.

'Then would you consider marrying me? I have waited patiently for you to make a career for yourself, for it seemed to me that that was what you wanted more than anything else. But there is a limit to a man's patience and I am at the end of mine. But you have only to say, Go away, and I will go.'

Julia sniffed back tears as she mumbled, 'Don't go. Please don't go.' And then, 'You shouldn't be here; its seven o'clock in the morning. And if you love me, why didn't you say so? And I don't want to be independent. Only there wasn't anything else and I thought you didn't like me.'

'My darling,' said the Professor soothingly. 'Let us get one thing straight. I fell in love with you when we first met, although perhaps I didn't realise that at once. I have never stopped loving you and I never shall.'

'Really?' She looked up into his face and smiled at what she saw there.

'Really,' said the Professor, and bent to kiss her.

It was quite a while before she went upstairs to dress, leaving Gerard to put the kettle on and let the dogs into the little back garden. Her head was a jumble of thoughts: they would marry just as soon as possible; she would go back to London with him that morning; she was not to worry about the shop, he would deal with that; they would live in his lovely old house in Amsterdam. But none of these were important. The one thought which filled her head was that he loved her. She bundled up her hair, dashed powder on her nose and ran downstairs to tell him once again that she loved him too.

*We hope you enjoyed
An Independent Woman
by Betty Neels.*

*Read on to discover some top tips which
will make your Valentine's Day one to
remember and then flip the book for another
classic romantic tale - Husband For Real
by Catherine George.*

Are you a chocolate lover?

Try WALDORF CHOCOLATE FONDUE
a true chocolate decadence

While many couples choose to dine out on Valentine's Day, one of the most romantic things you can do for your sweetheart is to prepare an elegant meal – right in the comfort of your own home.

M&B asked John Doherty, executive chef at the Waldorf-Astoria Hotel in New York City, for his recipe for seduction – the famous Waldorf Chocolate Fondue…

WALDORF CHOCOLATE FONDUE
Serves 6-8

2 cups water
1/2 cup corn syrup*
1 cup sugar
8oz dark bitter chocolate, chopped
1 pound cake*
2-3 cups assorted berries
2 cups pineapple
1/2 cup peanut brittle

UK readers can try golden syrup and Madeira cake

Bring water, syrup and sugar to boil in a medium-size pot. Turn off the heat and add the chopped chocolate. Strain and pour into fondue pot. Cut cake and fruit into cubes and I-inch pieces. Place fondue pot in the centre of a serving plate, arrange cake, fruit and peanut brittle around pot. Serve with forks.

An
Invitation
for Love

Romantic Tips

Find a special way to invite your guy into
your M&B moment. Letting him know you're
looking for a little romance will help put his
mind on the same page as yours. In fact, if you
do it right, he won't be able to stop thinking
about you till he sees you again!

You could send him a long-stemmed rose tied to
an invitation that leaves a lot up to
the imagination.

♥

Autograph a favourite photo of you and tape it on
the appointed day in his day planner. Block out the
hours he'll be spending with you.

♥

Send him a local map and put an X on the place
you want him to meet you. Write: "I'm lost without
you. Come and find me. Tonight at eight." Use
magazine cutouts and photographs to paste images
of romance and the two of you all over the map.

♥

Send him something personal that he'll recognise
as yours to his office. Write: "If found, please
return. Owner offers reward to anyone returning
item by 7.30 on Saturday night."
Don't sign the card.

Looking for a seductive cocktail?

Romantic Tips

★

Try Ero-Desiac – a dazzling martini

★   ★

With its warm apricot walls yet cool atmosphere, Verlaine is quickly becoming one of New York's hottest nightspots. Verlaine created a light, subtle yet seductive martini for us: the Ero-Desiac. Sake warms the heart and soul, while jasmine and passion fruit ignite the senses…

★ The Ero-Desiac

Combine vodka, sake, passion fruit puree and jasmine tea. Mix and shake. Strain into a martini glass, then rest pomegranate syrup on the edge of the martini glass and drizzle the syrup down the inside of the glass.

M&B on location

Whatever your dream date location, pick a setting and a time that won't be interrupted by your daily responsibilities. This is a special time together. Here are a few hopelessly romantic settings to inspire you – they might as well be ripped right out of an M&B novel!

Bad weather can be so good.

Take a walk together after a fresh snowfall or when it's just stopped raining. Pick a snowball (or a puddle) fight and see how long it takes to get each other soaked to the bone. Then enjoy drying off in front of a fire, or perhaps surrounded by lots and lots of candles, with yummy hot chocolate to warm things up.

Candlelight dinner for two...in the bedroom.

Romantic music and candles will instantly transform the place you sleep into a cosy little love nest, perfect for nibbling. Why not lay down a blanket and open a picnic basket at the foot of your bed? Or set a beautiful table with your finest dishes and glowing candles to set the mood. Either way, a little bubbly and lots of light finger foods will make this a meal to remember.

A wild and crazy week night.

Do something unpredictable...on a week night straight from work. Go to an art opening, a sports game, the local playhouse, a book signing by an author or a jazz club – anything but the usual blockbuster movie. There's something romantic about being a little wild and crazy – or at least out of the ordinary – that will bring out the flirt in both of you. And you won't be able to resist thinking about each other in anticipation of your hot date...or telling everyone the day after.

We hope you enjoyed Husband For Real
by Catherine George.

*Read on to discover some tips which will
make your Valentine's Day one to remember
and then flip the book for a classic
romantic tale from perennial favourite
author Betty Neels.*

Two Unforgettable Love Stories

Valentine
LOVE
AFFAIRS

An Independent Woman by Betty Neels

Julia Gracey has always stood on her own two feet,
but lately Professor Gerard van der Maes is always
on hand with a perfect solution to every problem.
And now, when she loses her home, he sweeps her
off her feet with an irresistible proposal – marriage!

&

Husband For Real by Catherine George

Years after their wedding of convenience, Rose
could admit that she *had loved* James. But she
didn't expect him to turn up on her doorstep
to say that he wanted to *stay* married to her.
Their physical attraction was undeniable, yet she
needed more than just a Valentine lover...

*Read one novel then flip the book
and read the other.*

*And don't miss our romantic, hot tips
for your own Valentine's Evening!*

Betty Neels spent her childhood and youth in Devonshire before training as a nurse and midwife. She was an Army nursing sister during the war, married a Dutchman, and subsequently lived in Holland for fourteen years. She lived with her husband in Dorset, and had a daughter and grandson. Her hobbies were reading, animals, old buildings, and writing.

Betty started to write on retirement from nursing, incited by a lady in a library bemoaning the lack of romantic novels. She then became one of Mills & Boon's most prolific and best-loved authors. Over her thirty-year writing career Betty wrote more than 134 novels, was published worldwide and brought pleasure to millions. She has left us all the lasting legacy of her heart-warming novels.

Catherine George was born in Wales, and early on developed a passion for reading which eventually fuelled her compulsion to write. Marriage to an engineer led to nine years in Brazil, but on his later travels the education of her son and daughter kept her in the UK. And instead of constant reading to pass her lonely evenings she began to write the first of her romantic novels. When not writing and reading she loves to cook, listen to opera, browse in antiques shops and walk the Labrador.

Valentine
LOVE
AFFAIRS

BETTY NEELS
& CATHERINE GEORGE

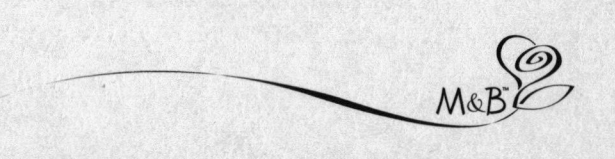

M&B

*M&B™ and M&B™ with the Rose Device
are trademarks of the publisher.
Harlequin Mills & Boon Limited, Eton House,
18-24 Paradise Road, Richmond, Surrey TW9 1SR*

VALENTINE LOVE AFFAIRS © by Harlequin Books SA 2006

Husband For Real and *An Independent Woman* were first
published in Great Britain in separate, single volumes.

An Independent Woman © Betty Neels 2001
Husband For Real © Catherine George 2001

ISBN 0 263 84982 1

118-0206

*Printed and bound in Spain
by Litografia Rosés S.A., Barcelona*

HUSBAND FOR REAL

CATHERINE GEORGE

CHAPTER ONE

WHEN a crimson envelope arrived among the morning post she was amused at first. But her smile faded when she took out an unsigned Valentine card painted with a single red rose. Frowning, she examined the typed envelope, but the postmark was so illegible it gave no clue to the sender's identity.

Rose stood lost in thought for a moment or two, then took her usual stack of mail into the small office at the back of the bookshop and propped the card up conspicuously as something to joke about. Which it had to be. She dismissed it with a shrug, switched on lights, computer and point of sale, chose some Schubert for background music and unlocked the door, ready for the first customers of the day.

As usual these were mostly mothers straight from the school run, needing books for their young. For the first half-hour Rose was kept busy looking out the required titles, or ordering them for delivery next day, at the same time exchanging conversation and offering opinions on the newest craze in children's stories or the latest paperback fiction. Interest in her customers, coupled with pleasant personal service, which came easy to Rose, were a necessary asset for a privately owned bookshop, even if in Chastlecombe only the supermarket and the various newsagents offered anything by way of competition.

When Rose's friend arrived for her part-time stint at the shop she crowed with laughter when she spotted the card.

'Lucky old you! I'm envious, boss. My beloved isn't

5

the sentimental kind.' Bel Cummings's eyes sparkled as she made the fresh pot of coffee they tried to share before she started. 'I suppose it's from Anthony. Though I would have expected something more impressive—'

'In the unimaginable event of his sending me one at all at his age,' Rose finished for her.

Bel smiled in full agreement. 'So who's the secret lover, then?'

'Haven't a clue.'

'Then it must be Anthony,' said her friend, disappointed. 'Get the thumbscrews out and make him confess over dinner. You are seeing him this weekend?'

'Yes, but tonight for a change. He's tied up with Marcus tomorrow.' Rose finished her coffee quickly. 'Right. I'd better get on with this lot before the day's book consignment arrives.'

After Bel went off to greet a customer Rose began to sort out bills and invoices from the usual heap of junk-mail, feeling out of sorts as she worked. And, though the anonymous card was mostly to blame, some of her mood was reluctance to break her routine. She preferred Friday nights on her own. After an hour or so's paperwork she liked to linger in the bath, eat something easy on a tray in front of her television and get to bed early with one of the latest additions to stock. But this weekend Anthony's teenage son would be home alone. Marcus had stayed in Chastlecombe with his mother after the divorce. And because Liz Garrett was spending this weekend away, her ex-husband, determined to keep his son happy at all costs, would devote Saturday as well as his usual Sunday to him.

Rose liked Marcus well enough, and from the little she knew of him didn't think he actively resented her. It surprised her that a young teenager preferred his father's company to going out with friends, but she was perfectly

happy for Anthony to spend Saturday night with his son. Tonight, too, if she were honest. Her week had been gratifyingly busy, and by the time she finished work she wouldn't feel like dressing up and dining out. Her original offer of supper for two upstairs in her flat—a first in their relationship—had been turned down in favour of a table at Chastlecombe's most fashionable restaurant.

Rose had known Anthony Garrett by sight when she was in her teens, but she met him again socially just after his divorce came through. He was an accountant promoted from a small Chastlecombe branch to the London head office of his company. And since the divorce he came back to stay at the King's Head on some weekends, to see his son and spend all the Saturday evenings with Rose that she would allow. She was well aware that Anthony's choice of someone local to wine and dine was deliberate. The injured party in his failed marriage, he'd remained firmly entrenched in a circle of friends only too ready to inform the ex-Mrs Garrett of every known detail of his connection with the new young manager of Dryden Books. Anthony was openly proud of his relationship with an attractive woman so much younger than himself. And if Rose sometimes felt like a trophy, it amused more than annoyed her.

Lunch-hour was busy, as usual, and it was late before Bel could be persuaded to go out for something to eat. During the post-lunch lull Rose finished checking the consignment of books newly arrived that morning, sorted out customer orders to file on the shelves kept for the purpose, then went into the office to eat the sandwich Bel brought for her when she got back.

It was Rose's habit to catch up on reading from new stock over lunch, and she was chuckling over one of the

latest children's books when Bel popped her head round the door.

'Delivery for you, boss.'

'I'm not expecting anything—' Rose stared in surprise when Bel handed over a long, beribboned package. Then swallowed convulsively when she took out a long-stemmed crimson rose.

'Hey, are you all right?' said Bel in alarm.

'Ate my lunch too quickly.'

'I think the rose was meant to be romantic, not give you indigestion,' teased Bel. 'Who's it from?'

'Let's find out.' Rose picked up the phone to ask the local florist.

'No idea, sorry,' was the response. 'Your secret admirer pushed a typed note through the door this morning, with instructions and the exact amount of money.'

When Rose rang off Bel patted her shoulder in concern. 'Are you all right, boss? You've been a bit abstracted all day.'

'I'm fine.' Rose eyed the flower with dislike. 'But I detest mysteries. If all this Valentine nonsense is Anthony's idea I'll have words with him tonight.'

'But surely he would have phoned the order through in the usual way?'

'He's got plenty of contacts in the town. Anyone could have put the money through the door of the flower shop for him.'

'Well I think it's *very* romantic,' declared Bel, then left to deal with an influx of customers, and Rose shut the door on her mystery tribute and went off to help.

After Rose locked up for the night she scanned through the pile of invoices and school orders waiting to be dealt in the office, hesitated, then abandoned her Friday routine.

She would be alone for Saturday evening this week. The paperwork could wait until then.

The phone rang when she arrived upstairs, but when she picked up the receiver the only sound on the line was heavy breathing.

'Who *is* this?' she demanded angrily. A voice whispered her name, raising the hairs on her neck, then the line went dead. Shaken and furious, Rose punched in the numbers to identify her caller, but the number had been withheld. Some stupid fool playing a prank, she assured herself, and made herself some lethally strong coffee to calm herself down.

She filled an empty milk bottle with water, thrust the rose in it and put it on the window-sill of her small kitchen, her eyes brooding as she gazed at the beautiful, perfect bloom. A rose for Rose, said a voice in her mind. A male voice. With the merest hint of Scots. Odd. She could hear the voice so plainly its owner could have been in the room with her. But normally she flatly refused to allow herself the indulgence of thinking about him. The wretched Valentine card was to blame, reminding her of things best forgotten. The phone-call hadn't helped, either. But the rose was the real culprit. Its relentless, heady scent brought memories rushing back like persistent ghosts determined to haunt her. And, as she got ready for the evening, for the first time in years Rose let them stay.

Rose Dryden had gone off to university just after her eighteenth birthday. Eager to embrace everything student life had to offer, she'd been a little wary at first when she'd found she was to share a college flat with two girls who'd been to school together. Cornelia Longford and Fabia Dennison, both a year older than Rose, possessed an aura of self-confidence she envied. But they were

warm, friendly creatures who had taken their younger flat-
mate under their combined wing, and from the first had
seen to it that Rose took full advantage of every social
diversion college life had to offer.

Rose, grateful to be accepted as part of a trio, had
quickly become accustomed to evenings spent in the students' union with a boisterous, rowdy crowd of both
sexes. Envious at first of Con's blonde, thoroughbred
looks, or the brain Fabia kept hidden behind a flippant
manner, even their names, which were so much more
glamorous than her own, Rose had quickly blossomed in
their company. By the end of term she'd attended every
possible festivity available, including the Christmas ball,
and had been as ready as any of her peers to contribute
to heated discussions on how to improve the world.

Determined to get a good degree, Rose had worked
hard. But at the same time she'd learned how to make
half a pint of lager last all evening, how to flirt, and how
to avoid danger when some importunate male misread the
signals.

'It's common-sense,' Con assured her. 'If you fancy a
bloke you go out on a twosome. If you don't, stick with
the crowd.'

Rose never let on that the only men in her life up to
that point had been friends of her unmarried aunt, plus
one or two brothers of girls from school. Nevertheless,
she had enough common-sense to know that a twosome
might involve a lot more than just a pizza and a trip to
the cinema. And, because she wasn't attracted to anyone
enough to risk finding out, her attitude challenged those
among the male student body who considered themselves
irresistible.

'Idiots,' said Rose irritably, during the first days back
after Christmas. 'I just don't fancy any of them that way.'

'You will, eventually,' warned Fabia, immersed in painting her toenails different colours. 'Mother Nature gets us all in the end. You'll see. One look across a crowded room and, wham, you're done for.'

Rose giggled. 'No way—not me!'

'She's right, you know.' Con looked up from her books. 'But most of them just want a fun night out, plus some hanky-panky at the end of it if they're lucky.' She paused dramatically. 'The trick is to make one of them fall in love so violently he'll be your slave.'

Fabia collapsed with laughter, lying flat on her bed with her legs in the air as she waggled her toes to dry them.

'You can't *make* someone fall in love with you, Con,' said Rose scornfully.

'How do you know? Have you ever tried?'

'Well, no, but—'

'Then keep quiet and listen.' Con's smile sent shivers down Rose's spine. 'Come sit at Mama's knee, children, and imbibe the knowledge. I'm the neurobiologist, remember, and this is scientific stuff. I read about it while I was having my hair cut yesterday. It's a proper game plan. No black magic involved,' she added, laughing. 'You don't need eye of newt or anything, Rosie, so don't look at me like that! Trust me. Are you two game?'

Fabia nodded so eagerly that Rose, afraid that dissent would be taken as cowardice, gave a reluctant nod.

'Good girl, Rosie,' approved Con. 'Don't look so worried. This will be fun.'

The first step was for each of the trio to write four men's names on separate pieces of paper, and put the folded scraps into a hat.

'Now we shake it up and draw one out—only one each, mind, and if we hit on the same one as someone else we draw again,' instructed Con.

The three of them thrust fingers into the hat simultaneously but Con raised a peremptory hand before they opened them.

'This needs a bit of ceremony. You first, Fabia.'

'Will Hargreaves,' announced Fabia with satisfaction, then grinned at the other two. 'I didn't cheat, honest. Just luck of the draw.'

Con groaned as she read hers. 'Joe Kidd.'

'But he's been chasing you ever since freshers' week,' objected Rose. 'That's no contest—' She stopped dead, her face flushing crimson as she saw the name on her own slip.

'Who on earth have you got?' demanded Con, taking the paper from her. 'Crikey—James Sinclair.' She raised an eyebrow at Fabia, who shrugged defensively.

'Why not? You said any name we like.'

'So we did,' agreed Rose, the light of battle in her eyes. 'Luck of the draw, just as you said. The legendary Sinclair is only captain of the rugby team and so brilliant he's bound to get a double first—not to mention being a good looking hunk *and* in his finals' year. Piece of cake. I'll have him slavering after little old first-year me in no time.' She thrust her hands through her hair in despair.

Con patted her shoulder soothingly. 'Steady on. You don't have to go through with it if you don't want to.'

'Of course not—it was just my stupid joke,' said Fabia, remorseful now. 'Pick another name, Rosie; you can't possibly go after Sinclair.'

'Why not?' demanded Rose hotly. 'You don't think I'm sexy enough to attract a man like him, I suppose!'

'*No*, love! It's not that.' Fabia hesitated. 'The thing is, rumour has it he might be gay.'

'That's just gossip, because he doesn't chase after every female in sight,' scolded Con.

Rose sighed glumly. 'Any female at all, the way I hear it.'

'How do you know?'

'When I went to a rugby match with Ally Farmer—she's going out with the full-back—she told me that Sinclair isn't interested in women.'

The other two exchanged a look.

'I'd forgotten you liked rugby,' said Con thoughtfully.

'I went to a couple of matches when you two were off shopping...' Rose trailed into silence, eyes suspicious as the others looked at her in speculation. 'What?'

'Sinclair must have seen you,' Fabia pointed out.

'Transfixed by my beautiful blue eyes while he was charging up the field with half the opposing team hanging from every limb,' said Rose scathingly. 'I wish!'

Con, diverted, tilted Rose's chin up. 'He could have been, they're big enough, *and* unusual, sort of navy blue.'

'Nice,' agreed Fabia. 'But, as I keep saying, you should use some paint on them, Rosie, you don't do them justice.'

'They've got twenty-twenty vision, just the same, and I assure you that the mighty Sinclair did *not* notice me.'

'He will if we carry out the plan scientifically,' Con assured her, 'so here's what we do...'

Rose crawled into bed that night utterly convinced of her own insanity. Because she had flatly refused to renege on the task of ensnaring James Sinclair, Con and Fabia had abandoned their part in the scheme in favour of forming a back-up team for the project Rose had referred to as mission impossible. According to Con it would have been child's play to enslave Messrs Hargreaves and Kidd. Sinclair, on the other hand, constituted a challenge Rose could hardly be expected to tackle single-handed. So Con

and Fabia would research every last thing about Sinclair's tastes, family background and relevant details, taking care not to give the game away. Then when Rose was in Sinclair's actual company—a prospect that rendered Rose sick with apprehension at the mere thought of it—she could drop casual phrases into the conversation that would indicate like tastes and interests of her own, and thus convince him she was a soul-mate.

But first, Con had instructed, Rose must run into Sinclair by accident.

'Where?' demanded Rose.

'When I said "run" I meant it,' said Con ruthlessly. 'At the stadium the town council lets us use. Get yourself there early in the morning. Very early. Joe Kidd says Sinclair runs at the track there most mornings about seven before anyone else does.'

'I have to *run*?' gasped Rose.

'At seven?' said Fabia, equally horrified.

'Rose must be there well before that,' said Con cruelly. 'He must come upon *her* by chance, not the other way round.'

'Not *much* before,' wailed Rose. 'Or I'll be dead before he even gets there.'

Tossing and turning in her bed, Rose decided that the whole scheme was madness. In the morning she'd tell the others she'd changed her mind. She fell asleep at last for what felt like a split second before Con was shaking her awake again, deaf to all protests as she thrust her victim into a track-suit, found socks and trainers and, while Rose pulled them on, twisted the tumbled black hair into a hasty plait. Con crammed a scarlet sweat-band low over Rose's eyes, then pushed her out of the door.

'Coffee when you come back,' she promised in a whisper.

'*If* I come back,' said Rose bitterly.

The stadium was deserted when she got there. She brightened. Perhaps he'd gone already. It was a grey, damp day, but thankfully no actual rain. Praying that Sinclair wouldn't turn up for once, Rose jogged up and down on the spot for a bit, then with zero enthusiasm began to run round the track. Three times max, she promised herself, then back to bed, no matter what. For the first circuit Rose, unaccustomed to serious running, thought she might possibly expire before she completed it. But during the second lap she gradually mastered the art of breathing and running at the same time and felt a little better. Then she heard footsteps behind her, and her heart lodged in her throat and she could hardly breathe at all. She stared straight ahead, the breath whistling through her lungs as a tall figure in a dark track suit ran past, eyes turned towards her for an instant. Sinclair acknowledged her existence with the slightest of nods, then raced on down the track.

Now her quarry was in sight, flowing round the track with coordinated grace, Rose summoned up her last shreds of stamina to keep going. Instead of leaving at the next exit she ran on to make another circuit of the track to allow the legendary Sinclair to lap her. This time he gave her a fleeting smile as he passed, and Rose, feeling she'd done all, and more, that could be expected of her, left Sinclair to it and dragged herself back to the flat, hoping her heart would slow down to a normal beat some time in the foreseeable future.

'Mission…accomplished.' She panted, chest heaving.

Con and Fabia pounced on her with cries of delight, demanded every detail, then hustled her off to shower.

'Can't have you too stiff to run next time,' said Con firmly.

'Next time?' gasped Rose. 'I've got to do this again?'

'Yes. But not tomorrow. Give him a day to miss you.'

'Oh come *on*! He barely noticed me.'

'Trust us older women, Rosie,' said Fabia, grinning. 'Sinclair will look for you tomorrow.'

The night before her next run Rose stayed in. 'If I'm running in the morning I need an early night,' she told the others. 'And I've got a tutorial tomorrow, so I must finish this essay, anyway. Try not to wake me when you come in tonight.'

Con woke her at six-thirty the following morning instead. 'Come *on*, Rose,' she whispered, shaking her. 'Up you get.'

Once again Rose was bundled, yawning, into running gear, but this time she'd braided her hair the night before, and only had to brush her teeth and throw cold water on her face before Con thrust her out into the chilly morning like a mother sending a reluctant child off to school.

Rose arrived at the stadium a little earlier than before, but this time Sinclair was there before her. She cursed him in fulminating silence. Now she'd have to run extra laps just to save face. The familiar, lean figure soon flowed past with its usual grace, and a slight smile came her way before Sinclair raced off into the distance, gathering speed. Rose gritted her teeth and pounded doggedly on until sweat soaked from her hair into the towelling band and each breath was like a spear through the ribs. Her running companion lapped her with increasing ease, but Rose forced herself to look straight ahead, counting the circuits until the magic number four released her from torture and she could escape.

This time the others were worried when Rose collapsed, crimson-faced and sweating, on Con's bed.

'No need to kill yourself, love,' said Fabia, pulling her shoes off.

'Was he there?' demanded Con.

'Of—course he—was there!' Rose heaved in a deep breath, eyeing the others malevolently. 'Before me. I had to do *four* circuits.'

'Brilliant,' crowed Fabia. 'Think how fit you'll be—and I bet he noticed you this time.'

'He could hardly fail to; he lapped me often enough.' Rose dragged herself up, groaning. 'Right. For pity's sake make me some coffee while I shower, please.'

Rose was allowed a run-free morning next day, purely, Con decreed, because it was a Saturday, and she could watch Sinclair play rugby in the afternoon instead. 'And just to fog the issue a bit we'll come with you, and cheer on Will Hargreaves. Someone's injured, so Will's got a place on the team today. *So* useful.'

Fabia was all for Rose turning up in her running clothes, complete with red sweat-band, so Sinclair would remember her, but Con wouldn't hear of it.

'Much too obvious. Rose can wear whatever she usually wears to stand ankle-deep in mud in a howling wind. Oh, how I wish it was summer, and Sinclair played cricket!' She sighed regretfully. 'Actually the whole scheme would be better in hot weather. You could strip off a bit, Rose. When the male of the species registers bare female flesh he gives off more pheromones—'

'Stop it,' howled Rose. 'I don't want to know!'

Normally she bemoaned her lack of inches, but at the match she was only too pleased to tuck herself between her tall friends, with lanky Joe Kidd and a few more yelling males for cover as they cheered the home team on to victory over a neighbouring college. Sinclair, at outside half, played with a brilliance which roused a frenzy of

appreciation in his fans on the touchline, but Rose's gloom deepened with every penalty he kicked between the posts. If only she'd set out to capture some ordinary mortal's interest she might have at least had *some* chance of success. But with Sinclair she hadn't a hope. She could just give up, of course. But her Dryden backbone stiffened at the mere idea. When the referee blew the whistle after Sinclair threw himself over the line to score a final try, Rose watched the mud-covered hero leave the field surrounded by shoulder-slapping team mates, and made herself a solemn vow. She would succeed. Somehow.

While the trio were thawing out over mugs of coffee back in the flat later, Will Hargreaves rang with the news that the rugby crowd would be in the Sceptre in the town that night.

'Thanks, Will,' said Con triumphantly. 'Keep us a seat.'

Fabia turned to Rose with a militant gleam in her eye. 'Right. Let's get to work. By the time we finish with you, Rosebud, the great Sinclair can't fail to notice you.'

Deaf to her protests, Con and Fabia curled up Rose's newly-washed hair, bullied her into a skinny-ribbed sweater of Con's and a pair of Rose's own denims discarded as too tight. Then they sat her down in front of a mirror and went to work on her face with the intentness of Renaissance painters creating a masterpiece.

'My word,' exclaimed Fabia when they'd brushed Rose's hair into a rippling waterfall down her back. 'Didn't we do well?'

Rose eyed her reflection with a touch of awe. Outlined in black, violet shadow in the hollows, her eyes looked larger in her small, triangular face, balancing the wide, full-lipped mouth Con had outlined with a pencil then painted with natural lip-gloss to leave the eyes to dominate. 'I look so different—'

'You look gorgeous, Rose,' said Con, so obviously sincere that Rose relaxed.

'Not too much over the top?'

'No,' said Fabia, patting her shoulder. 'We just added a few touches. The basic material was there to start with.'

The Sceptre was crowded by the time they arrived, but Will and Joe had kept places for them at a corner table near the bar. Rose spotted her quarry the moment she arrived. The thick dark hair and honed bone structure of his face were unmistakable. Even laughing among a group of his friends he stood out from the rest; something so mature and self-contained about him Rose felt a sudden stab of panic, glad to slide into a seat with her back to the room.

'Don't look at him,' whispered Con. 'We'll tell you what to do next.'

'Dance on the table?' snapped Rose.

'If you like! But first I'll tell you when it's your round so you can go up to the bar.'

Rose suddenly regretted the cheeseburger she'd wolfed on the way back from the match. She smiled her thanks when Miles, one of her most faithful admirers, put a glass of lager in front of her, but the very thought of it made her gag. She turned to Joe Kidd determinedly and began to discuss the match, but for once Joe, normally a devotee of Con's, was more interested in chatting Rose up than talking rugby.

There was an unmistakable gleam in his eye as he looked her up and down. 'What have you done to yourself, Rosie? You look—'

'Back off, Joe,' whispered Con urgently, glaring at him. Then, in an undertone reminded Rose of her priorities. 'Sinclair's just gone up to the bar to get a round in. On your bike.'

'But we've all got drinks,' muttered Rose wildly.

'Buy some peanuts, or something.' Con tugged her to her feet. 'Go.'

Rose pushed her way through the crowd and, conscious that her eagle-eyed mentors were watching, managed to wriggle eventually into a space alongside Sinclair. He glanced down at her and, as instructed, Rose gave him a cool little smile, then looked away, stomach churning. Her heart leapt as she felt fingers brush her arm. Pulse racing, she turned to look up into eyes the colour of burnished pewter.

'Hello,' said Sinclair. 'Don't I know you?'

CHAPTER TWO

THE deep voice held a trace of Scots accent which did alarming things to Rose's knees. Heart thumping under the clinging pink sweater, she somehow managed to follow Con's instructions and frowned, pretending to think, but before she could mention the stadium he snapped his fingers.

'Pocahontas with the rope of hair!' he exclaimed, and gave her a slow smile which put a final end to any nonsense about giving up her scheme. 'I've seen you at the track.'

'Oh, right.' Rose returned the smile, deeply grateful that he hadn't needed a reminder. 'I'm not there often enough, I'm afraid.' She took the bull by the horns. 'I watched the match this afternoon, by the way. Congratulations.'

'Good game,' he agreed. 'You like rugby?'

Rose nodded, then drew his attention to the barman, who was waiting for payment. Before Sinclair handed over the money he turned to her in enquiry.

'Let me buy you a drink.'

'I already have one, thanks. I just wanted some nuts.' She gave a surreptitious glance at the table in the corner, where everyone was watching, riveted, as Sinclair insisted on paying for the packet of nuts Rose didn't want, signalled to a friend to take the tray of drinks away, then leaned against the bar with the air of a man prepared to linger.

'What's your name?' he asked.

Nerves rendered her answer so quiet Sinclair had to bend his head to hers.

'I didn't hear you.'

'Rose,' she said in his ear. 'Rose Dryden.'

'Mine's Sinclair.'

Fascinated to find he pronounced it to rhyme with 'sprinkler', Rose gave him a polite little smile, thanked him for the nuts, then went back to her table.

'That went off well,' said Con in her ear.

'Yes. He remembered me from the track.'

'I *knew* he would!'

Normally Rose would have enjoyed the evening, but suddenly the crowd she was with seemed immature and noisy, and the usual overtures from the male contingent, more persistent tonight due to her new look, failed to amuse. After an hour or so she'd had enough.

'I'm going,' she whispered to Con. 'Headache.'

'Want me to come with you?'

'No, it's early. You stay. I just need fresh air.' Rose chose a moment when everyone was embroiled in a heated argument, made for the cloakroom, then changed direction and slid through the exit door unnoticed.

Rose had never walked back to campus alone at night. As she left the town to climb the hill to the college she heard footsteps behind her and felt suddenly afraid. And at last began to run, her worst fears confirmed when someone began to run after her.

'Rose—Rose Dryden,' called an unmistakable voice, and she whirled round to find Sinclair gaining on her.

'Sorry,' she said breathlessly, and tried to smile, but her lips felt stiff. 'I didn't know it was you.'

'I saw you leave and came after you.' He wagged an admonishing finger. 'You shouldn't wander around alone at this time of night.'

'It's quite safe,' she said defensively.

'Then why did you run when I followed you?'

Rose shrugged. 'Instinct, I suppose.'

'I'll see you to your door. Are you in hall?'

'No, one of the college flats.' She fell into step with him, hardly able to believe her luck. Con and Fabia would be over the moon.

'So tell me about yourself,' ordered her companion. 'How old are you?'

For a moment Rose thought of lying, but something about James Sinclair decided her against it. 'Eighteen,' she admitted reluctantly, certain that from the lofty heights of twenty-two he would instantly lose interest. Then she remembered her coaching. 'And, if you want my CV, I'm reading English Literature, like foreign films, and go for the occasional run to keep fit. Sorry you asked?' she finished, laughing.

'Not at all.' He smiled down at her when they paused at the entrance to her building.

'How about you?' she said casually.

Sinclair hesitated, then gave her the information she already knew, that he was doing business studies and economics.

Time to go before he got bored. Rose smiled at him and held out her hand. 'Thank you for troubling to come after me. I appreciate it. Goodnight.'

His eyes narrowed in warning. 'Before you go, Rose Dryden, promise you won't walk home alone at night again.'

She nodded obediently.

'Say it,' he ordered.

'All right—I promise.'

'Good. See you on the track some time.' He shook the hand solemnly, gave her the slow-burning smile, and

Rose, heart thumping at the sight of it, managed a friendly little nod and went inside.

When Con arrived, earlier than usual, she checked to see Rose was awake, then beckoned Fabia into the room with her. 'Are you all right, Rose?'

'Fine.' She abandoned her book and sat up cross-legged on the bed, grinning like a Cheshire cat.

'Someone looks pleased with herself!' said Fabia, lolling at the foot of the bed. 'Mind you, I would be too, if Sinclair had bought *me* some nuts. Have you eaten them?'

Not for the world would Rose have admitted that the unopened packet was zipped safely away in her tote bag. 'I think I left them in the pub.'

Con settled herself in the room's only chair. 'Admit it, Rose, the plan's working like a charm.'

'Better than you think!' said Rose in jubilation.

The other girls stared, wide-eyed when they heard Sinclair had gone after her to see her home.

'Did he kiss you goodnight?' demanded Fabia.

'Of course not!' Rose smiled demurely. 'We shook hands.'

The other two laughed their heads off, then Con got up to make some coffee, respect in her eyes. 'I never thought you'd pull it off, you know. Sinclair's immunity to our sex is legendary.'

Rose pulled a face. 'I don't think he sees me as one of the opposite sex, exactly.'

Fabia shrieked with laughter. 'Are you kidding? With all that hair and the magnificent paint job we did, not to mention a shape to die for in that sexy little sweater of Con's—of *course* he thinks of you as a girl.'

'But a very young one,' said Rose, depressed. 'He gave me a right old lecture about walking home alone.'

Con was undeterred. 'Sinclair noticed you, remembered

you, wanted to buy you a drink, then came after you to make sure you were safe. Don't worry about the little girl aspect, ducky—remember Lolita!'

Embarking on phase two of Con's plan, Rose missed the next day's run, but after completing a third circuit in solitude the following morning had begun to think all the heart-pounding effort was in vain by the time the familiar athletic figure appeared. She returned the smile Sinclair gave her as he passed, completed the circuit, then left before he could lap her, or she fell in a heap. Whichever came first.

She wouldn't have admitted it to the others, but it was an effort of will to stay away from the track next morning. But none at all to stay in the same night.

'I must do some work,' she said firmly. Because Sinclair never patronised it, an evening at the students' union no longer held the same allure.

Rose no longer needed a morning call for her run. Next morning she was out of the room by six-thirty, shivering in the cold half-light as she hurried to the stadium, openly looking forward, now, to her early-morning glimpse of Sinclair. To her horror he was there before her again. She groaned. Now she'd have to do even more circuits just to keep up the myth that she liked running. She jogged up and down on the spot for a moment, to warn muscles of the coming ordeal, then started down the track at a speed moderate enough to give her any hope of staying the course long enough to look convincing.

When Sinclair passed her this time she was rewarded with a 'Hi!' to go with the smile as he went flying by.

'Hi,' panted Rose, and ran on, making no attempt to catch up with him. This, she soon found, wasn't neces-

sary. The next time Sinclair caught up with her he slowed down and ran with her.

'Come on, try to speed up a little,' he exhorted, not even out of breath.

Rose did her best to obey, but after three gruelling circuits she flung up her hands in surrender and slumped down at the side of the track, her head on her knees as she tried to get her breath back.

Sinclair hunkered down beside her, looking concerned. 'Hey, sorry, Rose. I didn't mean to finish you off.'

She turned a crimson, sweating face up to his. 'I'm not—in your—class,' she gasped.

'You easily could be. Come every morning for a while. You'll soon get into shape. Not,' he added, with the smile that was no help to Rose in trying to breathe normally, 'that there's anything wrong with yours.'

She scrambled hastily to her feet, glad that her crimson face could hardly turn redder. 'Time I got back to shower.'

'Ah. You don't care for personal remarks.'

She liked his a lot. Rose smiled non-committally as he fell in step beside her, wondering if he meant to see her back to the flat again.

'I bring some kit and have a shower here sometimes when I've got lectures,' he said casually. 'If you do the same tomorrow we could have breakfast afterwards in the transport café down the hill.'

Rose felt a rush of excitement, wondering if this would be Con's idea of progress. Not that it mattered. By this time, plan or no plan, Rose Dryden was totally committed to her crusade to make the lofty, uninterested-in-women James Sinclair fall in love with her. Nothing was going to persuade her from it until she either succeeded, or he told her to get lost.

'If it doesn't appeal to you, don't worry,' he said curtly, and turned away.

Rose came to with a start. 'It appeals very much. I'd like that.'

'Right, then,' he said briskly. 'See you in the morning.'

Rose passed acquaintances by unnoticed as she jogged back to the flat in a dream. Her reception committee was waiting impatiently, as usual, demanding every last detail of the encounter.

'Wow,' said Fabia in awe. 'You're definitely winning, Rose.'

'But the prize is breakfast in a transport caff after slogging round the racetrack, not a candlelit dinner for two,' Rose reminded her, deliberately prosaic to hide her elation.

'Where Sinclair's concerned,' said Con, laughing, 'it probably counts for the same thing.'

When Rose arrived at the stadium next morning, sports bag in hand, Sinclair was racing round the track at a speed that exhausted her to watch.

'Hi,' he panted, coming to a stop beside her. 'Come on, a slow turn or two to warm up, then speed up a bit each circuit as you go along.'

When they took off round the track together Sinclair somehow managed to restrain his long stride to keep up with Rose as they ran, and to her surprise her technique improved so much with Sinclair for coach and pacemaker she even managed to stay upright when he called it a day at last and let her stop.

'Into the shower,' he ordered. 'Don't be long.'

Inside the deserted women's section Rose swathed her hair in a towel and leaned into a spray as hot as she could bear, then towelled herself hastily, slapped on some of the body lotion Fabia had provided, zipped up a yellow

hooded sweatshirt and wriggled into the clinging jeans. Con had ordered her to use eyeshadow and mascara, but Rose was so eager to rejoin Sinclair she didn't bother. She loosened the braid, tied her hair back with a velvet ribbon and put some lipstick on as a gesture to the occasion. When she joined Sinclair outside her entire body simmered with excitement which increased when she saw the gleam of approval in his eyes.

'If you feel as good as you look,' he told her, taking her bag, 'the run was a success.'

'I feel great. And *very* hungry,' she added, almost dancing along beside him as they hurried down the hill to the town.

The transport café was packed, and full of steam and the smell of frying, and Rose loved every last thing about it. Sinclair exchanged greetings with some of the long-distance drivers who formed the majority of the clientele, seated Rose in a corner near the fogged window, then without consulting her went off to collect their meal.

'Bacon sandwiches—the staff of life,' he announced as he returned with the food.

Rose, who rarely ate any breakfast at all, fell on her sandwich ravenously. 'That was fabulous.' She sighed, as they drank strong tea afterwards. 'But if I lost any ounces on the track I've put them all back on now.'

'Is that why you run? To lose weight?' The assessing grey eyes scanned her from head to toe.

'No,' said Rose with complete truth. 'I just want to get fitter, release the endorphins and so on. Isn't that supposed to help the brain to function?'

'It does it for me,' he agreed. 'But it's part of my training. I should really have given up rugby for my finals' year, but the season will be over soon; then I'll channel all my energies into the last push to the exams.'

'No more running?' she said involuntarily.

Sinclair regarded her in silence for a moment. 'If I gave it up,' he said slowly, 'I think I'd miss my morning run. Now.'

Rose gulped down the last of her tea and stood up, afraid he'd tune in to her excitement if she stayed a second longer. 'Could I pay my share, please?'

'No.' Sinclair got up, smiling at her indulgently. 'You can pay next time.'

Next time! Rose's heart sang as she walked briskly up the hill with Sinclair, ignoring the awed, disbelieving looks of her peers as they recognised her companion. When they arrived at her entrance Rose thanked Sinclair for the meal and turned away quickly so he wouldn't suspect how much she longed to linger, but he caught her arm.

'Rose, wait a second. We've got another home match the day after tomorrow. Will you be there again?'

Again! So he had noticed her.

'I don't know. It depends,' she said vaguely.

To her delight he looked slightly put out. 'If not I'll be running on Sunday, same as usual. Come and try for an extra circuit and I'll buy you two bacon sandwiches this time to compensate.'

'OK,' she said casually, and forced herself take the stairs without a backward glance.

Con was full of admiration when she heard that Rose was neither turning up at the Saturday rugby game, nor going to the pub later on.

'Good move. Fabia's meeting Hargreaves at the Sceptre after the match, but I'll go to the flicks with you instead, Rose,' she added nobly.

'In the afternoon, if you like. The Cameo's showing one of those French films I'm supposed to like, so I'd

better see it to impress Sinclair. But in the evening you
have fun in the pub with Fabia and the others, as usual.
I shall stay here and watch TV. Or even do some work.'
Rose grinned, her eyes dancing.

'Clever little bunny! You don't need teacher any more.'

'I'm grateful for all the help I can get, but I do have
the odd idea of my own, Con. Sinclair let slip that he
noticed me at the match, and he definitely saw me at the
pub, so this week I shall be missing from both. But I need
you and Fabia and the rest there in force to make my
absence marked. And a detailed report when you get
back.'

During Saturday evening, while the comings and goings
outside early on made it difficult to concentrate on a
Shakespeare essay, Rose was almost sorry she'd had the
self-control to stay behind while the others went out. But,
quite apart from wanting Sinclair to note her absence, secretly Rose had worried that he might do no more than
give her a casual wave anyway, if she'd turned up at the
Sceptre. And no way was she willing to risk that.

'Sinclair was there, right enough,' said Con breathlessly, the moment she came through the door with Fabia.
'Flushed with victory, after his usual star turn on the
rugby pitch. He saw us arrive, *and* craned his neck to see
if you were with us. Then afterwards he kept glancing
over to our table to see if you'd put in a late appearance.
It's working, it's working!' She seized Rose's hands and
yanked her off the bed, whirling her round like a dervish
until they collapsed in a heap with Fabia, laughing their
heads off.

'What are you two *on*?' demanded Rose, giggling help-
lessly.

'Adrenaline,' gurgled Fabia, and eyed her with envy.

'Damn. I wish I'd drawn Sinclair's name out of the hat myself now.'

Con threw back her head with a yelp of laughter. 'Come *on*, Fabe, can you honestly see yourself pounding round the track at dawn?'

Fabia joined in the laughter good-naturedly. 'Not a chance. No man is worth that kind of effort.'

'I rather enjoy the running now,' confessed Rose. 'It gives a terrific buzz.'

'And ruins the mascara!'

'Never wear any.'

Con patted her hand. 'You don't need it, anyway. Is Sinclair still treating you like a kid, by the way?'

Rose thought it over. 'No,' she said slowly. 'I don't think he is.'

'I bet he's wondering where you are tonight, and who with,' said Fabia with relish. 'He'd never believe the truth.'

'He's about the only one who might,' said Con. 'Sinclair's got tunnel vision when it comes to the study bit, according to our faithful researchers. Will and Joe give off gamma rays of hero-worship whenever his name is mentioned.'

Rose felt a sharp twinge of conscience. 'I just hope he never finds out what we're up to.'

'He won't. Neither of them knows him well enough for intimate little chats. Besides, we have enough relevant information by now.' Con ticked off her fingers. 'Sinclair comes from somewhere near Edinburgh, lives in digs here in the town, likes foreign films and excels at almost every sport—as if we didn't know—but apparently he likes fishing, too, and holidays on Skye, and, of course, ambition is his middle name. There.'

'When did you find all this out?' demanded Rose.

'I had to be dangerously sweet to Hargreaves on the way home from the pub to wheedle the home background out of him.' Fabia batted her eyelashes. 'I stopped short of surrendering my virtue, but only just.'

'Good,' said Con approvingly. 'Keep him on the boil in case we need his help again. And don't even *try* to look noble—you know perfectly well you fancy him.'

'A good thing I do in the circumstances!' Fabia pulled a face. 'Though he's now convinced I've got a crush on our hero. Not that it matters. Will told me tonight I don't stand a chance in that direction, because Sinclair, I quote, "has no time to spare for girls".'

'Except at dawn's early light for Rose,' said Con, laughing.

CHAPTER THREE

NEXT morning Rose woke before the alarm went off, deeply depressed to find rain streaming down her window. Moving quietly to avoid disturbing the others, she got into her running gear, collected a yellow slicker from the hook behind the door, picked up her bag with the change of clothes, then shut herself in the bathroom for the rest of her preparations. She hurried out eventually into rain so heavy she was sure Sinclair wouldn't bother to turn up. But when she got to the stadium he was there before her, tall and faintly menacing in hooded black until his teeth showed white in the smile she was beginning to know so well.

'Hi. I didn't think you'd come.'

'I had my doubts,' she admitted, smiling cheerfully in response. She eyed the water-covered track with apprehension. 'Can we run on that?'

'I vote we don't in this weather.' He took her bag. 'I've got a suggestion.'

'Bacon sandwiches with no run for starters?' she said hopefully.

'Something like that. But there's a problem. The café doesn't open this early on Sundays.'

'Oh. Never mind,' said Rose, swallowing her disappointment. 'Some other time, then.'

'I live in digs in the town,' he said quickly, the faint trace of Scots in his accent more pronounced. 'And I make a great bacon sandwich. My landlady's away this weekend, babysitting, but she gives me the run of her kitchen.'

33

'Does she do that for all her boarders?'

'I'm her one and only.' His expression was hard to make out in the gloom. 'Will you join me for breakfast, Rose?'

Excitement swept through her like a tidal wave. 'Yes, I will. Thank you.'

He smiled. 'Come on, then, let's make a run for it. We've got a way to go before you get anything to eat.'

'And I thought I was let off for today!'

By the time they reached a crescent of solid Edwardian houses they were drenched. Sinclair unlocked the door of a house halfway along and hurried her into a mosaic-tiled hall, switched on lights and yanked off her dripping slicker.

'Take your shoes off,' he ordered, 'then go straight up the stairs to the bathroom and get into some dry clothes.'

'How about you?' She panted.

'I'll strip off in Mrs Bradley's bathroom down here— go on, hurry up. I'll start grilling the bacon while you change. My room's first on the right. Wait for me there.'

Wishing she could avoid getting sweaty and red-faced just once now and again in Sinclair's company, Rose stripped off her outer clothes in a blessedly warm bathroom, then pulled on dry socks, old, comfortable denims and an outsize baggy white sweater which grew larger every time she washed it. She dismantled her damp plait, rubbed her hair dry with her own towel, rather than mar the immaculate ones on the rail, used a hairbrush vigorously, then added the usual token touch of lipstick to her mouth and packed her wet things in the bag.

Rose felt like a trespasser when she ventured into Sinclair's room. There were piles of books everywhere. The sizeable table he used as a desk had obviously been cleared of them to make room for a large wooden tray set

with tea-things, but books lay in stacks under it, and on shelves and on the floor either side of a big sofa. To her relief there was no bed. He obviously slept somewhere else. Through the rain sluicing down the big window at the back of the room Rose could see a drenched garden backing onto gardens in the street behind. Pleasant on a better day. And she envied him the room, which was three times the size of hers at the flat. She put her bag down and went to look at his books. Her aunt maintained that you could tell a lot about people from their taste in reading. But there was little to be learned from Sinclair's collection, which was all textbooks, bar a couple of volumes on fly fishing.

Rose turned guiltily as Sinclair came in with a platter of sandwiches. 'You were quick!' she exclaimed, hoping he couldn't tell how shy she felt now they were alone together.

Sinclair switched on a couple of lamps and plugged in a kettle. 'I put everything ready before I went out. I just had to light the grill and abracadabra, everything was ready in no time.' He handed her a length of kitchen paper in lieu of a napkin, and gave her a plate with two sandwiches on it, then made a pot of tea and sat down on a straight chair at the table and began to eat. Rose munched in silence for a lengthening interval, wishing she could think of something brilliantly clever to say.

'What's the matter, Rose?' he asked bluntly.

Her eyes met his with candour. 'I was just thinking that this isn't what I expected when I started out this morning.'

He raised an eyebrow. 'You'd prefer the transport café?'

'No, of course not.'

'Then don't look so scared. I'm perfectly harmless.'

She grinned involuntarily. 'So I've heard.'

He glared, his eyes suddenly wintry. 'And just what *have* you heard, little girl?' he drawled, ice in every word.

Rose blushed to the roots of her hair. 'Only that you're more interested in getting a double first than chasing after girls.'

His eyes softened. 'True enough. My surplus energies expend themselves on the track and the rugby pitch. The rest goes into this lot here.' He waved a hand at the encroaching books, then gave her the slow smile which made her insides dissolve. 'The rumours about my sexual preferences are false, by the way, in case you're wondering, spread in my first year by a female who resented my lack of interest.'

'I wasn't wondering,' she assured him blithely, and began on her second sandwich with more relish.

'Why not?'

Rose regarded him steadily. 'Because it's none of my business.'

Sinclair stared back in surprise. 'You're very blunt. Want some tea?'

'Yes, please.' He filled a beaker, added a splash of milk and handed it to her, pleasing Rose enormously because he'd remembered how she liked it.

'So you don't care whether I'm gay or not?' he demanded.

'No.' She shrugged. 'I fail to see why race, religion or sexual leanings should matter when it comes to friendship.'

Sinclair leaned forward, his hands clasped between his knees as he peered down into her face. 'You really mean that, don't you?'

'Yes.' Rose gave him a crooked little smile. 'Wet behind the ears I may be in your eyes, but I have my beliefs.'

'Your parents fostered them?'

Her face shadowed. 'They began the process, but they died when I was fourteen. I live with my aunt. Minerva holds strong views on everything, so I suppose I've taken some of them on board myself without even realising it.'

Sinclair got up, seeming taller than usual to Rose from her seat on his sofa. He took her mug and plate from her and put them on the tray, then to her astonishment he sat beside her and took her hand.

'Would you like to tell me about your parents?' he said gently.

Rose gave him a startled, sidelong glance, deeply conscious of the hard, warm hand grasping hers. Then after a moment's hesitation she told him about the joyrider who'd put an end to her parents' lives one afternoon on a narrow country road in Warwickshire.

'They were on their way to fetch me from school.' Rose bit her lip. 'For a long time I just couldn't accept that they were gone, even after I went to live with my aunt. Minerva owns a bookshop in a small town in the Cotswolds, and after—after the accident I moved into the flat over the shop with her.'

'Poor little kid,' said James quietly. 'It must have been tough for you.'

'I won't pretend it wasn't. But I've been fortunate, too. My father was a lot older than Minerva, so I look on her more as friend than aunt now I'm older. And I still have my memories of a happy childhood, and the holidays I spent with Mother and Dad.' Feeling horribly guilty, she recalled herself to the matter in hand. 'We even went to Scotland once, to Skye.' The last bit, a vital part of Con's strategy, was her first real lie, and she gulped down some tea to cover the rush of guilty colour to her face.

'Skye!' exclaimed Sinclair. 'When my father was alive

we went there once a year. I love it there. How about
you?'

'I don't remember much about it. I was quite young,
and it rained a lot,' said Rose, deliberately vague. 'My
father went fishing, and Mother and I visited woollen
mills.'

'Did your father do much fishing?' he asked with interest.

'Yes. When he could. Trout, like you.' She went cold
for a moment. 'I saw the books on your shelves,' she said
hurriedly, and went on talking to cover her blunder. 'Dad
made the most beautiful flies. He'd sit with a special little
vice at the kitchen table, listening to opera tapes while he
created tiny works of art. I still have some of them. The
fishing flies, I mean. His rods were sold.'

The grasp tightened. 'You still miss him.'

'I miss them both.' Rose hesitated. 'But it comforts me
to know that they're together.'

'You really believe that?'

'Yes.' Her chin lifted. 'Because I need to believe it.'

There was silence between them for a while.

'My father died when I was twelve,' said Sinclair
abruptly.

Rose sat perfectly still, hardly daring to breathe. In her
wildest dreams she'd never imagined he'd confide in her
in return.

'He died in his sleep,' he went on. 'When my mother
woke up one morning he was just—gone. Dad was a
workaholic with a heart problem. Fatal combination.'

'I'm sorry.' Rose tightened her fingers in sympathy.

'When I was eighteen my mother married again. He's
a good man, and they're happy together. But...' he
paused.

'You feel left out?'

He frowned thoughtfully. 'I've never thought of it in quite those terms, but, yes, I suppose I do. That's why I applied for a college down here. I could have gone to Edinburgh or St Andrews, but I opted to get right away to leave the newlyweds in peace. I even took off for a year between school and college. Went backpacking round Australia.'

'Sounds wonderful. I've never done anything adventurous like that,' said Rose enviously. 'Do you mind? That your mother remarried, I mean?' Then she held her breath, afraid she'd trespassed.

But Sinclair shook his head. 'No. I don't mind at all. She waited until I was ready to leave home, though Donald would have married her long before then from choice. My mother was only fortyish when they finally tied the knot. And even in a son's eyes a very attractive lady.' He gave her a wry look. 'Donald's a successful advocate, and a very self-contained sort of bloke, but it was obvious, even to me, that he was mad about my mother from the moment he met her. Still is. Mother sold our home when she moved in with him. His house is a big, rambling place, and there's a room in it kept solely for me, but I can't help feeling like a visitor there—' He stopped dead, shaking his head.

'What's the matter?'

'I can't believe I'm telling you all this stuff. I don't usually bore people rigid with my life history.' He squeezed her hand. 'You must be a very good listener, young Rose.'

Now, she thought reluctantly, would be a good time to leave. She detached her hand gently and got up. 'I'd better leave you to your books. Thank you for breakfast, and— and for talking to me.'

Sinclair got to his feet and stretched, suddenly so over-

poweringly male in the small room Rose felt a sudden urge to run, like an animal scenting danger.

'The average man doesn't need much persuading to talk about himself,' he said wryly.

'Average' was the last word Rose would have applied to Sinclair. 'I must go—or should I help you wash up first?'

He ruffled her hair, smiling. Like petting a puppy, she thought, resigned.

'I've got a better idea. Stay and have some more tea. It's still hissing down out there.'

Rose glanced at the window. 'You're right. OK. Then I really must get back.'

'Rose, it's only half-eight, and it's Sunday. What's the rush?'

'I must be keeping you from your work.'

'I've got the rest of the day for that.' His eyes narrowed. 'Or is there someone waiting for you?'

He didn't like the idea!

'A playmate of my own age, you mean?' she said, smiling.

'Hell, Rose, you're not *that* much younger than me,' he said irritably, and raised an eyebrow. '*Is* there someone?'

Afraid he might wash his hands of her if she even hinted there might be, Rose shook her head. 'No. Only my flatmates. And I doubt if they're even awake yet.'

'Right.' He picked up the kettle. 'You sit there for a minute, and I'll go and fill this again.'

'Can't I wash the plates, or something?'

'I'll let you off as it's your first visit. Next time you can do the catering.'

Next time! Rose sat deep in thought after he'd gone. It seemed Con might be right. It actually *was* possible to

deliberately rouse a man's interest. Though it was impossible to imagine James Sinclair as any woman's slave. Nor falling madly in love with Rose Dryden, either, however faithfully she followed the plan of campaign. But he was definitely taken with her a little bit. Enough to invite her back here, and coach her on the track. Which was way beyond anything she'd expected.

When Sinclair came back he gave her a searching look as he plugged in the kettle. 'Where were you last night, Rose?'

'Working.'

He frowned. 'A part-time job? Where?'

'No job. I was writing an essay. I went to the Cameo in the afternoon, then caught up with some work afterwards. Why?'

'I noticed you weren't in the pub. I wondered if you were ill.' He made two more beakers of tea, and handed her one.

She shook her head, full of secret jubilation. 'Since I've taken up running again I'm fighting fit.'

'I said you would be. So what film did you see?'

'They were showing a re-run of *Manon des Sources*. It's one of my favourites,' she added, crossing mental fingers.

His eyes lit up with enthusiasm. 'Mine too. I never managed to catch the prequel—what was it called?'

'*Jean de Florette*. That's on this week for three days— then it's *Belle du Jour*,' Rose added hastily, afraid she'd been too obvious. She sighed. 'Catherine Deneuve is so beautiful.'

Sinclair shrugged. 'Not my type. I prefer my women dark.'

'Sounds as though you own a harem,' said Rose flippantly, and drained her mug to avoid looking at him.

'Your face is very expressive, Rose,' he teased. 'What are you thinking?'

'I just wondered if you had someone—a girl, I mean—back home. Which is absolutely none of my business, of course,' she added in a rush, wishing she'd held her tongue.

'I don't have a woman back home, or anywhere else for that matter. The grapevine is absolutely accurate,' he said mockingly. 'I've got no time for girls.'

'Which is a cue for this one to leave, if ever I heard one,' she said promptly, and jumped to her feet. 'Rain or no rain, it's time I was off.'

He ran down the stairs ahead of her to fetch her shoes and slicker. 'Shall I call a cab?'

'No. The exercise will do me good.'

'Hands up.' He put the slicker over her head, then drew the hood over her hair. 'See you on the track in the morning, then.'

Rose smiled non-committally as she stamped her feet into her damp track shoes. 'Thanks again for my breakfast,' she said, when he opened the front door. 'Goodbye.'

'Goodbye, *James*,' he corrected.

'Everyone else calls you Sinclair,' she pointed out, careful to pronounce it as he did.

'Exactly.'

Rose smiled uncertainly. 'Goodbye, then—James.'

'See you in the morning. Don't hang about on the way back, and straight in the shower when you get there.'

She saluted smartly, gave him a cheeky grin, then took her bag from him and went off down the path at speed, turning to wave at him as he stood at the open door.

When she arrived at the flat, sodden, out of breath, and utterly triumphant, she dumped the dripping slicker in the bathroom, then went to join Con and Fabia.

'Where on earth have you been until now?' demanded Con.

Fabia eyed Rose's glowing face with suspicion. 'You can't have been racing round that track all this time!'

'No, I haven't.' Rose began stuffing her shoes with kitchen paper to dry them out. 'There was so much surface water James said it was unsafe to run so he took me back to his digs for breakfast.' She looked up, laughing at the identical look on both faces.

'At his digs?' said Con faintly. 'Like in his *room*?'

Rose nodded gleefully. 'His landlady was away for the weekend, and he's the only lodger. We had the house to ourselves.'

Fabia blew out her cheeks and sat down abruptly. 'You've cracked it, then!'

'Hold on. I haven't achieved that much,' warned Rose. 'James isn't in love with me—'

'Not yet,' put in Con, eyes gleaming, 'but he's interested enough to ask you back to his place for breakfast.'

'For which I was truly thankful,' said Rose piously. 'I think my efforts on the track entitled me to a couple of bacon sandwiches at the very least.'

'Did you have to make them?'

'No. *James*,' she said with emphasis, 'made them with his own fair hands.'

'Did he ask you to call him that?' demanded Con, impressed.

'Yes. Sinclair to everyone else; James to me.'

'So what happens next?' said Fabia eagerly. 'Has he asked you for a proper date?'

Rose's face fell. 'No. Though heaven knows I hinted enough—told him about the film we saw, and the one showing this week. He may like foreign films, but he's not taking me to see one.'

'Never mind. I think you've worked miracles as it is,' consoled Con. 'When do you see him again?'

'He said he'd see me at the track in the morning, but I suppose I'd better give it a miss until Tuesday.'

Con shook her head. 'If he wants to see you tomorrow, be there.'

'Won't that be overkill?'

'No. This, my pet, is phase three. Time to hot things up.'

'I just hope it doesn't end in tears!'

Fabia frowned. 'Why should it? It's just a game.'

Rose thought about that a lot later that night, once she was in bed. Since the exchange of confidences with James it no longer felt like a game. Which lay on her conscience so heavily sleep was elusive. But next morning she got up early, just the same, and let herself out into a cold, but thankfully dry morning to join James at the stadium, smiling in welcome.

'Hi! I've done my bit,' he informed her. 'Ready to try for an extra lap today?'

Rose nodded eagerly, went through a few warming-up exercises, then set off with him round the track. Under his tuition she found herself running a slightly faster circuit every time, exhilarated by her success, until halfway round for the fourth a sudden, stinging pain in her foot ruined her balance and she fell heavily, her momentum sending her rolling over and over to land flat on her back, completely winded.

'*Rose!*' James fell on his knees beside her. 'What the hell happened? Are you all right?'

Rose had no breath to spare for talking. While she fought to get air in her lungs he ran his hands over her arms and legs, probed her ankles, found nothing broken and pulled her carefully to her feet.

'Come on, breathe. Deep, even breaths. That's the way. Good girl. Lean against me for a bit.'

Rose obeyed gratefully, heaving in gulps of air, but soon grew much too conscious of the heat and scent of his body, the heart beating like a drum against her cheek. She pulled away, smiling shakily. 'Stupid—thing—to do. Sorry.'

'There must have been water on the track,' said James gruffly. 'Are you sure you're all right?'

She nodded. 'Embarrassed, that's all.'

'Here, take my arm. I'll help you back to the flat.'

Rose stared at him, horrified. 'No, please! You don't need to. I'll be fine.'

He scowled down at her. 'Be sensible, Rose, you're limping.'

'There's something in my shoe.'

James sat her down on the track and removed the shoe, swearing under his breath when he found a small nail sticking up inside it. He removed her bloodstained sock and located a puncture on the sole of her foot. 'No wonder you fell, Rose. What the hell was something like this doing on the track?'

'Maybe it got washed down from somewhere in that weather yesterday.'

'In which case there may be more. I'd better report it. In the meantime you need a dressing. Wait there a minute. I'll raid the first-aid box in the men's showers.'

While he was gone one of his rugby team mates appeared for a morning run, and hurried to Rose in surprise.

'What's wrong, love? Sprained your ankle?' said the large, amiable giant.

'No, I trod on a nail,' she confessed, feeling horribly self-conscious.

'Bad luck! I'll get you something to put on your foot,' he offered, then stared in astonishment as James appeared.

'Sinclair? A bit late in the day for you, isn't it?'

'Hi, Greg. Be careful on the track. There may be more like this.' James held up the nail he'd taken from Rose's shoe.

Greg looked on, riveted, as a sticking plaster was applied to Rose's foot and her sock and shoe carefully replaced.

'There,' said James, pulling her to her feet. 'Can you stand on it, Rose?'

She tried the foot gingerly. It was sore, but she could walk. 'It's fine,' she said firmly. 'Sorry for all the fuss.' She gave a smile that encompassed both men. 'Thanks a lot. I'd better get back. Bye.'

'Look, I could easily carry a little thing like you back to campus,' said Greg, with enthusiasm which evaporated as he met Sinclair's ferocious glare.

'It's very kind of you, but I can manage. Really.' Rose limped rapidly from the stadium in embarrassment, her morning utterly ruined.

When she got back to the flat the others were still in bed. Rose went off for a shower, choking back a sob as she dried herself. It had ended in tears after all. Because there'd be no more running for a bit. And no hope of seeing James again until she could.

Fabia burst in suddenly, scaring Rose to death. '*Run—* phone call.'

Wrapping herself in a towel as she ran, Rose flew to the sitting room, afraid something had happened to her aunt. 'Hello?' she gasped into the phone.

'Rose? James.'

Her eyebrows shot to her hair. When she nodded silently in answer to the incredulous question in Con's eyes

her friend gave a triumphant thumbs-up sign, and whisked herself from the room.

'Hi,' Rose answered, when she had herself in hand.

'I wanted to make sure you got back in one piece. How's the foot?'

'OK. The nail wasn't big enough to go in very far.'

'Good. But you'd better not run on it for a while.'

'No.'

There was a pause.

'Rose.'

'Yes?'

'You took off so suddenly I didn't have a chance to ask just now.' This time the pause stretched Rose's nerves to breaking point. 'Are you doing anything tonight?' James asked at last.

Rose clamped her teeth together to stop them chattering. 'No,' she said after a pause of her own, hoping he thought she'd been leafing through her diary.

'The French film you mentioned—' He paused.

'Jean de Florette?'

'Right. I thought we might see it together.'

'OK,' she said, hoping she sounded casual.

'Good. I'll pick you up outside the flat at seven.'

'No need to come out of your way,' she said quickly. 'I can meet you at the Cameo.'

'You can't walk down here on that foot, Rose. I'll fetch you in the car.'

Car?

'See you later, then.' She put the phone down in a dream.

'What did he want?' demanded Con, rushing in.

Rose turned dazed eyes on her friend. 'He's taking me to the Cameo tonight. In someone's car.'

'Fabia,' yelled Con in triumph. 'Get your self in here. Phase three is up and running!'

CHAPTER FOUR

ROSE came back to the present with an effort, annoyed to find she'd been daydreaming so long the bath water was cold and so was she. With no time to iron her original choice for the evening, she pulled on a black jersey dress with a long skirt slit to to the knee, and swiftly brushed the thick, glossy hair which these days stopped short just above her shoulders. She did her face with swift, practised skill Fabia Hargreaves would have been proud of, and as the finishing touch sprayed herself with perfume and slid her feet into low-heeled black suede shoes. Because Anthony Garrett was very conscious of his height, which at best could only be described as medium, Rose left her high heels at home when she went out with him.

On normal Saturdays Anthony usually arrived in Chastlecombe long before she closed the shop, and arrived to collect her punctually at eight. But by the time he rang her private doorbell that night he was almost an hour late.

'Traffic bad, Anthony?' said Rose, as they went upstairs. 'Have a drink.'

'Thanks. You're an angel.' He dumped a suitcase down, then slumped on Rose's sofa with a sigh, looking tired, and consequently every year of his age for once. 'Sorry I'm late. My blasted phone had run out of juice, so I couldn't let you know I was held up by an accident. The Friday traffic was bad enough before then, but I've been crawling along for the past hour.' He accepted the whisky gratefully and tossed it back in one swallow. 'I

needed that.' He smiled up at her in appreciation. 'You look wonderful, Rose.'

'Thank you, kind sir. I rang the restaurant to say we were delayed, by the way, but they're holding the table. Not,' she added, 'without reluctance.'

Anthony frowned. 'Why? We eat there often enough.'

'It's Valentine's night.'

He clapped a hand to his forehead and groaned. 'Hell and damnation—I meant to buy you some flowers, but I forgot. My apologies again, Rose.'

Her eyes narrowed thoughtfully. 'In that case, Anthony, I take it you didn't send me that card over there, either.'

He eyed the card with unmistakable hostility. 'No, I damn well did not. Who did?'

'No idea.' Rose went into the kitchen to fetch the rose. 'This arrived, too.'

Anthony jumped to his feet, scowling. 'Your old pal Mark Cummings, I suppose.'

So he hadn't sent the rose, either.

'I have no idea,' Rose assured him. 'We really ought to get going, Anthony.'

'Yes, of course.' He looked down at his rumpled suit with distaste. 'Look, could I have a swift shower and change? I was too late to get to the King's Head first.'

Rose had been wondering about the suitcase. She waved him off to the bathroom, then stared down at the card again. If Anthony hadn't sent it—not that she thought he had—who *was* her unknown admirer? If it was the joker with the heavy breathing the idea was so disturbing Rose found it an effort, later, to be bright, animated company over dinner in a restaurant which had pulled out all the stops for Valentine's night. Anthony, smart in a new suit, did his best to make up for his late arrival, and ordered expensive wine to go with the meal. But when they

reached the coffee stage he downed his accompanying cognac with uncharacteristic speed.

'Rose,' he said, leaning forward to avoid being overheard. 'There's something I want to ask.' His eyes, still bloodshot from driving, locked with hers with an intensity which made her apprehensive.

'In that case,' she said lightly, 'let's go back to the flat. There's too much noise here.'

It was only a short walk back to the cobbled arcade where Dryden Books rubbed shoulders with shops which sold antiques and expensive clothes. But because Anthony made no attempt to talk on the way Rose felt on edge by the time she unlocked the private door alongside her double-fronted shop.

'Coffee?' she said brightly, when they reached the flat.

'Not for the moment. Come and sit down.' He took her hand and drew her down beside him on the sofa. 'Look, Rose, we've been seeing each other on a regular basis for some time now,' he began.

'An occasional Saturday evening over the past month or two,' she amended quickly, not liking the sound of this.

'Almost three months,' he corrected. 'More than long enough for me to know my own mind, and, hopefully, yours.'

Rose eyed him warily. 'What's this leading to, Anthony?'

'Surely you can recognise a proposal when you hear one! I'm asking you to marry me,' he said, and tried to kiss her, but she dodged away and went to sit in a nearby chair.

'Why?' she asked quietly.

'*Why?*' Anthony stared at her, affronted. 'Because I care for you, of course, and I believe we could be happy together. Don't you enjoy time spent with me?'

'Well, yes. But I had no idea you were thinking about marriage.' Rose raised an eyebrow. 'Tell me the truth, Anthony. Isn't this sudden talk of marriage just a deep-seated need to show your ex-wife you can attract a younger woman?'

'That's unfair!' Colour flooded into Anthony's face, then receded again, leaving him pale. 'In the beginning there was an element of that,' he admitted at last, gaining her respect. 'But it soon changed into something very different. When I saw that stupid card earlier I felt so jealous it stampeded me into wanting to make our relationship official.' He looked at her in appeal. 'Will you at least consider the idea of marrying me, Rose?'

'I don't think so,' she said gently.

Anthony jumped to his feet, so obviously thunderstruck by her refusal he couldn't sit still. 'Why not?' he demanded. 'Is there someone else?'

Rose sighed. 'Not in the way you mean.'

'What other way is there?' he shot at her, pacing up and down. 'I suppose it's Mark Cummings. Your old pal with his sob story. Do you really want to tie yourself to a man with a failed marriage and a child—' He stopped dead.

'Both of those things apply to you, Anthony,' she pointed out.

'That's different,' he said, discomfited. 'I'm legally divorced, at least, and Marcus is a teenager, not a toddler like the Cummings child.'

Rose nodded. 'Nevertheless, any marriage between you and me, Anthony, would present certain problems.'

'If you mean Marcus, I don't foresee any trouble there. He wouldn't be living with us. Besides, he likes you, Rose.'

'Good. I'm glad.' She eyed him questioningly. 'But if,

by any chance, I did consider marrying you, where would you expect me to live?'

He frowned, taken aback. 'Why, with me, naturally.'

'In London?'

'Is that a problem?'

'It's certainly could be. My life is here in Chastlecombe now, with friends and familiar faces round me, and a livelihood which gives me pleasure. And independence.' Rose hesitated, then decided to tell him the truth. 'But the major obstacle between us is a secret from my past.'

Anthony's eyes narrowed. 'A secret?'

Rose nodded, glancing involuntarily at the rose. 'Yes.'

'Are you talking about a lover?'

She nodded. 'Or to be more accurate, the consequences of having a lover.'

He swallowed convulsively. 'You mean you had a child?'

'No, Anthony.'

'Then, what *is* this mysterious problem?'

She turned away wearily. 'I can't marry anyone at this moment in time, Anthony, because I'm still married to someone else.'

'*What!*' He spun her round, his face dark with anger. 'And you've never seen fit to tell me?'

Rose lifted her chin with sudden hauteur. 'I've never told anyone. Ever. Not even Minerva. I wouldn't have told *you*, believe me, if you hadn't talked of marriage.'

'What else did you think I had in mind at my age!' he demanded furiously. 'I'm too old to be your boyfriend—'

'I think the word's ''partner'' these days.'

'Partner implies a hell of a sight more privileges than I enjoy,' he snapped. 'And now I discover there's a whole area of your life I knew nothing about.'

'Why should you? It's my business entirely, Anthony. But if it's any consolation, no one else knows, either.'

'Aren't you forgetting someone?' he demanded. 'This mysterious husband of yours?'

Rose's lips tightened. 'Of course I haven't forgotten him.'

Anthony threw out his hands. 'Then what's the problem? Won't he agree to a divorce?'

'I don't know.'

'You don't *know*? Why the hell not?'

'I've never asked him.'

Anthony exerted control with visible effort. 'Rose,' he said at last. 'How old were you when you got married?'

'Eighteen.'

He stared at her incredulously. 'Ten years ago?'

'Yes.'

'Then why in heaven's name haven't you got round to a divorce?'

'Because our parting was so hostile I swore he'd be the one to ask first,' said Rose with passion.

'Why hasn't he?'

'No idea. It certainly wouldn't have cost him financially.' Her mouth tightened. 'I wouldn't have touched a penny of his.'

Anthony eyed her thoughtfully. 'It sounds to me, Rose, as though you need to be free of this man, regardless of your intentions towards *me*.'

'You could be right.'

'Can you tell me about it?'

Her face shuttered. 'I'd rather not discuss it.'

'Whatever you say, Rose.' He hesitated. 'Just answer one question, then I'll go. Did you leave this man, or was it the other way about?'

'I left him.'

'Not that it matters, after all this time.' Anthony gave her a bleak smile. 'As you well know, I'm clued up about divorce. Mine, due to Marcus and the house, was more complicated. But are you aware that after ten years apart the court will grant you a divorce whether your husband agrees to it or not?'

'Really?' Rose frowned. 'Then it's strange that he's never got round to divorcing *me*. Perhaps he has and forgot to notify me.' She shrugged. 'Or maybe he's just forgotten he was ever married to me.'

Anthony shook his head, looked depressed. 'No man could forget he'd been married to *you*, Rose.'

When she was alone at last Rose was amazed to find it was still a few minutes short of twelve, the time Anthony always left her. As far as the world knew, or cared, he could have been making mad, passionate love to her in the interval between dining together and his departure every time they met, but Anthony Garrett, deeply conventional at heart, always returned to the King's Head before midnight. And until tonight had never attempted to put their relationship on a more intimate basis. For which she'd been grateful. She liked his company well enough in small doses, but there was nothing sexual in their relationship. On her side, at least. Nor did she mourn the lack. She'd been through all that before, and it had never turned out well for her.

It could have been two in the morning by the way she felt when Rose got ready for bed. Desperate for sleep after the emotional drain of the past hour, she was about to switch off her light when her bedside phone rang. Thinking it might be Bel, to say she couldn't get in next day, Rose picked up the receiver, then almost dropped it again when someone whispered her name and rang off. Hand

shaking, she pressed buttons frantically, but the number had again been withheld.

Trembling, and this time more frightened than she cared to admit, Rose pulled on her dressing gown and went to make herself some tea, then took it back to bed and sat propped up against all her pillows with the lights on, feeling furious as well as frightened. Just minutes ago she'd been struggling to keep awake long enough to get to bed, but the phone call had changed all that. Speculation on the identity of her caller would do no good at all. Probably give her nightmares. Rose sighed, resigned. There was one infallible way to occupy her mind, of course. Talking about her marriage to Anthony had brought it all back in full force. And perhaps this was a good thing. If she recalled the past so that every aspect of it was clear in her mind, it might make things easier when she broached the subject of divorce. As she should have done long since.

CHAPTER FIVE

ROSE had forced herself to walk downstairs sedately for her first real date with James Sinclair. Refusing all offers of help from Con and Fabia, she'd worn her own clothes, made up her own face, and tied her hair back with a scarf in preference to anything more elaborate. But because none of this took very much time she was ready and waiting far too soon, and felt almost sick with suspense by the time James rang their bell to say he was waiting downstairs.

Waved off by her friends as though she were going away on honeymoon, Rose found James leaning against an elderly sports car.

'Hi,' she said breathlessly. 'Nice wheels.'

He patted the bonnet possessively. 'She's been out of commission for a while, waiting for spare parts. I've just got her back from the garage.' He held the door for her. 'I put the hood up to make sure you stay dry for once tonight.'

Knowing that Con and Fabia were glued to the window two floors up, watching them as they left, Rose huddled down in the bucket seat, simmering with the secret excitement that affected her from time to time in present company.

'How's the foot?' James asked. 'No infection?'

'No. It's fine. A bit sore, but I'll live.'

The lights had already gone down at the Cameo before they arrived. Once they were seated in the dark together Rose sat perfectly still, staring at the screen, hardly able

to believe this was happening. Gradually her excitement subsided, allowing her to translate the subtitles sufficiently well to follow the plot. If James discussed it afterwards, she reminded herself, the so-called fan of foreign-language movies had better be able to make intelligent responses.

When the film was over they went outside to find rain coming down in sheets again.

'Can you run for the car on that foot, or shall I carry you?' James asked as they stood in the foyer.

'I can run,' she assured him, and he took her hand and raced with her to the car.

'It's early,' he said as he drove off. 'Fancy a drink and a sandwich?'

Did she!

'Yes, please,' said Rose with enthusiasm.

'We could go to a pub, or you could come back to my place again, if you like,' he said casually.

'Your place,' she said promptly. By some miracle they hadn't seen anyone from college at the cinema, but it might be a different story if they went to a pub in the town. And Rose couldn't endure the thought of other people watching them, speculating on their relationship. Which wasn't a relationship, really. Not yet.

When they arrived outside the familiar house the door flew open as James hurried Rose towards it, revealing an elderly lady with grey curly hair and a beaming smile of welcome.

'I heard the car,' she explained. 'Come in quickly out of that rain. Now then, James, introduce me.'

'Mrs Bradley this is Rose. Rose Dryden. She's a student up at the college.'

'How nice to meet you, my dear. Let me take that wet coat.'

Rose murmured something polite, and obediently surrendered her jacket, feeling a little shy as James's landlady cast an approving eye over her.

'We decided on coffee and a sandwich here instead of a pub, Mrs B,' said James, smiling.

'I should think so, too, the prices they charge. There's some ham in the fridge, James, and cheese and salad greens. Take what you want.' Mrs Bradley gave them a motherly smile. 'I'll leave you to it, and get back to my television.'

James took Rose into the immaculate, modernised kitchen at the end of the hall and handed her a loaf. 'Can you cut bread?'

'Not unless you want doorsteps. You slice, I'll butter and fill.'

'Done.' He ruffled her hair indulgently, then took a selection of sandwich ingredients from the fridge and laid them out on the counter. 'No bacon tonight.'

'Which of this lot do you fancy?'

'Everything.'

While they discussed the film Rose assembled thin wafers of ham and cheese, watercress, chives and two varieties of lettuce, used some dressing she found in the fridge, then fastened the creations together with toothpicks James produced from a cupboard.

When she'd finished Rose wasn't given long to wonder where they were expected to eat. James put the platter of sandwiches on a tray, added a couple of plates, some linen napkins provided by his landlady for the occasion, then told Rose to go upstairs ahead of him to his room.

So Mrs Bradley had no objection to female visitors.

James eyed his guest closely as he switched on lamps. 'What's the matter, Rose? Would you prefer to eat down in the kitchen?'

'Is that what you normally do?'

'No. Apart from the Sunday roast I fetch my meals up here on a tray.' He shook his head in mock reproof. 'Stop worrying, Rose. You look good enough to eat, it's true, but I promise I'll restrict myself to the sandwiches. You could have chosen the pub instead of coming here,' he pointed out.

Crimson-faced, but comforted by the thought that at least she wasn't sweaty with it for once, Rose smiled at him in contrition. 'Sorry. I was just wondering about your Mrs Bradley's views on female visitors.'

'Pleased as Punch when I warned her that I might be bringing you back tonight. Apparently she thinks it high time I had a "nice young lady".' He put a sandwich on a plate and handed it to her. 'Surely you've been in some other guy's room on campus?'

'Yes, but not on my own.'

James waved her to the sofa and sat down beside her to eat. 'I can't believe one of those hopefuls buzzing round you hasn't asked you out.'

Rose nodded, mouth full.

'Did you go?'

'No.'

'Why not?'

Rose glared at him. 'You ask a lot of questions!'

James grinned. 'Sorry, sorry. Just interested.'

'Edgy, you mean, because I said yes to you but refused the others,' she said bluntly.

He threw back his head and laughed. 'Straight between the eyes!'

Rose went on with her sandwich, then gave him a side-long look as he sobered. 'I suppose it's my turn to say "stop worrying", now.'

'I'm not worried,' he assured her. 'But I can't help wondering why I got lucky when the others didn't.'

Rose bristled. 'Unlike you, they don't share my taste in films.' Then, casting caution to the winds she said, 'And now you've brought the subject up, James Sinclair, your interest in girls is so famously non-existent how come *I* "got lucky", as you so charmingly put it.'

'Ouch—the rose has thorns!' James gave her a very straight look. 'Because you're different. No artifice, no tricks. Not like a girl at all, in fact.'

No tricks! Rose burned with guilt. 'I'm a very normal sort of female,' she warned him.

'Don't think I hadn't noticed,' he said dryly, and got up. 'Which would you like, tea, coffee or beer?'

'Tea, please.' She pulled a face. 'I drink lager when I go out, but I don't really like it.'

James wagged a finger at her. 'Then don't drink it, for Pete's sake. Go for mineral water or fruit juice.'

'It seems so childish!'

He smiled as he made the tea. 'What does that matter, Rose? Be yourself. And remember,' he added, 'it's a great advantage for a girl with your looks to keep a clear head when the men you're with are drinking.'

'True,' she conceded, elated by the casual compliment, 'but the ones I know best are a *fairly* temperate bunch— most of them too broke to drink all that much, anyway.'

'But there's a Valentine dance in the union shortly. If you're going, take care. It's been a pretty rowdy occasion in the past,' he warned, and handed her a mug of tea. 'You haven't finished your sandwich.'

'Give me time.'

James sat down beside her, patting her knee. 'Are we friends again, then?'

'Of course we are,' she said cheerfully. 'Can't alienate my coach!'

He eyed her askance. 'Is *that* how you think of me?'

'Not entirely.' Rose munched deliberately for a while before giving him a demure little smile. 'You've been so kind to me I suppose I look on you as a sort of older brother.'

James spluttered violently, spilled some scalding tea in his lap and leapt up with a howl.

Rose jumped up to dab him down with Mrs Bradley's linen napkin, but with a choked sound he thrust her hands away and raced from the room. She stared after him blankly, then sat down again to drink tea until James came back, wearing battered old cords.

Rose eyed him warily. 'Are you all right?'

'Yes. My jeans suffered the most—I'd just washed the damn things, too.' He sat down again, arms folded, his straight black brows drawn together in a heavy frown. After a while he turned towards her, and took her hand. 'Look, Rose, I think we'd better have a little talk.'

She stiffened. Had he got wind of the plan somehow? 'What about?'

To her surprise he shifted uneasily, his eyes glued to their clasped hands. 'Look, from what you told me I take it there hasn't been much of a male presence in your life, right?'

Rose relaxed a little. 'Right.'

'This aunt you live with, does she have any male friends?'

'Yes, several,' she said, surprised. 'Minerva goes out quite a lot. Dinner, concerts, that kind of thing.'

'But I assume you went to a girls' school?' he went on doggedly.

'Yes, I did. What *is* this?'

'Bear with me. Did you know any boys?'

'Of course I did. Blokes from the neighboring school. One of them was even my boyfriend at one time—brother of my best friend, Bel.'

He relaxed a little. 'Nice lad?'

'Mark's very nice indeed.' Rose turned dancing eyes on him. 'James, I do know about the birds and the bees, if that's where this is leading.'

'I'm sure you do. But in my opinion you need a bit of advice from the male point of view.' He cleared his throat, still staring down at their hands. 'Rose, are you a virgin?'

She tore her hand away and jumped up, her eyes blazing. 'What business is that of yours?'

James leapt to bar her way to the door.

'Out of my way!' she ordered furiously. 'I'm going.'

'Calm *down*, Rose. Let me explain. I can't help worrying about you.'

'Well, you needn't,' she snapped. 'I can take care of myself.'

He thrust his hands through his mop of dark hair. 'Hell, this is embarrassing. Listen! Why do you think I rushed out of the room just now?'

Rose simmered down a little. 'Because you spilt your tea, of course.'

James smiled ruefully. 'That was part of it. But the main reason was my—er, response when you touched me in that particular danger zone. You just can't do that kind of thing. Oh, God, now you've gone red again. Does it help that I'm hot under the collar, too?'

Rose didn't know whether to laugh or cry. So she laughed. And James laughed with her, relieved, and caught her in a hug.

'Promise me you won't do that with anyone else!' he ordered.

That was an easy one.

'I promise.' She gasped, her eyes dancing as they met his. 'And just so you won't stay awake all night wondering, I am.'

'You're what?' he said huskily.

'What you said.'

Suddenly neither of them was laughing any more. Rose tensed as she saw the grey eyes narrow to a gleam which rang alarm bells in her head. But she couldn't have moved to save her life. Time seemed to stop as James slowly bent his head to hers. When he kissed her at last the touch of his lips on hers was gentle enough, but it triggered a response that swept through them both like a bush fire. He pulled her close and kissed her again, no longer gentle, and she leaned into him, her lips parting in welcome to his tongue, and instantly both of them were breathing harder than at any time on the track. James picked her up and sat down with her on his lap, his mouth moving over her face, feature by feature, as he undid the scarf to run his hands through her hair.

'This wasn't supposed to happen,' he whispered.

'I know,' she said breathlessly. 'You've got no time for girls.'

'Other girls,' he corrected, and kissed her with renewed heat.

Rose, in seventh heaven, thrust guilt from her mind and gave herself up to the utter joy of James's lips on hers and his body hard and hot against her own as he fought to restrict himself to kisses. She realised, deeply touched, that he was gripping her waist tight to prevent his hands moving higher, and returned his kisses with such wanton fervour by way of appreciation he broke away at last and sat with his head in his hands, breathing raggedly.

'I swear I didn't bring you here for this,' he said hoarsely.

Rose, speechless for a variety of reasons, put out a hand to touch his. He seized it without looking at her.

'Are you all right?' he asked eventually.

'Yes,' she managed.

James turned with a questioning look which made Rose conscious of hair all over the place and a mouth that felt swollen. 'Has that happened before to you?' he asked harshly.

She pretended to misunderstand. 'I've been kissed enough. But never like that.'

'What *was* it like?' He eyed her challengingly. 'Do you still think of me as a brother?'

He needed to *ask*? Rose gave him a crooked little smile. 'I just felt as though I'd die if you stopped kissing me.'

His eyes shut in such obvious anguish she put up a hand in alarm.

'Hey—don't worry, James. It was just a few kisses. If that's a problem for you just drive me back and I'll forget they ever happened.'

He raised a dark, disbelieving eyebrow. 'Can you do that?'

'If I have to.'

'Like hell you will!' He yanked her onto his lap and began to kiss her again, pushed her sweater aside to kiss her neck: swift, travelling kisses that set her heart hammering as he slid his hands beneath the heavy white wool to cup her breasts. Rose gasped as he laid them bare and caressed nipples which hardened at their first contact with a man's experienced, coaxing fingers. Streaks of fire shot through her, and she thrust herself against him, locking her hands behind his neck as she gave him back kiss for

open-mouthed kiss, until at last it was she who pulled away, and he buried his face in her hair and held her close.

'This is all wrong,' he groaned. 'I shouldn't be doing this.'

Rose stroked his hair. 'It was just a kiss or two, James.'

'But I wanted—still want—a lot more than that.'

'So do I.'

He sat up abruptly, his face stern. 'Don't say things like that, Rose.'

She met his eyes head-on. 'I'm just making it clear I'm as much to blame as you.'

'If I hadn't started it would you have kissed *me*?'

'No way!' Rose smiled crookedly. 'I didn't think you—well—thought of me that way.'

'I didn't think I did, either.' James shook his head slowly. 'It's Greg's fault.'

'Your friend at the track?'

'Yes. When he offered to carry you back this morning I could have thumped him. I almost told him to take his hands off—because you belonged to me.' He smiled a little. 'You can laugh if you like.'

Rose shook her head, a dazed look in her eyes. She slid off his lap and stood up, at a loss how to respond to his mind-blowing revelation. 'It's getting late. I should go.'

James eyed her moodily as he got up. 'You won't be able to run with that foot for a day or two.'

'No.' Rose began tying back her hair to hide her desolation.

'What do you usually do in the evenings?'

'Go for a drink in the union, or see a film. Con's got a VCR so sometimes we rent a video instead.' Rose gave him a wry little smile. 'And sometimes, believe it or not, I just stay in my room and work.'

He smoothed a stray lock of hair back from her fore-

head, his smile so openly possessive her pulse-rate rocketed. 'So you're not here just to have a good time like some of the others. What do you have in mind to do when you—?'

'Grow up?' said Rose tartly.

'I was going to say qualify, Miss Dryden,' he contradicted, in such ultra refined Morningside accents Rose giggled.

'Miss Jean Brodie to the life.'

'Doubting my sexual preferences again?' he growled, and pulled her into his arms. 'I thought I'd convinced you.'

'Convince me again!' she whispered, and he let out an explosive breath and kissed her so fiercely the difference in their height almost overbalanced them.

'I was wrong,' James groaned at last. 'You're very definitely a girl, complete with a full set of everything to drive a man crazy. And now it *is* time you went.' He thrust her away. 'Go and tidy up in the bathroom. Mrs Bradley will probably want to say goodnight.'

On the short journey back to the flat both of them discussed the film with determination, doing their best to behave as though their passionate exchange had never happened, and when James parked at the entrance to the building Rose said goodnight, shot out of the car and ran up the stairs as fast as her sore foot allowed.

'You're late,' said Con, looking worried.

Fabia pulled Rose into their room, her eyes sparkling. 'How was it? Did he hold your hand in the dark? Did he kiss you goodnight this time?'

'For heaven's sake,' said Rose, laughing. 'I don't ask what you're up to when you're out with Will.'

'Just as well!' Con rolled her eyes, then smiled affectionately. 'You obviously had a great time.'

Rose nodded blissfully. 'We went back to his place. His landlady's nice. She had things ready for us to make sandwiches.'

Fabia pounced. 'Where did you eat them?'

'In his room again.'

'Are we talking bedroom, here?'

'No. It's just a sitting room. He must sleep somewhere else.' Rose yawned. 'Now, if it's all right by you, I'd like to go to bed and get off this foot.'

'Is it still sore?' demanded Con. 'Sit down and show me.'

Rose obediently removed sock and shoe and tore off the dressing, wiggling her foot at the others.

'Seems all right,' said Fabia. 'A bit red and tender-looking, though. I'll slosh on some antiseptic and stick another plaster on for you.'

'You definitely can't go running again for a bit,' said Con regretfully. 'Has Sinclair said anything about another meeting?'

'No.' Rose looked guilty. 'I got out of the car in a rush so he wouldn't think I was hinting at one.'

The phone saved her from a storm of scolding from her friends.

'Yes, she's here,' said Con, eyes sparkling. 'Hang on a second.'

She tossed the receiver to Rose, hauled Fabia bodily out of the room and shut the door.

'Why the blazes did you chase off so fast, Rose?' Demanded James irately. 'You didn't even give me a chance to kiss you goodnight.'

Rose said nothing.

James waited, then sighed in exasperation. 'It's like getting blood out of stone.' He paused. 'I suppose I frightened you silly.'

Was he serious?

'No,' Rose assured him.

'So if I promise to stay at arm's length you'll come out with me again?'

To the ends of the earth, if he liked.

'Yes.'

'Is there someone else in the room?' he demanded.

'No.'

'Then *talk* to me, Rose.'

'What do you want me to say?'

'That you enjoyed our evening as much as I did.'

'You know very well that I did. Every single minute of it,' she added fiercely, in case he was in any doubt.

'That's *better*,' he said with satisfaction. 'So listen. To-morrow I train with the team, but how about the next night?'

'OK.'

'What would you like to do?'

'Would Mrs Bradley object if I just came round to your place for an hour?' And if he took it for granted she wanted him to make love to her again she didn't care. It was the truth.

'Mrs Bradley thought you were a very charming young lady,' he said, in refined Edinburgh accents again, and Rose giggled. 'I'm in full agreement,' he added, his voice deepening. 'I'll come for you at seven.'

'I'll look forward to it.'

'So will I,' he agreed, with a note in his voice that brought the colour rushing to her cheeks. 'Goodnight, Rose.'

Restless at the memory, Rose got out of bed and went to the kitchen to make more tea. How naive she'd been all those years ago. Young and so trusting she'd been caught

in her own snare. With not the slightest hope of success to start with she'd deliberately set out to make James Sinclair fall in love with her, and succeeded beyond her wildest expectations. But in the process she'd fallen help-lessly in love in return. Which had been inevitable. If she hadn't had a secret crush on the legendary Sinclair from the start nothing would have induced her to fall in with Con's plan. But that, in common with many other aspects of her love affair, was a secret she'd never shared with anyone. Not even with James.

From the first Rose was obdurate about going out in pub-lic with James. Their morning runs and the brief hours spent in his room were the only meetings she would agree to, even repeat trips to the cinema were vetoed in case they were less lucky than the first time, and met someone they knew.

'Why are you so dead set against being seen with me?' he demanded irritably.

'Because you're Sinclair, famous for not socialising with girls. And I'm a lowly first-year. So all your friends—not to mention mine—would be watching every move, tongues hanging out, if they saw us out together.' Rose touched his cheek with a placating hand. 'I just can't bear the idea of everyone speculating about us, spoiling things. Making more of our—our friendship than it is.'

'Friendship,' he growled, and pulled her onto his lap. 'Is this how you behave with all your friends, Miss Dryden?' He kissed her hungrily, his hands busy with her shirt buttons, and Rose moaned as his fingers found her nipples, her response arching her back. James bent his head to take instant advantage, his grazing teeth and clever fingers causing pleasure so intense she could hardly endure it.

Because this was the night Mrs Bradley went to her bridge club they had the house to themselves, a fact Rose was burningly aware of as James made love to her with mounting demand. They had cooked supper together in the kitchen and eaten it there for once, but, sitting knee to knee at the table, the tension between them had increased steadily throughout the meal until by the time they'd reached the privacy of his room they had fallen on each other the moment they were through the door. Kisses and increasingly intimate caresses were the extent of their mutual exploration of each other. So far. But by this time Rose was so madly in love she knew that if James wanted more she would give him everything he wanted. Because she wanted it too. So much it kept her awake at night.

After a while James thrust her from him and retreated to the far corner of the sofa, breathing raggedly. 'This is dangerous,' he said hoarsely.

Rose turned her head away, letting her streaming hair hide her face from him. 'Why?'

'You know very well why.'

'Are you saying I'm a tease?'

'No. But I'm not made of stone. So we can't see each other alone like this any more or the inevitable will happen.' He slanted a half-veiled glance at her. 'I suppose there's no chance of your turning up at the Sceptre on Saturday after the away match?'

Rose shuddered. 'No fear.'

James got up to tower over her, his eyes slitted. 'Why not?'

Rose shook her hair back, turning her face up to him in appeal. 'I keep telling you why not. I'd rather people didn't know we're seeing each other.'

'Is that what we're doing?'

She flushed. 'Sort of.'

'Which just about sums it up.' He glared at her. '*I* would be only too happy to be seen out with you. While you can't stand the thought of it, which does damn all for my self-esteem, lady. I suppose if you lived in actual hall, instead of the flat, I wouldn't even be allowed to pick you up and take you home.'

'No,' she admitted miserably.

'In that case what the hell's the point of it all?' He scowled. 'I refuse to be the skeleton in your cupboard, Rose Dryden. So it's ultimatum time. Come and join me at the Sceptre on Saturday, in front of your friends *and* mine. Or we pack it in—stop seeing each other altogether.'

Rose gazed at him, stricken. Then she got up and took her coat from the back of a chair. 'I just want to stay as we are,' she said miserably, hoping he'd sweep her into his arms and kiss her senseless.

But James did nothing of the kind. His face set in grim lines she'd never seen before, he preceded her down the stairs and took his car keys from the hall table. He opened the front door, and ushered her through it in a hostile silence he kept up all the way back to the flat. When he stopped the car outside her entrance Rose unfastened her seat belt, purposely taking time over it for once to give him a chance to thaw.

'Goodnight, James. Thank you for supper.'

'Goodbye, little girl,' he said coldly, and, far from thawing towards her, drove away the moment Rose closed the passenger door.

Because the flat was empty when she got in, Rose went to bed without interrogation, and cried her eyes out, unheard. Next morning she got up as usual for the early-morning run, but this time James wasn't waiting for her, and it was Greg Prosser, James's rugby-playing team

mate, who joined her on the track after she'd completed four endless circuits. Rose gave him a cheery wave and left before she could burst into tears again. When she got back to the flat she took a long shower, then had toast and coffee waiting when her yawning flatmates joined her.

'Right,' said Rose, cutting straight to the chase. 'I think we can all agree that the plan worked?'

'It certainly did—like a charm,' said Con, pushing her hair out of her eyes.

'Mission accomplished, then. But now it's over. If you remember, the idea was to make James Sinclair fall in love with me, not the other way round. So that's it.' Rose smiled brightly. 'Time I got myself back into circulation again.'

Con and Fabia were loud with argument against this, but Rose was adamant. She would not, she declared, be seeing James Sinclair again. And did her utmost to hide her desolation every time the phone rang for one of the other girls. But James, it soon became evident, was not a man to waste time on lost causes. Rose reverted to evenings spent in the union, but by the weekend she was missing James so badly she was willing to agree to anything he wanted, just as long as they could be together again. To demonstrate her change of heart she went to the Sceptre with the others, on fire with barely contained impatience as she waited for the rugby crowd to arrive. But when they did James wasn't with them. Rose's disappointment was so intense she felt physically ill. She forced herself to laugh and flirt as though James's non-appearance was the last thing on her mind, but inside she was hurting badly. And Con, whose eyes saw more than most, tapped Rose on the arm and suggested they left.

'Fabia's coming back with Hargreaves, as usual,' she said. 'So come on. Let's get out of here.'

On the way home Rose confessed that it was Sinclair who'd put a summary end to things between them. 'He wanted us to go out together like a normal couple.'

'And you *refused*?' said Con incredulously. 'Are you out of your mind? Most girls would jump at the chance.'

Rose nodded miserably. 'I know. And I'm sorry now, believe me. But at the time I couldn't bear the thought of everyone watching and making bets on whether we were sleeping together. No one would care a damn if it was some other bloke, of course. But because it's Sinclair it's different.' She swallowed hard. 'I never dreamed he'd stop seeing me altogether, Con. Which serves me right.'

'So ring him.'

Rose's eyes lit with a steely gleam. 'No, I can't do that. Not now.'

'Why not, for heaven's sake?'

'If Sinclair had really wanted to see me he'd have turned up tonight on the off chance I'd be there. He didn't, so that's that. I've got my pride.'

Con smiled in approval. 'Good girl. He's not the only man in the world, Rosie. And it's Valentine's day next week. You'll be knee-deep in partners at the dance.'

To Rose's surprise she received as many cards as Fabia and Con. The flat was awash with red hearts and sentimental verses alongside jokier offerings with messages ranging from the cute to the downright rude. But the card that Rose liked the most was an exquisite watercolour of a single red rose, with no verse at all. And to add to her secret excitement a matching live bloom arrived for her during the morning.

'A rose for Rose,' said the message on the florist's card.

'Dear me, I wonder who that's from?' said Con, smiling.

'No point in wondering,' said Fabia with relish. 'Mystery is the point of it all.'

Rose tried to convince herself that neither card nor rose was from James. Miles Challoner, who fancied himself as a Byronic type, was probably responsible. A thought which dissipated her excitement very thoroughly. In comparison with James Sinclair all other males in her immediate vicinity seemed immature and uninteresting, and with no chance of seeing him there she got ready for the dance later without much enthusiasm. Her dress, bought in Chastlecombe during the January sales, was a little sleeveless number sprigged with rosebuds on black silk, with fluted hem and plunging V-neck, and was pronounced such a success by her friends Rose's spirits lifted a little as Fabia did her make-up. Tonight she would have fun and enjoy herself. And forget James Sinclair.

CHAPTER SIX

TO MAKE the evening more of an occasion Con and Fabia had persuaded Rose it would be a good idea to invite a few people round first for a snack supper. By early evening the small flat was a crush of young men in dinner jackets and girls in party frocks. The three hostesses passed round bits and pieces bought from a supermarket to accompany a sparing supply of bubbly wine from the same source, and by the time they got to the dance the entire group was in tearing spirits. While Rose, if not quite as carefree as the others, was feeling a lot better than she'd done for a while, and knew she looked good, for the simple reason that so many of her partners told her so. Miles, as expected, was much in evidence, and extravagant with his praise of her dress.

'Clever girl—roses for Rose,' he whispered in her ear, unaware that he'd damped his partner down so badly she wanted to run from the floor in tears.

Of course James hadn't sent the rose. But like a fool she'd let herself hope he had. Just for a while. She smiled up at Miles with such determined animation he responded with enthusiasm, crushing her so close against him the studs of his dress shirt prodded her painfully through the silk. When the band finished the set Miles put a possessive arm round her to steer her back to the noisy group at their table and Rose slid into a chair next to Con to join in heated, laughing speculation about who had sent Valentine cards to whom. When the college band started up again with a slow number, Will Hargreaves pulled

Fabia to her feet, then stood rooted to the spot, staring at a new arrival near the door. Con muttered incredulously as all eyes turned in the same direction. But Rose couldn't hear a thing over the heartbeat drumming against her ribs at the sight of James Sinclair in formal black and white. With a red rose in his lapel. He began to thread his way through the crowd, causing an audible stir when he came to a halt in front of her.

'Dance with me, Rose?' he said, smiling.

In a flash the evening was transformed. She nodded formally in assent, and went into James's arms like a homing bird, never even noticing the stricken look on Miles Challoner's face.

The knowledge that they were attracting attention on all sides no longer mattered a jot to Rose. Now she was in James Sinclair's arms again the rest of the world could go hang. Unsurprised to find that someone as co-ordinated as James moved well, for a while she just gave herself up to the bliss of the moment, but when they were far enough way from the band to talk she looked up into his intent face.

'You dance well, Sinclair.'

'The academy in charge of my education insisted on such niceties,' he informed her, in mock-refined accents she found so irresistible. Rose gave a bubbling little laugh and he smiled down at her in response as he held her closer, and for a moment they could have been alone in the crowded room. 'Are you having a good time?' he asked politely, his eyes saying something so completely different Rose's breathing quickened.

'The best,' she assured him, which was the simple truth now she was dancing with James Sinclair. 'We had a sort of supper party before the dance to put everyone in the mood.'

'You didn't invite *me*!'

'Of course I didn't.'

'Why not?'

'You know perfectly well why,' she said, her eyes flashing, and he smiled, in the slow, igniting way that took her breath away.

'Do you know how much I've missed you, Rose?'

She gazed up at him steadily. 'Half as much as I've missed you, maybe?'

His eyes blazed as he bent closer. 'Let's go home.'

'Now?'

'Right now. Mrs Bradley's away on holiday, and...' he bent to whisper in her ear '...as you know very well, I make a great bacon sandwich.'

Rose looked up at him for a long considering moment, then noticed a pulse throbbing beside his mouth. So he wasn't sure she'd say yes.

'Ah, well, I never could resist a bacon sandwich,' she said lightly. 'I'll fetch my coat.'

The light in his eyes set Rose on fire. 'I'll be outside. Hurry,' he added urgently.

They were the centre of attention as they parted in the middle of the floor, but Rose didn't even notice. When she emerged with her coat Fabia and Con were waiting for her, looking anxious, their relief touching when Rose told them she was leaving with James.

'Don't wait up,' she said blithely.

'Be careful, love,' said Con, plainly worried by Rose's undisguised radiance.

'Don't be such a killjoy,' admonished Fabia. 'Our little flower has been wilting a bit lately. I prefer her this way. Have fun, Rosebud. See you tomorrow—or whenever.'

James was waiting outside by his car. He settled Rose in the low bucket seat, then got in and leaned over to kiss

her fiercely before starting the car. 'Are you angry with me?' he demanded.

'For giving me a kiss?' Rose could afford to be facetious now that all was right with the world again.

'No. For making the next best thing to a public declaration in there just now.' He slanted a triumphant look at her as he drove off. 'I decided it was time to take the war into the enemy's camp.'

'I'm not your enemy, James.'

'You defeated *me*.' He smiled straight ahead. 'I retired to plan new strategy, and decided the best thing was to give you no choice. If I came in black-tie gear to the union—which is not a habit of mine—and asked Miss Rose Dryden to dance, I knew no one would be left in doubt about our relationship.'

'Except me,' said Rose.

'If you wait until we get home I'll explain in full.' He touched a hand fleetingly to hers. 'I've missed you at the track.'

'Not every day, you haven't,' she said tartly. 'I went there the first morning. After our—our disagreement. But you were missing.' She turned accusing eyes on his profile. 'Was that a little dressage, to show me you were calling the shots?'

'Right.'

'It worked.'

'Wrong. I had to fight myself tooth and nail to keep from ringing you afterwards.'

'But you won.'

'On the contrary. I lost.' He shot her a brooding look as they arrived in the familiar house. 'After a couple of days without seeing you I was tempted to ring you and say I'd play it any way you wanted. But, chauvinist that I am, I needed you back on my own terms. My campaign

was to be subtle. I'd send you the card and the rose, and then, when you were in a totally weakened state of resistance, I'd invade the dance, complete with rose in my buttonhold like a total idiot, and carry you off the field—what's the matter? Why are you looking at me like that?'

Rose gazed at him with eyes like stars. 'You sent me the card with the rose on it? *And* the rose from the florist?'

He gave her a wry grin. 'Don't tell anyone! My street cred would suffer if it came out that Sinclair sent flowers and Valentine cards.'

'In the plural?'

'Hell, no! Just to you, Rose.' He scowled. 'And just who *did* you think sent them?'

'Miles Challoner.'

'The twit who was all over you tonight?'

'He was certainly *not* all over me,' she retorted hotly.

'It looked like it to me. But why did you think it was him?'

'I suppose he was just referring to my dress. He said something about roses for Rose, like the message on the card, so I crossed you off the list.' She smiled at him demurely. 'He must have sent one of the other cards. Yours was only one of half a dozen I received, Mr Sinclair.'

James leapt out of the car and strode round to pull her from her seat. 'Rattling my cage, Miss Dryden?' He hurried her into the house, then stood looking at her under the hall light. 'Do you want that sandwich?' he whispered.

Rose shook her head impatiently. He drew in a deep breath, removed her coat, then took her hand to pull her upstairs with him, both of them stumbling in sudden haste. When they reached his room James lifted her off her feet against him, backing into the door to close it as he kissed

her with an unrestrained longing Rose responded to in kind, her caressing hands as demanding as his.

'Wait!' gasped James, and held her away from him, turning her so that he could slide down the zip of her dress. 'My instinct is to tear it off you,' he said into the back of her neck, 'but it seems a shame when you look so good in it.' He kissed the hollow behind her ear, sending a great shiver through her as he lifted her clear of the dress. Then he stood utterly still, his eyes devouring her as she took the pins from her hair. 'You look even better out of it,' he said hoarsely.

Instead of her usual chain-store underwear Rose was wearing brief scraps of pearl-coloured silk Minerva had given her at Christmas, and felt passionately grateful for her forethought when she saw James couldn't take his eyes off her.

'Are you just going to look at me all night?' she asked unsteadily, shaking her hair back, and he closed the space between them, holding her so close their combined heart-beat thumped in unison.

'Tell me this is what you really want, Rose,' he said, his face oddly stern as his eyes locked with hers.

'I do. More than anything in the world,' she said, with such utter certainty he picked her up, laid her on the bed and stripped off the shirt she'd been trying to pull off him with such haste a moment before.

Rose smiled with sudden delight as she realised where she was. 'This is your sofa, James!'

'By day,' he agreed, responding with the slow smile she'd missed so badly. 'At night it's a bed. My bed. And,' he added softly, letting himself down beside her, 'you're the first to share it with me.'

Rose gave a deep, relishing sigh as his arms locked around her. Then she remembered something his ought to

know. 'James,' she whispered, then buried her face against his chest.

He tensed. 'What is it, sweetheart? Second thoughts?'

'No!' Rose drew away and met his eyes, her face hot. 'But now seems a good time to mention that Minerva sent me off for contraceptive pills last summer, before I came here.'

His eyes lit with laughter. 'How very practical. Your aunt was obviously a student herself, once.'

Rose nodded, rubbing her flushed cheek against his. 'She warned me that the main student pastimes are drinking and sleeping, quite a lot of the last bit with each other.'

'I'd like to meet this aunt of yours!' James looked amused. 'Though wasn't she worried you'd rush off to put the pills to the test?'

'No. Minerva made it plain she expected me to be— well, discriminate.'

'And you have been?' he said softly.

'Up to now, yes,' said Rose candidly, and smiled into his eyes as she wriggled closer. 'I've certainly never slept with a man before.'

'Did I mention sleeping?'

'No. Which is just as well—I'm not the least bit tired.'

James gave a smothered, delighted laugh, and kissed her, and Rose locked her hands behind his head, surrendering her mouth and body to him with trusting lack of restraint as he removed the last of their clothes. But when they held each other close in full, naked contact, for the first time at last, Rose was startled to find that James was shaking almost as much as she was.

'I haven't done this before myself, but I was rather hoping *you* had,' she said in dismay.

'Of course I have.' He kissed the hollow between her

breasts. 'But never with someone new to it all. At this moment I want you more than I've ever wanted anything in my entire life, but I can't make it perfect for you because I'll have to hurt you.'

'It can't hurt that much,' she said, with a confidence which proved misplaced, because though James kissed and caressed her at such length she thought she'd die if he didn't take her at last, Rose couldn't control an involuntary gasp of anguish when he did.

'Sweetheart,' he groaned, and lay very still, giving Rose time to adjust to the overwhelming intimacy of physical possession.

'I want you to move,' she said gruffly after a moment or two, and James obliged, with a lack of haste which took superhuman effort, Rose could tell, as her hands smoothed the knotted tension of his shoulders. But when she began to experience delicious ripples of sensation in response to the rhythm of his loving James kissed her fiercely, moving with new, demanded urgency, and Rose thrust her hips against him in instinctive, wanton response. But all too soon he groaned like a man in pain as the inexorable delight defeated him, and he buried his face in her neck and gasped in the throes of release as she held him tightly, glorying in the fact that he was suddenly so helpless in her arms.

At last James raised his head and looked deep into her eyes. 'I'm so *sorry*, sweetheart. I wanted it to be so good for you—'

'Oh, but it was,' she assured him, with such fervour she felt him relax against her.

'Next time,' he assured her, 'it will be as wonderful for you as it was for me, I promise.'

And, sooner than Rose had thought humanly possible, even for a superbly fir specimen like James Sinclair, he

began to make love to her again. And this time the heat built up slowly, mounting inside her until every inch of her responsive, throbbing body took fire as he coaxed her to heights of physical pleasure which left her lying limp in his arms afterwards, sated from her first experience of sexual fulfilment.

'You were right,' she breathed against his chest. 'It *was* wonderful. Out of this world.' She took a deep, relishing breath. 'I had no idea it would be like that.'

'Neither had I.' James drew the covers over them and held her close, but Rose drew away to look at him.

'You must have known!'

He shook his head, his eyes so gloatingly possessive she shivered with delight. 'This was different. Just knowing that everything we did was the first time for you rocketed me to such an incredible state of arousal it was all new to me, too. But second time round I managed to stay in control. For a while, at least.' He smoothed the tumbled hair from her face, and sighed heavily. 'Rose, it's very late. I don't want to let your go, but it's time I drove you back.'

'I suppose so,' she said without enthusiasm, and wriggled closer.

'If you do that,' he said breathlessly, 'I'll never let you go.'

On the way back to campus later James sprang a surprise. 'Mrs Bradley's away at her daughter's place for a week. Come and stay with me until she comes back.'

'Won't she mind when she finds out?' said Rose, utterly ravished by the idea.

'I don't know. I've never had anyone to stay before. But I'm sure she won't.' James slanted a grin at her. 'As I told you before, she thinks it's high time I had a "nice young lady" like you.'

If only the young lady were as nice as he believed, thought Rose guiltily, fighting off a sudden need to confess.

'Well? Will you come?' he repeated.

She eyed him doubtfully. 'Won't I interfere with your work?'

'Bring some of your own. And if we don't get much work done a little break won't do either of us any harm. In fact,' he added, as he drew up outside her building, 'the kind of break I've got in mind will do me a hell of a lot of good. Will you come?'

'Try to keep me away!' said Rose recklessly, and kissed him with a fervour which met with such approval it was a long time before James let her go.

'I'll be round for you in the morning,' he said huskily. 'About ten. Be ready.'

When Rose crept into the flat it was in darkness. She collected pyjamas and dressing gown, then lay in a hot bath, her eyes dreamy as she relieved the incredible events of the night. So that was what it was all about. Viewing it from a theoretical point of view in the past, Rose had always found it difficult to understand why the act of love was something people wanted to do so much. Now she knew exactly why. And pitied females who'd learned about it from lesser men than James. How lucky she was. Though she didn't deserve to be. She'd deliberately set out to make James want her. And, miraculously, he did. Enough to come to the dance tonight and demonstrate it so plainly that now everyone on campus knew that Rose Dryden had somehow managed to bag Sinclair, the man with no time for women.

Rose sat up at last and began to soap herself, her face hot as she found her skin marked with fingerprints in places, which clenched inner muscles at the memory of

how she'd acquired them. She dried herself quickly, pulling on pyjamas in a sudden hurry to get to bed and go through every detail of the enchanted night again.

But when she opened the bathroom door Rose found Con waiting for her, looking anxious.

'Come into our room for a bit, Rose. Fabia's making hot chocolate. Once we heard you come in we just had to know you were all right before we could get some sleep.'

'Everything's fine. Wonderful, in fact,' said Rose, her eyes shining.

'Yes.' Con sighed heavily. I can see that. I just wish I hadn't been responsible for it all. I feel like Dr Frankenstein.'

Rose shook her head. 'It isn't your fault. You didn't force me to carry out your plan. And no offence, Con, but it's James who's responsible for my present state of euphoria.'

'I know!'

'Everyone at the dance knows now,' said Fabia, coming in with a tray. 'Miles looked ready to slit his wrists when you left.' She sighed gustily. 'It was so romantic. Just like Richard Gere and Julia Roberts in *An Officer and a Gentleman*—only Sinclair didn't actually carry you out.'

'And it was Debra Winger not Julia Roberts,' said Con dryly, handing a steaming beaker to Rose.

'Whoever. The effect was the same.' Fabia patted the bed beside her. 'Come and sit down, Rosie. I take it that you and Sinclair are now officially a couple?'

'I suppose so.' Rose took refuge in her drink. 'Actually,' she said into the mug, 'I'm going to stay with him at his place for a few days. His landlady's away.'

Con stared at her aghast. 'For pity's sake, Rose, isn't that going a bit far?' She thrust her hands through her

pale hair. 'Damn. I feel so *responsible*. I wish I'd never mentioned that wretched plan.'

'I'm very glad you did,' said Rose dreamily. 'Otherwise—'

'Otherwise you'd never have come into contact with Sinclair, and I'm beginning to think that might be a jolly good thing!'

'Why, Con?' demanded Fabia. 'Rose had to—er—cut her teeth on someone, some time. So why not Sinclair?'

'Because,' said Con patiently, 'he'll be leaving in the summer, and Rose won't.'

'I'll meet that problem when I come to it,' promised Rose. 'And don't worry, Con. It's no big deal—just a college romance like everyone else's.'

'Not quite! If it hadn't been for that hare-brained plan of mine it would never have happened.'

Rose gave her a reassuring smile. 'Nothing would have made me go along with it if I hadn't wanted to.' She raised her right hand. 'And I solemnly swear I won't drown you both in tears when it's over.'

The following morning Rose told James to come up when he rang the bell, and not only introduced him formally to Con and Fabia, but made coffee for everyone. The four of them spent a lively half-hour together before Rose handed over her bag to James and said she was ready to leave.

'So,' said James, in the car, 'I take it my relationship with Miss Rose Dryden is now well and truly out in the open?'

'Yes,' said Rose serenely. 'At least, I told Con and Fabia to give truthful answers if—when—questions are asked.'

'And what will they say? That I'm your lover?'

Rose shot him an outraged glance. 'No way! They were instructed to say we're just good friends.'

'Which means everyone will definitely think we're lovers,' he said with satisfaction.

'The circles I move in refer to it as "going out together",' said Rose primly.

James gave her a leer. 'Whereas in actual fact we're going to stay in together.'

'All the time?'

He stopped the car in Henley Crescent and reached in the back for her bag. 'We can go to the cinema, if you like, or out for a meal. Never let it be said I'm a skinflint. But it's my turn, now, to draw the line at any venue where we're likely to run into mutual friends. And *not*, like you, because I don't want to be seen in public with you. I don't care a damn about the things that cause *you* such hang-ups. But right now we've got the chance of a whole week together, Rose, and I'm damned if I'm going to waste a second of it with other people.'

'Did you mind staying for coffee at the flat, then?' she asked as they went indoors.

James dumped down her bag and took her into his arms. 'No, because I knew you were showing me that you've finished with all that hole-and-corner stuff you were into before.' He kissed her nose. 'When Mrs Bradley's back you can invite your friends round here, if you like.'

Rose leaned back against his linked hands. 'No. I'd rather not. This is our special, private place. Come to the flat instead, If you'd like to.'

'Of course I'd like to.' James pulled her close. 'I didn't sleep much last night,' he said into her hair.

'Neither did I.' She let out a deep, euphoric sigh. 'I was happy just to stay awake and dream.'

For the first time since either of them had started at university neither James Sinclair nor Rose Dryden did a stroke of actual work for an entire week. Instead they cooked meals together, talking on every subject under the sun, and if the weather was fine they drove out of town to find a place to walk, or if it was wet stayed indoors and listened to music or watched television. On two of the evenings James went off to train with the rugby team, but otherwise they were never apart for more than a minute. And, as though it was something too precious to squander, they made love only at night when James converted his sofa into a bed.

Rose soon learned that her first experience of sexual love had been a mere foretaste of the delight possible when two people came together intent on giving each other pleasure.

'Though pleasure seems a milk-and-water kind of word to describe what happens between us,' said Rose one night, and turned her head to meet the half-veiled eyes intent on her face.

'You're the English student. What word would you choose?' asked James, smoothing a hand down her spine.

'You'll laugh.'

'No I won't.'

She kept her eyes on his. 'For me what happened just now was sheer rapture. And if that sounds too mushy and over the top, you did ask.'

'It sounds exactly right,' he said huskily. 'And I have a theory as to why.'

'Yes?'

'Is there a possibility that what we feel for each other is something a tad more cerebral than lust?' he said gravely.

Rose bit her lip, afraid to commit herself.

'Cat got your tongue?' he asked affably. 'Don't be frightened, Rose. I was merely pointing out that maybe we're attracted to each other for more than just our bodies. Or am I imagining the rapport we enjoy out of bed as well as in it?'

'No.'

James shook his head, resigned. 'Just no?'

'Yes. I mean you're not imagining it.'

'Good.' He trailed a finger down her cheek. 'You do realise that we've spent five days—and nights—in each other's company, now, and except for a heated argument or two on world issues we've lived together in remarkable harmony?'

As if she needed reminding!

'I'm very easy to get on with,' said Rose demurely.

'While I'm anything but, as a rule.'

'I think you are,' she said fiercely, and kissed him.

'Thank you.' He held her closer. 'But if you talked with some of the people I roomed with when I first came here they'd disagree, I promise you. I shared a student flat something like yours, only with three other guys. They were younger than me, straight out of school, first time away from home, and hell-bent on drinking and womanising. While my sole interests were study and sport. It made for a bad situation all round.'

'So what happened?'

'I looked around for lodgings and found this place before my second term. Mrs Bradley was newly widowed, and had decided to let a couple of rooms to students.' He paused. 'I persuaded her to make it one student only. Unlike most students, I had some money of my own.'

'From your father?'

'No. He left everything to my mother. But when she sold the family home Mother made the proceeds over to

me, and Donald put me on to a financial adviser who helped me invest it in a way which gives me an income. Not vast, but enough to compensate Mrs Bradley for taking me on as her sole lodger.'

Rose was impressed. 'Most boys of eighteen with cash would have gone on a spending spree.'

James grinned. 'I was normal enough to splurge on the car when I got back from Oz.'

'That's a relief—nice to know you're human.' She rubbed her cheek against his thoughtfully. 'So you're the only lodger Mrs Bradley's ever had, then?'

'Right.' He turned her face up to his. 'Though I prefer to think of myself as the only lover Rose Dryden's ever had.'

She gazed back at him speculatively. 'You like to be first, or the best, at everything, don't you?'

'I suppose you're right,' he agreed, after thought.

Rose eyes him militantly. 'Is that why you made love to me? Because you knew you'd be the first?'

'Hell no! It was part of it,' he added honestly. 'But the main reason was my gut feeling that you and I belonged together. I just couldn't handle the thought of you with someone else.'

'You wouldn't have had to,' she assured him. 'After meeting you I couldn't handle that, either.'

'Then you feel the same?'

Rose nodded. 'Haven't I demonstrated that with unmaidenly lack of inhibition?'

'Yes. But you haven't said so in as many words.'

'What do you want me to say?'

James pushed her flat and knelt over her, a lock of dark hair falling over his forehead as he captured her hands to spread them wide. 'Tell me exactly how you feel about me,' he demanded.

Rose felt like a moth pinned to a board by the relentless, glittering eyes. 'This isn't fair,' she protested.

'All's fair in love and war,' he assured her, and let himself down on top of her, taking her breath away. 'And this, my darling Rose, is love. On my part, anyway.' He kissed her hungrily, his fingers moving over her in sweeping arpeggios of such exquisite sensation she yielded herself up to him helplessly. Then his mouth followed his fingers to shock her with a caress so new and intimate she gasped and writhed, until at last he surrendered to her frantic pleas and surged between her parted thighs to take them rapidly towards climax.

But at the very brink James held her there, his body suddenly still.

'Say it,' he commanded hoarsely, and Rose, totally beyond coherent thought, obeyed.

'I *love* you,' she gasped, raking her nails down his back, and with a growl of triumph James kissed her fiercely and brought them both to glory.

CHAPTER SEVEN

ROSE woke with tears on her face, aching with the familiar feeling of loss and regret ten years had never managed to dispel. And realised she was propped upright against the pillows with all the lights on. When she remembered exactly why, she noticed the time, and shot out of bed, cursing the anonymous pest as she rushed at top speed instead of making her usual gradual transition into the working day.

'Gosh, you look a bit frazzled,' said Bel, when Rose let her in. 'Good thing I start work early on Saturdays. Here, take the post and shut yourself in the office with some coffee. Late night?' she added archly.

'No. Usual time. I just couldn't get to sleep.' Rose pulled a face. 'But if I look that bad I'll take advantage of your offer. Wouldn't do to frighten off the customers.' She hesitated. 'Look, this is for your ears only, Bel. I've had a couple of anonymous phonecalls.'

Bel grinned. 'Querying your taste in underwear?'

'No. Just a bit of heavy breathing, then he whispers my name and rings off. And, before you ask, the number was withheld.' Rose pulled a face. 'It seems silly now, in broad daylight, but it wasn't at all funny late last night.'

'I should say not! That's *nasty*, Rose. Any idea who it could be?'

'No. But coming on top of the Valentine card and the rose, I don't like it one bit.'

Bel eyed her warily. 'I asked Mark if he'd sent the card, by the way.'

'You did *what*?'

'It wouldn't be the first time.'

'We were just kids then,' Rose protested.

'A fact my brother pointed out. He promises to remember next year.' Bel looked worried. 'But where the heavy breather's concerned unplug the phone tonight and use your mobile instead. What did Anthony say about it?'

'Haven't told him.'

Bel looked disapproving. 'I suppose he denied sending the card and the rose?'

'Emphatically.' Rose smiled wryly. 'In fact he was quite hacked off about the whole thing.'

'I bet he was.' Bel swallowed her coffee and patted Rose on the shoulder. 'I'll hold the fort out there. You stay in here and recover.'

By the end of the day Rose was so tired she couldn't bring herself to cope with the paperwork left from the night before. Sunday morning without fail, she promised it, and went upstairs to fall apart for a while before she even thought of making herself some supper. When the phone rang her heart skipped a beat—until she heard Anthony's voice on the message.

'How are you, Rose?' he asked when she picked up.

'Tired. But otherwise, fine. Busy day today.'

'Rose, have you thought any more about contacting your husband?'

Oh, yes. She'd thought of it. 'I'll get round to it eventually.'

'Remember that you're not obliged to *speak* to him, Rose. After all these years you can just inform him of your intention. Or have a solicitor do it for you.'

'I know all that, Anthony.'

'Do it, then,' he urged. 'I'll call you on Monday.'

Much as Rose rather objected to his peremptory attitude, she knew Anthony was right. It was high time she set herself free. But not to get married again. Once was enough.

She'd known where James Sinclair worked ever since his promotion before the age of thirty to executive vice-presidency of a prestigious merchant bank. Fabia Hargreaves had sent her an article about him she'd cut out from the financial section of one of the Sunday papers. And had unsettled Rose for days afterwards. She knew perfectly well she should to have done something about divorce years before. But the article had revived her stubborn determination to make James the first to act.

While Rose ate her supper she came to a decision. She would write to James at the bank. Then the ball would be in his court. And if he chose not to reply, she would just carry on with the divorce now she knew the court would grant this whether James agreed or not. Not that he had any reason to refuse. He must surely be as eager to be free as she was by this time.

Rose got out her laptop and composed a brief, purposely formal letter, informing James Sinclair of her intention. Then, before she could change her mind, went out in the early evening quiet to post it. After the shops closed Chastlecombe always enjoyed a lull before it came to life again for Saturday night, and the only person Rose met was Elise Fox, who sold expensive clothes and jewellery at the other end of the cobbled arcade. After they'd chatted together for a few minutes Rose went back home, unlocked her private door, then stopped dead in her tracks. A fresh red rose lay on the floor. And it very definitely hadn't been there when she'd left. Rose snatched up the flower with a shaking hand, her heart thumping as she looked up the stairs. Could someone have got in while

she was out? No. Of course not. Her tormentor must have pushed the rose through the letter box while she was talking to Elise.

Suddenly Rose lost her temper. The man might be intent on frightening her, but no way was she going to let him succeed. She slammed the door shut, stormed up the stairs and hurled the flower in the bin to join the other one. Then she unplugged the phone and turned her radio on at almost full volume while she made herself supper. And later that night, when Rose went to bed, she pushed the extra pillows away and switched off the light, determined to sleep.

Sunday lunch with Minerva and her husband, Henry Beresford, was congenial as usual, and afterwards Minerva sent her husband off for a nap so she could catch up on shop talk with her niece. But instead of giving her aunt an update on business at the shop, after a few stops and starts Rose finally came out with her long overdue confession.

Minerva, elegant in tailored trousers and dark blue roll-neck sweater, showing only a few threads of silver in her black Dryden hair, heard Rose out in astonished silence. 'My poor child!' she said at last, giving Rose a compassionate hug. 'I knew there was something desperately wrong that summer, of course. But when you came back from Portugal you looked so much better I assumed you'd recovered from what I took to be a college romance gone wrong.' Cobalt-blue eyes twinkled at Rose. 'I'd had a few myself, remember. Though marriage was the last thing on the agenda with any of the wretches lusting after *me*. Anyway, don't worry about it any more, pet. Henry will see to everything for you the minute you give him the go ahead.'

Feeling as if a burden had been lifted, Rose decided to

wait for a few days to give James Sinclair time to reply to her letter. If he didn't, the following Monday she would instruct Henry to start divorce proceedings anyway. Decision made, she felt better. There were no more menacing phone calls, no more roses pushed through her letter box. Life, decided Rose, had returned to normal. On the Thursday evening she dealt with paperwork for an hour after shutting up shop, ate a substantial meal for once, and was just clearing away after supper when the bell rang below on her private door.

Rose hesitated. At one time she would have run down to open it without a second thought. Instead she went into her bathroom, the only place with the necessary view. But under one of the artistic street lights in the cobbled courtyard the only thing visible was the top of an unknown male head, and a second ring of the doorbell sent her hurrying downstairs to open the door as far as the safety chain allowed.

'Yes?' she said, with a polite smile, her eyes widening in sudden shock when her visitor turned to face her. White streaks in thick black hair gave a fleeting impression of age quickly cancelled by a lean, instantly familiar face. And from the hot surge of excitement thrusting up inside her Rose realised that this was exactly what she'd hoped for when she'd written the letter. She stared at her visitor in wordless recognition, while ten years vanished in the wink of an eye. Then excitement gave way to remembered pain and humiliation, and her eyes narrowed in hostility as they met her visitor's assessing gaze.

'Hello, Rose,' said James Sinclair at last. 'I was in the area so I thought I'd take a chance on finding you in.'

At the sound of his voice Rose recovered her own. 'James Sinclair, no less.' She gave a swift look round the

arcade, and unhooked the chain. 'I suppose you'd better come inside,' she said coolly.

'Thank you.' He waited in the small entry until she'd locked and bolted the door, then followed as she led the way up to the sitting room.

'Can I get you a drink?' she asked, caught so much off guard she cursed James Sinclair for surprising her at the end of a working day. After all these years, it would have been good to have brushed her hair, at least, before coming face to face with him again.

'Thank you. I'm not driving, so a finger of Scotch would be good if you have it.'

Not driving. Was he staying at the King's Head, then? Rose poured whisky into a tumbler, strangling a hysterical laugh at the idea of James Sinclair in the same hotel bed Anthony Garrett used.

She handed over the glass, sat down in her usual chair and waved James to the sofa. 'Do sit down,' she said, icily polite.

'May I take off my jacket?' he asked, equally courteous.

'Of course.'

James unzipped a suede windbreaker, laid it aside and sat down, looking so much at ease Rose felt fiercely resentful. Instead of the city suit expected of the well-dressed banker, he wore a heavy fawn sweater with khaki canvas jeans, and looked altogether far more comfortable and relaxed than she felt he had any right to. But even at twenty-two James had always been self-contained. Except in bed.

'You wear your hair shorter now,' he commented, surprising her.

Rose thrust it behind her ears impatiently. 'So what

brings you here, James? I never imagined you'd come in person when I wrote the letter.'

'Why not?'

'Lack of time—and interest, maybe?'

'I was due a break. And I own to a great *deal* of interest about your reasons for waiting so long to divorce me.' He finished the contents of his glass, looking at her over the rim. 'You could have done that any time this past five years with no problem. Why didn't you?'

Rose shrugged indifferently. 'A very childish reason, I'm afraid. I always promised myself you'd have to ask first. I never bothered to research the subject, so I've only just found out you had no need to ask by this time.'

James smiled. And she wished he hadn't. The smile was familiar. So, to her dismay, was its effect on her.

'For my own part I've never had the slightest desire for a divorce,' he informed her.

Rose raised a scornful eyebrow. 'You surprise me. At one stage weren't you worried I might start proceedings and demand half your worldly goods?'

'By the time I had any worldly goods to speak of too much time had elapsed for you to do that. Actually,' he added blandly, 'I've always found it rather an advantage to be married.'

'Saves trouble where women are concerned, I suppose.'

'Exactly.' He gazed at her in silence for a while, until Rose began to feel restive under the bright, searching scrutiny. 'So tell me. Why *do* you want a divorce, Rose?'

'For the obvious reason. I'm thinking of getting married. Again, I mean.' Which was an outright lie. Anthony was the only one thinking of marriage.

'Just thinking?' He raised an eyebrow. 'Does this mean you're already co-habiting with someone?'

CATHERINE GEORGE 99

'No,' she said evenly. 'I've tried that in the past. It was a mistake.'

His face hardened. 'Unflattering.'

'I wasn't referring to *you*, James.' She smiled coldly. 'Other men have featured in my life over the past ten years.'

His eyes roved over her impersonally. 'Which have been kinder to you than to me, Rose.'

'Your hair surprised me,' she admitted. 'How long has it been like that?'

'I wish I could be melodramatic and say the white streaks arrived overnight after you left me,' he said sardonically, 'but they started creeping in about five years ago. Not that I mind,' he added. 'They lend suitable gravitas to someone bent on a fast-track career in banking.'

'You're determined to be the youngest chief executive ever, I suppose?'

'Something like that.' James eyed her assessingly. 'How did you know where to contact me?'

'Fabia Hargreaves—she was Dennison when I shared a flat with her—sent me a cutting about your promotion. So I just had to check you were still with the same bank before I wrote.'

'I see.' He looked round at the room. 'You live here alone?'

'Yes.'

'What happened to your aunt?'

'Minerva surprised everyone by getting married last year. When she asked me if I fancied managing the shop for her I jumped at it. She still owns it, but to all intents and purposes it's mine to run as I like.'

He sat looking at her in silence for a while. 'And is life in a small country town like this satisfying for you?'

'Yes. I'd had enough city lights by the time I came

back here. I'd lived in London ever since I left college. Which,' Rose added, 'is more than enough about me. So tell me, James, are you getting married, too?'

'No. I was tricked into marriage once.' The grey eyes were steely. 'I rarely make the same mistake twice.'

'I didn't trick you,' she said wearily.

'That's a lie, Miss Dryden.' His mouth tightened. 'I doubt you've ever called yourself Mrs Sinclair.'

'Absolutely not.'

There was silence in the room for a while, until at last Rose couldn't help repeating her question. 'What's your real reason for coming here, James? We could have settled all this by letter.'

He looked at her levelly. 'When I saw your signature on that terse little missive it reminded me of unfinished business between us.'

Suddenly the air crackled between them, all pretence of civility vanished.

'It all seemed very final to me!' Her eyes flashed malevolently. 'You told me to get out of your life, so I did. What's unfinished about that?'

'I wasn't thinking straight at the time,' he rapped. 'I was only twenty-two, for God's sake—'

'And I was only eighteen,' she cut back. 'No match for you at all. I would never have dreamed you could be so vicious.'

His mouth tightened. 'I was hurt, and angry, and so bloody disillusioned I hit out in the worst way I could think of.'

'The very worst,' she agreed stonily. 'Your timing was diabolical. In the middle of my first-year exams. You'd done yours, of course. Belated congratulations, by the way. I heard you got your double first.'

'And despite everything you passed *your* exams, too.'

'Just. Which was something of a miracle under the circumstances. And such a struggle I didn't do as well as forecast. I took off abroad for the entire summer to try and get over you.' Her lip curled. 'Looking back, it seems such utter nonsense now. That I could have let a man affect me so badly, I mean. But at the time all I wanted was to forget I'd ever met you, let alone married you.'

'Did you succeed?'

'Oh, yes.' Rose gave him a frosty smile. 'Hearts mend. Though nothing would have convinced me of that at the time.'

'So where did you go? When I couldn't find you I contacted your aunt, but she just said you were working abroad.'

'Minerva knew someone who needed a nanny for the summer in Portugal. The family offered me the job, and, painful as it was in one way, I jumped at it, desperate to get away.'

James Sinclair's hard eyes narrowed. 'Why was it painful?'

Rose controlled herself with effort. 'Sensitive soul, aren't you? I had honestly believed I was expecting a baby shortly before, if you remember. When I found I wasn't I was utterly shattered. And bitterly disappointed. Unlike you,' she added bitterly. 'You said some foul, unforgivable things last time we met.'

His face set. 'Would it make you feel better if I told you I regretted them later?'

'Please don't bother. It's a very long time since any of that mattered in the slightest to me.' Rose got up, sure he'd take the hint and go if she offered him another drink. 'Can I give you a refill?'

'Thank you.' James surrendered his glass, ignoring the icy look she gave him as she took it. 'Rose,' he said

slowly, when she'd given him a meagre half-inch of single malt, 'hearing from you out of the blue reminded me of some loose ends I'd never tied up. I won't pretend I've been thinking of you *all* the time over the years, but from time to time I'd remember, and wonder.'

'About what, in particular?'

'Don't pretend you don't know!' His eyes speared hers. 'Tell me the truth at last, Rose. Did you really set out to trap me?'

'Oh, all that nonsense.' Rose shrugged airily. 'I certainly tried hard to make you fall in love with me, but there was no trap involved. The master plan was Cornelia Longford's brainchild, in actual fact, but I plead guilty to carrying it out.'

The cold eyes narrowed dangerously. 'So you really did follow a plan!'

'To the letter. Con worked out a sort of blueprint. Phase one, phase two, and so on. It all worked like the proverbial charm, too.' She felt a surge of primitive satisfaction at the look on his face.

'You deliberately baited your hook, and I swallowed it, line and sinker,' he said in disgust.

Secretly revelling in the effect her information had on her listener, Rose described the way her friends had gleaned information about the legendary Sinclair's background and tastes so she could pretend common interests. 'I must have been mad,' she added wryly. 'Up to then my sole effort at keeping fit was an occasional aerobics session. But Con insisted I went to the track to run into you accidentally.'

'You actually took up running that early in the morning just to bump into me?' he said blankly.

'I blush to think of it now,' she admitted. 'Up to that time I'd only run for a bus. I pretended to like foreign

films, too, which I didn't all that much, and holidays on
Skye, though I'd never actually been there. But perhaps
you've forgotten all that.'

'I remember every last thing,' he said grimly. 'My God,
I've often thought since that I'd been too ready to con-
demn. But that poisonous little tick was right after all.
You were guilty as charged.'

'Who do you mean?' she said swiftly.

'Fair-haired twit, always mooning after you.'

'So Miles was the culprit,' said Rose with relief. 'I'm
so glad.'

'*Glad!*'

'At the time I suspected Fabia, even Con, because they
were the only ones in the know.'

'Your precious Miles managed to find out, too. He took
great pleasure in cornering me to tell me about your plan,'
said James grimly. 'I didn't believe him at first, told him
to get lost before I rearranged his face—'

'But when you confronted me with it I confessed, of
course, and topped it by giving you the glad news that
you needn't have married me after all,' said Rose with a
brittle smile.

James finished the drink and stood up. 'Oddly enough,'
he said, his eyes wintry, 'I didn't regret marrying you,
Rose. I was crazy about you. But at that point I was so
dog-tired from working my brains out I just couldn't handle it when you hit me with the news about the false alarm
only minutes after Miles had told me about your famous
plan. It was a double body blow to every illusion I had.
Which is why I went berserk.'

Rose went to the door. 'Look, James, I confess I did
set out to make you fall in love with me. Though, heaven
knows, it just seems like a silly student prank now.' She
turned to face him, her eyes as cold as his. 'But think for

a minute. No one can really make another human being fall in love. Not that you did that, of course. If you had you'd have listened to me, trusted me, and found out what really happened.'

His eyes narrowed. 'I'm listening now. I've come a long way to listen. So go on. Tell me your side of it.'

'You know it already,' she said impatiently. 'I was late one month. I panicked.'

'But you were taking contraceptive pills. Or told me you were.'

'I was. Religiously. But, if you remember, I had a stomach bug which laid me low for a few days. I knew that could stop the pills from doing their job. So when—when my period was late, which had never happened before, I was in such a state I was convinced I was pregnant.'

'But I thought the tests were pretty accurate.'

Rose flushed hectically, and looked away. 'It sounds brainless now, but it never occurred to me to get one. I was even throwing up by that stage—sheer nerves, as it turned out—so I was convinced. By the time I told you I was in a terrible state.'

'And I was such a stiff-necked, high-minded idiot,' said James without emotion, 'that I did the time-honoured thing and married you the first moment I could. I was so shell-shocked I never even asked if you'd had a test.'

Silence fell between them, lengthening until Rose's nerves were stretched to breaking point by the time James spoke again.

'One thing I'm still in the dark about, Rose. When you were concocting this famous plan, why the hell did you choose me?'

'Oh I didn't *choose* you.' She gave him a patronising little smile. 'In the beginning all three of us were going

to try the plan out with different men, so we wrote names on bits of paper. I drew yours out of the hat.'

'Good God!' His brows drew together incredulously. 'You mean that everything that happened was just by chance?'

'Afraid so.' There was little point, now, in admitting that she'd had an outsize crush on him long before Con's famous plan. He was no more likely to believe her now than he would have back then, on the never-to-be-forgotten day when he'd heard his quixotic chivalry had been unnecessary after all.

'Amazing,' said James, shrugging into his jacket. 'Two lives changed out of all recognition by the luck of the draw.'

'Fate has a strange sense of humour,' agreed Rose coolly.

James looked at her for a long, contemplative moment. 'I'm glad I made the effort to come and see you. You've grown into your bones, Rose. You look good.'

'So do you,' she said, magnanimous now he was leaving. 'I rather like the hair.'

'Thank you.' He gave her the slow, inflammatory smile she'd never quite managed to forget. 'How very civilised we are!'

'That was my aim when I wrote to you,' she pointed out. 'To go about things in a civilised way, instead of informing you through a solicitor.'

When the phone interrupted them Rose excused herself to pick it up, then breathed in sharply as the caller whispered her name and rang off.

'What's the matter?' asked James, as she crashed the receiver back. He grabbed her by the wrists. 'Rose, for God's sake what's wrong? You're as white as a sheet!'

She gave him a shaky smile. 'Nuisance phone call.'

James released her to stab in the recall numbers, but again the number had been withheld. 'Has this happened before?' he demanded.

'Yes. This is the third. But there are the roses, too.'

'What roses?'

Seized by a sudden need to unburden herself, Rose explained, then gave James a wry little smile. 'At least I know it's not you.'

'Me?' His eyes narrowed ominously. 'You actually believed I'd deliberately frighten you like this?'

She shrugged. 'After a silence of ten years it seems a silly idea now, but I couldn't help wondering for a moment or two. By coincidence the card was very much like the one you sent me once. But the choice of a rose is pretty obvious for someone who knows my name.'

He eyed her warily. 'Your new man couldn't be the culprit?'

'Certainly not,' she snapped. 'Anthony was very annoyed by the card. And the first of the roses. But I haven't told him about the calls, or the second flower.'

'I think you'd better. What does the caller say?'

'Just breathes a bit and whispers my name.' She shivered. 'I sat up all night with the lights on when he rang after midnight the other night.'

'Tell the police,' James ordered brusquely. 'It may be just a rose and a phone call at this stage, but stalking can lead to something a hell of a sight more serious.'

'You think it's a stalker?' she said, horrified.

'It could be.' James looked at her with open concern. 'Rose, I don't like the thought of leaving you alone after this. Isn't there someone who could come to stay with you tonight?'

'Of course there is. Or I could go to Minerva if I wanted

to. But I don't.' Her jaw tightened. 'I flatly refuse to let this joker affect my life.'

He smiled wryly. 'You were always a feisty little thing.'

'Obstinate's the word,' she said, pulling a face, then shivered a little. 'But I admit to being a bit spooked by this.'

James looked grim. 'So tell the police. In the meantime, I'll stay for a while. At least until your colour comes back.'

'Thank you. I could do with some company. Even—' Rose halted, flushing at the gleam in the grey eyes.

'Even mine, Rose?'

'I don't mean to be rude,' she said stiffly. 'I've tried not to let this business get to me, but it's difficult. I thought it was amusing in the beginning, but it isn't any more. I really loathe the feeling that somebody's out there, watching me.'

'If he's watching you tonight at least he'll know you're not alone. And if the phone rings,' he added with menace, 'I'll answer it, and make sure your caller thinks twice about ringing you again.'

CHAPTER EIGHT

OF ALL the things she'd intended to do that evening, drinking coffee with James Sinclair was the last Rose had pictured when she'd shut up shop for the night. Taking time out for repairs to her face and hair, she went back to the sitting room eventually, armed with a tray.

'The coffee smells good,' he commented. 'Is there somewhere I could buy some brandy to go with it?'

'Yes, but you don't have to. Minerva's husband gave me two bottles of cognac for Christmas.'

James looked amused. 'You're that fond of it?'

'No, but Henry is. I ask them round for a meal every so often, so this is his way of saving me expense.'

'You like him.'

Rose nodded. 'Very much. Henry was a widower for years, and always the most determined of Minerva's men-friends. I'm glad she finally gave in and married him. And, far more important, so is she.'

'It must have been a surprise to her, all those years ago, when you told her *you* were married,' he commented.

'I never did tell her. At least not at the time.' Rose kept her eyes on the coffee she was pouring. 'Until last Sunday Minerva knew nothing about it. Henry's a solicitor, and I asked him to handle the divorce for me.' She looked up to meet the watchful, narrowed eyes. 'But before I could talk about divorce, of course, first I had to tell Minerva I was married.'

James whistled. 'That must have come as a shock after all this time.'

'It certainly did. Though Minerva always takes everything in her stride. She's the one person in this world,' said Rose deliberately, 'who I can trust to be there for me, no matter what.'

'Unlike me, you mean,' said James without expression, and took the coffee cup she handed him. 'If it's of any interest to you, Rose, I never told anyone about our marriage, either.'

'Not even your mother?'

'No one,' he repeated curtly. 'So what happened to break your silence after all this time?'

'Anthony asked me to marry him.' Rose shrugged. 'So I had to explain why that wasn't possible. I didn't tell him *why* I got married,' she added.

'Did you give your aunt the reason for our rush?'

'Yes.'

'But not Anthony.'

'No.'

He smiled a little. 'I'd forgotten how monosyllabic you get at times. Am I allowed to ask why you're keeping the man in the dark?'

Rose thought for a moment. 'I see no reason to tell him something which happened in the past, long before I met him.'

'Have you known him long?'

'I knew him by sight when I was young. But the present arrangement started a couple of months ago.'

'Do you love him?' probed James.

Rose looked away. 'I'm—fond of him.'

'That isn't what I asked.'

'Would you like more coffee?'

'In other words I should mind my own business,' he said wryly. 'But yes, I would like more coffee.'

Rose refilled their cups, aware that the truthful answer

to James's question was in the negative. Not that her feelings for Anthony Garrett, or any other man she knew, were anything to do with James Sinclair.

James took his coffee from her then sat down, his face sombre. 'I apologise. I've no right to intrude on your private affairs.'

She shrugged it off casually. 'Let's have some of Henry's cognac.' She gave him a wry look. 'Have you had dinner, by the way?'

James looked amused. 'Yes. Have *you* eaten, Rose?'

'Rather well, as it happens, a very conventional meat and potatoes kind of meal for once. Not that I bother with that kind of thing often. Normally it's just a salad, or—'

'Bacon sandwiches?'

Not for the world would Rose have told him that the very idea of a bacon sandwich had been anathema to her from the day they'd parted.

'I took a chance when I decided to knock on your door,' he said, as Rose poured brandy for him. 'But I was pretty sure that if I'd rung first you'd refuse to see me.'

'Why should you think that? I contacted you first.'

'But only by letter, which you signed very formally as Rose Dryden. You refused to speak to me often enough in the past, remember.' The grey eyes took on a cold, metallic gleam. 'Our parting was so acrimonious that even after all these years I wondered if you'd slam the door in my face tonight.'

Her chin lifted. 'I've grown up a bit since we last met, James.'

'You have, indeed.' He gazed at her thoughtfully. 'You know, Rose, I've often thought of how it would be if we met again.'

So had she. 'But obviously this isn't the scenario you pictured.'

'No. I assumed it would be in court, or some lawyer's office.'

'I'm surprised you came here in person, then.'

James shrugged. 'I acted on impulse. I was long over-due for a break, a colleague of mine knows this area well, so after I got your letter I decided on a trip to the Cotswolds.'

Rose raised an eyebrow. 'I'm surprised. The letter was pure formality. I didn't expect a reply, let alone the honour of a personal visit.'

James gave her a very unsettling smile. 'I decided it would be interesting to meet you just once again, Rose, before our lives are officially detached. A whim, I suppose. Only keep that fact to yourself. Professionally I'm not famous for whimsy.'

'Guarding your street cred again,' she said without thinking.

'Like another memorable occasion. No wonder you thought I sent you the card and the rose again,' he said, with an indulgence which irritated Rose considerably.

'Only for the briefest of moments,' she lied, and frowned. 'I just wish I knew who had.'

'But if someone's buying roses locally, surely you can find out?'

Rose explained how the first rose was ordered. 'But the second one could have been bought anywhere.'

James frowned. 'This is obviously getting to you, Rose. Have you no idea at all who could be doing this?'

'I did wonder if it was someone I knew in my time in London,' confessed Rose after a pause.

'What were you doing in London?'

Trying hard to forget James Sinclair, thought Rose with secret rancour. 'The usual things,' she told him. 'Earning a living, acquiring a succession of boyfriends. For a very

brief time I even shared a flat with one of them—just before Minerva made me the offer I couldn't refuse. At which point the relationship came to an abrupt end.'

'Because you opted for the business?'

'Right. Rob had apparently been expecting me to marry him.'

'You didn't want that?'

'No.' Rose looked at him steadily. 'Oddly enough the encounter with you, James, put me off marriage for good.'

His mouth tightened. 'You've changed your mind now, obviously.'

'Actually, I haven't.' Rose shrugged. 'But Anthony's very conventional.'

'I see.' James swirled the brandy in his glass thoughtfully. 'Where's he based?'

'London,' she said, after a pause.

'In that case won't there be a conflict of interests again?' He raised an eyebrow. 'Something tells me this Anthony of yours doesn't really know very much about you, Rose. Have you talked this through?'

'Not yet. He mentioned marriage for the first time only last week.'

'But you obviously like the idea or you wouldn't have contacted me about the divorce.'

It had been dawning on Rose all evening that she'd made a very bad mistake in writing to James Sinclair instead of just instructing Henry to do it for her. His unexpected presence, here on her own private territory, was disturbing in the extreme.

'It merely nudged me into doing something I should have done long ago,' she said curtly. 'I'll make more coffee.'

Alone in her small kitchen, Rose faced the truth. There was no point in pretending she felt only indifference to-

wards James Sinclair. Just having him in the same room smacked of danger. Even at twenty-two James had been a mature adult compared with the other students she'd known. But ten years on from that he was a formidable man who, as far as Rose could tell, still harboured resentment towards her. So before he caused any more damage to her life she needed to send him on his way, complete with an apology for any wrongs he felt she'd dealt him. Then both of them could get on with their lives, free of any emotional clutter left over from the past.

When she rejoined him, James watched in silence as she refilled their coffee cups.

'Before you leave, James, I'd like to get one thing straight,' Rose looked at him steadily. 'I didn't lie to you. I truly believed I was pregnant.'

'I know that,' he said, surprising her.

'You didn't believe me back then.'

'I've had a lot of time to think in the intervening years.'

'You said you haven't thought of me much.'

He smiled crookedly. 'Economy with the truth. I have my pride.'

'So have I.' Rose looked him in the eye. 'You hurt me badly, James. But at least I've matured enough to realise I hurt you equally as much.'

'More,' he contradicted. 'I was so crazy about you I wouldn't listen at first when that little reptile told me you set out to trap me. But then you admitted it was true, worse still told me there was no baby, and my world just fell apart. One minute you were the sweetest thing on God's earth; the next you seemed like the most conniving little witch I'd ever had the bad luck to encounter.'

Her eyes flashed. 'So you told me at the time. With colourful repetition.'

He winced. 'I'm not proud of the way I behaved, be-

lieve me. But I was so cut to pieces I hurled every insult at you I could think of, and took off to Scotland to cool off while you sat your exams. But you were my wife, Rose. It never occurred to me that you'd vanish into thin air by the time I got back.'

'I was obeying orders,' she reminded him. 'You told me to get lost, so I did. Right out of the country for the entire summer. When I came back Minerva told me you'd rung quite a lot, so I said you were a boyfriend I'd dumped, and if you rang again she was to say I wanted nothing more to do with you.' Rose's mouth twisted in self-derision. 'My own form of hubris, I suppose. Which didn't do me much good when I went back to college.'

His eyes softened. 'Was it difficult for you?'

'Difficult! A few months as the legendary Sinclair's girlfriend had boosted *my* street cred a sight too much. For a while I was hounded by men panting to find out what you found so special about me.'

'And did any of them succeed?'

Rose gave him a scathing look. 'Certainly not. Eventually even the persistent Miles got the message. My great good fortune was having two friends like Cornelia Longford and Fabia Dennison. They knew nothing about the wedding, of course, but Con, in particular, felt desperately responsible because you dumped me the minute you found out about her famous plan. I had to seem to get over you just to reassure her. So in time I did.'

'How much time?' he demanded.

'At lot more than I would have liked.'

James nodded. 'Likewise.'

'But you had your job in the City, and a whole new life. I doubt that you thought of me for long,' she said scornfully.

'I did my thinking at night. In bed.' His eyes met hers. 'We were very good together, Rose.'

So good that she'd never found anyone to take his place, thought Rose, suppressing a shiver. She'd thought for a while she'd succeeded with Robert Mason. Until marriage had been mentioned.

Rose jumped to her feet. 'I'm sorry to be rude, James, but it's getting late and my day starts early.' She smiled politely. 'At least it isn't much of a walk for you to the King's Head.'

'I'm not putting up there.'

She frowned. 'But you said you walked.'

'I did. The colleague I mentioned owns a weekend place, a cottage down by the river. It's a fine evening. I was glad of the exercise.' James smiled as he stood up. 'I'm there for a few days for some much needed R and R. You look surprised, Rose.'

Dismayed, not surprised. 'How pleasant,' she said politely. 'I'm sure you'll enjoy it there.'

He took his wallet from his jacket, extracted a business card and scribbled a number on it. 'There's no phone at the cottage, but you can reach me on my cellphone number any time you need to. Let me know if your stalker steps up his attentions.'

'Thank you,' said Rose.

They were almost at the door when James stopped suddenly, and held out his hand. 'Ten years ago, Rose, I said a great many things I would have given a lot to retract afterwards. I can't take them back, but at least I can tell you how much I've regretted them since. I know the apology's long overdue, but I'm sorry I hurt you so badly.'

With reluctance Rose put her hand in his, wary even now of touching him. 'Apology accepted. It was all a long time ago. Let's put it all behind us.'

'There's a snag,' said James, in a tone that quickened her pulse. 'Now I've seen you again it doesn't feel like a long time ago.'

'Nevertheless,' Rose said woodenly, 'it is. But now we've made our apologies at last, and washed away any bitterness.' Which came out sounding a lot more biblical than intended. But it was impossible to behave, or sound, natural when the mere touch of James Sinclair's hand on hers was rousing feelings she had never experienced in the most passionate of lovemaking with anyone else.

And James knew it, she realised, as she met the blaze of triumph in his eyes.

'Rose.' He smiled slowly, and brushed a lock of hair back from her face. 'Surely a kiss goodbye is permissible in the circumstances?' He drew her resisting body into his arms and kissed her, taking his time over it, the shape and taste and touch of his lips so frighteningly familiar she had no defence against the hot, consuming pleasure of the kiss. When the phone interrupted stridently, bringing her back to earth, she wrenched away to answer it, but James grabbed her hand, shaking his head. He snatched up the receiver and snarled a response.

Rose waited, tense, as he listened for a second.

'Who the hell is this?' James demanded roughly. 'Whoever you are you can stop your game right now. I've informed the police, so this call is being traced as we speak—' He broke off, lips twitching as he listened. 'Ah! I see. Sorry. Of course. I'll hand you over right now.'

'Who the devil was that?' howled Anthony in Rose's ear.

'I've been getting anonymous phone calls,' she said breathlessly, avoiding amused grey eyes. 'James assumed you were the culprit.'

'And who, may I ask, is James?'

'He called to discuss the divorce.'

There was a pause. 'Are you talking about your *husband*?' said Anthony in outrage. 'Why the blazes did you invite him to your place?'

'I didn't do that,' she retorted, struggling to keep her temper. 'Anyway, I can't talk now, Anthony. I'll—I'll ring you later.' She put the phone down to find James eavesdropping shamelessly.

'Sorry about that, Rose,' he said, shrugging. 'I heard dead silence on the line for a minute—'

'Shock at hearing a man where Anthony least expected one,' said Rose tightly.

'I thought it was your stalker. I hope I haven't made things difficult for you,' James added, with such patent insincerity Rose clenched her teeth.

'Not at all,' she said crisply. 'I'll show you out.' She marched down the steep flight of stairs ahead of him. 'I'm glad we've cleared things up at last. Henry will keep you up to speed on the divorce. Goodbye, James.'

'Wait.' He stood close in the small lobby, his eyes intent on hers. 'Will you really be happy, Rose?'

She dropped her eyes. 'My life is nothing to do with you any more.'

He smiled slowly. 'After meeting you again I somehow find it hard to get my head round that. Goodnight,' he added, a caressing note in his voice which made Rose unwilling to trust her own as she opened the door to let him out.

'Lock up securely,' James ordered, as he went out into the cobbled street. 'Disconnect your phone and get some rest.'

Easier said than done, thought Rose, almost tearful with resentment as she got ready for bed. After years of believing she was over James Sinclair, the discovery that

she was anything but was no preparation for a good night's sleep. She was an adult now, for heaven's sake, not a starry-eyed teenager to be bowled over by a kiss. Rose groaned in despair. Divorcing James Sinclair might be easy enough, but trying to forget she'd ever been married to him would be harder than ever now she'd met up with him again.

CHAPTER NINE

ROSE felt on edge all next day, half expecting to see James Sinclair walk in every time the shop door opened. But when there was no sign of him by the time she locked up at five-thirty, she shut herself in her office, mortified by her own disappointment.

As punishment for her absurdity she forced herself to do twice her usual session of paperwork, then had a shower and dressed in faded old jeans and yellow sweat-shirt, but paid close attention to hair and face afterwards, just in case James reappeared on her doorstep later.

Rose tidied her sitting room at top speed, threw a salad together, switched on her television and sat down on the sofa to eat her supper, with one of the newest arrivals on the bestseller list beside her. If James did come—not that she really thought for a moment that he would, of course—she would convey the perfect picture of someone enjoying a cosy evening, perfectly happy with her own company.

She had barely started on her salad when her private doorbell rang, and a triumphant smile curved her mouth as she pushed the tray aside. Elation surged inside her as she ran downstairs, then evaporated sharply when she opened the door.

'Anthony!' exclaimed Rose.

He eyed her truculently. 'I waited up for hours for you to ring me back last night. When you didn't I decided to make a personal visit today instead. May I come in, or would I be intruding?'

'No you wouldn't,' she said crisply, and turned to go ahead of him up the stairs. 'I was in the middle of supper. Shall I make some for you?'

'No, thanks,' he said, his mood lightening when he spotted a tray very obviously laid for one. 'Marcus is meeting me at Orsini's for dinner shortly. But you carry on with your meal, of course.'

'It won't spoil. I'll eat it later.' In peace, she almost added. 'You didn't tell me you were coming tonight.'

'I drove down on impulse,' he said quickly.

Other people's impulses were playing havoc with her life at the moment, thought Rose irritably, and gave her visitor a sweet little smile. 'Are you taking a chance on having your room free tonight at the Kings Head, then?'

'I rang them first to make sure,' he admitted, flushing. 'I knew you'd be busy in the shop so I didn't bother to interrupt with a phone call.'

But he'd rung Marcus. And booked a meal at Orsini's. So Anthony had obviously called on her unannounced because he'd hoped, or feared, to catch her entertaining James. 'I might not have been in,' she pointed out.

'In which case I would have rung from the hotel and left a message on your machine,' he said, after a pause that convinced Rose he'd only just thought of it.

'So,' she said briskly, 'is there a specific reason for seeing me tonight, Anthony?'

'Yes, a very important one.' He stood very erect, squaring his shoulders in a mannerism Rose knew well. 'I came to let you know I've engaged my own solicitor, so you needn't worry your head about it any more. Emerson will see to the divorce proceedings.'

Rose stared him in outrage. '*What* did you say?'

His eyes flickered. 'I've simply set the ball rolling for you.'

Her eyes flashed ominously. 'I can't believe you did that without consulting me, Anthony.'

His chin came up. 'It seemed to me you'd go on shilly-shallying indefinitely if I didn't take a hand in it. Anyway, it's all settled with Emerson now—'

'Then get it unsettled,' she snapped. 'I'm putting everything in Henry Beresford's hands on Monday.'

'Henry's semi-retired,' said Anthony impatiently. 'Besides, he's not experienced in divorce. Emerson will get it sorted out far more quickly.'

'Not in my case,' said Rose, ice dripping from every word. 'I wouldn't dream of hurting Henry, which, in case you've forgotten, would also hurt Minerva. In fact, Anthony, I deeply resent your interference.'

His colour deepened hectically. 'I meant it as *help*, Rose, not interference.'

'Really! And when, exactly, did you decide to consult this Mr Emerson?'

'Today. Though I don't see the relevance—'

'Do you think I'm stupid, Anthony?' Rose eyed him with scorn. 'You discovered that James was here last night and acted on another of these impulses of yours.'

'All right! Now you've brought the subject up, what exactly was he doing here?' demanded Anthony, a vein standing out on his temple. 'Do you expect me to believe that after ten years he just turned up on your doorstep out of the blue?'

Rose looked at him in distaste. 'I don't expect you to believe anything.'

'So you were lying—'

'I am not lying,' she said, with such icy emphasis Anthony Garrett backed away a little.

'I'm sorry,' he said, raking a hand through his hair.

Which showed Rose how upset he was. Anthony was particular about his hair.

'You'd better go,' she said coldly. 'Otherwise you'll be late for Marcus.'

'Look, I admit I went about this the wrong way. We'll discuss it tomorrow night, Rose.' He smiled cajolingly. 'I'll take you up on your recent offer of dinner here instead of going out.'

'Certainly not!'

'All right,' he said quickly, looking crestfallen, 'let's keep to a meal at Orsini's, then, and talk over coffee here later.'

Rose sighed impatiently. 'You don't understand, Anthony. I can't see you at all tomorrow.'

He glowered at her. 'Are you doing this just to punish me over the solicitor?'

'It's part of it. But I also resent the fact that you assume I'm at your beck and call just because you take it into your head to come down this weekend,' she said hotly, then tensed at the look of rage on his face.

'It's this husband of yours, isn't it?' he demanded. 'You're seeing *him* tomorrow, I suppose!'

'Don't be childish,' said Rose, and regretted it when Anthony seized her by the shoulders and shook her so hard her teeth rattled.

'You were lying when you said you hadn't seen him all this time,' he snarled. 'After ten years he suddenly turns up last night? Do you think I'm a fool? No doubt you slept with him for old times' sake—'

'Let her go,' rapped a hard, frozen voice.

'And who the hell are you?' said Anthony in outrage, his hands tightening on Rose's shoulders as he glared at the tall man standing in the doorway.

'I think you know very well who I am. My name's

Sinclair. Take your hands off my wife.' James shook his head at Rose. 'You shouldn't leave your door ajar. Any riff-raff could have got in. And obviously did.'

Scarlet to the roots of his hair, Anthony Garrett clenched the hands he'd dropped from Rose's shoulders, so patently wanting to hit James that Rose felt a fleeting pang of sympathy for his frustration. But something in James's attitude warned that her enraged assailant would do well to make himself scarce.

'You'd better go, Anthony,' she advised.

'Very well.' He pulled himself together with difficulty. 'I'll—I'll ring you tomorrow, Rose. When you're in a more reasonable frame of mind.'

'I'll see you out,' she said promptly, but James put out a peremptory hand.

'No. Stay where you are, Rose. I'll see your visitor off the premises. And make sure your door's locked securely while I'm at it.'

Rose slumped down on the sofa as her visitors went downstairs. She tried to make out what was being said, but all was ominously quiet before the outer door banged shut.

'Are you all right, Rose?' said James, when he rejoined her.

'Yes.' She rubbed at her shoulders, smiling ruefully. 'A bit bruised, but otherwise suffering mainly from temper.'

'Because the bastard manhandled you?'

'No. Though I didn't care for that very much, either.' Her eyes flashed coldly. 'Anthony made a colossal mistake today. He actually engaged his own solicitor to see to the divorce. Without consulting me.'

'Brave man!' James sat down beside her, eyeing her closely. 'You objected?'

'Of course I objected,' she retorted. 'I refuse to be pushed into anything.'

His eyes gleamed. 'So you're not as keen on the idea of divorce as your friend believes?'

Her chin lifted. 'On the contrary. I'm very keen on it indeed. But my aunt's husband handles all my legal affairs, so naturally I'll ask Henry to see to the divorce.' She frowned. 'That was a rather dramatic appearance just now, by the way. What brings you here again so soon, James?'

'I happened to be passing—' He grinned at the scathing look she gave him and raised his right hand. 'I was, I swear. I booked dinner at the Italian restaurant and I was quite literally on my way past your shop when I saw your private door was ajar. So mindful of your stalker, I came rushing to your rescue. And not before time, either,' he added grimly. 'Your friend looked ready to do you a mischief.'

'He was just jealous,' said Rose dismissively.

James sat back, arms folded, looking smug. 'Of me?'

'Yes. He didn't take kindly to your presence here last night.'

He smiled evilly. 'He didn't take very kindly to it tonight, either.'

'Do you blame him? For a moment there I thought you were going to knock him down.'

'So did I.' James shook his head in wonder. 'It's not a habit of mine to go round throwing punches, but I came very close with your little friend.'

'James!' protested Rose. 'Anthony's not *little*.'

'He's smaller than me.' He sighed regretfully. 'Which meant I couldn't indulge myself by throwing him down your stairs.'

'Are you into violence a lot these days?'

'No. And in the past only on your behalf, if you recall.'

'I can fight my own battles, thanks just the same.' She looked at her abandoned supper. 'What time's your reservation?'

'Half an hour ago.'

'Ring them and explain.'

James eyed her tray disparagingly. 'I've got a better idea. I know there's no point in asking you to keep me company at the restaurant, but they do food to take out. Ask them to send dinner for two here.' He smiled into her startled eyes. 'No one will know exactly *who* you're entertaining, Rose.'

'True. But at Orsini's they'll know who I'm *not* entertaining. Anthony's dining there tonight with his son.'

'Public opinion has always been such a huge thing with you,' he said impatiently. 'At university I had to make a total spectacle of myself before you'd agree to let the world know we were—'

'Going out together.'

'Only we didn't go out very much.'

'Better if we had,' said Rose bleakly.

James changed tack. 'Right. If you won't go out, and you won't order anything in, there's a third option.'

She eyed him suspiciously. 'What is it?'

'Come down to the cottage and I'll cater for you there.'

Rose's first reaction was to refuse. Last night was meant to be a one-off, she reminded herself, since James Sinclair represented such a clear and present danger to her peace of mind. But she was sorely tempted by his offer, just the same. After the excitement of the past half-hour an evening on her own would be anticlimax. She smiled a little. 'Is having dinner together accepted behaviour for people about to divorce?'

He shrugged. 'No idea. Your letter started me on a bit

of research to get up to date on the subject, but I don't remember any veto on a friendly evening spent in each other's company.' His eyes locked with hers. 'We were good friends, once, Rose. Did I alienate you too much, all those years ago, for us to be friends again?'

She met the look head-on. 'I certainly thought you had at the time.'

'Do you still feel the same?'

Rose shook her head. 'Ten years is a long time to nourish hatred. I couldn't sustain the emotion indefinitely so I concentrated on forgetting you instead.'

'I hope you succeeded better than I did.' His mouth twisted. 'When I finally calmed down enough to engage my brain all those years ago I soon realised the truth of what you told me last night. No one can *make* someone else fall in love. I rushed back from Scotland to tell you that, to say that I loved my little wife so much I didn't care why we'd got married as long as we stayed that way. But the bird had flown.'

'To look after a couple of toddlers for the rest of the summer,' said Rose huskily, and looked away, not wanting him to see how much his words had moved her. 'It takes a lot of energy to look after children all day. I was so tired most nights I fell asleep the moment I got to bed.' Which told him she hadn't lain sleepless, agonising over the treatment he'd dished out, for the simple reason that she'd made very sure she was too exhausted to stay awake.

'By that time I'd been accepted by the bank I joined straight from college,' said James, watching her like a hawk. 'Which was another reason why I went rushing back to you. I wanted to share my pleasure in getting my first job. Maybe you didn't realise it, Rose, but when your

aunt eventually told me you wanted nothing more to do with me, you had your revenge in full.'

'Exactly as I intended.' Rose shivered suddenly. 'But I don't want to drag all that up again. Let's change the subject.'

'Done. Come and spend the evening at the cottage. It's very peaceful on that stretch of river.' He got to his feet, his eyes gleaming in a way that did serious damage to her heartbeat. 'All you're agreeing to is a scratch meal, Rose, and a couple of hours of catching up on our lives.'

'Why not?' she said casually, ignoring fierce urgings of caution from her brain. 'I'll drive; you give directions. I haven't been down that way for years. It's a long time since I went walking by the river with Mark Cummings.'

'Does this mean you're actually willing to be seen in my company as far as the public car park?' said James caustically.

'No.' Rose gave him a seraphic smile. 'There's a back door in the store room behind my office. My car's parked just outside.'

'So you can smuggle me out with no one the wiser!'

She bristled. 'Amusing though it may be to you, James, I don't keep my car in the back for secrecy. Like everyone else with a shop in the arcade here, it's merely the most convenient place to park.'

The small, stone-built cottage James directed her to was reached by a narrow track leading off a road so minor they almost missed it in the dark.

'I had a hell of a job finding it the first time,' he said, as Rose came to a stop beside the house. 'There were no lights on like this when I arrived, so even with the map I drove past several times in the dark before I made it. But

if you want peace and quiet this is certainly the place to come.'

'Is that why you came here?'

'No. I came to see you.' James unlocked a door beneath a stone lintel, and ushered Rose into a welcoming, lamp-lit room with an inglenook fireplace. A laptop sat on a large leather-topped desk beneath the front window, and the chairs and sofa grouped around the room were well-worn and comfortable.

'This is lovely,' said Rose, as James stooped to light the fire.

'To add a little cheer,' he announced, as realistic flames danced on equally realistic logs.

'Not town gas as far out as this, surely,' said Rose.

'Bottled.' James grinned. 'Nick's wife likes the look of a fire, but not the mess that goes with it.'

'She doesn't object to the isolation?'

'No. They're still at the honeymoon stage. They both work hard during the week, and escape down here when-ever they can just to be together in peace. Like most nor-mal newly-weds,' he added deliberately.

'We were studying too hard to be normal newly-weds,' said Rose, refusing to rise. 'Our marriage was only on paper. We never did live together properly.'

Once James had organised a licence they'd been mar-ried very early one wet May morning at a register office, with only cleaners for witnesses. Afterwards the bride-groom had rushed off to sit an exam and the bride had returned, alone and disconsolate, to her college flat. Their nearest thing to a honeymoon had been spent beforehand, during the Easter vacation, when James had taken her to stay for a week in the Lake District, in a cottage not unlike this one. It had rained so much most of their time had been spent in bed.

'It amazes me,' he said, after a while, 'that you never told your aunt we were married.'

'There didn't seem much point. If you remember, I was adamant about keeping it from any of our friends at the time—'

'Of course I remember,' he said scornfully. 'You were so hysterical about your secret I felt like a murderer.'

Rose eyed him uncertainly. 'What do you mean?'

'Can't you imagine how guilty I felt about getting you pregnant? How the responsibility of it all weighed down like a ton?' His mouth twisted. 'I couldn't even enjoy the privileges of any normal bridegroom because I was working like a maniac—spurred on to do well in my finals so I could get a job good enough to support you and the baby.'

Rose had never looked past the rage and humiliation of their last meeting to consider this point of view. 'I caused you a whole lot of trouble, didn't I?' she said after a while.

James smiled a little. 'Not all trouble. All right, if you hadn't embarked on this famous plan of yours I probably wouldn't have noticed you. But the fact remains that when I did I fell crazily in love with you. I had no objection at all to marrying you, Rose, ever. Only the reason for the rush.'

'Fatherhood thrust upon you and all that,' she said sadly.

'No,' he said forcibly, and put a finger under her chin to turn her face up to his. 'I was appalled because I'd forced motherhood on *you*.'

Rose returned the look steadily. 'There wasn't much forcing about it, James. I was very much in love, too. Which is why—'

'Why I hurt you so badly,' he finished for her.

'But hurt heals. And I'm not in love with you any more,' she said flatly, 'so let's forget the past.'

James studied her face at length, with a look far too much like a jungle cat about to pounce on its prey for Rose's liking. 'Right. If the past is taboo we'll discuss supper instead, Miss Dryden—' He stopped, smiling crookedly.

'Keep to Rose,' she advised, determinedly prosaic. 'And lead me to the fridge. It's long past my suppertime. I need food.'

The galley kitchen was very modern, and very small, and James refused to let Rose set foot in it.

'There's no room for two of us. I promised you dinner, so I shall provide it,' he said firmly. 'You sit down in front of the fire and relax with a book, just as you were doing earlier on before the fun started.'

'An offer I can't refuse! Sitting down is my favourite pastime after a day on my feet.' Rose left James to his labour and retreated to the sitting room, where alcoves with well-stocked bookshelves offered literature very much to her taste, as long as she was happy with something she'd read before.

She chose a worn volume of Jane Austen's *Persuasion*, and curled up in the corner of the sofa, her eyes on the man-made flames. She read a page or two, then stiffened as the scent of grilling bacon came drifting from the kitchen. Not the famous sandwiches! Surely James had more subtlety than that.

Rose soon found that he had. In a remarkably short time she was provided with a plateful of pasta mixed with diced pancetta and tangy tomato sauce.

'Thank you! I'm impressed. How on earth did you manage all this so quickly?'

'I brought a few basics with me.' James put a glass of

wine on the table beside her. 'But Becky Henstridge's store cupboard provided the sauce and the pasta. And Nick keeps a fair selection of wine on hand.'

'Do you cook for yourself a lot?'

'No more than I have to. I eat out, or get a meal sent in.'

'When I smelt the pancetta cooking I thought I was getting one of your celebrated bacon sandwiches,' Rose informed him.

His jaw tightened. 'My enthusiasm for those vanished the day you left me.'

Suddenly all pretence of harmony was gone. They went on with the meal in silence, the remembrance of things past raw in the air between them.

'I've often thought of contacting you again, Rose,' said James after a while. 'Then I'd remember how you refused to speak to me, and my ego baulked at the idea of more rejection.'

While she, unable to accept that all was over between them, had watched for every post, and tensed every time the phone rang once she was back in college, or even at home, in spite of her instructions to Minerva.

Rose smiled politely, and pushed her plate away. 'I'm afraid you were over-generous, James. This is delicious, but I can't eat any more.'

He got up at once and took their plates into the kitchen, then came back with a bottle wrapped in a napkin. 'You haven't touched your wine yet,' he pointed out as he re-filled his glass.

She sipped obediently, and smiled. 'I never developed much of a palate, but this is wonderful. Is it a *rosé*?'

James lips twitched. 'Close.'

'What, then?'

He removed the napkin to reveal a staggeringly expen-

sive brand of pink champagne. 'Don't worry, I'll replace it before I go. But in the circumstances it seemed an appropriate choice to celebrate our reunion. I always hoped that one day we'd be in contact again, over the divorce if nothing else.' His smile clenched her stomach muscles. 'Old flames are normally easy to put out the minute the affair is over. But you and I were actually married, Rose, which made you a tad harder to extinguish than the others.'

How many others? wondered Rose, giving him a hostile look. 'You could have divorced me any time you wanted, James.'

'I've explained my reasons for being quite happy with the status quo,' he reminded her blandly. 'But let's not waste time on recriminations. This kind of occasion can hardly be repeated now you're thinking of marrying again. What's the man's surname, by the way? Referring to him as Anthony sounds too damn friendly on my part.'

'Garrett,' said Rose, digesting the fact that this evening was to be a one-off in the lives of James and Rose Sinclair. What had she expected? she thought impatiently, astonished to find a lump in her throat at the thought of the name she'd never used. Rose Sinclair sounded so utterly right. But it was no use thinking of that now. After tonight she might never be in touch with James again, other than through a solicitor. She finished her champagne hurriedly, and James got up to refill her glass.

'I shouldn't,' she said with regret. 'I'm driving.'

'It's a very quiet road back. I doubt you'll meet a policeman desperate to breathalise you. Besides,' he added, 'two glasses of wine won't do much harm.'

'I know. That's my usual allowance when I'm wining and dining.'

'With Garrett, of course.'

'Not exclusively. I get asked out to dinner parties some-times, and I enjoy the occasional date with one of the solicitors in Henry's chambers. And I often make up a four with Mark and Bel Cummings and her man.'

James's eyes narrowed. 'The name Cummings rings a bell.'

Rose nodded. 'Mark was my first boyfriend. He teaches history at his old school. He's a single parent now, with a small daughter he's bringing up with help from his mother and Bel, and even me, sometimes, when he's stuck for a babysitter.'

'What happened to his wife?'

'She took off with someone else before Lucy learned to walk.'

James gave her a searching look. 'Was that before you came back to take over the bookshop?'

'Long before.'

'Cummings must have welcomed you back to the fold with open arms, then.'

'Yes, he did. We're old friends.'

'Does he know about me?'

'No.' She gave him a taunting little smile. 'Everyone has a skeleton in the cupboard, James. You're mine.'

'Nothing's changed, then,' he said curtly. 'I assume I can't tempt you to more champagne?'

'No, thanks.'

James poured the last of the wine into his glass, looking down into it with a brooding look Rose remembered well. 'So when are you going to come out of the closet, Rose, and tell the world you've been a married lady all along?'

'I don't imagine the world is all that interested!'

'I meant this pretty little town of yours.'

'I don't expect anything more than the merest ripple of interest,' said Rose firmly. 'No one knows *you* here. And

I was quite respectably—if briefly—your wife; nothing remotely newsworthy.'

'You still *are* my wife,' James reminded her, his eyes clashing with hers.

She looked away. 'Only in the eyes of the law.'

'I wonder how it would have been,' he said musingly, 'if we'd stayed together.'

Rose shrugged carelessly. 'Who knows? The marriage success rate's not very high these days, and we were very young. We would probably have split up long before now.'

'Do you really believe that, Rose?' he said, startling her.

She gave him a long, analytical look. Seeing James Sinclair as he was now, even more attractive in her eyes than before, it was hard to believe that she would have ever left him willingly. 'I don't know,' she said honestly. 'Nor does it matter. It's all academic now.'

'If you say so. Tell me,' added James, 'having met the man, I can't believe you really want to marry Garrett, Rose. You must have other reasons for wanting a divorce.'

She frowned. 'What do you mean?'

'This Mark Cummings. It seems to me he's in need of a wife and a mother for his child. Has he cast you in the role?'

'Heavens, I hope not,' said Rose involuntarily.

'You don't care for the idea?'

'No. And not,' she added tartly, 'because I'm still married to you, either. I just don't care for Mark that way. Besides, I think he still lives in hope that his wife will go back to him some day.'

His mouth twisted. 'I can understand that.'

Her eyes flew to his in astonishment.

'For a long time after you left me,' James told her, his eyes locked with hers, 'I hoped we'd get together again.'

'Did you?' she said huskily.

James nodded. 'I even came here to Chastlecombe, determined to mend things between us. And caught sight of you walking down the street with a stocky, fair-haired man. You were laughing together, and so obviously a pair I dodged out of sight. After that I felt fate was telling me to give up. I didn't try again.'

Rose stared at him wordlessly, feeling her heart contract. 'It must have been Mark. How strange.' She dropped her eyes to hide sudden moisture on her lashes.

James turned her face up to his. 'Don't, Rose. That's the way I've remembered you all these years, in floods of tears during that gut-wrenching fight just before we split up. This time I want a happier picture for a keepsake.'

'I'm not crying,' she assured him, and smiled crookedly. 'Just mourning for what might have been.'

'It doesn't have to be in the past tense,' he said with sudden force, and pulled her out of the chair and into his arms. He tipped her face up to his, his eyes glittering with a heat that made her tremble. 'Look me in the eye, Rose Sinclair, and tell me you feel absolutely nothing for me.'

CHAPTER TEN

HELD so close to him, Rose knew there was no point in trying to lie. 'I can't do that,' she said, resentful of her body's treachery. 'Though, Lord knows, I'm entitled to feel enmity, James, if nothing else, after the things you once said to me. Which hurt all the more because some of them were true.' She looked up at him in appeal. 'Though in the beginning I didn't dream that Con's blueprint for seduction would succeed.'

'But it did—God, how it did,' he said bitterly. 'How I passed my exams I'll never know. All the time I was revising I just wanted to be with you, making love to my wife.'

'I followed orders faithfully—kept away from you the whole time,' she protested, wishing she had more control over her pulse.

'True. But just because you weren't there in the flesh—' He stopped, jaw clenched, and Rose swallowed hard, conscious that her breasts were hardening in response to his nearness, and a secret liquefying feeling lower down gave humiliating proof that James Sinclair still had the power to arouse her in ways no other man had ever done. And knew this only too well by the look in his eyes.

'Let me go, James,' she said quietly. *Please* let me go, she begged silently, before I do something I'm sure to regret later when you're gone.

'I don't want to let you go. I've always been curious to know if the chemistry would still be there. And it is.

Don't try to deny it.' His arms tightened instinctively. 'You owe me the truth.'

'I don't owe you anything!'

'Oh, yes, you do.' His eyes bored into hers. 'You're the reason I'm still on my own, lady. I've never been able to commit to the other women in my life because there you were in the background, reminding me of what happens when a man loses his head.'

'That's nothing to do with me,' she said, angry at the mention of other women.

'Of course it is.' He slid a hand down her cheek. 'I suppose I always knew what type of woman you'd become. You're not beautiful, but there's something about that face and body of yours that still gets to me like no other woman's ever has. Not that it matters to you now, of course,' he added suavely. 'Because you're not in love with me any more.'

'Exactly.' Rose shoved him away and stood back. 'Just how many women have there been, as a matter of interest?'

'It matters to you?' he demanded in triumph.

Oh, yes. It mattered.

'Of course it doesn't,' she assured him, and turned to pick up her glass. 'I was angry when I first saw you last night. But I'm not any longer. In fact I think it's a good thing we met up one last time to discuss the divorce in an adult, civilised way.'

'Civilised!' he growled, and snatched the glass away from her. 'I don't feel civilised, Rose. I don't know what there is about you that's so different from—'

'The others?'

He smiled slowly, and Rose quivered inside as he pulled her against him. 'Can you honestly say there's nothing happening between us? And,' he added, in a tone

which turned her bones to jelly, 'I'm not discussing things cerebral here.'

Without waiting for a reply James ended the argument in the way he had ended many an argument between them in the past. His lips took possession of hers, parting them, urging a response, his seducing tongue sending heat rushing through her body. He scooped her up and sat down with her in his lap, enclosing her in the embrace she had missed as much his lovemaking once it was no longer part of her life.

'In that get-up you look like the teenager I was so crazy about. It's hard to realise ten years have elapsed, Rose.'

'But they have,' she said in alarm. 'And you promised this wouldn't happen!'

He smoothed her hair back, his eyes hot on hers. 'Nothing has happened. Yet.' He pulled her close to kiss her, one hand sliding down her back. 'I shouldn't have mentioned the word "flesh",' he said against her mouth.

'Very evocative word,' she agreed with difficulty as his exploring fingers played havoc with her resistance, his touch burning through her shirt.

'And if I am trying to seduce you, it's only fair.' He put a finger under her chin. 'Isn't that what you did to me all those years ago?'

Rose thrust him away. 'I never imagined for a moment that my plan would entail carnal knowledge of my quarry, Sinclair.'

He raised a cynical eyebrow. 'But isn't that what you intended?'

She shook her head. 'I never aimed so high—or do I mean low? The idea was to make you fall in love with me; that's all.'

'The two are not mutually exclusive! Once I'd kissed you all I could think of was teaching you everything I

knew about the rest of it. I'm amazed I held off as long as I did.'

Rose gazed into his relentless eyes for a moment, then, summoning every shred of self-control she possessed, she stood up. 'Time I went home.'

His eyes hardened so suddenly she backed away as he leapt to his feet. 'You don't mean that, Rose.'

'I do, you know!'

His mouth twisted. 'Delayed retribution?'

'Nothing so dramatic. Just common sense.' She squared her shoulders. 'I'll be honest, James, and admit that part of me, the physical part, wants to give in to whatever you have in mind. But my brain tells me you can't walk back into my life after ten years and expect me to jump into bed with you at the snap of your fingers just because you fancy a little payback of some kind. I'm human enough to be flattered that you want me, of course.'

He leaned an elbow on the stone ledge above the fireplace. 'Are you still saying you feel nothing in return, Rose?'

'No,' she said unwillingly. 'But there are several reasons why I won't go to bed with you—'

'You mean make love with me.'

'For one thing,' she said, ignoring him, 'it could complicate the divorce.'

'Ah, yes, the divorce.' James's eyes narrowed to a predatory gleam. 'Tell me, Rose, what would happen if I informed your solicitor that I wanted a reconciliation?'

'This isn't something to joke about,' she snapped.

'Who says I'm joking?'

Rose turned away in angry defeat. 'It's too late for all this, James.'

'It's only a little before eleven, Rose.'

'I mean it's ten years too late.' She turned to face him. 'Or is all this just to queer Anthony Garrett's pitch?'

The surprise on James's face was genuine. 'I never gave him a thought,' he assured her. 'I don't think he's right for you, but if you tell me you love the man I'll never darken your door again. But you don't love him, Rose. And you know it.' He moved from the fireplace and took her by the shoulders, then dropped his hands, scowling when she flinched. 'The bastard hurt you—let me see.'

Rose slid the sweatshirt off one shoulder, craning to see the damage, then caught her breath as James laid his lips to the bruise, his tongue licking in deliberate caress as his hair brushed her skin.

'Don't worry,' he whispered, 'I'm just kissing it better.'

She covered herself hurriedly, and collected her bag. 'Goodnight, James. Thank you for dinner.'

'Wait.' James took her hand. 'When can I see you again?'

'I don't think that's a good idea, James.'

'Why not?'

Rose regarded him steadily. 'Because underneath all the blarney you're still angry with me, aren't you?'

'Do you blame me?'

'No. But it makes me uneasy. So it's best we say goodbye, James.'

'You've grown into a hard woman, Rose Sinclair,' he said, shaking his head.

'Don't call me that!'

'It's your name. In the eyes of the law you're still my legally wedded wife, remember.' His eyes held hers. 'If I'd carried you upstairs just now, as I wanted to, there would have been nothing against an old married couple sharing a bed together.'

'That's sophistry—' She turned away, unable to face

the mocking grey eyes a moment longer. 'And time I went. Thank you for dinner.'

He was frowning as he walked with her to the car. 'Rose, I'm not happy about your driving home alone. I'll come with you and walk back. Or I can just follow you in my car until I know you're safe.'

'Thank you, but no,' she said decisively. 'I can't go on jumping at shadows, James. And I have to live here after you're long gone, remember.'

'But I haven't gone yet, so ring me as soon as you get home and confirm you're safe and sound.'

'All right. I will. But I warn you, I'm a slow, cautious driver.' Rose smiled up at him, then drove off quickly, before James discovered how much she wanted to stay.

Rose parked her car in its usual niche behind the shop, let herself in through the back door and turned on the hall light. And found another rose lying inside her private door.

She raced upstairs, and rang James's cellphone number with a shaking hand. 'I'm home,' she said tersely. 'But I don't feel safe and sound. Another rose was waiting for me.'

James cursed colourfully. 'Rose, call the police right now,' he ordered.

'Not tonight. I'm tired; I need to go to bed. I'll call them tomorrow.'

'Then I'll come and sleep on your sofa—'

'No way, James.' No point in exchanging one danger for another. 'I'll be fine now. Everything's locked, bolted or disconnected. All I have to do is get myself to bed.'

'All right, have it your own way,' he said impatiently. 'But ring me if the least thing disturbs you. However late it is. And give me your cellphone number so I can check

on you in the morning. Are you seeing Garrett tomorrow night, by the way?'

'No way! He wasn't due to come down this weekend. I was so furious with him about the solicitor I turned him down flat when he took it for granted I'd be available just because he was.'

'This man hasn't got a clue where you're concerned!' James paused. 'Look, Rose, now I'm here I want to see you again before the law separates us for good. I assume there's no point in asking you to go out somewhere, so come here for a meal again tomorrow. Look on it as a kind of farewell party, if you like.'

Rose hesitated. Another evening in that cosy, isolated cottage would be asking for trouble. But there was no point in deluding herself. She wanted—needed—to see James again. Just one last time. But here on home ground, on her own territory. 'Come and have dinner here, instead,' she said casually.

There was dead silence for a moment. 'With the greatest of pleasure,' said James, openly surprised. 'Do I slink from the car park in disguise?'

'No. Just arrive brazenly at my door as usual. About eight?'

'Eight it is. Rose,' he added swiftly, 'do you feel better now?'

'Yes, I do.' The mere sound of James's voice had dispelled her panic. 'Goodnight.'

Before disconnecting her phone Rose listened to three consecutive messages from Anthony, begging her to change her mind about their Saturday night arrangement.

No chance, thought Rose, as she got ready for bed. Whatever happened from now on, Anthony Garrett was history. She put him from her mind and thought about

James at length instead, and eventually slept until the phone on the pillow beside her woke her up.

'Good morning,' said James. 'Did you sleep?'

'Gosh, you're early.' Rose yawned, peering at her watch. 'Amazingly enough I slept very well.'

'While I tossed and turned in my cold and lonely bed,' he said, sighing.

'How sad!'

'Unsympathetic creature. Now then, Rose,' he added, suddenly businesslike, 'phone the police this morning.'

'No. It's exactly the sort of publicity I could do without. And in broad daylight it just seems silly. No actual crime has been committed. It's not against the law to send roses.'

'I don't like it, just the same.'

'Neither do I. But if I ignore it, and keep my phone disconnected out of business hours, I'm sure the culprit will give up in the end.'

'If I were your husband for real I'd insist on notifying the police.'

'Possibly. But don't even think of trying it, Sinclair.'

'I won't. But only because I know how you react when people try to run your life. Don't work too hard, Rose. See you later.'

Rose dressed at top speed, ate some breakfast, and before she opened up hurried along the arcade to do some shopping for her unexpected dinner party, wondering if she'd lost her mind as she selected a meal likely to please her guest. She knew very well she should be wary of the underlying resentment James so very obviously harboured along with the desire he still felt for her, but in some ways it just added an extra spice of danger to the pleasure of seeing him again. Much as she loved Chastlecombe, life

there tended to be on the quiet side. And right now the sun was shining, a touch of spring was in the air, and, whatever happened afterwards, tonight she would enjoy spending time with James just once more. Because, quite apart from reviving old hurts, meeting him again had reminded her of a very important aspect of her relationship with James Sinclair. As well as being crazy about each other, for a few short, sweet months they'd been best friends as well as lovers. A combination that had made James such a hard act to follow.

Rose stowed her shopping away, then went to collect the post and start the day.

'Goodness me,' said Bel soon afterwards. 'You look very bouncy today, boss. What's put the sparkle in *your* eye?'

'Promise of spring in the air.'

'Wish it would do the same for me. Seeing Anthony tonight?'

'No, not tonight.' Rose hesitated, then decided on the truth. 'I've invited an old college friend to dinner,' she said, smiling.

'An old *male* college friend, I trust?'

'Absolutely.'

'Close friend?'

'Used to be.'

'Brilliant!' said Bel, who disapproved of Anthony Garrett. 'Have fun.'

The day was busy, as most Saturdays were, and the morning passed so quickly Rose was remorseful when Bel had to beg off for lunch and shopping.

'Sorry, sorry. I didn't realise it was so late. Bring a sandwich back for me. Something extravagant.'

While Bel was away Rose's heart sank as she saw Anthony come in. He gave her a brooding look, then

turned his back to browse round the shelves while she was busy with customers, but the moment the shop was empty he pounced on her belligerently.

'Where the blazes were you last night, Rose? I rang several times.'

'I know. I got your messages.'

'I asked you to ring back.'

'It was too late when I got home—'

'Where from?'

'I don't have to give you details of my movements, Anthony,' she said curtly, then looked up with a smile of relief as Bel came rushing back.

'Sorry I took so long,' Bel said breathlessly, handing over a paper sack. 'Crab salad, and it's fab. Hello, Anthony,' she added, offhand.

'Bel.' He nodded distantly. 'A word in private, Rose, if you would.'

She nodded, resigned. 'Come in the office, then, while I eat my lunch.'

'Can't we go up to the flat?' he complained, as he closed the door behind him.

'Not on a Saturday. Bel could be inundated any minute.' Rose took an appreciative bite of her sandwich. 'Talk away,' she said indistinctly.

'You know why I'm here,' he began, very obviously irritated by her attitude.

Rose shook her head. 'Actually, I don't.'

'Of course you do. To change your mind about tonight.'

'Sorry. No can do.'

His lips thinned. 'You're just being childish, Rose.'

She shook her head at him reprovingly. 'Your powers of persuasion need work, Anthony. Besides, I'm doing something else tonight.'

'But when I'm here you spend Saturdays with me!'

'Not every Saturday, and certainly not tonight.' Rose looked at him squarely. 'In fact, not any more. I'm afraid it's over between us, Anthony.'

He stared at her incredulously. '*Over?* What are you talking about? Only a short while ago we were discussing marriage—'

'No, Anthony. That was your idea, not mine.'

'Oh, I get it!' His face suffused with angry colour. 'Sinclair's to blame for all this, isn't he? You're still in love with him.'

'No,' said Rose curtly. 'That's nothing to do with it. You and I just wouldn't suit on a long-term basis, Anthony, so it's best to end things now before either of us gets hurt.' She held out her hand. 'Can we at least part friends?'

He gave her a look of burning dislike, brushed the hand aside and wrenched open the door, forcing a smile when he spotted someone he knew amongst the people browsing along Rose's shelves.

'I've been dying to ask all afternoon, but we've been too busy,' said Bel, as she was getting ready to leave for the day. 'By the look on Anthony's face earlier I assume all is at an end?'

Rose heaved a sigh. 'Afraid so.'

'Can't say I'm sorry.' Bel gave her a swift, unaccustomed kiss on her cheek. 'Have some real fun instead with your friend. And tell me all about it on Monday.'

After Rose locked up the shop she did some swift housework, had a shower, did more to her hair with a styling brush than usual, then dithered about for a while in front of her open wardrobe. Nothing too special, she warned herself, and buttoned a thin, blush-pink cardigan to its plunging V-neck, pulled on navy linen drawstring trousers

she'd been keeping for the summer, then wrapped herself in a striped apron, and repaired to the kitchen to get to work.

Potatoes were scrubbed, hollandaise sauce prepared for the asparagus, and monkfish tails wrapped in bacon ready to roast by the time Rose laid a small table under a window which in daylight gave a view of rolling Cotswold hills. And realised she was in a state of excitement unknown since she was eighteen years old. When she'd been so young and vulnerable, and so hopelessly in love with James Sinclair. But all that was changed, she assured herself, as eight o'clock loomed nearer. Tonight she would discuss the forthcoming separation sensibly with James, and after that they could go their separate ways. Because spending time with a man who made it gratifying plain he both resented and desired her was asking for trouble, when the man in question was the husband she was still married to.

When the bell rang at last Rose went sedately down the stairs, unable to control her body's leap of response when she found James standing there, arms full of bottles, his eyes bright with sudden heat at the sight of her.

Warning bells in Rose's head. He was reading too much into her invitation to dinner. 'Hello, James,' she said, smiling politely. 'You're punctual.'

'I'd have been earlier if I'd thought you'd let me in,' he assured her, and closed the door behind them, slamming the bolts home with a finality far too symbolic for Rose's peace of mind. 'I brought some wine. If you want the red I need to open it for breathing space. Or you can chill the white instead.' He smiled down at her. 'Or we could drink both.'

Rose retreated up the stairs hurriedly, conscious that his eyes were on her rear view as she went.

'I already have some wine. But thanks, anyway. I'll keep yours for another time.' She waved him to the sofa. 'Dinner will be half an hour, so we could start on my wine now, if you like. Or I've got whisky, gin—'

'Rose,' he interrupted, and dumped the bottle down to take her hands. 'You're as jumpy as a cat.'

'Yes, I am,' she said bluntly. 'I think this may be a mistake.'

'You're worried I might try to get you into bed before dinner, or after?' he said affably.

Rose stared up into teasing eyes, then relaxed, and laughed. 'Something like that.' she admitted.

'Is that how Garrett behaves?' he demanded.

'Not with me.' She picked up the wine and went to the kitchen, then turned in the doorway to look at James over her shoulder. 'Which doesn't mean I've led a totally celibate life from the time you and I split up, Sinclair.'

'Likewise,' said James promptly. 'But I knew very well you and Garrett weren't lovers.'

'How?'

'Something in the body language.' He shook his head. 'He's not the man for you, Rose.'

'I'll get the wine,' she said firmly, and went to oversee her dinner preparations.

The meal was a success, and James sincere with his praise as he despatched his dinner with gratifying speed.

'That was fabulous. You're a great cook, Rose,' he said, sitting back at last.

She shook her head. 'Just a fan of TV cooking programmes. You were a guinea pig tonight. I've never tried monkfish before.'

'It was superb,' James assured her, and refilled their wine glasses. His eyes were intent as he leaned back in his chair. 'You know, Rose, I used to think about this a

lot. Meeting you again, sharing a meal like this—just being together.'

Rose eyed him cynically as she got up to take their plates. 'In which case you could have done something about it long before now if you'd wanted to. I wasn't exactly on another planet.'

'I was a coward,' he said flatly, and followed her to the kitchen.

'A *coward*? You, James?'

'I couldn't face more rejection.'

She gave him a scornful, disbelieving look as she handed him a platter of cheese and biscuits. 'You take these; I'll bring celery and grapes. No pudding. I did consider treacle tart from the bakery, then I remembered you weren't keen on sweet things in the past.'

'Only on you, Rose,' he agreed, standing aside to let her pass.

'"Sweet" wasn't one of the adjectives you flung at me during our final encounter all those years ago,' she reminded him acidly. 'So if you had come to see me again some time I suppose you're right. I might well have shut the door in your face.'

'After I saw you in the street with this Mark of yours I worked that out for myself.' James put the plates on the table, then took her hand. 'Could we eat this later?'

'OK. Coffee?'

'No. Come and sit down.' James led her to the sofa and drew her down beside him. 'Did you soften towards me after you left university?'

'I was in London by then, learning to earn a living, and far too busy to mourn for you.' She gave him a sidelong glance through her lashes. 'I admit I used to imagine, sometimes, that I spotted you in the street. But it was

always just some tall, dark stranger with a king-of-the-jungle walk like yours.'

James kept hold of her hand, his forefinger smoothing the back of it. 'So you're certain you'd have rejected me second time round, Rose.'

'Definitely.' Her eyes hardened. 'Like you, I rarely make the same mistake twice.'

James tensed, and for a moment she thought he was going to leap to his feet and stride out of the flat. Instead he raised her hand to his lips. 'I'm sure I could change your mind about that,' he said, in a tone that sent trickles of apprehension down her spine.

'I don't think so,' she said doggedly, and got to her feet, holding onto her resolve with both hands. 'I think it's time you went, James.'

He got up with the lithe grace she remembered so well, looking like a tiger balked of its prey. 'What if I don't want to go, Rose?' And before she could dodge away he pulled her up into his arms, kissing her with an abruptness that excited her so much she responded involuntarily, all her cool resolutions flying through the window at the first touch of his lips, her hands making only nominal resistance as he began to slide buttons from their moorings.

'You can't *do* this,' she gasped, trying to push him away. 'Do you really think you can march back into my life after ten years and straight into my bed?'

'Who said anything about bed?' he said, frustrating her attempts to free herself. 'What's the harm in a few kisses, Rose Sinclair?'

'Don't call me that,' she snapped, twisting in his arms, but he held her fast.

'It's your name. And I'm still your husband.'

'Only technically—' But the rest of her words were smothered as James began to kiss her again, making love

to her with a subtlety that broke down all the barriers she'd tried so hard to erect against him. Her mouth parted helplessly to his demanding tongue, and she sucked in her breath as he caught her flailing hands in one of his and bared her breasts to his lips and teeth and relentless, clever fingers, rousing hot, wet turbulence deep inside her as he bore her further down on the sofa, his breath coming in great gasps as he raised his head to look down into her flushed, desire-blank face.

'You still want me, admit it,' James said hoarsely, the breath rasping through his chest, triumph in his voice bringing Rose back to earth with a bump.

She shoved him away in disgust, and jumped to her feet, desire transformed to blazing anger. 'Is that what all this is about?' she threw at him. 'An ego-massaging exercise?' She let out a strangled sound of self-loathing as she put herself back together with shaking fingers, then shoved him away as he tried to take her in his arms.

'Rose,' he panted, capturing her hands. 'Don't look at me like that.'

She calmed down a little. 'It was my fault,' she said bitterly. 'I should never have asked you round here tonight.' She blinked away angry tears. 'Like a stupid idiot I thought we could just talk rationally, like adult human beings. Whereas you took it for granted I had a spot of auld lang syne in mind.'

James released her and stood back. 'I'm only human, Rose. And male. I needed to know if you still responded to me.'

'Well, now you do,' she said wearily. 'You've made the experiment and it worked like a charm. I hope your wilting ego is satisfied.'

He gave her a deeply disturbing smile. 'Bad choice of words, Rose. But if I promise not to come within a foot

of you until I leave could we still have that rational talk?
And maybe the coffee we passed on earlier?'

Rose stared at him, irresolute, then gave a deep, shaky
sigh. 'All right,' she said dully. 'Why not? We can discuss
the divorce.'

'What if I said I don't want a divorce?' he parried.

She swallowed, thrusting a hand through her tumbled
hair. 'Don't start that again. Because whether you do or
not, James, is immaterial. I can get one any time I want.'

His smile set her teeth on edge. 'In that case, Rose, tell
me what made you wait all these years before doing something about it?'

Good question, thought Rose, later that night, while sleep
became less and less of a possibility as the hours dragged
by. The coffee had been a mistake, since James had flatly
refused to discuss the divorce, and in the end had taken
his leave without kissing her again, but with a faintly om-
inous promise to be in touch.

And what, exactly, did he mean by that? thought Rose,
pummelling her pillow yet again. Tonight was meant to
be a full stop. A finale to the unfinished business between
them.

After a Sunday spent alone and restless, hoping James
would contact her again, halfway through Monday Rose
discovered exactly what James had meant by keeping in
touch when the local florist delivered a vast sheaf of
spring flowers.

'Thank you for a delightful evening. J.S.,' was the message.

'I assume J.S. is the old chum,' said Bel, eyes dancing,
'*Very* nice. You obviously had a good time together.'

Rose smiled in agreement, and took the flowers up to
her flat, glad that the rest of the day was busy enough to

keep her mind off James Sinclair. But later that evening the phone rang while she was deep in publishers' catalogues, checking on titles in the pipeline.

With the caution she'd acquired lately she waited until she heard James begin to leave a message before she picked up the receiver.

'How are you today, Rose?'

'Tired. We've been busy. I lost your phone number,' she fibbed, 'so I had no way of thanking you for the flowers.'

'Just a small token of appreciation. And for obvious reasons, not roses. It occurred to me that you don't have my home address. So grab a pen.' He gave her his home and mobile number, and his London address. 'Try not to lose them this time. Though in emergencies you can always reach me at the bank.'

'I doubt I'll need to do that! Future communications,' added Rose crisply, 'will probably be made through my solicitor.'

James laughed mockingly. 'You really believe that? Goodnight, Rose.'

Rose was very much aware that this was the day she should have instructed Henry to start proceedings, but she hadn't been able to bring herself to do it. Because in her heart of hearts she didn't want to be free of James. At least, not yet. Her intellect resented his assumption that he could just invade her life again and sweep her off her feet to show he still had power over her. But her errant heart, not to mention the body that throbbed at the mere sound of his voice, made it plain that only sheer force of will had helped her hold out against him. The sensible course would be to break all contact with him once and for all, and be safe. But then, when had she ever been sensible in her dealings with James Sinclair?

And James, she discovered, had no intention of letting her break contact. He phoned every night, ostensibly to check on her stalker, then to chat for a while, and if the intention was to keep Rose in a state of suspense every night until he called James was highly successful. She found it hard to settle to anything until she'd heard from him, and even refused Bel's invitation to a meal at the weekend in favour of staying in for the nightly conversation with James.

'I'm in bed, James,' she snapped, one night towards the end of the week, irritable because she'd been waiting on tenterhooks for what seemed like hours.

'If I woke you up it's your fault. Your line was engaged early on, before I went out. I've only just got back. Who were you talking to, anyway?'

'Let me see.' Rose relaxed, smiling smugly at the ceiling. 'Mark Cummings, Henry Beresford, oh, and Anthony Garrett.'

There was a tense pause. 'I don't know which one I object to most,' said James tightly. 'But on consideration perhaps it's Henry Beresford. Was the subject divorce, by any chance?'

She stretched luxuriously, deeply gratified by his tone. 'Yes.'

Another silence. 'And Garrett? What did he want?'

'In a word, me. He decided to overlook my aberration last weekend, and proposed marriage again.'

'Remind the bastard that you're not a free agent,' said James savagely. 'So what did Cummings want?'

'To talk about the bookstall I'm running at his school tomorrow night.'

'As long as that's all he wants.'

'My personal life is nothing to do with you any more, Sinclair.'

He laughed softly, with a mocking indulgence that clenched her fists. 'Goodnight. Sweet dreams. I'll call you.'

CHAPTER ELEVEN

ROSE went off with her wares to run the stall at Chastlecombe Grammar School parents' evening without hearing from James. Disappointed, and furious with herself because of it, she got through the evening with her usual smiling efficiency, accepted Mark's help in clearing up, and his company on the way home to help her take everything into the shop. Refusing her offer of coffee, Mark gave her a hug and a kiss on the front doorstep, told her to lock up securely behind him and went sprinting home to his little daughter.

Rose dawdled over her preparations for bed, but the longed-for phone call refused to materialise. She lay awake for hours, but heard nothing from James until he strolled into the shop next morning in person. Rose, bowled over at the sight of him, was involved with a customer, but Bel, in tune at once to the gamma rays sizzling between her boss and the newcomer, gave James a beaming welcome and volunteered her help in supplying him with the latest additions to their non-fiction section.

The moment the shop was empty Rose made the necessary introductions, and tactful Bel promptly took herself off to a very early lunch hour.

'You didn't say you were coming down again, James,' said Rose, eyeing him with resentment.

'If I had you'd probably have taken off somewhere else,' said James, and leaned against the counter to look into her eyes. 'We need to talk.'

Rose clenched her teeth against the wave of pure long-

ing that swept through her, and saw James's eyes dilate
as he sensed it. 'We can't talk here,' she whispered, as a
trio of customers entered the shop.

'Tonight, then.'

'No. I'm going out to dinner—'

'No, you're not. Cancel!' His eyes took on a steely
gleam. 'Do it, Rose. I'll be round later.' He picked up his
book and strode from the shop, leaving her in a state of
such tension she was glad the newcomers were content to
browse for a while before requiring her attention.

'That was the old college chum, I assume,' said Bel,
when she came back.

Rose nodded. 'I wasn't expecting him.'

'I could see that. I thought I'd have to scrape you up
from the floor.' Bel grinned. 'You're a dark horse, Rose
Dryden. No wonder you passed on my offer tonight!'

It was the longest Saturday Rose had ever experienced.
By the time she closed the shop she was tense with a
variety of emotions ranging from plain weariness to a state
of euphoria that made her feel sick. She went through the
motions of locking up and leaving everything secure for
the night, then trudged upstairs, wondering how soon
James was likely to turn up. This time she had no special
meal in readiness. If he wanted food James would have
to provide it. And probably cook it too, in her present
state of exhaustion.

Rose stood under the shower for a long time, dried her
hair, dressed in the navy linen trousers and a white cotton
sweater, added a few basic touches to her face, and made
herself some tea. She curled up on her sofa with it, but
before she'd taken more than a sip or two her phone rang.
She snatched up the receiver eagerly, expecting James,
then shuddered as she heard her name whispered before

the line went dead. She slammed the phone down, not even bothering to try and trace the call as she cursed the idiot who was frightening her. When the doorbell rang she raced down the stairs, then gave a gasp of horror as she stumbled over a newly delivered rose in her headlong flight. She flung the door open, tears streaming down her face, and James stared at slammed the door shut behind him.

'My God, Rose, what's wrong—?' He stopped short as she held out the flower, and with a savage curse he flung it down and took her in his arms, holding her close, murmuring wordless comfort into her hair as she sobbed her heart out against his chest. After a minute or two James picked her up and carried her up to the flat, and sat down with her in his lap, smoothing her head against his shoulder as he let her cry.

'Better now?' he whispered, when she was quiet at last.

'Yes,' said Rose thickly, and sat up, knuckling the tears from her eyes. 'Sorry to make such a fuss. It was a hard day, I'd just had another of those phone calls, and the flower was the final straw. I just hate this feeling of being watched.' She looked up into his eyes, trying to smile. 'I must look a mess,' she added, pushing her hair back.

'No, you don't.' James drew her down against his shoulder again. 'You look delectable.' He narrowed his eyes at her. 'Nor, I discovered last night, am I the only one who thinks so.'

Rose frowned. 'What do you mean?'

'I came round to see you last night the minute I arrived, and saw you in a clinch with another man.' His jaw clenched. 'I assume the guy kissing you was Mark Cummings?'

'Oh. Yes. He helped me home with my stock,' she said,

secretly euphoric. 'Why didn't you say something? I waited hours—' She stopped dead.

'What for?' he asked, so silkily she tried to pull away, but his arms tightened. 'Were you waiting for me to ring, by any chance? If I had I'd have blown my top, lady, after watching you kiss another man.'

'It was just a goodnight peck,' said Rose truculently. 'Mark's an old friend.'

'Which doesn't give him the right to make love to my wife.'

'I'm not—'

'Oh, yes, you are. I'm still your husband and you're still my wife, Rose Sinclair. I've got every right to make love to you,' he whispered, raising the hairs along her spine. 'And I want you. Now.'

Their eyes met. Rose could feel his arousal hard beneath her thighs, and her heart began to beat thickly, every nerve-ending heightened by recent fright, and present longing, and a deep, uncontrollable need to feel James's body joined with hers in the rapture she had never come near to experiencing with anyone else. Even if tonight was all she'd have, she wanted it. And wanted it badly. She shivered uncontrollably as James, eyes blazing with triumph, took her silence for assent.

He kissed her as though he was starved for her, and Rose surrendered to him with equal hunger, responding wantonly as their lips and tongues and importuning hands synchronised in a love duet which quickly threatened to reach crescendo.

'Wait,' gasped Rose.

'I *can't* wait!' James pushed her flat beneath him and smothered her protests with kisses that drove everything from her mind as their mutual need roared through them like a forest fire, consuming them so rapidly they clutched

each other close. As they shockwaves receded afterwards, their eyes locked in mutual awe.

Without a word James picked her up and carried her to the bedroom, where he relieved her to the remainder of her clothes at dizzying speed, then demanded a similar service in return.

'No,' gasped Rose, trembling under the eyes which caressed her body with tactile hunger. 'You do it. I'll be too slow.'

'I thought you'd lived with someone!'

'I didn't do that kind of thing for him.'

'Why not?' he whispered, stretching out beside her.

'I just couldn't,' she said impatiently, and lay with eyes closed for a moment to savour the bliss of head-to-toe contact again as he smoothed her body against his. The first time, James had removed only enough clothing to make their loving possible. But now they were together in full naked contact their bodies generated a heat that quickly rekindled their mutual fire.

'I've got a lot of time to make up for,' whispered James, his breath hot against her ear. 'And this time I mean to go slow, so pay attention.'

He began to make love to her in the way she'd so often dreamed of and longed for, his lips pulling on taut, hard nipples as his probing fingers caressed and cajoled. Soon she was one aching, shivering mass of hot, liquid longing as he deliberately inflamed them both to such unbearable heights of arousal he gasped her name at last and entered her with a sure, conquering thrust and united them again, as they were always meant to be, in one flesh.

Rose's breath was still tearing through her chest as James turned her face up to his afterwards, his eyes hot on hers. 'Now tell me you're not in love with me any more!'

She stiffened in his arms. 'Is that what all this is about? To make me admit I still find you irresistible, Sinclair?'

'Not entirely. I know your body responds to me, Rose.' He smiled a little. 'I tried to convince myself that I'd fantasised about what we had together. That it couldn't possibly have been as good as I remembered. And it isn't.'

She glared at him, and he laughed and kissed her heard. 'It's even better.' He sobered abruptly. 'But it was never just physical for us, Rose. I need to know you still care.'

Rose gazed up into his eyes for a long time, unwilling to commit herself, then threw caution to the winds. Of course she cared. So what was the point in pretending she didn't? 'Yes,' she said gruffly. 'I care.'

His engulfing kiss put an end to conversation for a while, until her stomach gave an unromantic grumble and James laughed indulgently.

'You're hungry. What can I do about it?'

Rose sat up, pulling the covers up to hide her breasts from grey, marauding eyes. 'One,' she said, ticking off her fingers, 'you can order in something from Orsini's and wait for hours until we eat, two, you could go out and buy fish and chips, or three, we can eat bacon and eggs right now.'

'Three,' said James promptly. 'I'm starving.'

A few minutes later, fully dressed and more or less in her right mind, Rose had bacon, eggs and mushrooms ready, accompanied by hunks of bread. They sat together on the sofa, and for a while James ate in famished, appreciative silence. But once the meal was over he looked at her with searching eyes.

'So what happens now, Rose?' He took her hand. 'Come and sit on my lap and let's discuss it.'

When they were settled together in familiar embrace,

with Rose's head on James's shoulder, he put a finger under her chin and turned her face up to his.

'Does this mean you've changed your mind about the divorce?'

Rose met his eyes steadily. 'Do you want me to?'

'What else did you think all that was about?' he demanded, then frowned. 'However, like the late, unlamented Mr Garrett, I'm based in London. Will this be a problem?'

'No, it won't,' she said emphatically. 'Because I'm not rushing into anything this time, James.'

He eyed her askance. 'I don't like the sound of that. Hell, Rose, we've wasted too much time apart already.'

'Nevertheless, I'm not a starry-eyed teenager any more, James. I've acquired at least *some* common sense since I saw you last.'

He kissed the lip she was biting. 'To hell with common sense. It's time you made up for all the years you forced us to spend apart.'

Rose drew in a deep, unsteady breath. 'James, we need to get to know each other again before I do that.'

'Why? Surely we've both matured into responsible adults.'

She touched a hand to his cheek. 'No one could have acted more responsibly than you did ten years ago, James, when I came crying to you with my little problem.'

His eyes darkened. 'It was no big deal, Rose. I knew you had no parents to turn to. It never occurred to me to do anything other than assume full responsibility.'

'And I was desperately grateful for that. But so guilty, too, about your finals.' She smiled a little. 'You were well-known for concentrating on books rather than girls.'

'Until I met you.' He kissed her again. 'And, just in case you're wondering, there's no significant female pres-

ence in my life, I promise.' He smiled crookedly. 'Though I confess to acquaintance with more than one lady not averse to the odd spot of wining, dining and bed, now and then.'

'Lord, you're arrogant!'

'Just truthful. I'm a normal male animal and own up to certain needs from time to time.' He smoothed her hair back from her forehead. 'If I had you all that would be over, I promise.'

'But living with someone can be tricky,' said Rose, resisting the urge to say yes to everything he asked.

'We managed it very happily during the brief times we managed to spend together,' he reminded her.

'Maybe because we never had enough of it—time, I mean,' she added, flushing.

'So let's make up for it now,' said James, his eyes locked with hers as he stroked a finger along the hectic colour in her cheek.

'Not so fast,' she said breathlessly. 'I think we should work up to it gradually, just seeing each other socially for a while. Going out to dinner—'

'Out?' he mocked. 'Did you actually say *out* to dinner?'

'I did.'

'Hallelujah!' James paused, eyeing her narrowly. 'Or did you mean in London where no one knows us?'

'Right here in Chastlecombe, too.' Rose smiled at him cajolingly. 'What do you say?'

'In what capacity am I to do this as far as this town is concerned?' enquired James. 'Officially as your husband, or just as a replacement for Mr Garrett?'

'I'll have to think about that,' she said, frowning. 'If this is to be a sort of testing period, to find out if marriage is a practical proposition for us—'

'Rose,' he said impatiently, 'We *are* married!'

'Only on paper.' She looked at him in appeal. 'But before I burn my boats I need you to be very sure about this, James. I don't mean what happened between us just now,' she added, colouring. 'In that way we're still totally compatible—'

'Agreed. So what's the problem?' he demanded.

'A very prosaic one.' Rose sighed. 'My only attempt at actually living with a man was a total disaster.'

'With me it will be different, I promise,' he said with supreme confidence, and kissed her as emphasis. He drew back to look down into her eyes. 'So tell me you're willing to take the chance, Rose.'

She looked at him in silence for a moment, then nodded slowly. 'Yes. I am.'

His eyes lit with satisfaction. 'But if I come courting for all your world to see, I need assurances. My ego couldn't take another hammering from you, Rose.'

'It won't have to.' She looked at him in sudden disbelief. 'James, we're going too fast—'

'Not fast enough for me!'

It was very late by the time Rose made a pot of coffee to drink with cheese and biscuits. 'A recipe for insomnia if ever I saw one,' she commented.

James smiled slowly. 'I know an infallible cure for that—or would you rather I slept at the cottage tonight?'

'When are you going back to London?'

'Tomorrow evening. After I've spent as much of Sunday as possible with you.'

Rose looked at him for a moment. 'Not much point in going back to the cottage, then. Stay the night.'

James reached for her and pulled her close, a look in his eyes that sent a cold shiver down her spine.

'What is it?' she whispered.

'I'm thinking of all the time wasted,' he said bitterly,

and held her face cupped in his hands. 'You owe me, Rose.'

After Rose had paid some of the debt to James's satisfaction they fell asleep in each other's arms, and woke to make love again in the early morning before the world outside was awake.

'Do you still have your wedding ring?' said James later, over the breakfast they'd brought back to bed to eat.

'Of course I have.' She frowned as she considered her hand. 'I was never able to wear it back then, so maybe it won't even fit me now.'

'If it doesn't I'll buy you another one,' he said promptly, but Rose shook her head.

'I want that one. It can be altered if it doesn't fit.'

'So when will you start wearing it again?'

'When we go public, I suppose. Which had better be soon, now Anthony knows about you. Minerva will be surprised. Henry's expecting to arrange a divorce.' Rose looked at him questioningly. 'How about you? Will you tell your mother?'

'Yes, but not over the phone. I'll go up to see her.' James leaned over to kiss a smear of marmalade from Rose's cheek. 'Messy eater,' he said indulgently.

'It's so difficult in bed,' she said, laughing. 'Look out, mind your coffee!'

'I vote we eat lunch elsewhere.' He brushed toast crumbs away. 'Sorry—you'll have to change your bed before you sleep in it again.'

'Pity,' said Rose with regret, and gave him a sparkling look. 'I was hoping to keep your smell to sleep with to-night.'

'My smell!'

'Scent, then.' She leaned nearer to nuzzle his shoulder, sucking delicately at his skin. 'I'd know yours anywhere.'

James gave a strangled sound, slid out of bed, removed the breakfast tray, then got back in and took Rose in his arms all in one movement. 'I'd know you anywhere, too, Rose Sinclair,' he whispered against her mouth. 'So, if you were intending to read the Sunday papers at this point, you're out of luck.'

CHAPTER TWELVE

WHEN James left her, far later that evening than he'd intended, Rose had time at last to think. Too much time. She felt restless, and roamed the flat like a lost soul, switching on the television, switching it off again, trying to read the Sunday papers neither of them had looked at. When her cellphone rang at last Rose felt limp with relief when she heard the voice she'd been waiting for.

'What have you been doing since I left?' he asked.

'Nothing much. I'm a bit tired.'

'Lack of sleep last night,' he said, audibly smug.

'Yes.' Rose heaved a sigh. 'I don't foresee sleeping all that well tonight, either.'

'Because you're head over heels in love with me?' he said swiftly.

'Something like that.'

'Good,' he said triumphantly. 'I'll remind you of that next time we meet. Talking of which,' he said after a pause, 'that won't be for a while. I'm afraid I'm off to Boston for the job on Thursday. I'll be up the following weekend.'

A whole fortnight. Which would be for the best, in some ways. 'In that case, James,' she said slowly, 'could I come down to you that weekend? If I am going to move in with you I'd like to see where you live.'

There was silence for a moment. 'Rose, could we postpone that for a while?'

'Of course,' she said instantly, rebuffed.

He swore softly. 'You're offended.'

'Not in the least. I'll come some other time. Or not, according to how things go.'

'Stop that right now, Rose! Come by all means. I just wanted the house to look less of a mess before you did. Until very recently I shared it with someone else.'

Who? thought Rose, picturing some voluptuous female making off in a huff with designer luggage. 'It's all right,' she said carelessly. 'It was just an idea. Let's leave it awhile.'

James let out an exasperated sigh. 'I shall expect you here a week on Saturday evening, Rose, so arrange it.'

Mondays in the shop were usually busy, and Rose was glad of it after the emotional ups and downs of her weekend. She had slept badly for more than one reason after the unexpected little tiff with James, and felt on edge until he rang that evening.

'I've rung to apologise,' he said without preamble.

'What about?'

'For not welcoming your visit with open arms.'

'It was certainly a bit off-putting after I'd—'

'Made mad, passionate love with me for most of the weekend?'

'Beautifully put,' she said acidly. 'Look, James, I don't have to come.'

'Don't dare back out now, Rose. I've organised a cleaning company to come in next week to make the place habitable. Just for you. It's going to be a hell of a long fortnight, so what time do I expect you? Early as possible, please.'

'Actually,' said Rose carefully, 'I could make it on the Friday evening. If you like.'

'Damn right I like!' He paused. 'Hopefully the cleaners should be finished by then, but I'll probably be working late with the risk management boys, so I'll send you a

key. You can let yourself in if you're before me. And explore Bluebeard's lair to your heart's content,' he added slyly. 'Who's minding the store for you?'

'Minerva's volunteered. She likes to keep a finger on the pulse occasionally, anyway. I think she misses contact with the general public.'

'Will you miss that, too?'

'Probably.'

'Enough for second thoughts?' he demanded.

'No.'

'Then tell me again you're still mad about me.'

'How many times do I have to say it to convince you?'

'A lot more yet, lady.'

'I'll tell you—no, I'll *show* you when I see you.'

The time dragged by while James was away, with only his phone calls to reassure Rose she hadn't dreamed the passionate weekend in his arms. By the time her train arrived at Ealing Broadway just under a fortnight later she was in such a state of tension her head was aching as she took a taxi to a house in one of the suburb's broad, leafy roads. Feeling rather furtive, she let herself into James's empty home, put her bag down in the square hall, then went exploring the large, conventional house. The sitting room was big, with rugs scattered here and there on polished wood floors, chairs and sofas covered in new-looking sand-coloured linen, paler curtains looped and swagged round a large bay window. Books filled the shelves in alcoves flanking a fireplace topped by a glowing oil of a Highland loch at sunset.

Rose looked round her with a sudden, fierce sense of possession. She liked it here. She wanted to live here. Whoever had lived here before.

After a moment's hesitation she went upstairs to look

into James's bedroom, which was spartan and very tidy. She looked at the wide bed, then wished she hadn't as a hot rush of excitement intensified the throbbing in her head. Wondering if James was ever in need of a painkiller she had a look in his bathroom with no result, then went back along the landing to the main bathroom. In a cabinet which held a sparse selection of male toiletries, she found a few basic medical supplies, and a box of tampons and a half-empty bottle of expensive French perfume. Rose clenched her teeth against a sudden rush of nausea. James had been frank about other women, but it was a shock to come face to face with such personal confirmation of his past. Did these things belong to the former tenant, or merely one of the women happy to share bed and board with James on a casual basis?

It has been ten years, she reminded herself stringently. What did you expect? She swallowed down a couple of painkillers with a glass of water, then went back into the master bedroom to examine the leather folder on James's dresser. It held two snapshots: one was of a lurcher, with a schoolboy James embracing it as he grinned at the camera, the other showed two people flanking young James with fishing rod, the woman's face obscured by a cotton sun hat, the tired man gazing down on his son with such deep affection Rose felt a lump in her throat. A third, unframed photograph lay face down on the chest. Rose turned it over, and eyed it with deep hostility. A young blonde woman of her own age, with expensively cut hair and a black dress which clung to every curve, lounged, laughing, on what looked like the sofa downstairs. The eyes held a smile of such confident, teasing allure Rose's fingers curled, wanting to tear the photograph in shreds.

Rose heard the door slam downstairs, and put the photograph down guiltily. She ran downstairs, and without a

word James dumped down his briefcase and swept her into his arms, kissing her with a hunger she responded to involuntarily, unable to control her body's reaction to his touch after so long.

'God, it's been a long time,' he said at last, rubbing his cheek over her hair. 'I wondered if you'd be here, after all.'

Rose stood back to look up at him. 'I very nearly wasn't. Your initial lack of enthusiasm was very off-putting,' she said frankly. 'I almost told you to get lost again then and there.'

'I could tell that,' said James, grimacing. 'So I re-grouped in a hurry. Come here. I've been thinking about this for two long weeks, woman.'

'So have I.' Pushing the photograph from her mind, Rose returned the kiss with such fervour James thrust her away at last, his breathing ragged.

'Let me take you on a tour,' he said gruffly. 'Otherwise I'm likely to carry you straight up to bed right now. And then you might think I'm only after your body.'

'You want more than that?'

'Damn right. I want every last thing you have to offer, Rose Sinclair,' said James, and shrugged off his long dark overcoat. 'How much have you seen?'

'Only your sitting room and some of the upstairs.' Which last had been a bit of a mistake. She smiled as they went into his sitting room. 'You must have found my place a bit claustrophobic after this.'

'You were there, Rose. I didn't notice much else.' He looked around him. 'The cleaning people seem to have done a good job. They've put the new covers on for me, I see. Alex left me a couple of chairs, so with a bit of input from my mother I had them married up with the same material.' His eyes returned to Rose, bright with

something she thought she identified as decision. 'But if you don't like anything I'll change it—in fact if you don't like the house we'll find somewhere else.'

'I love it here.' Rose reached up and kissed him, forcing herself to keep quiet about the woman in the photograph.

'Then come and see the rest of it.'

James took her on a tour of an empty dining room and a study at the back, which shared a view of the garden with a kitchen some former owner had been clever enough to enlarge and modernise without losing its character.

'When I bought the place Alex came in with me as my tenant, which helped with the mortgage. I lived downstairs, Alex up here,' he said, preceding her upstairs. 'But now the master bedroom's all mine.' James paused beside the large bed, his eyes intent on her face. 'Rose,' he said huskily, reaching for her, 'don't make me wait any longer—'

'Not so fast,' said Rose. 'First tell me who this is.' She detached herself and picked up the photograph. 'Is she the reason you put me off coming, James? Was she still in residence at the time?'

He stared blankly at the photograph, then back at Rose, his eyes narrowed to a gleam which sent a chill down her spine. 'No, she was not. What kind of a man do you think I am?'

'After ten years how should I know?' she said, all the more militant because she'd expected him to reassure her. 'Is she one of the dinner-and-bed brigade? Or is *she* this Alex of yours?'

'Neither,' said James flatly, taking off his jacket.

'So why the secrecy?'

James's face set into cold implacable lines. 'I've had only one guilty secret in my life.' He smiled grimly. 'That

was you. So if we're going to have any kind of viable relationship in future you need to take me on trust.'

'That's not fair!'

'Life isn't fair. I learned that early on at your hands, lady.'

Rose winced. 'Look, James, I came up here earlier. I had a headache and I was looking for painkillers. There's some perfume and—other things in your bathroom cabinet. Which made it obvious a woman's been in residence quite recently. Was that why you didn't want me to come?'

'No,' said James harshly. 'That wasn't the reason at all, but let's leave that for now.' He stalked across the room towards her, his eyes bright with such cold ferocity Rose had a sudden urge to turn and run. 'To set you right, my darling wife, no woman has ever lived here with me because I've never exposed myself to the dangers of a close relationship since the day I last saw you.'

Rose backed away, her headache suddenly excruciating. 'You haven't forgiven me at all have you, James?' she said unsteadily. 'So why in heaven's name did you have to make love to me if you felt like that? Punishment? Ego-boosting?'

'Before I saw you I didn't intend to make love to you at all,' he said bitterly. 'Once I did meet you, I was angry because I wanted you the minute I laid eyes on you again. So I hatched some crazy idea about turning the tables on you, making you fall in love with me. The way you'd done with me in the past.' He flung away to stare through the window.

Rose felt an icy chill seep through her as she stared at his back. 'That's why you kept on asking me to say I loved you,' she said dully. 'Why you never once returned the compliment. You just wanted revenge, didn't you,

James? All that talk about not wanting a divorce, living together, wedding rings, was just bait for the trap you set me.'

'*No*, it wasn't.' James turned sharply, and put out a hand in appeal, but Rose looked at it with such disdain he let it fall.

'If you'll call a cab I'll go home,' she said quietly.

His face hardened. 'Is that what you want?'

'It's not what I expected,' she said with a brittle smile, 'but under the circumstances it seems like a good idea.'

James shook his head. 'Look, we need to talk.'

'Too late for that,' she threw at him, and marched from the room, but he caught her back.

'Don't leave like this, Rose. Not now, when—'

'When what?' she said scornfully. 'You've had your fun with me, James Sinclair. Keep your wretched secrets. I wish you joy of them.'

'Oh, for God's sake,' he said in sudden fury. 'Alex is a hunk of Glaswegian testosterone by the name of Cargill. The woman in the photograph is his girlfriend. She was in and out of here all the time. The perfume must be hers.' He grabbed her by the shoulders. 'The cleaning people must have turned it up.'

Without warning Rose's headache suddenly reached crisis proportions, and with a gasped apology she fled into James's bathroom and parted with everything she'd eaten all day. When she emerged, ashen-faced and shivering, James put out a hand instinctively, then dropped it as she backed away.

'Sorry about that,' said Rose with what dignity she could muster.

'Would you like some tea?' he asked quietly.

'Thank you. I would.' She gave him a polite little smile. 'It's the travelling. I'm not good at it.'

'Go downstairs and curl up on a sofa while I change,' said James, suddenly all brisk sympathy. 'I'll make tea. Then we'll have that talk.'

'If we must,' said Rose listlessly, and drifted from the room, suddenly wanting to cry her eyes out at the way things had gone so contrary to the way she'd planned.

James came into the sitting room with a tray of tea, the investment banker metamorphosed into something more approachable in faded old sweatshirt and jeans. He poured tea into a beaker, added a splash of milk and handed it to her, then sat down beside her with his own. 'How do you feel?'

'Fragile,' said Rose, and drank some tea gingerly.

'Too fragile to listen?'

'I suppose not.'

'In that case let me explain in full.' James took the beaker from her and put it down on a table with his own. He took her hand in his. 'You remember your famous plan all those years ago, Rose?'

She gave him a derisive, sidelong glance. 'I'm hardly likely to forget, after the trouble it caused!'

'Right.' He frowned, looking down at their joined hands. 'I never forgot it, either. Nor you. Every time I met a woman I'd think I'd found the one to lay your ghost, Rose. But I never did. So when I received your letter I assured myself that I'd feel nothing for you after ten years. That you would be different. I'd be different. That we'd feel nothing for each other when we met again.'

He was wrong there, thought Rose.

'When we came face to face that night,' continued James, 'ten years disappeared like a flash of lightning, and the idea sprang fully-formed into my mind. Now it was your turn, I swore, before you'd even said a word. This time I'd be the one with the plan. I'd make you fall in

love with me all over again, no matter how many men you had in your life.' He gave a short, derisive laugh. 'So much for ten years' maturity. What a fool!'

'Not really,' said Rose very quietly. 'Your plan was highly successful.'

James looked down at her. 'Was it? Truthfully, Rose?'

Her mouth twisted. 'Oh, yes. Ten years hadn't done much for my maturity either.'

He winced, his fingers tightening on hers. 'The reason I hesitated about having you here in my house was sheer, native Scots caution. I wanted to be utterly sure, first, that you were going to come back to me for good. Because *my* plan backfired. Whatever your feelings on the subject, I was the one who fell in love all over again.' He paused. 'So are you still going home, Rose?'

She hesitated. 'Actually, I don't feel very wonderful, so I think I will.'

James's mouth tightened. 'Walking out on me again?'

Rose looked at him hard and long. 'Look, I know you want me, James—'

'Dammit, Rose, I *love* you,' he said, and tried to take her in his arms, but she held him off.

'I believe that, too,' she said, surprised to find this was true. 'But you haven't forgiven me, James. Not really.'

'That's nonsense,' he said roughly.

'I don't think so...' Rose swallowed hard. 'Sorry, I feel sick again—'

He pulled her up and raced with her to a ground-floor cloakroom, and this time held her head as she threw up. Afterwards he washed her face gently, and smoothed her hair back, then, ignoring her protests, picked her up and carried her upstairs to his bed.

'Rest there for a while,' he said urgently. 'When you

feel up to it come downstairs and I'll concoct something tempting for your supper.'

Rose lay where she was for a long time, her arm over her eyes, her mind going round in circles. She got up gingerly at last, decided her stomach intended to behave, then washed her face and went downstairs to find him waiting in the hall.

'I heard you get up, Rose. You're very pale. What can I do for you?'

She ran her tongue round dry lips. 'Would you call a cab? I want to go home.'

'You can't travel like that,' he said impatiently.

'If I've got a stomach bug I'd rather cope with it at home.'

James thrust a hand through his hair in exasperation. 'I'd forgotten how stubborn you can be. All right, all right,' he added, as her mouth set mutinously. 'If you must go I'll drive you.'

The late Friday night traffic was heavy enough to prolong the journey, and by the time James drew up in the niche behind the shop Rose felt like death. Neither of them had said much in the car, but the things left unsaid had hung heavy in the air, and when James put her bag down in the sitting room Rose took her courage in both hands.

'I need to be on my own for a while, James.'

'Shouldn't you call a doctor?'

'Not tonight. If I'm not better in the morning I will.'

They looked at each other in silence.

'I don't want to part like this. What the hell went wrong, Rose?' demanded James.

'A stomach upset,' said Rose woodenly. 'An unromantic complaint. It needs privacy.'

James stiffened. 'Are you suggesting I turn tail and

drive back to London? Is that the kind of privacy you mean?'

'Yes. That's exactly what I mean.'

For a moment he stared at her in utter disbelief, then with a smothered exclamation he strode from the room and ran downstairs, banging the back door shut behind him.

Rose forced herself to go down and check that everything was secure, then she rang Minerva about the change of plan. 'But I'd like the day off tomorrow just the same,' she added apologetically. 'I feel terrible.'

James rang late that night after he arrived back in London. 'You and I have things to discuss.'

'I know,' said Rose wearily. 'But not right now. I need some time to myself.'

There was a pause. 'How much time?'

'A week or two?'

'If you need that much time away from me perhaps we should just pack it in altogether and go for the divorce,' he said savagely, and rang off.

When a couple of days went by with no word from James, Rose began to think he'd meant what he'd said.

'I just can't see why you told James to back off,' said Bel, who was now in possession of most of the facts. 'The minute I saw you both together it was obvious you were meant for each other.'

When she'd asked for time Rose hadn't expected James to take her quite so literally, and slept badly, the resulting shadows under her eyes causing comment when she joined Minerva and Henry for supper a day or two later. When Henry, with his usual tact, left them alone for a while after the meal Minerva eyed her niece searchingly.

'You look terrible, Rose. You're obviously pining for this James of yours. So what's wrong?'

'I have this rather ironic little problem,' said Rose bitterly. 'When I went to Cheltenham last week I bought a pregnancy test, and found a little blue line in the right—or the wrong—place.'

'Darling child!' Minerva got up and sat beside her, patting her hand. 'Are you sure?'

'That's the whole point,' said Rose miserably. 'James married me the first time round over a false alarm, so I waited until I'm absolutely certain this time.'

'Do you mind?' said her aunt gently.

'I don't mind about the baby, Minerva. But I mind because it complicates things. Last time James spoke to me he was angry with me, even made noises about getting on with the divorce. Though I don't think he meant that. I think—I *hope*—he was just angry because I pushed him away. I went down to London determined to tell him. But we had a row. And in the end I couldn't.' Her eyes filled. 'The baby's all my fault, anyway.'

'Not quite,' said Minerva dryly. 'James is at least half to blame.'

'But in the heat of the moment I never told him I don't take the necessary pills any more.' Rose blew her nose angrily. 'So now I'm pregnant, which is like holding a gun to his head.' She shuddered. 'I wanted us to be together because we can no longer bear to be apart, not because of James's sense of duty all over again.'

'Does he love you?'

'He says he does.'

'Do you love *him*.'

'Of course I love him,' said Rose tearfully, and jammed her knuckles in her eyes. 'Otherwise I wouldn't be in this stupid predicament.'

Rose was in bed, feeling very sorry for herself that night, when her cellphone rang.

'How are you, Rose?' said James, and she closed her eyes in thanksgiving.

'Better.' Miraculously better just for hearing his voice.

'Thank God for that,' said James gruffly. 'Look, this has gone on long enough. You're coming between me and my work. My assistant keeps offering me medication and making noises about a holiday.'

'I'm sorry to hear that,' said Rose, brightening.

'So no more nonsense about giving you more time, lady. Time's up.'

'Yes, James.'

'I should bloody well think so. I'll be with you on Saturday evening, so just make sure your dancecard's empty.'

Rose blinked away the tears that never seemed far away lately. 'Right. I'll do that.'

'But until then I want you to keep one very important fact uppermost in your mind, Rose Sinclair.' James cleared his throat. 'I love you. I always have and I always will.'

Which, thought Rose, as she settled down to sleep, was the only thing that really mattered.

Until that point life had been hard, with everything a chore to be got through as best Rose could manage. But after talking to James her lift in spirits was so visible Bel was euphoric with relief when she arrived next morning. And Minerva, who dropped in later to check on her niece, expressed similar satisfaction when she heard James had been in contact and was coming up at the weekend.

'I take it that after Saturday we can all relax?' she demanded.

Rose nodded. 'I hope so.'

'In which case, Bel dear,' said Minerva, 'you and I must have a little talk. I'll be needing a new manager soon.'

James rang on Saturday from his car to say he'd arrive at seven, by which time Rose had groomed the flat, prepared a simple meal, and had worked herself up into a state of such anticipation she couldn't keep still. When her small French clock struck seven she rushed back to her bedroom to add a few finishing touches to face and hair, then stiffened in horror at the sound of breaking glass somewhere below. Rose raced downstairs to check the shop windows, blew out her cheeks in relief when she found them intact, and went to investigate outside in the arcade.

But as she opened her private door she gasped in astonishment as James thrust a youth through it and slammed the door shut behind him.

'Don't be frightened, darling,' he said swiftly, 'but I think it's time you met your stalker.'

Rose gazed in utter disbelief at the defiant, scarlet-faced boy James was holding by the scruff of his neck. *'Marcus?'*

'So you know him,' said James grimly. 'I thought you might. I caught him red-handed, posting a rose through your door.'

'Get your hands off me,' spat the boy furiously. 'I wasn't doing any harm—'

'Like hell you weren't! You've been frightening my wife to death with your nonsense,' said James with menace. 'You need a good hiding, my lad—'

'Let him go, James,' said Rose, pulling herself together. 'Marcus is Anthony Garrett's son.'

'Lord, I might have known.' James thrust the dishevelled boy away and brushed his hands together, as though

ridding himself of contamination, heightening Marcus's colour still further. 'I was just leaving the off-licence when I saw the young idiot sidling towards your door, rose in hand. I collared him, but lost a couple bottles of champagne in the process.'

'So that was the breaking glass I heard.' Rose gazed at the boy, baffled. She knew Marcus Garrett so slightly she had no idea how to deal with the situation. 'Did you send me a card, and make anonymous phone calls too, Marcus?' she asked after a moment, her eyes severe.

'Yes,' he said miserably, white as a sheet now. 'I didn't mean any harm, I swear. I just wanted to—I mean I needed to—' Sudden, racking sobs overtook him, putting an end to his confession.

Rose put an arm round him, pulling a face at James over the boy's dishevelled head. 'James, why not go and buy some more wine while I have a chat with Marcus?'

'Is it safe to do that?' James demanded, eyeing the slim, heaving shoulders with deep distaste. He sighed impatiently as he met the look in her eyes. 'Oh, very well, Rose. If I must. But you behave yourself, laddie,' he warned Marcus. 'I won't be long.'

When James had gone Rose put the distraught youth away from her a little. 'Come into my office, Marcus. I'll give you a drink.'

'Thank you. Sorry to blub like a baby,' he said thickly, following her. 'I suppose you'll tell my father now.'

'It depends.'

By the time Marcus had downed a glass of water, and splashed more on his face, Rose had reached a decision. She fixed the boy with a stern look.

'Right then, Marcus. I've decided I won't tell your father about this.'

His eyes lit with hope, then dulled in despair. 'But he

wants to marry you. You're bound to tell him—' He scowled suddenly. 'Wait a minute. That—that gorilla who mauled me about said you were his *wife*.'

'I am.'

Marcus looked bewildered. 'But you were seeing my father.'

'I've been separated from my husband for a long time,' said Rose gently, 'but we're together again now. Which naturally means I can't go on seeing your father. So I see no need to tell him about this. Or your mother,' she added, startling him. 'But I keep quiet on one condition, Marcus. I need your solemn promise you'll never make phone calls like that again. To anyone. Or keep sending roses all the time.' She shook a finger at him. 'One card, one rose, fine. But to someone more your own age. OK?'

Marcus nodded, then smiled soulfully. 'I'm not sorry about you and Dad. You're loads too young for him. I think you're really cool, Rose.'

'And in any case I'm married to someone else,' said Rose hastily, to stem further outpourings. 'Are you seeing your father tonight?'

Marcus looked at his watch, and swore in a way that would have shocked his parents. 'Sorry! I'm supposed to meet him at the King's Head any minute.'

'Off you go, then.' She opened the office door as she heard James come in. 'We're in here,' she called.

James strode in, carrying a wine-store bag clinking with bottles, his eyes steel-hard as they fastened on the youth. 'Have you called the police yet, Rose?'

'No,' said Rose swiftly, as Marcus turned a sickly shade of green. 'We're settling this out of court, so to speak.' She gave the boy a stern look. 'Right?'

He nodded dumbly, eyes averted from James.

'Right,' said Rose, purposely brisk. 'Have a nice eve-

ning with your father, Marcus. And don't worry. I won't
say a word, I promise.'

He gazed at her in worshipful gratitude. 'Thanks, Rose,
I mean Miss—'

'Mrs Sinclair,' said James very deliberately. 'I'll see
you off the premises. And let me add a piece of advice,
young Garrett. Make sure you never bother my wife
again.'

Rose stayed at the foot of the stairs while James thrust
the boy out, then bolted the door. He turned to look at
her, with a smile that turned her heart over.

'Are you all right?' he said, as he took her in his arms.
'If that young villain upset you I'll—'

'He didn't, and I'm fine.' she said and kissed him. 'In
fact,' she added breathlessly, 'I'm relieved to know it was
just Marcus, not someone with something more sinister in
mind for me.'

'That's what I thought.' James kissed her at length, then
held her close, his cheek rubbing hers for a moment, then
to her surprise he picked her up and carried her upstairs.

'I'm not ill any more,' Rose protested, laughing.

'I just like having you in my arms,' he said, grinning,
and sat down with her on his lap. 'God, I've missed you!'

Rose returned his kisses with ardour for a moment, then
came to a decision. No way was she going to be able to
cook dinner, or even just enjoy being with James again,
until everything was out in the open for good or ill.

'James,' she said, sitting up to look him in the eye.
'Before we go any further there's something you should
know.'

'Is there?' His eyes lit with a surprising gleam. 'Tell
me, then.'

Rose swallowed hard, feeling the colour rise in her
cheeks. 'Sorry to confront you with the same old problem

again, James.' She gazed at him in desperate appeal. 'Though it's not exactly the same problem, because this time—this time I really am pregnant.'

'I know you are, darling,' he said, taking the wind out of her sails. He caught her close, rubbing his cheek against her. 'I've just been waiting for you to tell me.'

'How do you know?' she demanded indignantly, pulling away a little.

'Minerva told me.'

Rose stared at him, utterly dumbstruck.

'When you told me to get lost for a bit I was worried sick,' he said hastily. 'I needed to know how you were, so I rang your aunt. Apparently she thought I had a right to the truth. I *like* your aunt, even though I haven't met her yet,' added James with feeling.

Rose didn't know whether to laugh or cry, so she laughed, and James laughed with her in relief, holding her close.

'I've been in a right old state,' she said unsteadily at last. 'All day I've been rehearsing ways to tell you. And you knew all the time!'

He raised her face to his, his eyes very sober. 'Rose, when I set out to make you fall in love with me again I was ready to go to every length I could to make it happen, but I swear this wasn't part of my plan. But when Minerva gave me the glad news I realised I'd been hoping against hope you might be pregnant. Lord knows, I was too desperate to make love to you again that night to do anything to prevent it.'

'And I never got the chance to tell you I wasn't doing anything to prevent it, either,' she said ruefully, then smiled at him. 'But while we're on the subject I may as well clear up a point or two about this plan of yours, Sinclair. You had no hope of making me fall in love with

again, darling, because I'd never fallen *out* of love in the first place.'

With a smothered sound James crushed her close, expressing his appreciation without words, but after a while he put her away from him to look down into her face. 'So clear up another point for me, Rose. Are you truly happy about the baby?'

'Of course I am,' she said joyfully. 'I wanted your baby all those years ago, James. I still do.' To her surprise she saw a trace of moisture in his eyes, and smiled shakily. 'How do you feel about it, Daddy?'

James took so long to tell her exactly how he felt in every detail, it was very late by the time they got round to eating the simple meal Rose had prepared earlier.

'So how soon can you wind things up here and come live with me, sweetheart?' he asked as they lay in each other's arms in bed later.

'Minerva's asked Bel to take over from me, so I'll need to stay to give her a teach-in for a while. After that I'm all yours.'

James gave a great sigh of satisfaction. 'You were mine from the first moment I set eyes on you, sweetheart.'

'Quite a bit before that, actually,' she informed him. 'I took one look at you during a rugby match one Saturday afternoon—'

'At a match?' He frowned. 'I thought you drew my name out of a hat.'

Rose smiled gleefully. 'I did. But I wouldn't have taken part in all that nonsense if I hadn't been madly in love with you to start with, James Sinclair. The three of us were supposed to write different names on each paper, but I wrote yours on all four of mine.'

James gave a shout of laughter and hugged her close. 'Little devil!'

'I still remember the state I was in as Fabia and Con drew other men's names out of the hat.' She smiled radiantly. 'But fate let me draw the slip Fabia had written your name on as a joke, so the others had no idea I'd shortened the odds. You never stood a chance, Sinclair.'

'Am I complaining?' he whispered, and switched off the light.